COWBOY, UNDERCOVER

LAZY S RANCH

VICKI THARP

JPC PUBLISHING

COWBOY, UNDERCOVER

1

WHEN IS ENOUGH, ENOUGH?

Is it when you put your back to a wall in every room you enter?

Is it when you look at a kind gesture with mistrust?

Is it when you can lie easier than tell the truth?

Or is it when your job literally almost kills you?

For former Marine and ATF agent Gil Brant, it wasn't any one of those things. But combine them all with a year and a half of working deep undercover—an assignment that had taken an exacting, exhausting toll on his soul—and he'd realized the price was too steep.

Turning in his resignation was the right decision.

Gil kept telling himself that as he walked into the Bison County Sheriff's Office, where the ATF had been given temporary accommodations until the building housing their new satellite field office could be renovated.

He knocked on the open door of a ten-seater conference room. Special Agent in Charge, SAC Rod Spinks, sat at the far end of the table, his back to the flat screen mounted on the wall. Being in law enforcement, it was hard not to put your back to the door, even here, where the men and women were supposed to be your allies.

"Got a minute?" Gil asked.

Without looking up, SAC Spinks fired his remote at the screen behind him, muting CNN. "Can it wait?"

Gil's resignation wasn't time critical, but now that he'd made the decision to quit, he wanted a quick, clean break. He stepped into the room and tapped the corner of the envelope he held on the edge of the table. "It'll be quick, sir."

Spinks' fingers flew across his laptop's keyboard, doing a damn fine impression of a court reporter. The clicking of the keys stopped, and Spinks finally looked up.

No smile.

Gil hadn't expected one.

"Done faffing about at that country club and ready to get your ass back to work?"

"Veteran therapy program. Not a—"

Nope. Gil cut himself off. He refused to explain himself to this man. That he'd needed time to heal physically, after being shot and almost killed, and mentally after his long stint undercover, shouldn't have come as a revelation. Gil held out the envelope. "I came to give you this."

Spinks appraised him. The SAC's cropped hair had gone straight to white, and the afternoon Wyoming sun streaming through the plate-glass window made it look like a crusty layer of ice. Instead of reaching for the envelope, Spinks folded his arms over his chest and leaned back in his chair. He didn't put his feet up on the table, he wasn't that kind of guy.

"What's that?" Spinks' tone held a note of impatience as if he wanted to rush to the punchline of the joke.

Gil dropped the envelope next to the laptop. "My resignation."

Spinks didn't look surprised.

He also didn't try to talk Gil out of it.

Spinks sat forward, his fingers working the keyboard again, his attention more on the screen than Gil. He stopped long enough to slide the envelope back toward Gil. "Talk to me when your leave is up."

"I'm not changing my mind."

Spinks glanced up, his fingers slowed but didn't stop. "Didn't ask you to. I told—"

"Yeah." Gil picked up the envelope and stuffed it into the rear pocket of his jeans. "I heard you."

He stood there a moment longer, not knowing quite what he'd expected or what he was waiting for. He turned to go.

He'd made it to the door when Spinks said, "Brant."

Gil stopped and glanced at his SAC over his shoulder, wondering if Spinks was going to toss in an obligatory 'great seeing you, man,' or an offer to buy Gil a beer sometime that he would never take Spinks up on.

"Close the door."

Spinks never failed to disappoint. "Yeah, sure."

Before Gil left, he stuck his head into the other conference room the ATF had on loan. The long table had been removed, and two sets of desks sat back to back, abutting the long window. Another desk was shoved up against the short wall. But instead of his fellow agents, all that greeted him were desks stacked with files and cold cups of half-drunk coffee.

It wasn't that he really missed anybody, being deep under-cover for as long as he'd been with only a handler for contact, had made it near impossible to maintain any work-related relationships, but it might have been nice to see a familiar face.

It wasn't until he'd made it outside, striding across the parking lot that he became aware of the *tink, tinking* of his spurs strapped to his dusty cowboy boots. He chuckled to himself, never in a million years did he think he would prefer that sound to the feel of his Glock 22 strapped to his hip.

He opened the door of his truck. He didn't click a key fob. The beast was too old of a vehicle for that. Not classic old where he'd have to worry about it getting jacked, but the kind of old where he could leave the windows down and the doors unlocked, and nobody bothered touching it.

"Hey, cowboy."

Gil turned at the sound of the familiar voice and broke out a genuine smile when he saw his buddy, and ex-handler, Isaac Lang jogging over to him.

Gil clasped Isaac's hand and brought him in for a warm one-armed hug and a clap on the back. "Hey Iz, how's it hangin'?"

Isaac smiled that cocky smile he never seemed to wipe from his face. "I don't think you really want to know."

"You're probably right." Gil leaned back against his truck. "Haven't seen you around lately. Tricks taking you out of town?"

There were lines at the corner of Isaac's eyes where a few months ago there hadn't been any. His usual laid-back lankiness held a hint of tension. Make that a lot of tension.

Isaac shrugged, but the gesture didn't come across as care-free. "Got a bit of a thing going on. Taking up a lot of our time. When are you coming back?" Isaac slapped a hand against Gil's right shoulder, and Gil couldn't hold back the wince. "Oh man, sorry, bud. I totally forgot that was your hurt shoulder."

"No worries."

"But seriously, man," Isaac said. "When are you coming back?"

"That's what I came to talk to the SAC about. I don't want word getting out yet, but I ain't coming back."

Isaac barked out a loud laugh. "Good one, man. No, seriously?"

Gil braced his hands on the tail bed behind him. "Seriously."

"Dude... That's not even funny." Isaac stepped back and ran a hand through his blond hair curling over the collar of his shirt. Isaac had height. But at six foot four, Gil had a half a head on him. "Look, we've got some shit starting, and we need a guy like you on our team. You can play cowboys and Indians on your own time. This shit is serious."

"That's the thing. This shit is always serious. You know that. And *I* know that."

"But this shit is big."

Gil was going to regret this, but he said, "What do you have?"

Isaac glanced around as if making sure no one was within earshot. "You know I can't talk about a case to someone who's not on it."

"Right." Gil climbed into the truck and glanced back at his friend. "It was great seeing you, man."

"Jesus, Brant." Isaac leaned on Gil's open window. "Spinks will kill me if I say anything."

Gil cranked the starter. The motor spun and chugged to life, sending a cloud of white exhaust through the open window. "Then don't say anything. I'm late."

Isaac didn't remove his hands from the door. He glanced off in the distance as if mulling something over in his mind. "How about I buy you a beer? For old time's sake? Tomorrow night?"

"Old time's sake." Gil couldn't keep the thick skepticism out of his voice. Isaac wanted to talk, just not here where there was a possibility they could be overheard.

Isaac shrugged like it didn't matter, though Gil knew it did. Isaac wouldn't have asked to buy him a beer if it hadn't. You didn't spend eighteen months with someone as practically your only point of contact with the outside world, and not get to know them inside and out. To live that kind of life, you have to trust, and trust wholly.

"I've got plans tomorrow night," Gil said. "At least I hope I will."

Isaac got a sly smile and leaned in. "Hot date?"

It was Gil's turn to shrug. His sex life wasn't up for discussion.

"Anyone I know?" Isaac shook a finger at him as if someone had come to mind. "Let me guess, that curvy DEA agent on the task force with the—" He held his hands out in front of him indicating someone with a big rack.

Forget the DEA agent. Gil had his sights on a certain helo pilot that rocked a flight suit the way most women rocked a little black dress.

"Sunday then?"

Officially, the Healing Horses therapy program had a no drug or alcohol policy. Unofficially, as long as you weren't in an alcohol or drug treatment program, what you did off the ranch was your own business.

With a crisp nod, Gil said, "Sunday. I'll call you."

Isaac tapped the roof of the truck and walked back into the station.

Gil tossed his resignation letter into his glove box. Already late, he beat it back to the Lazy S Ranch. He'd promised the Healing Horses program director, Jenna Nash, that he'd be back by four to help work the mustangs that had been turned over to the program for training.

He glanced at his watch. He had ten minutes to get back. He stomped down on the gas and leaned into the curves, accelerating through the twists and turns of the mountain roads paving a ribbon of asphalt through the shadows of the Rockies.

Behind the fences on the side of the road, cattle grazed, their heads down, doing their best to turn grass fields into hamburgers.

Gil was curious about what his buddy and the ATF had

cooking. But that wasn't his life anymore. He'd meet for the beer, settle his idle curiosity, then let it go.

You should have made Spinks accept your resignation before Isaac sucks you back in.

"I'm not changing my mind," he said to no one in particular, the wind whipping his words away as if they had no weight. As if he hadn't spoken them at all.

———

Lieutenant Tessa Sterling banked her UH-60 Blackhawk helicopter and headed south along the foothills of the Rockies. The bird was an older military helo that the task force had converted for its own purposes, part tactical, part rescue, part medical transport, a setup that served the community well.

The sun was on its downward arc, she blinked against the grit in her eyes as they headed back to the municipal airport on the outskirts of Murdock. Too much flying and not enough sleep.

The *whump, whump, whump* of the heavy rotor blades, and the steady drone of the twin engines worked together, lulling her senses. Tessa shook her head to clear out the cobwebs.

"Want me to take over?" Lieutenant Quinn Powell said from the co-pilot seat.

She glanced over at her copilot. They hadn't been flying together long, and Powell was new to the Blackhawks. The more time he had at the stick, the better for the both of them. "Sure, take it away."

After Powell had taken the controls, Tessa rung out the stiffness in her hands and settled more deeply into her seat. Agent Isaac Lang sat in the jumpseat behind her. They'd been short-handed, and he'd flown along with them as their spotter.

Over the comms, Tessa said, "What do you think, Lang? Any

of those landing strips or helo pads a good fit for these gun runners?"

Lang was slow to answer. "Any of those helo pads are a possibility, but if The Wolf is moving the merchandise by plane, he's going to need either a lot of small planes or a longer runway."

Powell eased back on their speed as they approached the municipal airport, spoke with the tower. Then to her and Lang said, "Until we have better intel on what they're trying to move, and how much, it'll be hard to narrow down possible locations."

He banked right as he maneuvered downwind of the airport's helo pad and came in for a landing. Tessa eyeballed their airspeed, the altimeter, and the fuel gauges. "At this point, I feel like we're wasting our time. Too many unknowns."

Powell eased down on the collective, their altitude dropped, and Powell landed the big bird with skill and grace. The task force had been lucky to snag Powell up after he'd discharged from the Marines. That man had been born to fly.

"Agreed," Lang's voice was low and thick with fatigue.

They'd spent the better part of the past week scrounging the foothills and surrounding areas for any landing zones or private airstrips that The Wolf—a heavy hitter in illegal arms dealing circles—could use for smuggling.

If helos were involved in the operation, an expensive halo pad wasn't needed to set down. All that would be needed was a patch of grass or dirt with enough clearing that the rotors wouldn't be caught in trees or high lines. The truth was, Wyoming was vast, and unless the task force could get someone on the inside, their chance of finding where the gun runners were taking off and landing was slim.

The Blackhawk's wheels had barely touched down when Lang slid the side door open and hung up his headset. He tossed a wave over his shoulder as he headed to the hanger for his debriefing with his SAC. She and Powell started their shutdown procedures. As the rotors spun down, Tessa removed her helmet, yanked her ponytail holder free, and scrubbed her fingers through her sweaty hair, scratching all the itchy spots. "Nice landing. Couldn't have done it better myself."

Powell opened his door. "Damn straight. Better watch out. I'll be sitting in the pilot seat in no time."

"As long as it's in your own bird and not mine, more power to you. But if you think you're going to pilot my bird, you'll have a fight on your hands." A good-natured threat.

Mostly.

Quinn flashed her an amused smile, his eyes unreadable behind his reflective aviator lenses. "Just you wait, Sterling. I'm gunning for you."

"Good luck with that." Powell was good. Great even. But she had seniority, and she was better.

That wasn't conceit. It was fact.

Still, knowing the task force was in the process of sourcing another bird didn't hurt either.

The fuel truck pulled up and started refueling. A cloud of JP-8 fumes tickled her nose. After she and Powell completed their shutdown procedures, they secured the helo for the night and headed back to the hanger themselves. Her legs were stiff, and her lower back bitched and complained. There was a hot bath at home with her name on it.

"You're coming with us tomorrow to run the cattle over to the other canyon, aren't you?" Powell asked. "With Jenna's grandparents and Pepita on their UK tour, we could use all the warm bodies we can get."

She got to the hanger doors first and held it open for him to walk through. "I don't know. My ex-husband skated on taking our son this weekend. I was thinking of sleeping in."

"He's welcome to tag along. Besides, he's seven years old.

You're kidding yourself if you think he's going to let you sleep late."

True, and her son would love nothing more than to go on a mini cattle drive, but he hadn't been riding horses for very long. Hell, she had only been back in the saddle in the past few months since she'd met Quinn.

This wasn't a pony ride. These were real cowboys, real cattle, real dangers. Someday she would take Jack, but neither one of them were ready for that adventure yet.

"I don't know…"

They walked over to the bank of lockers and stripped out of their flight gear. Powell slipped on a leather jacket. With night approaching, the temperature had dropped. She pulled a dark blue hoodie out of her locker and slipped it over her head.

"Brant's going." Powell wiggled his brows up and down. "You know you wanna."

That funny flutter hit her stomach at the mention of Brant's name. Kinda like that feeling she always got when she hit an air pocket, and the helo dropped fifty to a hundred feet. It wasn't an awful feeling, but Tessa wasn't sure if it was a good one either.

"I haven't missed that little flirt-fest you and Brant have had going on these past few months."

Tessa ducked her head and closed her locker, not wanting Powell to see the flush seeping into her cheeks. "Flirt-fest? What are you, thirteen?"

His smile went wide at her hesitation. "Got ya. We're heading out at seven. Don't be late." Powell turned on his heel and headed out the door before Tessa had a chance to weasel out.

GIL STOOD IN THE CENTER OF THE LAZY S'S ROUND PEN. A STOCKY sorrel mustang cantered around the rail, it's mane and tail blowing in the breeze, while Sidney Wilcox, the ranch's resident horse trainer, gave Gil instructions.

"That's it. Like that!" Sidney climbed up the round pen and draped her arms over the top rail. When the horse broke into a trot, she got on to Gil again. "Use the lunge whip to drive him forward. Don't let his feet stall out."

Gil slapped the ground with the lunge whip, and the horse cantered off again. The muscles in Gil's right arm ached where the bullet had ripped through the muscles several months ago. Physical therapy had been tough, but sometimes working the ranch was even tougher.

Unlike physical therapy, the ranch work wasn't an hour or two a few times a week. It was all day, every day. Hauling hay. Mucking stalls. Working the horses. Riding fence. And that didn't include the extra set of exercises his physical therapist had given him to work on in between their sessions.

"When did you say the other veterans were going to be here?" Gil's breath came out in harsh pants. His stamina sucked, but he was getting stronger every day. If Healing Horses didn't do anything else for him, it was at least helping him to physically get back to where he'd been before he'd been shot.

Jenna Nash stood beside Sidney, her arms on the rails and a boot on the bottom rung. "I'm expecting Mia Mann in the next day or two. But the other two have problems with their funding paperwork. It could be a couple of weeks or more before they're able to come."

"What's the matter, tough guy?" Sidney said. "You getting lonely out here?"

Gil stepped in front of the mustang's driveline and sent the horse back in the opposite direction. "Not lonely. I'm wondering when someone's going to get here to help lighten the load."

The wind whipped up and blew hair into Jenna's face. She wiped it away and mashed her hat down further on her head. "I don't know Gil, you seem to be doing a damn fine job all by yourself. You sure you haven't had prior horse training experience? Maybe you should think about giving up your day job."

Funny she should say that. Gil didn't comment. What he did with his life after Healing Horses wasn't anyone's business but his own.

"I think that's enough for one day," Sidney said as she stepped back from the round pen. She was a tiny thing, with short cropped red hair that she moussed up into short spikes, though it would be a mistake for anyone to let her size fool them. She was tough and probably had more true grit than John Wayne.

Gil stepped in front of the mustang's driveline again, turned his back to the horse, watching it over his shoulder. The horse stepped to the center of the pen and followed him around. They walked a few circles as they both caught their breath, then he stopped and turned, and the mustang stuck his head against Gil's chest.

He raised a hand to pat the horse's head. The horse shied, and its head came up, but as soon as Gil touched the broad forehead, the horse settled. Gil scrubbed his fingers through the cowlick between the horse's eyes. From what Jenna had said, a swirl smack dab in the middle of the horse's forehead was a sign of a good, levelheaded horse.

Gil didn't know about all that nonsense, but this mustang was going a long way to proving Jenna right. He retrieved the lead rope, clipped it onto the horse's halter, and lead him back into the large paddock where the other three mustangs grazed.

The sun dipped behind the mountains, casting long shadows on the ground. Sidney headed back up to the barn. It was her night to feed. Which didn't hurt Gil's feelings one bit. His stomach growled, and his muscles screamed, and all he wanted was hot food and an even hotter shower.

In the distance came the *clop, clop* of horse hooves as Alby and Santos, the Lazy S's resident ranch hands, came trotting up to the pasture gate after a long day out on the range.

Off to his right, from the back porch of the big house—an old two-story number with a wraparound porch—came the clank of the triangle as Jenna called everybody in for dinner. It had only taken a few days for Jenna to turn him into Pavlov's dog with that damn triangle, his stomach gurgling and his mouth salivating anytime he heard that bell.

After dinner, Gil didn't hang around and shoot the shit with everybody else. He hoofed it back to his cabin. He was tired and sore, and he had barn duty first thing in the morning.

Besides the big house, and the smaller foreman's house farther down the road, the ranch had two older cabins, two newer cabins, and two more nearing completion. One of the older ones Sidney's husband Boomer had expanded when they'd adopted their young teenage daughter. The other one was shared by Alby and Santos.

Gil was in one of the newer cabins. One room. A double bunk on either side. A kitchenette with a bathroom tucked behind. Footlockers and hooks on the wall were ample storage for his clothes and what few personal items he'd brought.

It wasn't the Ritz, but it wasn't meant to be.

This was a working ranch with a veteran therapy program. The veterans didn't need luxury. They needed healing. Somehow, the combination of open spaces, horses, and body numbing hard work all around a group of people who *got* him, had begun to change him in ways he'd never thought possible. That's how he'd known it was time to get out of the ATF.

After his shower, he dropped into one of the lower bunks with a groan. Would the day ever come when his shoulder didn't continually remind him how close he'd come to dying?

But he hadn't died.

Now it was time for him to do all the things his choice of careers hadn't allowed him the time to do. Like, have a relationship. A family of his own perhaps? Kids? Who knew. None of that had even been a thought or consideration eighteen months ago. But now that he had a second chance at life? He wanted all that.

And more.

2

THE ALARM ON TESSA'S CELL PHONE WENT OFF, AND LIKE THE starting gun on *Amazing Race*, Jack burst through her bedroom door, his kid-sized tactical backpack loaded up and strapped to his back. A flashlight and water bottle dangled from a couple of the loops on either side. You'd think he'd packed for a week in the Serengeti, not the weekend at her great Aunt Evie's ranch.

"Get up, get up, get up." Jack's boots slid on the wood floor, and his thigh thumped into the nightstand. Something slid off the paper plate he held in his hand. "Oops."

That can't be good. Tessa closed her eyes. When she opened them again, Jack was blowing on a piece of peanut butter toast. He held it out to her with pride. "I made you breakfast."

With the flight hours she'd been clocking, she couldn't remember the last time she'd swept or mopped. The hairy toast mocked her. "That's okay, buddy. I'm not that hungry. You can have mine."

"I already ate." He held the plate out to her again. If she blurred her eyes, she almost couldn't see the dust bunnies glued to the peanut butter. "And my teacher says breakfast is the most important meal of the day."

Jack hoovered up information faster than a Dyson, and he wasn't shy about sharing what he learned. Before he launched into the intricacies of the food pyramid, she plucked a stray hair off the top of her toast and took a big bite.

She choked it down, and he yanked the covers off her. "Hurry, we're going to be late."

"Okay, okay." Tessa laid her toast on the bedside table and rolled out of bed. "I'm hitting the shower."

"But, Mom—"

"Go," she said. "You can play one of your video games while you wait if you want."

Jack rolled his eyes, as he headed toward the door, his thumbs tucked in the shoulder straps of his backpack. "Billy's dad says that too much screen time rots brain cells. Do you *want* me to lose brain cells? I'm only seven. If I start now there's no telling how many I'll lose by the time I'm fifteen, and then if I start drinking young—"

"Ho, now. Since when were you planning on a life of underage drinking? That doesn't sound like you."

"I'm not. Pickling your liver is no joke." He grabbed the door as he slowly started backing out. "But statistically kids are starting to drink younger and younger, and it's inevitable–"

"Jaaack." *Statistically. Inevitable.* Who else's second grader argued like a seasoned lawyer?

"I'm just saying you can't fight statistics and—" She raised her brows, letting him know it was time to give up. "Okay, okay. I'm going."

Jack left and closed the door behind him. Tessa let the smile that she'd been holding back break free. Some days it was all she could do to keep up with him mentally. What was she going to do when he was fourteen, or sixteen, or eighteen? Dear Lord, she was in trouble.

Tessa was in and out of the shower in record time. She stood in front of her mirror, a towel wrapped around her body as she brushed her teeth and worked the tangles out of her hair. There came a faint knock at her bathroom door, and Jack poked his head in.

"I'm almost ready," she said. "Give me a few more minutes."

Jack came into the bathroom and held up the plate with her fuzzy peanut butter toast. "Don't forget this," he said. "Protein is a great way to help you keep full all day."

Tessa smiled, took her toast, and because he was watching, she took another bite. Who knew, maybe the dust bunnies would add a little fiber to her diet. Around the bite, she said, "Now go on. I need to get dressed."

Jack hurried out, his backpack flapping against his back. Tessa shoved the rest of the toast into her mouth. Her cell phone buzzed on the counter beside her. She groaned when she saw the caller ID and swallowed hard.

"Dad? Something wrong?" She held the phone away from her face, checking the time. It wasn't even six AM. "Why are you calling this early?"

"Been talking with your husband –"

"*Ex*-husband."

Her father talked over her as if she hadn't said anything. As if her divorce wasn't final. The fact that her father was still talking with Bradley left a worse taste in her mouth than the fuzz-encrusted peanut butter.

It was frustrating enough that her ex wanted back into her and Jack's life, but to have her father do her ex's groveling? Her father should be on *her* side. Not Bradley's.

She only half listened to her father talking because the gist of what he had to say never changed: Bradley was sorry. Bradley would try better. Her son deserved to have his father around.

Her father couldn't understand why she was so difficult, so selfish.

All those things were meant to pile on the guilt, to make her into the villain, to make her think she was the one who was going to screw up their child.

"Dad, stop."

"Be reasonable, Tessa. Bradley deserves—"

"Bradley deserves what he got. A divorce, and limited visitation."

"Your son needs a positive male role model. He needs his father. He needs—"

"Look, Dad, I gotta go." Tessa pinched the bridge of her nose to relieve the pounding behind her eyes. She didn't have the time or the energy to argue with her father. "I'm running late. I'll call later. Tell Mom I love her."

Tessa hung up, her hand shaking as she dropped the phone on the counter. Six years and her father hadn't accepted that she and Bradley would never, ever, ever be together again.

Bradley wasn't a good man.

He was a charmer. When it suited him. Especially with family court judges, she found. He could make you want to drink the Kool-Aid and jump off a cliff. How could her father not see past Bradley's bullshit?

Before Jack could come back into her room, she jumped into a pair of jeans, stomped into her boots and slipped on an old T-shirt and sweatshirt. Catching her hair in a ponytail, she called it good. The cows weren't too picky.

She dumped her paper plate in the kitchen trash, grabbed a quick cup of coffee in her travel mug and called out to Jack. He'd settled on the couch engrossed in one of his new books from the library. Harry Potter? Or maybe quantum physics? Who knew. Long ago, she'd quit steering him toward books geared for kids his age. With Jack, she picked her battles, and what books he read wasn't one she was going to win.

She plopped a Bison County Sheriff's Office baseball cap on

his head, the bill turned backward. "Come on, slowpoke, you're gonna make us late."

Jack grumbled and righted his cap. "Mom, that's not the way the pros wear their caps."

Heaven forbid her son does something against the "rules." And really? Was she complaining that her son follows the rules? What was the matter with her?

He scrambled to his feet, tried to stuff the book into his already overloaded backpack. When it didn't fit, he tucked it under his arm and ran out the front door. Tessa pulled up the rear and locked the door behind her.

"Uh, oh," Jack said.

Tessa turned, her purse dropping from her shoulder at the sight of her flat tire. "Shit."

"Mom, Billy's dad said that swearing –"

"Yeah, yeah." Tessa clicked her key fob and had Jack throw his gear in the back seat of her four-door Jeep Wrangler.

Jack closed the rear passenger door and grinned at her. "Does this mean I get to learn how to change a tire today?"

Tessa leaned over her tire and ran her finger along the one-inch gash in the sidewall. Her stomach shifted and the peanut butter she'd eaten stuck like glue. This wasn't a flat tire from a simple road hazard. Someone had slashed her tire. Tessa forced false cheer into her voice. "I guess, buddy. Help me get the spare off."

She glanced at her watch, she wouldn't make the Lazy S by seven. She shot off a quick text to Quinn and told him she had a flat and suggested they should go on without her.

The responding text came in as she busted the last of the lug nuts loose. Jack checked her phone. "Quinn said someone will wait and you can catch up."

She replaced the damaged tire with the spare and showed Jack how to tighten the lug nuts evenly. He pushed and pulled on the lug wrench getting the nuts as tight he could. She followed up behind him tightening them up the rest of the way.

"Take this," she said, handing him the lever for the jack. "Slowly turn it to the left until the hydraulic bleeds down and the tire is on the ground."

In a rush, she hefted the damaged tire in the back of her Jeep and tossed the tire tools in on top. "Saddle up, Cowboy."

After climbing behind the wheel, she wiped her grimy hands on her jeans and glanced over her shoulder at Jack. "All set?"

He fastened himself into his booster seat. "You know, the new guidelines on child safety seats—"

"Say you have ten pounds and an inch and a half to go."

"But Billy doesn't use a booster seat, and he only weighs—" Tessa cut him off with a narrow-eyed look in the rearview mirror. Jack blew out a breath. "*Fiiine.*"

Her headlights cut through the dull gray dawn as the low cloud cover kept well east of the Rockies. About fifteen minutes later, the Jeep rumbled over her great Aunt Evie's cattle guard. Jack giggled. The cattle guards always made him giggle. Sometimes she forgot he was a kid.

"That tickles my butt," he said.

Jack scrambled out of his booster seat as Tessa parked. He was out of the Jeep and running for Evie's front door before Tessa got the chance to pull the keys from the ignition. She reached into the back, shouldered Jack's backpack, and followed him to the front door. Jack raised his hand to knock, but Massey, Evie's grown grandson, pulled the door open before he had the chance.

"Hey, Squirt." Massey released the grip on one of his crutches and gave Jack a fist bump.

"Hey."

They both pulled their hands back and extended their

fingers like an explosion. Jack skipped into the house, and Massey pulled Tessa in for a hug. "Hey cuz, how you been?"

Tessa rolled her eyes. "If I didn't know any better, I'd say this was a Monday."

"That good, huh?" Massey chuckled and started crutching his way to the kitchen. Massey had Cerebral Palsy, but he rarely let that slow him down. When he spoke, his consonants came out soft. When she and Jack had moved to the area, it had taken them no time at all to get used to the way he talked. The local women had learned to appreciate it. He never seemed short of female companionship.

Tessa dropped Jack's bag on the couch on her way to the kitchen. Evie greeted her with a hug. Evie was a slight woman who had more steel in her spine than Lady Liberty.

"I thought this would be nice for your ride." Evie handed her a full thermos of coffee. "It probably won't warm up for another couple of hours."

With thanks, Tessa took the thermos. She glanced toward the table where a set of architectural drawings were spread out over the top. Massey bumped his chin toward the man standing in the kitchen. "You remember Wyatt Wolfe?"

"Sure." Wyatt and his new wife lived on a houseboat on Evie's large stock pond. When you pulled up to her aunt's house, it was kind of hard to miss. She stuck out her hand, and they shook. She leaned over and looked at the drawings for what looked like some sort of barn or warehouse facility. "What's this?"

Wyatt glanced at Massey. Massey shrugged as if to say, 'sure why not?'

"It's a training facility," Wyatt said. "For Steele-Wolfe Securities. I'm trying to keep it on the down low for right now."

In other words, don't tell anybody. Fine by her. "Ohhh," Tessa said. "I want to come play when you get it finished."

Tessa had known that the former detective with the Bison County Sheriff's Department was now a private investigator, but this was the first she'd heard about him opening a security firm.

"Who knows," Wyatt said. "Maybe you'll like the facility so much you'll want to stay on."

Tessa raised her brow. "I'm pretty sure you can't afford me. Or my helo."

Wyatt's warm smile said that maybe she didn't know as much as she thought she did. "We'll see about that."

Jack downed half a glass of the milk that Evie had poured him, leaving a white mustache on his upper lip. "You're going to be late, Mom."

"Is that your nice way of getting rid of me?" She ruffled a hand through his dark brown hair. She really needed to get him a haircut. "No crying, no whining, no Mom please don't leave me?"

"Nope." No thought. No hesitation. Tessa loved Jack's newfound independent streak, but sometimes a piece of her wondered what happened to that little boy that used to cling to her neck and never want to be put down. But this was good. This was really good.

She started backing out of the kitchen. To Wyatt, she said, "Hey I know a guy in construction if you're looking for bids."

Massey leaned against the counter, most of his weight on one crutch. "Who's that?"

"Boomer – I mean Brian. Brian Wilcox. He built a bunch of the cabins at the Lazy S. Quality work. I don't know if this job is too big, but you might think about giving him a call."

"Thanks," Wyatt said. "I'll do that."

To Evie, Tessa said, "You sure you don't mind keeping Jack for the weekend? I can pick him up tonight. I don't think we'll be super late getting back."

"*Mooom*," Jack complained. "You said I could stay all weekend. You promised—"

"It's fine." Evie patted Jack's shoulder. "We love having him."

"I've got my riding lessons." Jack drank the rest of his milk and used his sleeve to wipe the remains from his lip. *Boys.*

"And Jack was going to help me build that teeter-totter for the horses," Massey said. "Go on. Enjoy your time off. You deserve it."

She smiled, warmed by the way her extended family had embraced her and Jack when they'd moved to the area. What she wouldn't have given to have that kind of support when Jack had been younger, and Bradley had been nowhere around.

"Go." Jack waved his hand in a shooing motion.

"Okay, okay. I'm out of here. I have my cell phone if you need me. She pulled out a piece of paper from her pocket and handed it to Evie. "Here's the Lazy S's satellite phone number. You should be able to reach me there if need be, once I'm out of cell phone range."

Evie took the paper and slipped it into her back pocket. "Don't worry. Everything will be fine. Go have your fun."

———

At the Lazy S, Gil watched as the headlights from Tessa's Jeep popped over the gentle rise. His guts felt light and he tamped down on the thrill. Yes, Tessa was a beautiful, fascinating, intriguing woman, but a little flirting didn't mean she had any interest in a relationship with him. Gil pushed himself off the rails of the round pen and tightened Sierra's and Mr. Ford's cinches for the final time.

"You made it," Gil said, as she climbed out of the Jeep. He led the horses over to her. "I was about to give up on you."

"Sorry. I didn't mean to make you wait. I hate to hold you guys up."

"It's all good. They were a little late leaving anyways. A little trotting, a little cantering, and we'll catch up to them in no time."

She smiled, but it came off a little unsure. "Quinn did tell you that I'm just now getting back into riding, right? I don't have to go. I don't want to slow you down."

"You'll be fine. If we start going too fast, you let me know, and we'll slow down." He handed her Sierra's reins.

Sierra was one of the ranch's older horses, a babysitter, Jenna had told him. The kind of horse she could put kids and new riders on and the mare would pack them around and treat them like fine bone china.

"Where's your hat?" Gil bobbed his chin toward her head. "Your face is going to fry."

She glanced at her Jeep as if a hat would suddenly appear, then glanced back at him. "I'll be fine."

Her complexion wasn't too fair, but the sun at this altitude was strong. Stepping closer, he pulled his black-felt Stetson off the top of his head and plopped it down on hers, sorely tempted to cup her face, run his thumb over her plump bottom lip and lean in and taste for himself what he'd been missing. Would her kisses be sweet and tender? Or would the heat scorch them both?

Instead, he reached up and tugged on the end of her ponytail. "The hat suits you."

She pulled the hat off her head and held it out to him. "I can't take your hat."

"Don't argue." He took a step back, pulling an old beat up ATF baseball cap from his back pocket and tugging it down over his head.

The morning sun shone through the bullet hole in the brim.

Luckily, he hadn't been wearing the hat when the bullet had struck it. "Let's go, daylight's wasting."

She replaced his hat on her head. He liked seeing something of his on her. Not like he was claiming her. It wasn't like that, but it put a self-satisfied smile on his face.

They both swung into the saddles and trotted down the two-track dirt road, past the new cabins, and even further past the old ones. They continued on the trail leading down to the Lazy S's hot spring and rode on, their horses' noses pointing toward the foothills.

The horse he rode, Mr. Ford, seemed to know the way. They trotted for a mile or two, over scrub and scraggly grass, his saddle squeaking to the gentle rhythm. Gil kept Tessa ahead of him to make sure that she wasn't riding above her abilities.

But the truth was, he liked watching her ride from behind. He loved watching how her hips swayed in the saddle and wondered what it would feel like to have those lithe thighs wrapped around him. At a small creek, they slowed the horses to a walk, and let the animals catch their breath.

"Why were you late?"

Tessa remained quiet for a moment, glancing at him and then looking away as if deciding how much she was gonna tell him. The trail widened, and Gil trotted up and slowed Mr. Ford to a walk beside her. She rolled her head from side to side and said, "Flat tire." She didn't look at him when she said it.

"Something tells me there's more to that story."

"Maybe." She shrugged, but there was a stiffness to her shoulders. She wasn't as indifferent as she pretended. "I ... It's nothing."

"Whoa," Gil told Mr. Ford. The horse stopped, so did Sierra. "What's nothing?"

Tessa turned her horse to face him. "My front tire was slashed. But I don't live in the nicest part of Murdock. It could have been anyone. A bunch of kids on a dare. It doesn't mean anything."

By the way she scrunched up her face, he didn't think that she really believed that. Neither did he. She may not live in the affluent section of town, but while Murdock wasn't the slums of New York, it also wasn't the wild, wild, West. "Who was it?" He would bet his left nut that she knew who'd done it.

"It doesn't matter. I can't prove—"

"I'm not asking you what you can prove. I'm not a prosecutor. I want to know what you *think*."

She turned her horse and started walking off again. Gil squeezed Mr. Ford into a trot and pulled her to a stop by her reins. "Tell me."

"I really—"

"Tell me." There was no asking in his tone. He'd been in law enforcement long enough not to let something like this slide. He waited her out.

She scratched Sierra's brown and white neck and ran her fingers through the paint's thick mane. "I think it was my ex-husband. Or maybe one of his lackeys."

"What about security cameras? Is your house monitored?"

She laughed, it was a little sad, but sweet. "No. And before you ask, my neighbors don't have any either. It's not that kind of neighborhood."

They rode on toward the canyon again. If they didn't hurry, they'd never catch up to Quinn and the rest of them. Not that that would bother Gil any. He'd much rather spend a little alone time with Tessa, than ride at the back of the herd eating dust and wiping grit from his eyes. "Did any of the neighbors see anything?"

Far in the distance, a horse called out. Mr. Ford pricked his ears and returned the call. They must be getting close to the others. As they walked on, the scrub grass slowly gave way to greener pasture. With careful steps, they negotiated a steep downhill, crossed the shallow river, and trotted up the gentle slope of the embankment on the other side.

"I was in too much of a hurry to check with the neighbors."

"Check with them when you get home." It was an order. Even if it wasn't his to give. An ex, angry enough to slash a tire, could easily escalate. He'd seen it happen too many times. She bristled but didn't say anything. If she didn't do it, he would. She was living alone in a not good part of town with a young child. This wasn't the kind of thing where you shrugged your shoulders and dismissed it.

"Look, my ex is an asshole, clearly, but he's basically harmless."

"And angry. *Clearly*," he said, mocking her tone.

They came over a rise, and saw the rest of the group a few hundred yards ahead. This time it was Sierra who called out, but none of the other horses answered.

"Yeah, well, he thinks he can swoop back into his child's life after being AWOL for the past six plus years and get full custody. Not gonna happen. He's going to have to get over himself. As it is, the judge granted him limited visitation. Not as much as my ex would have liked, but more than I'd wanted." She stared off into the distance, where everyone from the Lazy S had gathered, but Gil could tell she wasn't seeing them.

"Who is this guy?"

She looked at Gil then. Eyed the embroidered letters on his baseball cap. She was law enforcement herself, but she flew helo's, she wasn't the kind to bust down doors, guns blazing. He was. The way her eyes narrowed, she'd guessed that about him.

"Why do you want to know? You going to bust down his door? Tell him to back off? Rough him up?"

Yes. Yes. And hell yes. "Maybe," he said, deciding to answer her honestly. She wasn't a damsel in distress, and he didn't have a white knight complex. She was tough, he could see that, but even the toughest people needed backup.

"I'd rather not say. I don't need you, or Quinn, or any of y'all's buddies making matters worse. It was a slashed tire. He made his point."

"Which is?"

"That he's not happy with me. Look, can we drop this? I want to enjoy the day. The last thing I want to do is to bring my ex on this ride with me. Think we can do that?"

"On one condition." He held back a smile. "Have dinner with me tonight."

She pulled Sierra up short. The horse tossed her head. "Aah... Look, Gil, I'm not looking for –"

"It's dinner, Sunshine. It's not a proposal. Even you have to eat sometimes, right?"

"*Sunshine?* I seriously don't think anybody has called me that before."

Up ahead Quinn broke away from the rest of the riders and trotted toward them on a heavily muscled black gelding. Despite what Tessa had said, Gil got the impression she kind of liked the nickname. Who would've thought? He'd been prepared for her to reach over and slug him in the shoulder.

Quinn hardly slowed down. He gave them a rash of good-natured shit for taking so long, then told them to get a move on. They spent the next hour rounding up the cattle before they could start pushing them toward the big box canyon.

By the time the cattle had settled into their new grazing spot, it was afternoon, and everyone pulled up to break for a late lunch. They dropped their reins, ground tying their horses. Quinn and Boomer unpacked the food from their saddlebags, while Jenna and Sidney passed out bottles of water.

Tessa pushed Gil's hat up high on her forehead, cracked open a bottle, and sucked down four long, gulping swallows. A few drops of water escaped the corners of her mouth, and Gil couldn't take his eyes off of the water as it dripped down her neck before disappearing beneath her shirt. Quinn stepped up beside him and bumped him in the shoulder. "Enjoying the view?"

Gil tore his gaze away from Tessa. Quinn had a shit-eating grin on his face. *Damn.* It's wasn't that he really cared if Quinn knew that he was interested in Tessa, but after years of working undercover, it was hard to get used to living a more public life.

In the past, he'd avoided any type of long-term relationships. They didn't work out when you couldn't be completely honest. If truth be told, the type of women he'd attracted while under-cover, weren't the type he'd wanted to take home to his mother. But Tessa... Tessa was a new and interesting wrinkle. "None better."

Quinn slapped two sandwiches in Gil's hand. Gil walked over, sat on the boulder next to Tessa, and handed over one of the ham and cheese sandwiches.

"Thanks. I'm starving." She unwrapped her sandwich and took half in her hands. These weren't your average sandwiches. The bread was homemade and thick, the ham piled high. He had to unhinge his jaw to take a bite.

He tore a section free and tucked it into his cheek. "What's the verdict on tonight?"

The more he'd watched her on the drive, the more he wanted to get to know her better. There was something about her, beyond the physical, a boldness perhaps, that intrigued him. It showed in the way she drove the cattle and handled the horse even though she'd had limited experience.

She took a bite of her sandwich and wiped away the mayon-naise from the corner of her mouth with her thumb. He captured her wrist, and brought her thumb to his mouth, sucking it clean.

He released her hand. "What do you say?"

Her gaze locked on his. He glanced at her lips, then lower, to the spot where her pulse thrummed at the base of her neck.

"Maybe that's not such a good idea."

"Why's that?"

"Look, I've got a kid…"

"You say that like he's a contagion."

She gave him a look he didn't know how to interpret. "Is your having a kid supposed to make me run for the hills?"

She took another bite, chewed it slowly as if chewing on her words. When she swallowed, she said, "I like you."

"That's a yes on dinner then?"

"No. It's not."

He washed down his sandwich with a big swig of water. "I'm not following you. I'm interested, so I asked you out. I may be reading this incorrectly, but when you say 'I like you' I'm thinking you're interested too. Explain why you're flashing a giant *Do Not Pass Go* sign? You have a thing against dating fellow LEO's?"

"I don't have anything against dating law enforcement officers."

Bold, like he'd thought. Tessa wasn't one to play head games. He liked the fact that she didn't deny she was interested. "Then what is it?"

"Five more minutes." Hank—the foreman of the Lazy S, and Jenna's father—started gathering their trash and stuffing it into his saddlebags. Alby and Santos had already finished eating and were tightening their cinches. Jenna drank the last of her water, and Quinn walked over and caught their horses.

Tessa handed Gil the last of her sandwich as if she'd lost her appetite. "My life is a little complicated at the moment. I don't need to throw a wrench in it and make it any worse."

He polished off the rest of her sandwich and brushed the

crumbs from his fingers. "It's not a complication, it's dinner. Think about it."

With that said, he gathered up Mr. Ford's reins, tightened his cinch, and swung up into the saddle. Sierra had wandered about thirty yards away from the other horses, and Boomer trotted over, ponying Sierra behind him.

"Thanks." Tessa took the reins but was slow to get up off the bolder. Her leg seemed stiff, and she looked a little bowlegged.

"How is your rear?" Boomer asked. "You sore yet?"

"Maybe a little." Tessa tried to put her foot in the stirrup, but her leg wouldn't bend enough.

Boomer chuckled.

"Okay," Tessa said. "Maybe a lot. But it's nothing I can't handle."

Boomer flashed a grin. "Never doubted that for a minute." Boomer squeezed his horse and trotted off to catch up with Sidney and Jenna.

Tessa gathered her reins, and with a soft groan, that made Gil's jeans a size too small, put her foot in the stirrup and gingerly settled in the saddle.

The day had been hot, and dirt clung to the sweat on Gil's skin. Grit ground between his molars every time he closed his mouth. He spat, trying to clear some the grime, but it didn't seem to do much good.

When they were almost back to the ranch, Boomer and Jenna galloped away on their horses, disappearing behind a rise.

Gil, Tessa, Sidney, and Hank rode four abreast. Alby and Santos brought up the rear about fifty yards back.

Sidney's horse jigged in place, his head high as if he wanted to run after the other horses. Mr. Ford and Sierra were content to plod along. "You'll have to excuse them." Sidney waved her hand, indicating Boomer and Jenna. "They have this little rivalry."

"I'm surprised you don't want in on that," Tessa said

"Oh, no." Sidney shook her head.

"That's kind of their thing," Hank said. "We stay out of the way and let them get it out of their systems."

A couple of rolling hills ahead, Jenna and Boomer popped into view, the sound of thundering hooves came to them even from that distance. Dual clouds of dust streaked behind them like dusty contrails from a jet's engines. Moments later they disappeared again, and Gil didn't see them again until they'd all made it back to the barn.

Boomer was all smiles, and Jenna had a playful scowl. The big blue roan Jenna had been riding blew a cloud of dust from his nostrils, his sides heaving, his nostrils flaring. Boomer's horse, a sorrel, was tied to a hitching post. The mare lowered her head and cocked a rear leg as she relaxed.

Boomer walked over and lifted Sidney out of the saddle and gave her a big smooch on her lips. "You were right, Irish. Bullet has jetpacks *and* a turbo drive."

He grabbed Sidney around the waist and spun her around before setting her down again. "I knew you could find me a horse that could beat Angel."

"That was a one-off," Jenna said. "Don't get used to winning."

Boomer jogged over to his horse that had managed to pull his rope free. "Never knew you were a sore loser. It's not a great feeling. But you're tough, you can deal."

They all went to work unsaddling their horses, hosing them down, and settling them into their pastures for the night. Mackenzie Nash, Hank's wife, stepped into the barn, a large wooden spoon in her hand. "Soup's on if any of you are hungry."

Hank walked over to her, tugged the USMC baseball cap off her head and kissed her on the lips. It wasn't quick. It was slow and—

"Ew, gross," Jenna said. "I would tell you to get a room, but we can all see what happens when you do that."

Hank grinned and splayed his hand over Mac's ever-expanding belly. He leaned over, his mouth at his wife's belly. "Hey, Littlebit. Have you been good to your Mom today?"

"The brat's been kicking my kidneys all afternoon, that's how he's been."

"*She*," Hank said. "She's been kicking your kidneys."

"It's a boy," Mac insisted.

"We'll see about that." Hank kissed his wife again. "Come on everybody, before it gets cold."

"Uh..." Gil hung back and glanced over at Tessa. "I think Tessa and I are going to head to the diner. Y'all go on ahead."

Tessa shot him a quick look but didn't contradict him. Smart woman.

Jenna opened her mouth to say something, but Quinn caught her hand and dragged her toward the big house. Mac took his announcement in stride. "Suit yourself."

"More for me," Santos called from the tack room.

Hank, Mack, Quinn, and Jenna headed off to the big house. Santos jogged after them. "Hey, wait up."

Alby clapped Gil on the shoulder. "You kids have fun. We won't wait up." He gave Tessa a wink and strode after the rest of them.

She turned to Gil and said. "I really should say no." She looked down at herself, her arms held out. "Look at me. I'm filthy." She ran a hand across her forehead, and held her fingers out, showing him the grime.

He took her fingers and wiped them on the front of his shirt, trapping her hand against his chest. He caught a finger under her chin and tilted her face up and pressed a light kiss to her lips. "It's the diner. Unless you would prefer my place. You could catch a shower, and I could cook."

"You cook?"

"I can microwave a hot dog with the best of them. Plus I think there are a couple slices of pizza in the fridge, but they've been in there a few days. It might poison you."

She glanced at his lips, then back at his eyes. "Tempting, but the diner seems less... dangerous."

Dangerous?

"Wait." He was a big man, but Tessa didn't strike him as a woman who was easily intimidated. Gil eased out of her space but didn't let go of her hand. "Are you afraid of me?"

Though it wasn't just his size that people found forbidding. He'd be lying if he said his overseas tours of duty and his time undercover hadn't blackened his soul.

He wasn't violent.

He wasn't mean.

But he'd done things he wasn't proud of and seen things he couldn't unsee. He would never be the man he was before he'd deployed, and that frightened some people. She of all people should understand that. Even if she'd spent her time in the military in the helo's and not on the ground, she knew firsthand what the men and women on the ground had faced.

"Should I be afraid?" An open and honest question. Her eyes narrowed. She expected the same honesty in return. He liked that she wasn't scared to ask the hard questions.

"No." He didn't elaborate. He figured the response was self-explanatory.

"A shower and the diner then," Tessa said. "Unless you want to rescind your offer."

"Not on your life."

3

———

Tessa wasn't sure why, but she'd agreed to drive them to the diner instead of them taking separate cars. Which meant she would have to go back to the ranch tonight to drop Gil back at his cabin.

Would he invite her in?

Did she want him to?

In front of the diner, she killed the engine and set the Jeep's parking brake. The saliva dried in her mouth as she looked over at him. "You know... If Pearl sees the two of us in there together, she's gonna start talking."

"I didn't take you as someone who cared about what other people thought."

"I-I'm not. Usually. It's just... With this thing with my ex, like I said, it gets complicated. I wouldn't want to give him any reason to take me back to court for custody."

"They're not going to give him custody because you went out on a date."

"No. Probably not. But... He's an asshole, remember? I wouldn't put it past him to try. Even though he's the one who ran out on us."

Gil took her hand off the manual shifter and held her hand in his, running his thumb over her knuckles, over the bumps, to the valleys, and back again.

"Look, I don't want to cause you any trouble." His voice went soft. "Your son is the most important person in your life. I get that. If you want, you can take me back to the ranch and we'll call it a night. No harm, no foul."

His eyes were stark but sincere. He wasn't blowing smoke. He meant every word he said. Tessa's heart kicked at her ribs. This man knew what he wanted, and right now for whatever reason, that was her. Yet he also saw *her* and seemed to understand how hard being a single mom could be.

"Do you have any kids of your own?"

"No. Not yet." The yet piqued her interest, but that was a conversation for another time. Her stomach rumbled, and Gil smiled. He had one of those smiles that could transform his whole face. He had a short, thick beard, a bump from a break on the bridge of his nose, and dark eyes that drew her in. He had an edge to him she'd seen in other military and LEO boys, but when he smiled like that... it did something sinfully wicked to her insides. She glanced down at his lips and back up at his eyes.

His grin got wider.

"Can I kiss you?" She got the words out before she lost her nerve.

"I'd like that," he said, though he didn't move any closer. Instead, he turned Tessa's hand over and massaged his thumb into her palm.

Her eyes fluttered closed, then opened again. That gentle massage shouldn't have felt as good as it did. Now if he could go a little higher until he hit that knot between her shoulder blades. That nagging, niggling knot that hadn't gone away since Bradley had gained visitation rights.

"I'll tell you what," he said. "You hold that thought while we eat dinner. If you're still interested when we're done, you let me know."

She gazed back at him, and Gil didn't break eye contact. He wasn't anything like she'd expected. "Deal." She held out her other hand for him to shake and he took it.

"Do you trust me?"

"That sounds ominous." She went to take her hand back, but he didn't let go. Despite what she'd said, this was the man who'd single-handedly held off a drug cartel's armed watchdogs, risking his life, while allowing Quinn, Jenna, and Pepita to escape a deadly situation. A situation that almost cost Gil his life. "Yeah, I trust you." She didn't say those words lightly.

He popped his door and released her hand. "Wait here."

Gil jogged up the steps of the old converted railroad car turned diner. The backside had been blown out and a kitchen added on. Through the windows, she saw that most of the booths were taken as well as the row of stools lining the counter.

It wasn't long before Gil returned with a large *To Go* bag. Her heart skipped like a giddy little girl let out for recess.

He climbed in and closed the door behind him. Tessa had been willing to go in with him, but the fact that he understood her hesitation spoke volumes to the type of man that he was.

"Why don't we head back to the ranch," he said. "I know a place we can eat that I think you'll really like."

She started the engine and backed out of her parking space. "I really appreciate you doing this for me, I—"

"Well, don't go polishing my knightly armor yet. It wasn't completely altruistic." He didn't crack a smile, but his teasing tone gave him away.

"Ulterior motives then?" Why was she hoping the answer was yes? She turned at the stop sign and sped back toward the ranch.

"I wouldn't mind having you all to myself. Then there's the

whole bit about not having to update the rumor mill if I decide next week I don't like you."

"I can see where that could be a hassle." She knew he was joking, but the doubts crept in. In all seriousness, she said, "Do you think you're going to change your mind next week?"

She expected him to deny it, she hadn't expected him to say, "pull over."

Where the shoulder widened for a row of mailboxes, Tessa eased the Jeep to a stop. While her foot was on the clutch, Gil popped the Jeep out of gear and engaged the emergency brake.

"Look, between my deployments and my stints undercover, it didn't leave me many opportunities for relationships, or even much of a chance to date for that matter. It made me very selective with who I wanted to spend time with."

"Which means?" She wasn't really getting impatient. She wanted to hear what he had to say, but the smells from the To Go bag where making her mouth water and her stomach grumble.

"The short answer to that question is no. I'm not going to change my mind next week. I don't ask random women out on a whim." It might have been the play of the lights from her dashboard that made his eyes look like they'd gone darker, as the conversation got much more serious than she'd ever intended.

"I'm just looking for some fun, Gil. I'm not looking for permanence."

The corners of his mouth twitched up, but somehow it came off looking like a frown. "Fun is good, too." The lightness in his words seemed forced, but it was late, and she was hungry so she didn't push him on it. He bobbed his chin toward the dark ribbon of road ahead of them. "Let's go. I'm starving."

Tessa shifted into gear, the knot between her shoulder blades twinged as an uneasy silence splintered and fractured the air around them. She reached for the volume on the radio when her cell phone buzzed.

She pulled it from her back pocket and glanced at the screen. There goes dinner.

"What is it?" Gil asked.

"Quinn and I got called in to fly cover for an op. I don't have time to take you back. I'll drive to the airport, and you can take my Jeep back to the ranch."

Her tires skidded and kicked up loose gravel as she pulled a U-ey and sped in the opposite direction toward Murdock's municipal airport.

"What's going on? I've been out of the loop."

She glanced over at him, not knowing how much she could tell him. Technically, he was part of her task force, but she suspected if Special Agent Spinks had wanted Gil involved, he would have contacted Gil as well.

She gave him the cliff notes version. "There's been chatter of a big arms deal going down. We think The Wolf has moved into our area."

"Way the hell out here? Wouldn't it be easier if he was closer to a port?"

"You would think, but the ports are under intense scrutiny. We're thinking The Wolf's going to fly the goods in and out. In that case, a remote area works in his favor."

They lapsed into silence as she sped down the road, her headlights cutting through the darkness. Without lights and sirens, her speed was limited. Quinn must have broken the land speed record because he screeched to a stop and jumped out of his truck moments after she and Gil had arrived.

She handed Gil her keys as Quinn clapped him on the back. "Are you our spotter?"

"He didn't get the call," Tessa said. "We can't take him out on this, without —"

"Screw that, Sterling. Another set of eyes on a cover op never hurt. It's not like he needs his medical clearance, or even to carry a weapon."

"Spinks will want to know," she said, even as the three of them jogged toward the helo. They didn't have time to jump into their flight suits.

There didn't seem to be a question of if Gil was willing to go. He beeped her Jeep locked and kept up with them.

"We'll tell him," Quinn was quick to assure her, "as soon as we land."

Gil grinned over at her and climbed into the Blackhawk and buckled into the jump seat behind the pilot's chair.

Tessa and Quinn ran through their preflight as fast as they safely could. The engine spooled up, and as soon as they received clearance from the tower, they lifted off and banked north and west.

Over the comms, one of the task force agents fed them coordinates to rendezvous with the rest of the team on the ground.

Quinn plotted their course, and Spinks filled them in mid-flight on the rapidly developing operation. Everyone was en route to a location where actionable intel had placed an arms deal going down. They had a guy on the inside of a local gang that was looking to carve a niche as a snitch.

The gang wasn't satisfied with a little drug running like a lot of the other low-level scum who had moved in to fill the void since El Verdugo's drug cartel had imploded. This gang had moved on to nastier things—guns and grenades. As much as the task force wanted to stop these guys, they weren't the ones that posed the most significant threat.

If everything went according to Spinks' plan, the gun buys might lead them to The Wolf. Mainly because if the scuttlebutt was correct, this guy had amassed the firepower to huff, and puff, and topple small governments, or at least supply the revolutionaries with enough firepower to do it themselves.

Even the most well thought out strategies never went off without a hitch, and as quickly as this operation had been pulled together, Tessa had a bad feeling...

"This is fucked up," Gil said from behind her over the internal comms, not the open mic to headquarters. There wasn't any distress or panic in his words, just an observation from a guy with enough life experience to trust his gut.

"Copy that," Quinn said. "But after months of little or no intel, at least we're not sitting here with our dicks in our hands waiting for something to happen."

Tessa made a noise in the back of her throat, not because she was offended, but because Quinn had reminded her what she might have missed if she and Gil had actually made it back to his cabin. It wasn't often she had a weekend without her son. And yeah, she really needed to focus on what was happening beyond her windscreen.

"You always talk like that around the ladies, asshole?" Gil's reprimand came through her headset, clear and calm beneath the beating of the rotor blades.

"Present company excluded," Quinn amended. "Sorry, LT, sometimes I forget I'm in mixed company."

"I'm not mixed company, I'm your teammate." To Gil, she said, "I don't need anyone to run interference for me either, special agent. Someone gets outta line, I'll tell 'em."

Gil's soft chuckle raised goosebumps on her arms, sounding much more intimate and more arousing than it should have. "Fair enough, *lieutenant*."

The way he said *lieutenant* almost sounded like an endearment. Her stomach had that falling-fifty-feet feeling, although a quick glance at her altimeter told her that their altitude remained steady.

Quinn glanced over at her from the left-hand seat, a stupid grin on his face that told her Gil's tone hadn't been a figment of her imagination. *Great.* Just what she needed was Quinn giving her shit about Gil. At least it was good natured.

Quinn had tried to warn her off Gil, but he'd been unable to hide the respect he held for the man who had helped save his life. Whatever faults Gil might have, whatever internal demons had brought him to the Healing Horses program, Tessa didn't doubt he was a good man at heart.

"Big Bird, this is Elmo. You got eyes on?" Agent Isaac Lang's voice came through Tessa's headset, with an edge to his voice that the crackle and hiss of the radio couldn't hide. Lang was the lead agent on the ground with eyes on the impending gun deal.

"ETA five minutes," Quinn confirmed for him.

The night was clear with good visibility. The plan was to keep the helo at altitude and out of sight. They were to keep their eyes on the truckloads of arms while Lang and his men would attempt to follow the sellers back to their hidey-hole.

"We don't have five minutes," Lang said. "This shit's going down now."

The rendezvous point was taking them far into the foothills where the houses and street lights gave way to rolling hills and trees and the cover of darkness. Tessa lowered her night-vision goggles, NVGs, pitching her world into an eerie green canvas. For some reason, the altered optics always made her think of an underworld of bridge trolls and fire-breathing dragons.

Beside her, Quinn lowered his NVGs as well.

"Sitrep, Elmo," Spinks ordered.

"I've got two—no, make that three enclosed trucks. White. No identifying marks. We're attempting to place trackers now. I thought this was supposed to be—"

At the same time Lang cut out, bursts of light flashed far ahead between the trees.

"Fuck. They've gone hot," Gil said, indicating shots being fired.

From the overwhelming spray of light coming from one direction and the intermittent, controlled fire coming from the other, Lang and his men were outnumbered and outgunned.

"Get me down there." Gil had slipped into a harness and tethered himself inside the helo. He slid open both rear doors, armed with an AR-15 he'd retrieved from a rack in the back.

"Command, this is Big Bird, request permission to assist."

"Negative. You're on overwatch—"

Quinn switched the comms and Gil's mic went hot. "Forget overwatch. Our men are going to get slaughtered if we don't get down there."

"Who the hell let you on that bird, Brant?" Spinks hollered.

Tessa was going to pay for allowing Gil on the mission. Probably with her job. But there wasn't anything she could do about that now.

"Man down," Lang reported. "They've got cop killers. I'm going in."

Cop killers. Armor piercing rounds. Those bastards didn't fool around.

"Put me down. *Now.*" Gil didn't leave any room for argument. One more guy might not make any difference, but then again, one more might. Tessa glanced at Quinn. Quinn nodded his agreement. After all, if they were going to disobey direct orders, both of their asses could be canned. She set the helo down in a clearing about one kilometer, one klick, away from the shooting.

"Coming your way," Gil told Lang. He ditched the harness, tossed on a bulletproof vest and clipped on a mobile radio. The armor wouldn't help him if he got hit with an APR, but it was better than nothing.

As soon as Gil was clear of the rotors, Tessa lifted off again.

She switched to the internal comms, so only Quinn could hear her. "I hope he knows what the hell he's doing."

———

Running a klick in the dark and over rough terrain got Gil's blood pumping and his heart thumping, as the steady drip of adrenaline seared his veins. Up ahead, more shots were fired, but the tempo had slowed. Headlights from one of the trucks came on. Gil ducked, and a bullet thumped into the tree right where his head had been.

Two trucks roared by, and Gil let them go. He didn't want to give up his position. From his location behind the tree, he could make out Lang holed up behind the rear axle of the remaining truck. One of the task force guys had taken cover to Gil's right behind another tree, and two others had found cover in a ditch.

On the ground, out in the open, was the agent who'd been shot. The man slipped his hand up under his vest, and said, "He shot me. The fucker shot me." The man groaned, pulled out his hand and stared at the blood. He chuckled. More pain, less humor. "*Motherfucker*. My wife is going to be pissed if I die."

"We're not going to let you die," one of Lang's men said, Joel Cook, Gil thought. "We're going to get you out of there."

Gil spoke into his radio, "Lang, coming up on your six. Don't shoot."

Over the radio, Lang told his men to hold their fire.

"Coming to you, buddy," Gil said. "Cover me."

Lang peeked around the bumper of the of the truck and laid down suppressive fire. Gil ran over to Lang and pressed his back against the rear wheel. "What's the plan."

"I gotta get Rivera before he bleeds out. They've got two guys behind that shack, one in the trees at about ten o'clock, and one I haven't seen for a while. I think he took off, but I can't be sure."

Rivera tried scooting backward, shoving at the ground with the heels of his boots. A shot rang out, the bullet hitting inches from Rivera's right boot. Rivera stilled.

"I can't wait any longer. You guys cover me," Lang said. "I'll pull him behind that rocky outcrop." Into his radio, Lang gave the orders. His men were to concentrate their fire on the shack, and Gil was to make sure the guy in the trees kept his head down. Lang counted down, and when he hit zero, Gil and the rest of the men started firing.

Lang sprinted in a half crouch over to Rivera and hooked his hands under Rivera's arms. Lang struggled as he dragged the dead weight toward the rocks. Gil cursed under his breath. Rivera was a big man, Gil should have been the one pulling him to safety.

Gil's AR-15 hit empty as Lang got Rivera behind cover. Gil dumped the empty mag and slapped a new one home. Lang shrugged off his backpack and pulled out a blowout kit, a first-aid kit designed to treat bullet wounds. A bullet rent the air, and Lang fell. Gil yelled into his radio, "Did any of you see where that came from?"

From beneath the back end of the truck, Gil watched as Lang writhed on the ground. "My legs. I can't feel my fucking legs."

Over the comms, someone said, "The shot came from that rise at Lang's nine o'clock." Meaning a position to Lang's left. From Gil's vantage point, the truck blocked his view. It was probably the guy Lang thought had run off. But instead of running off, the asshole had circled around and flanked them. Gil clicked the talk button on his radio, "Hang on, buddy. I'm coming for you."

"Stand down," Lang said, "No one is going anywhere until someone gets that motherfucker."

Lang and Rivera were screwed, and Gil wasn't sure why the

shooter hadn't wasted his teammates already. What was he waiting for?

Lang and Rivera were pinned down. If they moved around to the other side of the rocks, they would be in the direct line of fire from the guys behind the shack, yet staying where they were would likely get them killed. Lang's best hope for survival was for Gil to get the guy who'd ambushed Lang to surrender or end him.

At that point, Gil didn't care which.

Gil slid under the truck. With his rifle cradled in his arms, he crawled to the truck's right front wheel, the healing muscles from his old bullet wound bitched and complained and generally gave him hell like a bitter ex-wife on a rampage. The smell of gunpowder filled his nostrils and his ears rung from all the shooting.

From his new position, Lang and Rivera were directly in his line of sight. Lang had rolled to his side and applied pressure to Rivera's wound while trying to hold pressure on his own. Rivera was no longer talking, but the man's moans of pain set Gil's teeth on edge. If they waited too much longer, they'd be taking both guys out in body bags.

Into his radio, Gil hissed, "One of you guys try to talk to this guy. I'll see if I can locate his position."

"This is the Bison County Task Force. Drop your weapon, and come out with your hands up," Cook said.

Cook was one of the newer guys that had joined the task force shortly before Gil had been shot. From the direction of Cook's voice, he'd moved to a better vantage point as well.

A shot rang out and the tire Gil had been hiding behind hissed and went flat. The bullet pinged off the steel wheel and zinged past his head with inches to spare.

He returned fire. A double tap. A body hit the ground with a soft thud. Over his radio, he heard, "Target in the tree has been neutralized."

"Someone needs to secure those guys at the back of the shack," Gil ordered back.

"We're on it," that from Hugh Fisher, one of the guys who'd taken cover in the ditch.

Two shadows rose from the ditch and ran from cover to cover, making their way toward the shooters who had taken up positions behind the shack. No shots had come from that direction for a few minutes. Had those men taken off for the hills while they'd had the chance? A distinct possibility.

On the way to the shack, one of Lang's men knelt next to the guy Gil had shot, then kept moving. Dead, Gil figured. That left one more.

"Come out now," Cook ordered. "Unless you want to be dead like your buddy over there."

"You've got ten seconds. Come out, or we're taking you out. Your choice."

Not standard negotiating protocol, but Rivera and Lang were bleeding out, they didn't have the time to mess around.

"Nine, eight, seven—"

"I want—"

"You shot a cop. You don't get to negotiate," Gil hollered. "You come out, or you get dead. Don't matter much to me. Tick-tock, asshole."

"Five, four, three."

One of the agents slapped a new magazine into their duty weapon.

"Two, one—"

"Okay, okay." There was a clatter as what looked like an AK-47 hit the ground.

Gil rolled out from beneath the truck and got to his feet, the end of his barrel aimed at the guy's head as Gil stood.

"The back of the shack is clear," Fisher said over the radio. "They must have taken off. Want us to pursue?"

"Negative," Gil said. "It's clear out here, come on back."

The shooter stepped out, his hands on his head. "On your knees." Gil's aim didn't falter. When the shooter complied, Gil said, "Cuff him."

"Motherfucker," the guy screeched out when Cook yanked they guy's arms behind him and cuffed him.

"What's his problem?" Gil asked.

"Looks like he sprung a leak," Cook said. "A shame it doesn't look fatal."

Cook patted down the shooter and hauled him to his feet. Gil shouldered his weapon and hurried over to Rivera and Lang. Rivera had lost consciousness. Gil felt for a pulse, it was light, thready.

"Someone give me a hand over here," Gil called out.

Lang's blood-covered hand gripped Gil's arm. "I can't feel my legs, man. Holy fuck, I'm never going to have sex again."

"That's bullshit, and you know it." Gil couldn't say what he really thought. He couldn't say that Lang was probably right. He pulled off his outer shirt and held it against Lang's lower abdomen. "It's just a flesh wound."

Lang's chuckle came out strangled, and his lips pulled back in a grimace. "*Flesh wound.* You're such a prick."

"Don't you forget it." Even in the dark, Gil couldn't miss the pool of blood dripping down Lang's side. He loaded Lang's wound with Quick Clot from the kit he found in one of the pockets of Lang's tactical pants hoping to buy his friend some time.

Fisher dropped to his knees beside Gil and held pressure on Rivera's wound while Gil did the same for Lang. The bullet had struck low, beneath the bottom edge of Lang's ballistic vest, and buried itself deep into Lang's belly. With no exit wound, and Lang's inability to move his legs, Gil was concerned that the bullet had lodged itself against Lang's spine.

"Medevac is on its way," Fisher said, "but only one chopper was available."

As Fisher relayed the news, Gil heard the *whompa-whompa-whompa* of the medevac's rotor as the chopper flew in. Rivera was worse off, but Lang wasn't fairing much better. He'd started losing consciousness and he no longer grimaced as Gil held pressure on his wound. They didn't have time to wait for the medevac to come back.

"Cook," Gil hollered. "Have Sterling on standby, we'll evac Lang to the trauma center ourselves."

———

Tessa flopped down in the chair beside Gil in the waiting room at the trauma hospital in Idaho Falls. "How are you doing?"

Not worth a damn sprang to mind, along with a few other honest words that might make Tessa, and especially Spinks, question his ability to do his job. "Fine."

She gave his hand a squeeze but didn't hang on. Not with the rest of the guys waiting around. She wouldn't want anyone to know that something was brewing between them, and Gil couldn't blame her.

In his mind, there was no work conflict with him leaving the task force, but she didn't know his plans. Besides, he knew how much harder the women had to work to prove themselves to their teammates. He wouldn't want to make her professional life any more challenging for her than it already was. But to say he didn't want to wrap her in his arms and lose himself in her would be a damned lie.

And that wasn't the remnants of an adrenaline stiffy talking either.

"That must be hard." Tessa leaned in, her voice soft to keep it from carrying.

"What?" He glanced at her, but she wasn't looking at his crotch like he'd suspected. *Jesus Christ.* He needed to get his mind out of the gutter and off all of the delicious, delectable, devilish things he wanted to do with Tessa if he ever got her naked.

Now wasn't the time.

Anytime you cheat death is a good time, his body was quick to remind him.

Maybe, but he hadn't been the one shot this time. He hadn't been the one clinging to life as the helos motored to the trauma center at max rated speed. Rivera and Lang had.

"Saving your friend's life."

"That was the training." Uncle Sam had made sure he knew more than basic first aid. He could start an IV, administer plasma expanders, and manage sucking chest wounds at least until someone more qualified came along. Luckily, the task force helo was sometimes used for rescue work and was well equipped for medical emergencies. "The harder part would have been watching him die."

Tessa stood and held out her hand. He took it and allowed her to pull him to his feet. After coming off the adrenaline dump, his legs hung from his body thick and heavy as tree stumps. It was all he could do to put one foot in front of the other.

He didn't ask her where they were going. It didn't matter. He'd probably follow her through the gates of hell if she'd let him. None of the other agents in the room seemed to notice them leaving or that his hand engulfed hers. Or if they did, they were too caught up in their own heads to say anything.

She led him into one of those single, unisex wheelchair accessible bathrooms and closed and locked the door behind her. "Strip."

He arched a brow at her. "Excuse me?"

"You're covered in blood. Take your clothes off. We need to get you cleaned up."

He didn't really need help, but if a beautiful woman wanted him to undress, who was he to argue? Still, he hesitated.

She didn't.

She tugged his bloodstained undershirt shirt from the waistband of his jeans and pulled it over his head. The bathroom had a plastic chair in the corner. She pushed him down onto it and yanked off his boots. Then she made quick work of his jeans, taking out his wallet and keys and handing them to him.

"You want to keep these?" She held up his clothes.

Even if he could get all the blood out, they'd never get clean enough. Not in his mind at least. "Toss them."

There was nothing sexual about what she was doing but tell that to his super-charged body. He'd just *thought* the adrenaline had thoroughly wrung him out. He'd been wrong. The hairs stood up on his arms as if she'd run her tongue down his torso and his dick struggled against the virtual straitjacket that was his underwear.

She bobbed her chin toward his boxer briefs. "Those too."

He glanced down at his gray briefs that had become soaked with blood when he'd helped carry Lang to Tessa's helo. Even after several hours, they were still damp. He hitched his thumbs in his waistband, then stopped.

"What?" Tessa said. "Don't tell me you're shy."

"Hardly."

"Then off with them. Come on. Chop-chop."

Even though what was now happening beneath a thin cover of cotton had absolutely nothing to do with adrenaline and everything to do with Tessa, he said, "I should warn you. Adrenaline sometimes has this... uh... effect on guys—"

"Yeah, yeah, Brant, I deployed with a bunch of men. Trust me, I know more about adrenaline boners than any woman should. I know how it works, you don't have to worry about me thinking you're attracted and want to jump my bones."

"I didn't say that."

Her dark brown eyes caught his, her pupils expanding. She swallowed hard, then made a rolling motion with her hand, telling him to hurry up.

"Fine," he said. "It's not like I didn't warn you."

He lifted and shucked his underwear in one quick motion, balling them up and shooting them into the trash can for two points. It wasn't like he'd ever wear them again.

Her eyes went to his crotch, then darted away. "Yeah, well, you've seen one penis, you've seen them all." The words came out right, but her bravado and bluster were gone. A blush rose to her cheeks.

"Did you have a plan beyond getting me naked?"

Her eyes traveled up from his junk, up, up, up his long torso and finally met his eyes again. "What?"

"A plan. Do you have one? Or am I supposed to streak through the halls of the hospital?"

"I—" her voice squeaked, and Gil had to hold back the grin. He was a big man. He was a big man *everywhere*. She may have seen penises before, which for some stupid reason made him oddly jealous, but she hadn't seen his.

"I have a plan," she said. "Wait here. I'll be right back."

She left, then popped her head back in. "Maybe you should lock the door. You don't want to give some little old lady a heart attack if she stumbles in here."

"I've got it," he said. "Little old ladies aren't my thing anyway.

I prefer a woman who can control a stick." Did he just say that? Her face turned red again, so he must have.

He locked the door behind her, needing to get his head on straight. He was an adult, not some horned-up hound that had slipped its leash and was out on the prowl.

4

You've seen one penis, you've seen them all.

Gil had been quick to prove Tessa wrong.

As Tessa raided one of the hospital's supply closets, she tried not to think about how wrong she'd been. Tried not to imagine what he'd feel like in her hands, her mouth, and other places.

Tessa hurried back to the bathroom, fanning herself with a blue surgical towel about the size of a hand towel. She rapped on the door with her knuckles. "It's me, open up."

After a couple seconds, the lock clicked, and the door swung open. Gil stood behind the door to keep from being seen, though this late at night, the foot traffic was sparse.

Going in, she made a conscious effort to keep her eyes to herself, as she dumped the armload of supplies onto the counter. She handed Gil a pair of scrub bottoms. Without glancing over her shoulder, she said, "I hope these fit. I grabbed the biggest size I could find."

She waited with her back to him until he said, "I'm decent. You can turn around now."

He'd scrubbed a lot of the blood off his hands, but much of it remained in the creases and crevasses of his work-hardened hands. She pulled the plastic off a hand scrub brush—the kind surgeons use to scrub the dirt from their fingernails before surgery—and met him at the sink.

"Let me help," she said.

She turned both faucets on until the water ran hot, but not scalding. She took Gil's hands and placed them under the running water. From the soap dispenser on the wall, she put a large dollop on her hands, rubbing them together, then took his hands and started sudsing him up.

Her hands looked like a child's in his as she worked the lather between his thick fingers and over the callouses on the pads of his palms. Then she got the soft brush and scrubbed his hands until the suds turned a rusty red.

"I can do this myself," he finally said, though he made no effort to take the brush from her and do it himself.

"I know." She rinsed his hands, then wet the surgical towel. She pointed to the smears on blood on his chest. "Do you mind?"

He shook his head but didn't say anything.

With firm strokes, she wiped the blood from his chest and abdomen. She had to rinse the towel twice to get it all. She tugged on the waistband of the scrub pants and wiped a bit of blood from his V trail that disappeared beneath the fabric.

He caught her wrist with his hand and took the towel from her. "I can get it from here."

Holy moly, what was she doing? She held her hands up and took a step back. "Sorry, I was—"

"It's okay."

She shook her head that it wasn't, but he placed a finger under her chin and tilted her head up, forcing her to look at him. "I appreciate the help, but..." he glanced down at his crotch. The thin fabric of the green scrubs couldn't hide his arousal.

"That damn adrenaline," Tessa said, trying to give him an out.

He grinned, and his face softened. He was no longer a warrior, but a regular man. "No, Sunshine. That's all you."

She wasn't into head games, so she didn't fight the smile. "Good to know."

He stepped into her space and cupped one hand around the back of her neck, his thumb tracing the edge of her jaw.

She leaned into the touch. "You about ready to head back out there?"

"Give me a second."

"What for?"

"For this." He ducked his head and touched his lips to hers. Even with some washing, she could smell the gunpowder on his skin, and beneath that, the coppery scent of violence. The kiss wasn't hard or demanding as she'd expected it to be.

A fast-food worker would describe Gil as *super-sized*, but there was another side to this man. Different than what he projected to the outside world. Despite what this man did for a living, beneath the thick muscles and his intimidating exterior, behind the hard eyes, inside his protective shell, there was a softness, a gentleness to him that he couldn't hide. At least not from her.

Or maybe he hadn't tried.

Maybe like her, he'd found the one person he didn't feel like he had to put up a front and shield his true self from.

Yet he wasn't all mush behind the rugged exterior. You couldn't live the violent life he had and not have flame-hardened steel protecting your soul.

She rose up on her toes, deepening the kiss, and tasted the bitter hospital coffee on his tongue. She wanted more. Much more. Not because it had been too long since she'd been with a guy. She couldn't lie and say that it was. She'd been horny and lonely many times before and had managed not to throw herself at every handsome man that gave her a speck of attention. She was better—no, she was *stronger* than that.

But this man...there was something special about this man, more than just the way he tripped all her sex-starved switches.

You'd said the same thing about Bradley and look where that got you.

Yeah, well, she'd gotten Jack out of the deal. Despite how hard it was to be a single mom, she had no regrets. She wrapped her arms around Gil's neck, but he broke the kiss, caught her wrists and held them between them.

The thumping of her heart screeched, like a needle skipping across a record. "Something wrong?"

He touched his forehead to hers. "No. Something's right, and I don't want to screw it up by taking you against the wall of a hospital bathroom."

His directness, his honesty, was something she'd already fallen for. She couldn't, wouldn't fall for the man. A hot, sweaty affair? No problem. But after her experience with her ex, she was now deathly allergic to anything that resembled a commitment.

Besides, she already had a little man in her life that she'd given her heart to the moment she'd set eyes on him. Jack's happiness, Jack's safety, was all that mattered. There would come a time for her, but that time wasn't now.

"You ready to go back?" she asked.

He glanced down at the tenting of his pants, then back up at her. If he was embarrassed, he did a damn fine job hiding it. "You go ahead. I need a few minutes."

———

Lang and Rivera's surgeons came in together, their

surgical masks dangling around their neck, their caps still on their sweaty heads. The shorter and heavier of the two doctors addressed the room at large. "We've spoken with the families, and they've given us permission to update everyone. Rivera should make a full recovery. He lost a lot of blood, but the bullet went through and managed to miss anything vital."

The other doctor, a thin man with excess nervous energy, despite the hours in emergency surgery said, "Lang..." the doctor looked away, then met the eyes of the anxious men and women of the task force. "The family asked us not to sugar coat it. He's in rough shape and has a long recovery ahead of him. The bullet had lodged next to one of his vertebrae, at this point, he's lost all feeling in his legs, but it's too soon to know how much of the paralysis is permanent."

"When can we see them?" Gil asked.

"Tomorrow sometime," Short Doctor said. "They're in recovery, and we expect them to be in ICU at least for the rest of the night."

Gil let out a huge breath and scrubbed his hands down his face. Then he nodded his head. "Okay," he said, but to Tessa, it seemed like it was more to himself than to anyone else.

She reached over and gave his hand a quick squeeze.

He glanced at her then, blinking a few times. "This is good news." The tone of his voice was off, the hope false and manufactured. "Lang won't let a little paralysis slow him down. He's a fighter. It will take more than a bullet to stop him."

"Yeah," Tessa said, but the word came out strangled as if she really didn't believe her own words. "Yeah," she repeated with more conviction, for Gil that time.

He put his arm around her shoulder and pulled her in for a side hug. Quinn came over and clapped Gil on the back. "Nice job out there."

"Lang's paralyzed." The anger had crept into his voice, replacing the worry. "He may never walk again."

"Yeah, but because of you, he's not dead."

Gil pulled a face that said, maybe he hadn't done his friend any favors, but he didn't voice his concern.

The door to the waiting room burst open, and Spinks blew in, his face red, his hair on end, and his expression set on detonate. He looked like a man who'd almost sunk in a bureaucratic shit-storm.

"Sterling, Powell," he bellowed like an Eastern shore fog horn. Everyone in the hospital wing must have heard him. "Come with me."

Spinks turned on his heels and left the room.

"Aw, shit," Quinn said. "This can't be good."

Tessa went to follow Quinn out of the waiting room. She stopped and looked back at Gil. He gave her a wink, and she turned and followed Quinn down the hallway. They caught up with Spinks near the nurse's station. Their boss was pacing back and forth, his hands on his hips, with enough steam pouring out of his ears to pull a coal train from coast-to-coast.

Spinks stopped and narrowed his eyes first at Tessa and then at Quinn. "Give me one good reason why I shouldn't fire the both of you right here, right now." But Spinks didn't stop long enough for them to give him an answer. "You disobeyed a direct order."

Tessa knew there was no excuse, but the truth was, if they hadn't disobeyed, it was likely two good men would be dead. So yeah, she'd violated a direct order, but it was hard to argue with the outcome.

"It was my idea," Quinn said.

"What?" Spinks and Tessa said at the same time.

"That's not true," Tessa said. No way was she letting Quinn take the fall for this. "I was the pilot. I was the senior officer. If you want to blame anyone, blame me. It was my call. But if you want to know the truth, sir, given the same situation, I would do it again."

Spinks crossed his arms over his chest and rested his chin on his hand, contemplating her words. Spinks had a temper, and he could be an ass at times, but there was a reason he led the task force. "Explain."

Tessa didn't even look at Quinn. Like she said, this was on her. "Things were developing quickly, they already had a man down, and from the amount of suppressive fire, Lang and his men looked to be outgunned. Having another man on the ground could mean the difference between them walking away, or them all getting slaughtered. I took that chance."

"It wasn't your chance to take." Spinks stepped into her personal space, and she stared straight ahead, like the old days in basic training. "Luckily for you, it worked. The Brass wanted your ass on a platter, but I managed to talk them down. Don't make me regret it."

"No, sir," Tessa said. "I won't, sir."

Spinks focused his attention on Quinn. "And you, I expect you to keep her in line. You got me?"

"Yes, sir."

"You two get that bird back to the airport, pronto." Spinks stormed off, his boots echoing down the empty hall.

Tessa pulled her hair out of its messy ponytail, combed her fingers through it and tied it back up. "That was pleasant." She turned her back to Quinn and glanced at him over her shoulder. "Tell me, do I have any ass left?"

"Enough," Quinn said, as they started back toward the waiting room. "Gil won't be too disappointed."

Tessa came up short. "What do you mean?"

"I mean you and Gil were gone a long time."

Quinn kept walking, and Tessa had to jog to catch up. "I was helping him get cleaned up. He had a lot of blood on him and—"

"That explains the time, maybe. But it doesn't explain that flush on your face when you returned." If she'd had a baby brother, she imagined this was the kind of torment he'd have fun giving her.

They were almost back to the waiting room, and there was no way she wanted to discuss this with any more ears around. She grabbed his arm and pulled him to a stop. He wasn't exactly smiling, but he wasn't exactly *not* smiling either. "Nothing happened, and if you say anything to any—"

"Sterling," Quinn leaned in, his voice going low as if he were a confidant telling her all his dark secrets. "I'm giving you shit. Gil deserves to have something go right in his life." He bumped her with his shoulder. "You do too."

"Gil and I work together, we can't—"

"There are ways around that."

"Maybe, but I have a kid and an asshole for an ex and—"

"Sometimes you have to forget all the reasons why you *can't* and concentrate on all the reasons why you *should*. Think about it." Quinn backed through the waiting room door and disappeared inside.

The problem was, for the last couple months, sometimes that was all she could think about, even when the last thing a single woman needed to do was gift wrap another reason that could get her fired.

———

"Where's Spinks?" Gil asked when Quinn and Tessa entered the waiting room. Everyone else had left after getting the update from the doctors. There wasn't much they could do for Rivera and Lang besides work hard and catch the bastards that did that to them.

"I think he's heading back to Murdock," Quinn said.

Tessa went around the room and policed all the half-drunk cups of coffee the guys had left lying around. "We've got orders to head back ourselves. Are you coming with us or are you staying here?"

"I'll go with you. I'd rather not be stuck here without transportation. Can you give me a minute? I want to see if I can catch up with Spinks."

"Better hurry. Spinks was making tracks." Quinn headed for the door. "We'll meet you at the helipad."

Gil followed them out, then jogged through the mostly empty halls, taking the stairs down two at a time and bursting out of the stairwell and into the back parking lot. That late at night, the lot was nearly empty, except for what he suspected were employee cars along the back row. A black Bison County SUV's engine rolled over, and the headlights came on, but the truck didn't move. Spinks was on his phone, the blue glow of the departmental computer in the front passenger seat highlighted Spinks' grim face. No doubt Spinks had had better days on the job.

He hustled over before Spinks could finish his conversation and pull out. He knocked on the driver's window. The SAC didn't startle, but his lips got thinner when he saw Gil standing at his door. Spinks raised one finger in the universal sign to give him a minute.

Gil waited, hands on his hips as he caught his breath. He really needed to up his running game. He'd been in denial about his fitness since recuperating from being shot, but as the lactic acid slowly dissipated in his quads, Gil couldn't deny he'd been slacking.

Finally, Spinks hung up and buzzed down his window. That wasn't the face of a happy and content man. "What now?"

"Whatever you got going on, I want in."

Spinks studied him, the SAC's expression never wavered. "We'll see."

———

DAWN WAS A COUPLE OF HOURS OFF BY THE TIME THE Blackhawk's wheels set down at the Murdock municipal airport. Gil had managed a short combat nap on the way back, but it wasn't nearly enough. He shook his head to clear all the cobwebs as light from the helo pad lit the dim interior.

As the rotors slowed to a stop, Gil eyed the helo's cargo area. Disaster. War zone. You name it. In his effort to keep Lang alive long enough to get him into the hands of the surgeons, he'd dropped all the packaging from the medical supplies on the deck.

Mixed in with the trash were blood-soaked gauze and lap pads. You could read Gil's movements in the lines of bloody boot prints where Gil had waded through the pools of clotting blood.

The coppery stench was as thick as the helo's exhaust. His gut didn't turn. Gil had been around the spilled blood of his teammates too often for that to happen, but that didn't mean the sight of all that blood didn't affect him.

Tessa and Quinn climbed out of the cockpit, but the movement hardly registered with Gil. Then the side door slid open, and Quinn said, "You coming?"

"I think I'm going to stay and clean this up."

Quinn looked at him as if he'd grown a horn in the middle of his forehead. "You know we have guys for that, right?"

"Yeah, but I feel like this is something I should do."

"Okay then," Quinn said. "Should go fast with the three of us."

Before Gil could say anything, Tessa put a staying hand in

the middle of Quinn's chest to stop him from climbing into the helo. "You go on home. We'll take it from here."

"I'm not leaving you two here to clean up this mess on your own."

In no mood to argue, Gil went to the aft of the helo and left Tessa to deal with Quinn. Out of the corner of his eye, he saw Tessa pull Quinn aside, her words lost beneath the low growl of the oncoming fuel truck. Gil scrounged around until he found a trash bag in one of the storage compartments. He donned a pair of latex gloves and got to work.

The next time he glanced up, Quinn had disappeared, and Tessa was returning from the hanger with a sloshing bucket of water in one hand, and a work light in the other. He jumped out of the helo to help. Under her arm, she'd managed to carry a roll of paper towels and a scrub brush as well.

The work light made the task more manageable, if not more gruesome. They didn't talk. They worked and wiped and scrubbed and sweated. By the time they were done, the deck of the Blackhawk wasn't as good a new, but the inside no longer looked like the inside of a slaughterhouse.

He closed the helo door facing the hanger and went to dump the last bucket of blood-tinged water on the grass by the fence. When he returned, he boosted himself up onto the helo's deck, his legs dangling over the side. Tessa made a return trip from the hanger with a couple of paper bags. She handed him one. It was the *To Go* order from the diner. His stomach rumbled.

"Come eat." Gil dug into the bag. "We can finish that later."

"I want to replenish the medical supplies. Eat up. I'm almost done."

Gil laid out the sandwiches and limp fries, using the paper bag as a plate, but he didn't dig in. He'd waited that long to eat. He could wait a few minutes more.

At last, Tessa dropped down beside him with a groan. Sweat

was drying on her forehead and tendrils of wispy hair that had fallen from her ponytail framed her tired face. She looked done in. "The bottoms of my feet are killing me, and I'm pretty sure my heels have tarantula sized blisters. These boots may be great for riding horses, but they weren't made for walking."

"A good foot massage will help the soreness." He didn't mean it to come out as an invitation, but somehow it had.

She held his gaze for a beat or two. There was a shine in her eyes that wasn't there a moment before, like she wouldn't mind taking him up on the offer, but then she said, "My feet are sore, but it's my ass that may never be the same." She reached for her sandwich and took a bite.

"You get used to it. If you get desperate, I can help you with the saddle sores too." Yeah, it was a cheesy line, but it was meant to be funny, not as a come on. Though if she was inclined to take him up on his services, he most certainly wasn't opposed.

She laughed. Around a bite of her sandwich, she said. "Good to know my ass is in good hands."

"That's why I joined the ATF. To serve the community."

"Dork." The tension in her shoulders eased, and her smile widened. Not many people could get away with calling him a dork, but when she smiled at him like that, she could call him anything she damn well wanted.

His gaze dropped from her eyes to her lips. She swallowed hard and leaned in a fraction like she was going to kiss him. "Thirsty?"

It took him a second to switch mental gears. "Yeah."

She got up and rummaged around in the back of the helo and came back with a bottle of water. "Mind if we share? I don't want to have to restock the water supply as well."

"Sure."

She took two long swallows and passed the bottle to him.

The hanger and the mountains were to their back, and they

stared out over scruffy foothills that settled in the distance to flat plains. Nothing but the razor-wire-topped security fence marred their view as the coal black night lightened a fraction with the hint of dawn.

Besides a pair of security guards patrolling the grounds of the airport—who were off somewhere doing whatever the security guards did—he and Tessa were all alone.

The bottle of water she'd handed him was warm, but he didn't care. "You guys got a little bit of everything back there."

She waved her hand in the general direction of the Blackhawk's shadowed interior. "You'd be surprised at what we've got squirreled away back there. Sometimes we are tasked with search and rescue missions. You never know what you'll need in an emergency."

He was thirsty enough that he could have polished off the whole bottle without trying hard, but only drank half before passing it back to her. The silence wasn't awkward, but it also wasn't quiet. It hummed with the electricity snapping between them. She leaned in as close as she could without squishing the food and rested the side of her head on his shoulder, her thumbnail toying with the bottle's label. Despite their long day and intense night, frenetic energy wafted off her in tumultuous waves.

"Tired?" he asked around a bite of cold burger.

"Exhausted. Wired. Frustrated. Mad. Sad. Concerned."

"Rivera and Lang are in good hands—"

"It's not that." Tessa sat up straight, brushing away some of the stray hairs that had escaped her ponytail. "Don't get me wrong. I'm worried about them. They're my colleagues, my teammates, my friends. But like you said, they've got a great team of doctors."

"Then what *are* you worried about?"

"You."

"Me?" A strange warmth bloomed in the center of his chest. Unexpected. Foreign. But not outright unpleasant.

"It was a crap night. Lang and Rivera are in the hospital, you killed a guy—"

"You can't only look at the downside." He reached for the fries. They were limp and frigid. He ate them anyway. Beat the hell out of eating an MRE on the hairy ass end of the Hindu Kush. "You have to see the good, too. The good guys survived. Not all the bad guys did."

Tessa smiled, but it stumbled and fell far short of her eyes. "I never figured you for a closet optimist."

Gil shrugged. Optimist? Maybe. Not the unicorns that fart butterflies kind, but the good conquering evil kind. It took up too much of his mental energy to maintain pessimism. You couldn't survive the months deep undercover unless you believed in your heart that you would make it out the other side.

"If I asked you something personal, will you answer me honestly?" From the way she focused on the fence instead of on him, it wasn't going to be an easy question to answer.

Not knowing where she was going with that question, Gil popped the last bite of his sandwich into his mouth to buy him some time. Whatever this was starting between them, he didn't want to base the foundation on a bed of lies.

"Shoot," he said.

"How does it feel to kill a man?"

The one question everyone he knew in law enforcement or the military hated to hear. She didn't ask it the way most people did, with a morbid curiosity. She asked it like she didn't *want* to know but wanted to understand. He didn't get the impression she'd ever asked that question of someone before.

He usually avoided those types of questions, using humor to deflect. He'd come to terms with what his profession sometimes required of him. He was his harshest critic. But somehow, Tessa was different. If he told her the truth, no matter what he said, he didn't get the sense that she would pass judgment.

She turned and looked him in the eyes as if no answer would frighten her. She wasn't that kind of woman. She'd served in the military, was accustomed to being around people who had had to kill to protect themselves, their teammates, their country. If anyone could understand, she could.

Still, he hedged. "I'm not sure I have the right answer for you."

"I'm not looking for a right answer, just an honest one."

"Otherworldly," was the descriptor he settled on. "For me, there's this disconnect. Like I know it's me who's taken that shot, taken that life, and I think that I should feel guilty, that it should make me feel sick or twisted or *wrong*. But I don't. Killing doesn't thrill me or make me feel powerful. I did it because I had to."

Tessa reached over and rested her hand over his, her fingers fitting neatly between the grooves of his knuckles. He liked that she didn't pull away, liked that despite the literal and figurative blood on his hands, she saw a man and not a beast.

But there was something else to killing that he'd never tried to articulate before, but for her, knew he had to try. "But I'd be lying if I said there wasn't this heaviness, this blackness that has brushed my soul. Like I'm marked. Like killing has set me apart from the rest of the world."

"Does it give you nightmares?"

"Sometimes, but for the most part, no. I'm not saying it hasn't affected me because I'm not anywhere close to the same man I was before. But what gets to me the most, what fills me with the most guilt, is that it doesn't bother me the way it bothers a lot of my brothers and sisters in arms."

He turned his hand over and linked their fingers, her touch taking the sting out of his words. "There are many that have trouble coping, suffer from PTSD, and they drink and self-medicate, and even worse, commit suicide. I don't know how I've been lucky enough to escape the worst of that."

Her thumb rubbed soft circles on the palm of his hand. "What haven't you escaped?"

This woman got bonus points for her perception. He gathered his thoughts, then said, "The lies. You would think the killing would be the worst, but living day in and day out in a world where the truth will get you killed, where the people you interact with daily are the type to stab you in the back—not *have* your back—makes you jumpy and paranoid. Living in a place where trust is a four-letter word skews your perception of yourself and your world."

She turned her head, pressed a kiss to his shoulder. "Thank you."

He blew out a soft, self-deprecating chuckle. "What for? Depressing the hell out of you?"

"For telling me."

She rested her head on his shoulder again. He should pour her into her Jeep and take her home. But he was a selfish bastard and liked having her all to himself, especially now that there was the possibility of him disappearing under cover looming. If that happened, there was no telling when, if ever, he'd get her alone again.

Shifting, he turned toward her, intrigued by her answer. She was unlike any woman he'd ever been with. Not that he was *with* her, but—

One second, he was staring into her eyes, and the next, her lips were on his. Not tender or tentative. She fisted her fingers in his hair that had been due for a cut a couple months ago. Her teeth scraped his bottom lip and raked against his thick beard.

One of the security guards zipped by in a utility vehicle, the headlights blazing a trail in front of him. The guard either hadn't seen them or hadn't cared they were there. Cupping her cheeks, he pulled back.

"Whoa, now." He hated to stop her but needed to anyway. After the night they'd had, she was too vulnerable.

"Yeah...that would be a no." She reached across and ran a hand up his thigh.

If he were a *good* man, if he were a *smart* man, he'd stop her, despite what she'd said.

"You're not the bad boy you pretend to be, Gil Brant. You're a good man, an honest man. Two qualities that I admire."

By her open expression, she wasn't blowing smoke. That warmth he'd felt in his chest earlier, spread. *Admiration?* That's the last thing he'd expected after revealing a side of him he'd always kept to himself.

Most people couldn't handle his dark, sometimes depressing truth, but this strong, forthright, amazing woman *admired* it.

But there wouldn't be anything to admire if he took advantage of the situation. He had the experience. He knew what this moment between them was. This was the adrenaline, this was the relief, this was to forget, this was to feel alive.

This wasn't real.

This was something she was going to regret.

As she cupped him through his scrub pants, she deepened the kiss and shifted until she was straddling his lap. He scooped that luscious ass of hers and pressed her tightly up against him. She made a strangled noise at the back of her throat that made his heart trip, and his dick twitch.

Yeah, nothing here for her to admire, because though he knew it was wrong, he wasn't peeling her off him.

She grabbed the hem of her shirt and yanked it off her head. *Holy mother of all that's glorious and hot.* Turquoise looked damn good on her. He ran his hands up her sides, over her ribs, kneading her breasts. He leaned into the kiss, a hum, a vibration running through his body like the drone of the helo's engines only instead of putting him to sleep, the kiss woke him up.

It woke everything up like a jolt of nuclear strength caffeine mainlined into his veins.

She pulled away, her eyes meeting his. Dawn had pinked the horizon, highlighting the question in her eyes as if she was unsure what this was. This *thing*, this powerful thing that was growing between them. In Gil, it awakened the big beast of emotion he preferred stayed asleep. Could he slay the beast? Or would that beast rip and claw and tear him apart?

But then she took his head in her hands, and all higher thought vanished. All that was left to him were his senses. The faint scent of exhaust and bleach on the deck. The tang of the spicy mustard from her sandwich on her tongue. The grip of her fingertips on the back of his neck as she twisted her body and pulled him down to the hard deck of the helo.

Gil reached out for one of the thin wool emergency blankets stowed behind some cargo netting. It wasn't a cushy pillow top mattress, but if this thing was happening— and by the way her fingers fumbled with the drawstring of his scrub pants, this *was* happening—he wanted it to be as comfortable for her as possible. They broke the kiss long enough for him to lose his shirt and to scoot farther inside and the blanket was more or less beneath them.

"Don't stop now." She was laying on her back, he stretched out on his side along the length of her, his fingers drifting up her belly.

Beneath his touch, her muscles fluttered. "Trust me," he said, "I don't want to stop."

He pulled the black band out of her hair, slipped it over his wrist, and ran his fingers through her hair.

A smile lifted the corners of her mouth, and he couldn't keep from nipping at her bottom lip. She bit back, her teeth scraping against his beard.

He hadn't taken Tessa Sterling for the kind of woman who was a passive participant in life, and she didn't disappoint. She slipped a bold hand beneath the waistband of his scrubs, her fingers trailing up the hard length of his shaft, teasing, not timid. He hissed in a breath. Nope, not passive, which ramped up the *sweet baby Jesus* factor by a good eleven and a half points.

He rolled onto his back, taking her with him and settling her between his legs. Her pelvis aligned with his and he squeezed her ass and pressed her against him. She dropped her forehead on his chest, a moan of pleasure ripping from her throat.

She sucked in a breath. "Right there. Wait, no, higher."

He changed his grip, and the groan that ripped from her throat came out a mixture of pleasure and pain.

"Sore?" he asked.

"Stupid saddles. I don't know why they have to make them so hard."

Gil barked out a laugh, moving his hands a little higher on her firm ass, digging his thumbs into the sides of her glutes, his fingers digging into the dense muscle beneath her tailbone. She writhed, the meat of her fist tapping the steel deck. "Hurts," she managed as she buried her face into his chest. "Dear God don't stop."

He wouldn't, couldn't deny her. He massaged her sore muscles, the noises she made short-circuiting his brain and simmering his blood. Then the tenor of her moan changed and then all those little sounds had less to do with sore muscles and a lot more to do with a building need. He knew it because he felt it too.

5

____

As much as Tessa would love to lay on top of Gil all day and have him massage the soreness out of every muscle she owned, they didn't have that kind of time. It wouldn't be long before the tiny local airport opened. With the helo pad out of the way and off to one side, the likelihood they'd be discovered decreased, but was not eliminated.

Which kind of turned her on.

She worked her way down his body, nipping and licking at his flat nipples. His hand slid up her back, catching the clasp of her bra and snapping it free with an expert twist of his wrist. She slid her arms free of the fabric, and she tossed it toward the cockpit, refusing to dwell on his expertise. She didn't want to know how many women he'd slept with, because those women didn't matter. He was here. With her.

Her tongue trailed down his centerline, dipped into his belly button, then traced a lazy trail through the patch of hair north of his waistband. His fingers fisted into her hair, the gentle tugs electrified her scalp, sending salvos of need rushing south dampening her panties. She wanted him.

In her hands.

In her mouth.

In *her*. Now.

She tugged his scrubs down his legs, and he toed off his boots and kicked the clothing free.

"Much better." She slid a hand up the inside of his thigh, her fingers coming to rest at the root of him. He made a sound in the back of his throat that sounded more like frustration than lust.

He gripped the back of her neck. "Come here a minute."

Seriously? "You're kidding, right? I'm about to get to the good part."

She'd been cock blocked before, but never from the guy she was about to go down on. Did he not want this? She took a quick glance at his glorious erection, at the gleam of precum at the tip. No. It wasn't just her who wanted this.

She crawled up his body, laying on her side, her head in one hand as she gently stroked him with the other, the softness of his skin a stark contrast to the long, hard length of him.

He folded a hand behind his head and looked at her. "I know you're trying to distract me from what happened tonight. I appreciate the thought, but you don't have to do this."

She threw a leg over his and rolled against him as she kept up the slow, languorous, strokes, more amused than put off. He was a good man, the type that wouldn't want her to do anything she might later regret, but she wasn't that kind of woman. She knew what she was doing. She knew why she was doing it.

Did she want to help him forget, if only for a moment? Without a doubt. But having sex with Gil was about taking her life back. About staking a claim. About not letting what her ex had done to her hold her back from living her life any longer.

"You think I'm doing this all for you?" When he didn't answer, she said, "I'm not that altruistic. I'm a single mom who rarely gets the time away from her son to shop for groceries, which pretty much puts sex off the table."

"But that's what this is. Sex. Release. I don't want you doing this for the wrong reasons, because you think I need—"

She pressed a kiss to his lips. "That's some of it. But that's not all of it. Not by a long shot." Because he had gone all serious on her, she wanted to lighten the mood. "If the release was all I was after, I could take care of that by myself at home."

He closed his eyes, and his head fell back. "Quite the amazing visual." He thrust against her hand and huffed out a laugh. "You don't play fair."

"Nope."

He slid a hand up her arm, past her shoulder until his fingers brushed the back of her neck. He hooked his thumb under her jaw and tilted her chin up until she was looking him in the eyes. "What are you saying then?"

"Do I have to spell it out?"

He nodded, a tight, teasing smile on his lips as if the answer was more important to him than he wanted to let on.

"I like you, Gil Brant. Simple as that. It's not the dry spell talking either." Though she supposed it would have to have had a beginning and an end to be considered a *spell*. "Though in the interest of full disclosure, this *spell* is like the Mojave Desert. Hot, dusty, and ready to be quenched. Think that's in your skill set, special agent?"

Something stark and raw flashed in his eyes, but he ducked his head and kissed her until her senses sizzled and her thoughts fizzled. "At your service, ma'am."

"Hold that thought," she said as she sat up and leaned over his body.

This time he didn't stop her. She took him in her mouth, teasing the tip of him with her tongue, tasting the salt, the essence of him. One of his hands rested on her upturned ass, the other slid to the back of her head, fisting in her hair, keeping her there as he surged up. She relaxed her throat, taking him in.

"That's...Tess—" She pulled back and glanced up at him, his eyes dark with primal need. She licked his slit, then retook him. He groaned. "*Fuuck.*"

There was a faint thud as the back of his head smacked the steel deck, but it didn't faze him. He took his hand off her ass and fumbled with the button of her jeans. "Off."

She sat up and stripped. Boots and socks going one way, her jeans and underwear landing somewhere else. When she turned back to him, his hands were clasped behind his head, his eyes bold and brash, raking her body as intimately as if it were his hands that were touching her. She felt no shame, no embarrassment, no self-consciousness even though the men in her unit had teased her about her tomboy-esque body.

She may not have the tits of an exotic dancer or the hips of Marilyn Monroe, but the way he took all of her in, made her feel perfect, even if she was only perfect for him.

On her hands and knees, she crawled back to him, the cold steel biting into her knees until she reached the blanket. His hand skimmed down her side and over her hip, but instead of looking rapt, he shook his head and blew out a resigned sigh.

"What's the matter?" she asked.

"I don't have any condoms."

She thought for a moment, then couldn't help but smile when she remembered a conversation she'd had with Quinn on a late flight back to the airport one night. "Hang tight, I've got you covered."

She rummaged around at the back of the helo and found the thin box of condoms Quinn had stashed there. She tore the box open and tossed one to Gil.

"You've got to be kidding me," he said, though he didn't waste any time ripping the foil packet and sheathing himself.

Tessa went back, re-straddling his hips. Her hands landed by his shoulders, her long hair curtaining them. "Looks like we're not the only ones who want to have hot helo sex."

"Thank God."

"No. Thank Quinn."

Gil grinned and slid his hands up her waist until his thumbs hooked on the underside of her breasts. Squeezing the mounds of flesh, he rose up and sucked first one and then the other into his mouth. His tongue flicked and licked until she thought she might come from his mouth alone. But that wasn't what she wanted.

She reached down, taking him in her hand and placing him into position as the first chug of a single-engine plane sputtered to life. They didn't have much time. But before she could plunge down on him, he stilled her hips with his hands.

She stifled a groan. "What now? Is this where you tell me this is my last chance to stop you?"

A look of confusion crossed his face. "What? No. It's never too late to say no. I'm a grown ass man. You say stop, we stop. No questions. No repercussions. No—"

"No whining?"

He grinned at that. "No promises. It's just—"

She pressed a finger to his lips to shut him the hell up. This was happening, and unless he was the one who was going to say no, there was little else that would stop her. She sat back and sheathed him as the sun popped up over the distant plains, bathing her in heat and light. It took a moment for her body to adjust. Gil was bigger than her ex in breadth and length, and there was that whole not having sex for way, way too long going on.

He lay still beneath her, his body tense and tight, his breathing slow and controlled as if it was taking everything he had not to go all caveman on her. She liked that. She liked that very much. She braced her hands on his chest, her eyes going to his, checking back in with him.

The tension eased from his face, and he smiled as he slid his hands up her thighs and gripped her hips, the tips of his fingers pressing into her flesh anchoring her to him. To the present. "You good?"

Fantastic. Spectacular. Orgasmic. She'd scare him off if she admitted all that. "I'm good."

He raised her up, then with a slow, steady slide, plunged back in. She leaned back, catching her arms around his knees, taking him as deep as he could go. When was the last time sex had ever felt that good? Had it *ever* felt that good?

She didn't have time to contemplate that question. Gil amped up the speed and the intensity, until he had her breasts bouncing, her breath catching, her orgasm growing. Goosebumps rippled across her flesh as she met him brutal stroke for brutal stroke.

His rhythm faltered, and she knew he was getting close. He wrapped his arms around her, pulling her on top of him, their bodies melding and melting, slick with sweat and piping-hot passion.

He hooked his hands over her shoulders, plunging harder, deeper until her nerves pinged, and her body trembled as together they chased their climax. She squeezed her eyes tight, shutting out the past, wanting only what was here and now.

He brushed her hair aside, framing her face with his hands. "Look at me."

She opened her eyes.

He slowed, exchanging the fast, hard strokes for almost painfully tender ones. "There you are." His voice was soft and full of wonder. "Good Lord, if you only knew what you were doing to me." The way he said it, made her think he wasn't talking about the physical.

She was close, so close. And those eyes... the way he looked at her like she was the only thing that mattered, that she was what made the earth spin, the tides ebb, and his heart beat. Her eyes stung, and her chest got tight.

"Come with me," he said.

She did.

SOMEWHERE BEHIND THEM CAME THE RUMBLE AND GRUMBLE OF one of the fuel trucks as the airport woke to a new day. They needed to go. They were spent, tired, and hungry, but Gil wasn't ready for their time together to end.

Tessa lay on top of him as they caught their breath. He tightened his arms around her. Even though the morning air was crisp, his sweat-dampened hair lay plastered to his head. With the tips of his fingers, he traced light circles at the small of her back, liking the way goosebumps erupted on her skin and her body shuddered with the aftershocks of her climax.

The engine of another single-prop plane revved, and they listened as the throaty whine receded into the distance as the plane took off down the runway. They really needed to get up before someone found them wrapped together, naked and sweaty and sated.

"We should get going," he said, hating that he had to be the one to break up this...this...whatever this was. He didn't have a name for it. A one-night stand wasn't accurate because, if he had anything to say about it, this wasn't a one and done thing. On the other hand, it wasn't like they had a relationship. Yet. "We both need showers. Spinks will want reports ASAP, and I'm pretty sure we're all due for an ass chewing. Besides, I want to call the hospital, check on Lang and Rivera. But first, I need to take care of this condom before it's too late."

"Mmm," she mumbled, turning her head and pressing a kiss to the center of his sternum. "One more minute."

He could give her that. He was going soft, but that didn't make being inside her feel any less incredible. "Okay, one more minute." He kissed the top of her head.

Fifteen seconds into their minute, one of the security guards flashed by in one of the utility vehicles, the strobe light on top flashing blue and white. What the? A second utility vehicle sped by, a bullhorn in the driver's hand. "You. Get away from the fence. This is a restricted area."

Tessa popped up and rolled off him, scrambling for her clothes. He tied off the condom and tossed it into the empty food bags, making a mental note to come back for them as soon as they found out what the hell was going on.

By the time they climbed out of the helo, security was at the far end of the fence, a cloud of dust choking the air on the far side of the razor wire, the retreating vehicle already out of sight behind a gentle rise.

The security guards drove back toward the hanger at a more sedate speed. Half-way between the helo and the hanger, Gil and Tessa waved them down. "What's going on?"

"Kids, more than likely," the first guard said. The name on his name tag said 'Haggerty'. He had a bald head and a weapon wedged against his overabundant belly. "They come out on Saturday night. Smoke. Drink. Have sex. You know. Kid stuff."

"Shouldn't you go after them?" Tessa asked.

The second guard in the far vehicle said, "The only way through the fence is by the hanger. By the time we can get around, they're always long gone."

"What about security cameras?"

Haggarty shrugged. "I don't know what kind of security you two are used to, but this isn't Fort Knox. All the cameras along the fence face inward, and those on the outside of the hanger are too far away to be any good. Trust me, we've checked."

That all too familiar itch between Gil's shoulder blades was back. Some people had gut feelings. Gil had the itch. Or maybe it was that he and Tessa had been that close to getting caught naked in the helo that had him all out of sorts. Could be it. But Gil wasn't convinced. "Something doesn't feel right."

"It's kids, man," the second guard reiterated.

"Look." Haggarty lowered his voice and leaned toward Gil and Tessa as if he were the director of the CIA about to impart pearls of wisdom on the peon recruits. "I know you two had a terrible night last night, it was all over the scanners. Shit like that can make you paranoid. This..." He spread his arms meaning the airport in general. "This is a small-time muni airport, in the foothills of Wyoming. Nothing happens here. Trust me."

"You won't mind me having a look around." Gil didn't pose it as a question, because it wasn't one.

"Suit yourself." Haggarty gave them a mock salute and pressed his foot down on the accelerator, leaving him and Tessa on the black tarmac.

"What do you think?" she asked.

"I think I'll see what I can find out. You coming?"

"Go ahead," she said. "I'll close up the helo, and I probably should find my bra before Quinn does."

Gil glanced down and smiled, liking the way her bare nipples pressed against her T-shirt. "Good idea." He started heading toward the gate, and over his shoulder he said, "I'll meet you back at your Jeep."

They parted ways, and Gil strode around the perimeter of the fence, the sun climbing higher and higher, a reminder that the day was getting away from him. He wouldn't have time for that nap after all. The shower, though, was non-negotiable.

Past the far corner of the fence where the guards had stopped their chase, and out of sight of the airport, Gil came across a set of vehicle tracks. A mid-sized pickup maybe, from the axle width. The tires thick with nobbies. The tires had spun out and dug deep. The vehicle would have needed four-wheel drive to make it out of there without getting stuck.

The dust had already settled on the twisty dirt road. Gil walked up the road a short way. Not far from the car tracks, he found a set of footprints that tracked parallel to the fence line. He followed. The ground rose and fell, and for the most part, no one on the tarmac would be able to see him walking there. The boot prints were almost as big as his. This was no kid looking to party.

The tracks stopped at a narrow ravine. The ground trampled, with divots in the side of a sand dune as if someone had climbed up and knelt there. Who was this guy and what did he want with the airport?

Gil climbed up the dune, hand over hand, his feet sliding back in the loose sand. At the top where the divots were most prominent, Gil stood. A chill shimmied up his spine, drenching that itch between his shoulder blades with a cold sweat.

In his direct line of vision was Tessa in the open door of the Blackhawk. *Fucking hell.* He wasn't sure what it meant. Maybe nothing. But he didn't really believe that.

Had he and Tessa been seen?

If they had, *who* had seen them and what were the possible repercussions? Spinks wasn't too strict on inter-personal relationships between the team members. If everyone kept it professional at work and weren't in each other's direct line of command, Spinks let it slide.

Besides, Gil wasn't planning on staying in the task force long term. He was going to get the bastards who left his partner paralyzed and then he'd be out.

———

After dropping Gil off at the ranch, Tessa headed home, calling Evie along the way because, after all that had happened, she needed to talk to her son and hear his voice. Evie picked up on the third ring.

"Hey Tessie," Evie said. "Are you on your way?"

"Aah... About that." Tessa turned down Main Street in Murdock, driving past the tourist shops, the mom-and-pop restaurants, the hardware store with the front window plastered in tool advertisements. "Look we had this thing go down last night—"

"You mean the gun raid?"

"How did you hear about that?"

"We had an early breakfast down at the diner," Evie said. "You know how news travels around here. Everyone okay?"

Not by a long shot. But Tessa wasn't in the mood to get into all that now. She turned off Main Street and down the long road heading to her house.

The lightning speed with which good and bad news traveled around her town was even worse than the Army. "More or less," she said. "I've got a crazy day ahead of me. Is there any way Jack could stay with you guys until this evening?"

"Whatever you need. Family is always here for you. Don't you forget that."

Tessa pinched her nose to stave off the sting in her eyes. She never expected this kind of support when she moved to Murdock. After all, before she'd moved to Wyoming, Evie had only been someone to whom her mother had sent Christmas cards. A branch of her father's family tree that had pulled up their New England stakes and rooted themselves near the base of the Rockies.

The years of going it alone had been tough, and it was such a relief knowing someone had her and Jack's back. She heard Jack's voice over the phone. "Mind if I talk to him?"

"Here he is," Evie said. "Don't worry about a thing. We'll see you tonight."

"Hey, Mommy." Jack sounded his usual bright and chipper self. All she wanted to do was drive to Evie's and scooped up her son and hold him tight and never let go. But that wasn't in the cards for today.

"Hey, baby. I've got to work today. You're going to stay with Evie and Massey and I'll pick you up tonight. Sound okay?"

"Yea! That means I can ride horses again. You should see me, Mom. I can go super-fast," Jack said, making super and fast sound like one word as if saying it faster helped her understand. "Massey says I'll be a cowboy in no time."

"That's terrific, baby. Hey, I'm almost at the house. I want to hear all about it when I pick you up tonight. Sound good?"

"Okay. Bye."

Tessa clicked *End* on her phone and pulled into her driveway. Bone weary, from the horseback riding, the late-night...

The sex.

She smiled thinking about Gil. He hadn't as much rocked her world, as much as he'd introduced her to a whole new universe. He was a man unlike any other that she'd ever been with. Not that he was perfect. Nobody was. But there was something about the way they... the way that they fit, that made her wonder if maybe he was the perfect man for her.

That was crazy talk. She shook her head as she unlocked her front door. She was looking for a distraction. A little *something-something* to combat the loneliness. She would have plenty of time for romance, for relationships, when Jack was grown and out of the house.

She pushed the door open, but it stopped midway. *What the?* She pushed harder, but the door wouldn't budge. She put her shoulder into it, and she managed to open it enough to squeeze through.

Holy hell. Tessa stared at the destruction that used to be her living room. The couch lay on its back, the cushions sliced open and the stuffing strewn everywhere. Her TV lay on the floor, the screen smashed and spider-webbed. Her stomach fell, dragging her heart down with it.

She tried to take in a deep breath, but her lungs seized, and she sputtered. *Bradley.* It had to be. The rat bastard. First her tire this morning. Then her house broken into, vandalized. No, she didn't live in a Manhattan high-rise, but she didn't live on the streets either. Stuff happened, but two incidents this close together reeked of her ex's vindictiveness.

Instead of getting scared, she got pissed. What was Bradley after? What did he want with her?

He was the one who'd left them.

He was the one who'd wanted no contact.

Him.

If this was what it meant to have him living the next county over and back in their life again, she wasn't having any of it. She would rather quit her job and move halfway around the world if it meant getting distance from him.

Could she tear her son away from family? He liked it in Murdock. For once, he had friends. He wasn't the lonely little boy on the playground that nobody knew and nobody wanted to play with. No. She couldn't do that to Jack. She would find a way to make this better. She had to.

First, she needed a shower. She needed food. She needed to get back to the station. The break-in wasn't an emergency. She'd file a report when she got back. Besides, the mess wasn't going anywhere.

The rest of the house hadn't fared any better. Her mattress had been upended and thrown against the wall, her dresser drawers pulled out and dumped, the sheetrock scraped and dinged. Her clothes lay strewn on the floor.

As she showered, her frustration built. As she dressed, her anger simmered. As she tried to wedge the back door against its shattered frame, her determination cemented. Somehow, someway, she would get Bradley out of their lives. The cautionary tale that had been her life with her ex had to stop.

End of story.

In the kitchen, she stepped over the broken plates, the smashed glasses, the food smeared on the floor, and grabbed a box of crackers out of the pantry and a drink out of the fridge. It wasn't much. But it would do for now.

On the way back to the station, she chugged her soda and stuffed crackers into her mouth and tried to get her head back into the game. She knew Spinks wasn't done with her, and if she wanted to keep her job, she needed to have her shit together.

———

Tessa strode into the station and brushed past a couple of sheriff's deputies heading the other way. There was a general buzz in the station, the kind that you get when things have gotten a little exciting, and in a tiny Wyoming town, where moose and bear and drunk tourists were sometimes as heart-stopping as it got, a gun bust was electrifying.

She walked through the station's bullpen, where a few deputies were hanging around. One of them gave her a chin bob as if to say, 'good job.' She nodded back but didn't have the time nor the inclination to stop and chat. She had other, more important, things on her mind.

She walked down the hall to the rooms the task force had been assigned. Spinks' office was closed, his blinds overlooking the hallway shut tight. A raised voice came from inside. Not

Spinks'. Great. Looked like she wasn't the only one who was due for an ass chewing.

Tessa walked into the converted conference room where many of the agents had their desks. Gil was already there, hunched over a keyboard and typing away. He glanced up, gave her a quick "hey," then went back to typing.

It was the first time she'd seen him since that morning. She hadn't known what kind of greeting to expect, but the casual way he treated her surprised her. But really, what would she expect him to do in front of their colleagues? Jump up, wrap her in a big bear hug and tell the boys they'd be right back? No. Gil wasn't that kind of guy. Good thing. In fact, Gil acted like she would have wanted him to, but a little recognition, a secret smile, something, *anything*, that said they had shared a moment might have been sweet.

Along with Gil, Quinn and some new task force pup were also there, all hard at work. Tessa assumed the rest of the agents were out working the case. Tessa slid into a chair at an open desk and logged into the system to write her report.

She hadn't heard an update yet on the guy the task force had taken into custody, or on the gun truck with the tracker that had driven away, but that wasn't really part of her job description. She was a pilot. Not an investigative person on the task force. Her job was to fly them in and fly them out, nothing more. But that didn't mean she didn't want to know.

"Lieutenant Sterling," Spinks hollered from down the hall, making Tessa's back go stiff and sweat pop out on her upper lip.

Taking a deep breath, she rolled her chair away from the desk. Quinn stood and waited for her at the door.

Gil glanced up and gave Tessa a wink. "Give 'em hell, lieutenant."

Right. She'd be lucky if Spinks didn't skin her alive. "Thanks."

Quinn followed her out. Tessa stopped and pulled him aside. "Where are you going?"

"Same place as you."

She narrowed her eyes at him, recognizing and understanding that Quinn had gone into protective brother mode. She'd been on the receiving end of a lot of that in the Army. But this screwup was all on her, not Quinn. "I didn't hear Spinks call your name."

Quinn shrugged and continued down the hall, leaving Tessa to follow him. He entered Spinks' office first as if he could protect her from Spinks' wrath with his body. She stepped out from behind him and said, "You wanted to see me, sir?"

Spinks glanced up from his computer screen. "You. Not him." Spinks eyed Quinn, but was talking to her when he said, "You always let your subordinates fight your fights, lieutenant?"

Quinn stood taller. "Sir, I—"

"I wasn't speaking to you, Powell. In fact, you shouldn't even be here. You should be home, catching up on your sleep."

"I'm finishing up my report, sir. Then I'll be headed home."

"You've got ten minutes to get that report on my desk and get your ass out of here. Clear?"

"Yes, sir."

Spinks dismissed Quinn, who gave Tessa a half shrug as he left as if to say, "I tried."

In his squeaky chair, Spinks leaned back, his hands locked behind his head. Before he could speak, she took ownership of her actions. "I know I was out of line, allowing Brant on the flight and disobeying orders, sir. I'll do my best not to let it happen again."

Spinks dropped his hands to his desk. He didn't have a smile on his face, but his features softened a tad, making it read as one. "You'll do your best? But you can't promise me you won't violate a direct order again?"

Tessa didn't answer right away, not wanting to lie straight to the SAC's face. "No, sir. I can't promise. I know going against a direct order is grounds for termination, but I did what I thought was best for everyone involved. That's not an excuse, it's an explanation. If this is where you tell me I'm off the task force, or out of a job, I understand."

Please don't fire me. Please don't fire me. Please don't fire me.

Sweat formed at the base of her spine. What the hell would she do if she got her ass fired? No doubt Bradley would find a way to take advantage of her problems and use that against her.

"Disregarding a direct order is a serious concern. I can respect your honesty and the way you own up to your responsibilities. But let there be no mistake," Spinks leaned forward, the tension back on his face, his jaw jutting, his voice stern. "You disobey me again, and it won't matter how good of a pilot you are, you'll be off this team and be lucky to find a job hauling tourists over the Tetons. You hear me?"

"Yes, sir." Tessa managed to keep the tremor out of her voice. Mostly.

"I want your report on my desk ASAP. Then I want you catching up on your sleep, lieutenant. You look like hell, and I won't have my pilots flying on no sleep." Spinks leaned back in his chair. "Dismissed, lieutenant."

Tessa had almost made it out the door when Spinks added, "This is your one and only warning. There's no three-strike rule here. One more mistake, one more screw-up, and you're done."

Her throat tightened, but she nodded her assent. She didn't *do* being in trouble well. In the Army, she'd never been written up. Her parents had never grounded her. Never had a reason to. Now she was one screw-up away from losing all that she'd worked extremely hard for.

She wouldn't let Spinks down. She couldn't let herself down. Most of all, she couldn't let Jack down.

By the time she made it back to the other conference room, Quinn and the other agent had cleared out. Gil sat at his desk, deep in thought as he plucked at the thin black hair tie around his wrist. *Her* black hair tie. She didn't ask for it back. She liked that he'd kept it. Liked that maybe their time together had meant something to him.

Gil glanced up. "You still have a job?"

Tessa huffed out a laugh and plopped into the chair at the desk behind him. "Barely."

Gil spun his chair around, and wheeled himself over to her, trapping her between the wall and the desk. "Don't let Spinks get to you. He's a hardass, but even he knows you did the right thing, the *only* thing you could have done. That's why you're still here."

"Maybe." She didn't want to think about it, much less talk about it. She pointed at the computer. "I'd better finish my report."

"Sure," Gil said, turning back to finish his own work.

After she'd hit Send on her report for Spinks, she scrubbed her hands over her face. Sleep, she needed sleep. She groaned, thinking of the mess back at her house that she didn't have the energy to clean up.

Spinks had been clear about her getting some rest. That's what she'd do. She'd drag her mattress back onto the bed frame, she'd dig up some clean sheets, and she'd sleep like the dead until it was time to pick up Jack.

The springs on Gil's chair squeaked, and she glanced up to see him watching her. He tilted his head and gave her the once-over. Not like he was undressing her with his eyes—because there was nothing sexy about the old pair of jeans and the wrinkled T-shirt that she'd pulled out of the crumpled mess of clothes on her floor—more as if he was assessing her and trying to determine how well she was holding it all together. "What's up?"

She guessed that meant she didn't pass inspection.

Tessa picked up a paper clip off the desk, straightened it, then bent it in thirds, debating what she was willing to say. Everything that had to do with Bradley was like this vortex of trouble, and she didn't want any other innocent bystander to get sucked up into it. She went with the obvious. "I can't afford to lose my job."

"I get that. But that's not all that's bothering you."

She did a double take which was enough to tell Gil he was onto something. He probably hadn't needed to be a trained agent to figure that one out.

The paper clip was utterly mangled now, nothing more than a twisted hunk of wire. Gil took it out of her hand. "Spill."

The last thing she wanted to do was drag Gil into her personal mess with her ex. Gil was supposed to be a little fun. A distraction. Not someone she brought into her inner circle. But what Gil was *supposed* to be, and what he was turning out to be, were two entirely different things.

"You promise you're not going to go all *special agent* on me?"

Gil raised a brow and considered her. She figured he hadn't managed to stay alive all that time undercover by speaking without thinking first. "Well...when you put it like that...definitely not."

Uhhh...she needed clarification. "No, you don't promise?"

"Hell, no." No anger. Gil wasn't a rash man. "But now you have to tell me."

She didn't, but it wasn't like she could keep it a secret for long. As soon as one of the deputies came out to her house to file a report, word would get around the station. Best if he heard it from her. "Someone broke into my house."

"What did they take?"

"Nothing that I know of. More of the same. Vandalism. Television trashed, couch cushions cut, drawers dumped, dishes destroyed. Petty stuff."

"What do you mean, *more* of the same?"

Crap. Tessa hadn't meant to say that. Leave it to an undercover guy to pick up on the little things. He leaned forward, his forearms on his knees, his eyes searching hers for answers.

She glanced at his lips, remembering how they'd felt on her as he licked and sucked and brought her pleasure. All she wanted was to sink into him, to go back to that morning when Bradley and Lang and Rivera were, for a few glorious minutes, the last things on their minds.

Gil had the beginnings of a caught-ya smile on his face. "Focus, Tessa."

She nabbed a new paper clip off the desk and proceeded to murder it. "I think it was my ex."

Gil bowed up and before he could say a word she said, "I'm still not telling you his name."

"You could get a protection order."

"Not on suspicion and supposition, I can't. Besides, an order of protection only works on guys who follow the rules. My ex doesn't. You don't build the kind of business he does in such a short amount of time by sticking to the letter of the law."

"What kind of business?" The way he asked was casual as if he was only asking to be polite.

She almost spilled the beans, that's how tired she was, and that was how talented Gil was. "I'm not saying. You don't think I know that if I did, that as soon as I left this room, you'd be on your computer hunting down every possible business trying to hunt him down?"

He looked affronted. Tessa was pretty sure he wasn't. "I'd never—"

Spinks popped his head into the conference room. "Sterling, what are you doing still here?"

She popped out of the chair. "I was just leaving."

Gil laid a staying hand on her arm and to Spinks said, "I need a few minutes of your time."

Spinks glanced at his watch. The knot of his tie was loose, and his eyes were bloodshot. Like the rest of the task force, he wouldn't have gotten any sleep. "I have to get to the hospital. The suspect is finally awake enough to talk. Make it quick."

After Spinks left, Gil let go of her arm and said, "I don't want you going back to your place alone."

"It's all I've got."

"Do the doors lock?"

"The back door was damaged, but I was going to put a chair under the doorknob."

"Perfect. No one has ever gotten past a door with a chair under the knob." He laid on the sarcasm thick as sorghum syrup. "You got a gun?" A muscle twitched by Gil's right eye, the only outward indication that he was losing his cool.

"No. But—"

"That's gonna change." He said it like he had a say in the matter.

"I've got a kid—"

"We'll make sure he can't get to the gun. Until then, go to the ranch, crash at my cabin. I'll call Mac and tell her to expect you."

If he was trying to get on Tessa's good side, ordering her around wasn't the way to do it. She would deal with that later because the thought of not having to go back to her place eased the knotted muscles between her shoulder blades. Besides, she was too wrung out to argue anyway. "What about you?"

"I have some things I need to do here, and I want to hit the hospital, see how Lang and Rivera are doing."

"That's a long drive on little sleep."

He shrugged. "That's what coffee's for."

She took a step to leave, but he caught her hand and tugged her back to him. He glanced out the door, but he must not have seen anyone because he stood and pressed a kiss to her lips. "I'll catch up with you tonight."

6

———

GIL WATCHED TESSA LEAVE, NOT SURE WHAT HE WANTED TO DO more, kick her ass or kiss it. A little of both, he decided. He shook his head as he walked to Spinks' office. *Put a chair under the door.* What the hell was she thinking? There was no way she was going back to her place before he got Boomer to fix her back door.

He rounded the corner of Spinks' office. Since he wasn't officially back on duty, he hadn't been updated on what had happened in the case. But being out of the loop was about to change if he had anything to say about it.

Spinks was on the phone and motioned for Gil to take a seat. He did. Spinks didn't even get the phone back into the cradle before Gil leaned forward and said, "I want in on this. I'll go to the interview with you. I'll type up reports, or hell, put me on the damn phones if that's all you've got, but I want those bastards who stole Lang's legs."

"You're too close to this."

"Fuck that, SAC." Gil popped out of his chair, paced to the door and back again. "We're all too close to this. You'll have to put together a whole new task force to find anyone who isn't. We are the ones you want out there finding these guys. *No one* is more motivated than we are."

"You tried to give me notice, and now you want in? I don't need someone on my team who doesn't want to be here or who wants to be here for all the wrong reasons."

Gil held Spinks' gaze, not willing to beg, but not willing to back down either.

Spinks let out a begrudging breath. The first indication he might relent. "That was Finn on the phone."

Oliver Finn had been the FBI agent in charge of a joint task force between the FBI, and the DEA when Gil, as a deep undercover ATF agent, had been shot and almost killed a few months before. Finn was one of the top interrogators on their side of the Rockies. "Finn was close to the hospital, and since the information is time sensitive, I had him go to the hospital and lean on the guy the gun runners left behind."

"Seriously? You called in the FBI?"

"Finn. Not the FBI. He owes us one."

"Who is this guy and what did he say?"

"Drew Ross is his name. Ex-Army from what we've been able to dig up. Dishonorable discharge. Waiting on the particulars. Long and short, the guy's too afraid someone will go after his family to talk. We're looking at the idea of leaking to the media that he died from his wounds. Get some heat off the guy, maybe he'll feel like talking. From what Ross has said, Finn thinks he might have found a way to get an agent on the inside. But nothing definite yet."

Gil's mouth dried up. One of the reasons he wanted out of the ATF was because of all the undercover work. He was good at it. Very good. Which was why he'd continually been tasked with it. He was an accomplished liar and had come to not like what that said about him. But this was Lang they were talking about.

For Lang, he could do it.

For Lang, he could dance with the devil one last time.

"What about the weapons? What did they find in the truck that got left behind?

"M-4s, mortar rounds, a couple Stinger missiles, shoulder-fired anti-aircraft guns, enough ammo to supply an army. Surplus from the looks of it. We're working on the tracking numbers."

"That's a lot of firepower," Gil said. "You thinking home-grown terrorists?"

"Possibly, but if the other two trucks were similarly packed, you can't rule out export to other countries. Somalia, Syria, Yemen. Many options."

"When you have something definite on getting an agent on the inside," Gil ordered his boss. "You come find me."

"You only recently got out of a long stint undercover. I've done my share of undercover work in my time. I'm not insensitive to how tough of a life that is. You sure you're the right guy for this?"

"Can you think of anyone on this team who would be better?"

When Spinks didn't answer, Gil turned to leave.

Spinks said, "Not so fast."

Spinks pushed a sheet of paper at Gil. "Sign this."

Gil stepped over and picked up the paper. "What is it?"

"Papers saying your medical leave has ended and you're back to full duty status."

He hadn't passed a physical yet, but Spinks was fully aware of that. Gil grabbed a pen, then noticed the date. "This is back-dated two days before the shooting."

Spinks raised his brows. "And?"

"You're telling me to falsify an official document?"

Spinks stared at him. "No one is telling you anything."

Maybe not, but there was no question that if he didn't sign it, there was no way he'd be let back on the task force. Not now. Maybe not ever. Spinks was covering his ass. Gil's ass, too, in a way.

If the Brass found out that Gil hadn't been authorized to be on that helo, that he'd killed a man while not officially back on duty, there would be a lot of hard questions asked that would put Spinks' career in a sling.

Lying while undercover was one thing. Signing his name to a backdated document was another, but this was for Lang. Gil didn't have to like it to sign it.

"I'm going to the hospital this afternoon to see Lang. I can talk to Ross and—"

"You're on leave until the shooting is investigated *and* you pass the psych evaluation.

"Psych eval. Are you kidding me?"

"Does it look like I'm smiling?"

No, no it didn't.

"Look, Brant, you've been through a lot these past few months. It stands to reason—"

"I'm fine." Gil dropped back into the chair, the long hours with little sleep were catching up to him with a vengeance. This wasn't the quick conversation he'd expected. Wasn't there somewhere Spinks had to be or someone he'd needed to talk to?

"Then you should have no problem passing the evaluation."

"It's not like he's the first man I've killed. I'm not some rookie who's never discharged his weapon."

"I'm not violating protocol." Spinks raised his hands as if to say the requirement was out of his control.

Funny that Spinks had no qualms asking Gil to falsify documents, but Gil wasn't going to push his luck by trying to bypass the psych eval. The shooting had been justified, and being an accomplished liar, he knew what he needed to say to pass the evaluation. He'd be back on the team in no time.

If the internal investigation went as smoothly as it should.

———

THE LAZY S WAS QUIET WHEN TESSA PULLED PAST THE BIG HOUSE and the barn, but then again, it was Sunday, and from what Gil had told her, it was the one day that everyone had off. Which was okay with Tessa. She didn't want anything or anyone getting between her and a bed.

She climbed out of her Jeep, trudged up the steps, and walked through the unlocked door. For a bachelor, Gil kept his place relatively neat. There was a dirty coffee mug in the sink, a rumpled T-shirt on a footlocker. The bed was made, but no military corners and no quarters would bounce off the multicolor quilt covering the bed. But it wasn't like there were empty beer cans strewn about or dirty underwear littering the floor.

On the opposite side of the cabin was an identical set of bunk beds. On the left, Gil's bed was the one with sheets. Since there were no other linens or even a linen closet, she gave up thinking she'd sleep in a different bed.

She opened the windows in the stuffy cabin to catch a breeze. Then she stripped off her boots and jeans and slid between the sheets with a grateful groan. She reached over to her jeans and pulled her cell phone out of her back pocket and set the alarm for two hours.

Two hours wasn't much of a nap, but she had a house to clean and Jack to pick up. Afraid she'd hit snooze and sleep through her alarm, she climbed out of bed and put her phone on the dining table.

Nestling into Gil's pillow, she lay awake long enough to catch

Gil's scent, to remember their tryst in the helo, to wish he was there, and not just for the sex. She didn't have time to analyze what that meant before sleep pulled her under.

She woke to the sound of someone pounding on the door, and her alarm bleating on the table demanding attention. Her head swam as she tried to shake the cobwebs. Again, the knocking. "Brant? You in there? It's Mac," came the voice on the other side of the door. "Everything okay in there?"

Tessa flopped back on the bed wishing her phone would shut the hell up, but not willing to get up and make that happen. "Come in."

The door swung open, and Mac walked in. For Mac, she was dressed up. Starched jeans, clean boots, her little baby bump pressed against a button-up shirt, her hair down and her usual USMC baseball cap nowhere to be found. Mac swiped the phone off the table and silenced the alarm.

"Thank you." Tessa scooted up on her elbows and brushed the tangle of hair out of her face. "This isn't what it looks like. Gil isn't here."

"Pity," Mac said, a mischievous smile on her face.

Tessa shook her head. Did Mac imply what Tessa thought Mac had? "*What?*"

"If I wasn't married," Mac put her hand on her bump, "or pregnant..." Mac ended the sentence with a one-shouldered shrug and let Tessa fill in the rest.

"It's not like that. With Gil and me I mean." Well, it was, but a fast fuck in a helo at dawn didn't a lasting relationship make. Tessa tried to sit up, but the room spun, and she grabbed her head.

"You okay?" Mac sat on the edge of the bed and put a hand on her forehead. "You don't feel like you have a fever, but I'm not a mom yet. Maybe my thermo-*mom*-meter isn't fully functional yet."

"I'm not sick, just sleep deprived."

Mac sneaked a glance on the other side of the bed as if wondering if Gil were the reason for Tessa's lack of sleep. Which got Tessa wondering. "You think Gil's hot?"

"I'm married and pregnant, not in a nunnery. Let's say there was a time when hot monkey sex might have been on the menu if I'd met a guy like Gil."

Tessa laughed. "Better not let your husband hear you say that."

"Hank knows he's got nothing to worry about. Besides, you're more Gil's type anyway."

Gil had a type? She was about to ask when Mac got up and said, "Anyway, I was in town for a prenatal appointment. Heard about the gun bust. I wanted to check on Gil, see how he was handling the shooting."

Tessa shrugged. "He says he's okay, but he doesn't really want to talk about it."

"That's what worries me. Gil's quiet when it comes to his past. He tends to hold it all in. Maybe he's okay. Maybe he's not. Either way, I'm glad he has you to talk to."

"I'm not really sure our relationship is at the skeleton revealing stage."

"Just the sex stage?"

Tessa didn't bother denying it, especially when the heat rushed up her neck and settled in her cheeks. There didn't seem to be a point. "It's not serious."

Why couldn't she keep her mouth shut? She and Mac were friendly, but she didn't think they'd advanced to friend status yet. Definitely not to a confidant. Did she really need a friend who could read her with no effort?

"Is that him talking, or you?" Mac tone seemed casual as she reached down and tossed Tessa her jeans, but Mac's face had shifted. It reminded her of Quinn's expression earlier that day when he'd tried to protect her from Spinks. Instead of protective brother it read protective sister.

Tessa got dressed as she thought about what she wanted to say. Mac patiently waited her out. When Tessa finished stepping into her boots, she said, "Is this the 'if you hurt him I'll hurt you' speech?" Tessa was fit enough and could probably hold her own in a fair fight, the trouble was, she had the feeling that if it came down to someone Mac cared about, Mac wouldn't fight fair.

"Gil is a good man with a bunch of walls he's had to build for his own protection. But I've seen the way he looks at you, like you're knocking on that wall with a sledgehammer, and he's too taken with you to stop the destruction. All I'm saying is don't break the walls down for sport."

Tessa should have been mad. What business was it of Mac's who she slept with or why? Then again, with Gil being in the Healing Horses program, maybe on some level Gil's welfare was Mac's business.

"Point taken," Tessa said. "Does he know he's got friends protecting him, watching his six?"

"I'm not sure he's at a place where he would appreciate the sentiment. All that time he's spent undercover, he's gotten used to relying on himself."

"Like a lone wolf?"

"Make that the Lone Ranger."

"Hell," Tessa said, "Even the Lone Ranger had a sidekick."

"Yeah, but Tanto didn't have the power to rip out his heart."

They'd had sex, not professed their undying love, or hell, even had a real date. Tessa wasn't sure what Mac wanted to hear. That she'd leave Gil alone? That she *wouldn't* leave him alone? That she wouldn't break his heart? With a clear conscience, she couldn't make any promises.

Tessa quickly made Gil's bed, the silence growing awkward. She had about decided to find another place to stay for the night, but Evie's house wasn't really an option. As it was, Jack had to sleep on the love seat in Massey's office when he spent the night. No way could the two of them fit on it together. With all the money she would have to spend replacing damaged items, a hotel wasn't in the budget either.

Tessa's phone rang, and she snapped it up without checking the caller ID, surprised she had enough reception for a call to go through. It was always hit or miss out there at the ranch. "Hello?"

There was a lot of static, and the voice on the other end was broken up and garbled, but Tessa knew who it was. *Bradley.*

The revulsion must have shown on her face, because when she went outside to get a better connection, Mac followed her out and leaned against the Jeep with a scowl on her face and her arms crossed over her chest. Tessa would have told her it was a private call, but one look at Mac told her Mac didn't give a freaking flying fuck.

"Why are you calling?" she asked Bradley.

"I want to speak to my son." Bradley sounded reasonable. He always did until he didn't get his way.

"If you hadn't backed out on your visitation this weekend, you could have talked to him all you wanted." She knew she shouldn't provoke him, but *really*?

He hollered something, and Tessa held the phone away from her ear until he'd calmed down. Mac frowned.

"Are you finished?"

"Put him on the phone."

"He's not here. He's with a sitter." Tessa didn't elaborate. With Bradley's limited custody, he wasn't authorized to pick Jack up from summer camp, but she didn't trust him not try to shove his way into Evie's house if he got determined enough. Evie didn't need that.

"A sitter? A fucking sitter? It's Sunday. The boy should be with his mother—"

"Or his father," Tessa said. "Something came up with work. The same way it did with you this weekend. It happens."

Bradley let out a big sigh. Tessa knew that sigh. It was his I'm-trying-to-be-reasonable-when-you-aren't-reasonable sigh. It used to make her feel guilty or less than, but she'd heard it many times over the years and it had lost its effectiveness. "Meet me tonight. We need to talk."

"I've got nothing to say to you."

"It's about Jack. Mariano's. Six o'clock."

She didn't have time to respond before he hung up the phone. One of the many reasons why she'd divorced Bradley. "Sorry about that," Tessa said to Mac.

"Trouble?"

"Nothing I can't handle." Now not only did she have to get the house cleaned, but she had to meet Bradley before she picked up her son. She could have refused to go. But she knew her ex. He'd find a way to make her life even more problematic if she didn't show up. It was easier to meet and be done with him.

Which brought her back to the reason she was sleeping in Gil's cabin to begin with.

"Hey," Tessa said, "I had a break in overnight. The rear door frame was shattered. Gil invited Jack and me to stay in one of the cabins until I could get my back door fixed. He said he'd call and smooth things over with you, but if you prefer we stay—"

"No. Gil's right. You two stay here. One of our new veterans is supposed to come in sometime today, and we were going to put her in the other cabin, but don't worry, you can share, or we'll figure something out."

Tessa was confused. First Mac was warning her away and the next, inviting her to stay.

Mac walked backward up the road toward the big house.

"Just to be clear, I don't have anything against you. In fact, I like you, Tessa. I think you could be good for Gil. He's a special person, who nearly got himself killed protecting our family. I'm trying to return the favor."

———

TOO MANY TIMES GIL HAD DRIVEN THE MOUNTAIN PASS OVER THE Idaho-Wyoming border on his way to the hospital in Idaho Falls, the hospital closest to Murdock with a top-rated trauma center.

After parking, he threw his empty coffee cup in the trash can near the lobby entrance and made a beeline for the nearest coffee pot before hunting down Isaac's room.

Word from Isaac's parents was that he had been moved out of ICU, though they'd kept him sedated. The door to Isaac's room stood open. Inside, Isaac's father lay sleeping in a recliner, his mother sat in a chair by the bed, one hand on Isaac's, the other held a book.

Gil tapped on the door with his knuckles.

Rita Lang glanced up from her book, and Howard startled awake.

"Gil," Rita said, "Come in, come in."

Rita stood and gave him a hug. The woman barely came up to his chest. Her clothes were rumpled, and her gray hair disheveled as if she hadn't had a chance to clean up since she'd gotten the call that her son had been shot.

Howard rubbed his hands over his face and came over and shook Gil's hand. "Good to see you, son."

"How has he been?" Gil asked.

Rita pasted on one of those smiles, the devastated kind that said her heart was broken and that she was holding on to hope with both fists. "They started weaning him off the sedatives.

They're expecting him to start waking up within the next hour."

"Does he know yet? About his legs?"

Isaac's father shook his head. The man was an ex-cop. If Gil hadn't already known, he could have told by the way the man carried himself, and how he seemed to be able to take blow after blow and keep standing. "Not yet. We're not looking forward to that."

"Do the doctors know if the damage is permanent yet?"

"It's too early to tell," Rita said. "But Izzy is a fighter."

Gil figured she'd said that more for herself, than for him. She was the type who grabbed on to hope and positivity and refused to let go. But even the strongest people needed a break, and Rita and Howard looked like they needed one. "Have you two gotten any sleep? How about food? Or a shower?"

"It can wait," Howard said.

"Tell you what." Gil took Rita's book off the chair and sat. "I'll stay with him for a while. Go get a hotel room and get some sleep. Or a shower, or food, if nothing else. I'll let you know when he wakes."

"We can't—"

Howard took Rita's hands in his. "Gil's right. We won't be any good to Izzy if we don't take care of ourselves, too." Howard stepped toward the door and gave her hand a little tug. "Go on, grab your purse."

Rita gathered her things and left the room. Howard was at the door when Gil asked, "If he wakes up, and asks about his legs, do you want me to tell him?"

Howard grabbed onto the door jamb, and Gil could see the man's internal struggle. How does a father tell his only son that he might never walk again? "I... We... I don't know what to tell him." Howard's voice shook, and Gil wasn't sure any more words would get past the stricture in Howard's throat. As it was, Gil's own throat was tight.

Gil swallowed hard. "If he wakes up, I'll tell him. You good with that?" In some ways, Gil hoped like hell Isaac didn't wake up on his watch, because how was he going to give his friend that kind of news? But at the same time, he hoped it was him that would deliver that blow and save his parents from any more heartbreak.

Howard's throat worked, but no words came after several tries. Then Howard nodded to him and disappeared around the corner.

Though Gil doubted Isaac could hear him, he said, "I've got news for you, Iz. But it can wait."

Gil slumped into the chair, took a sip of his now lukewarm coffee, and stared at his buddy as a machine beeped a steady beat. Isaac's chest rose and fell, his breathing slow and steady. There was no bruising on his face, and since his abdomen was covered with the hospital gown, it looked as if Isaac was sleeping. Not laying there, broken.

Gil polished off the rest of his coffee and killed the overhead lights, leaving the one on over the bed. There was nothing he could do besides wait Isaac out. He kicked off his boots, propped his feet on the edge of the bed, and settled his head against the back of the chair. He would take a quick combat nap, and then he'd be as good as new.

Gil didn't know how long he'd been asleep when he heard a muffled moan coming from the bed beside him. He sat up and patted Isaac's shoulder. "Hey, Iz? You going to wake up, buddy?"

Isaac tried to open his eyes, then squeeze them shut again against the light. "Fuck me, man." Isaac's voice was thick and raspy. "How much did I have to drink last night?"

Isaac held his hand in front of the light and tried to open his eyes again. Gil jumped up and clicked off the lights above the hospital bed. The light from the hall streamed through the open door. "That better?"

Isaac tried to sit up, groaned, and wrapped a hand around his belly. "What the... Who..." He held a hand over his stomach. "Did I get in a fight? Feels like someone beat the crap out of me."

Gil pushed him back into the mattress. "Lay back. You weren't out drinking. You're in the hospital."

Gil let that sink in. Waited for the memories to return. For Isaac to figure things out on his own.

Even with the sedation, it didn't take Isaac long to snap to. "The gun bust."

"Yeah."

"Rivera?" Leave it to Isaac to be thinking about his teammates first.

"In ICU, from what I've been told. I was going to check on him next. But the consensus is that he should pull through, barring any complications."

"Did you get them? Did you get those bastards?"

Isaac wasn't up for a full debrief. Gil kept it to the basics. "Some. Not all. One's dead. One's wounded. The team is on the case. Hopefully, we'll know more soon."

Isaac reached a hand out, but Gil didn't know what he needed. "Can I get you something?"

"Water."

On a rolling table, there was a pitcher of water and a plastic cup with a lid and a straw. Gil filled it, buzzed the head of Isaac's bed up, and held the straw to his lips. "Drink up."

After several long swallows, Gil pulled the cup away. He didn't want Isaac throwing up. "Let that settle, then we'll try some more."

Isaac leaned back against the pillow, and his eyes drifted closed. Gil thought he'd fallen back asleep when his eyes opened a fraction and Isaac said, "Okay, hit me with it. All of it."

Seconds ticked by as Gil tried to form the words, the sentences, that would deliver the devastating news. Gil was now seriously questioning his offer to tell Isaac about his paralysis. To buy himself more time, Gil sent off a quick text to Isaac's parents to let them know Isaac was awake.

"That craptastic?" Isaac asked.

"It's not good."

"I can't move my legs. I feel nothing from the waist down." Isaac's voice didn't break, it was this dry monotone. "Answer my question." Isaac closed his eyes again as if that would make what Gil had to say less heartbreaking to hear.

"What question was that?"

"The one I asked you out in the field. Am I ever going to get laid again?"

"Look, buddy, you have more important things to worry about."

Isaac opened his eyes again "Maybe. But if I can't have sex, what's the point?"

Gil popped out of the chair and paced to the far wall and back. "Are you fucking kidding me? There is more to life than sex."

"Spoken like a man who can have it."

"Fine," Gil raised his hands in defeat. "Say you're right, say the worst happens. Say you never walk again. Say you never have sex again. You're still alive. You can still love, you can still work, you can still—"

"Yeah, yeah. I hear you." But by Isaac's tone, Gil wasn't convinced Isaac had heard him at all.

"You were the one who always preached that satisfying your partner was what was most important to you. You have your hands, your mouth. You don't need a dick to make a man happy. Not the right one anyway."

"Is this you offering to help me update my Tinder profile?

We can say: Looking for the right man, who likes half a man, one who doesn't need a di—"

"You're awake." One of the male nurses walked into the room. He was young and fit, and the type of guy Isaac would normally go after. From the subtle way he checked Isaac out, the nurse might have been the kind of guy to take Isaac up on his offer. "How are you feeling? Can I get you anything?"

The nurse put a blood pressure cuff on Isaac's arm and stuck the stethoscope into his ears.

"You can settle an argument for me." Isaac's tone came across as light and unaffected.

"*Isaac*," Gil warned.

Isaac ignored him.

The nurse held up one finger as he slowly let the air out of the blood pressure cuff. If Isaac had seen him at the bar, he would have been quick to buy him a drink, and knowing Isaac, try to take him to his bed.

The nurse pulled the cuff off Isaac's arm and jotted something on Isaac's medical record. "What's your question?"

"Say you met a guy, a good-looking guy, and you liked him. Would you go out with him?"

The nurse looked from Isaac to Gil and back again. He hesitated, then said, "Probably." The nurse knew something was up. "What's this about?"

"I'm getting there," Isaac said. "Let's say this guy that you like, this cute guy, charming guy, asked you out, and you said yes. Say you guys got along, and let's say you decide, you want to have sex with him—"

"Where are you going with this?" The nurse leaned in. He had one of those interested smiles on his face.

"Hang with me, I'm almost to the point." When the nurse nodded for him to go on, Isaac said, "Then say you found out his dick was dead, would you want to have sex with him?"

He took a step away, his hands on his hips. He glanced over his shoulder at Gil again, who gave the nurse the slightest nod. He knew what Isaac wanted and needed to hear. "For the right guy? Sure. Why not. You wouldn't be the first impotent man in this world. There are other ways to please your partner."

Isaac barked out a laugh, then grabbed at his stomach and groaned. "You're saying that because you feel sorry for me."

"Maybe," the nurse said. "Maybe not. You'd have to ask me out if you want to find out for sure." He checked a few other vitals, then said, "I'm going to go call your doctor, and let him know you're awake."

"Yeah, sure."

He had almost made it to the door when Isaac said, "Were you serious? About me asking you out?"

He pulled out his pen and strode back to the bed and scribbled his number on the palm of Isaac's right hand. "You tell me."

He turned and gave Gil a wink on his way out. Gil wasn't sure if the nurse was being genuine, but he didn't care. The man had given his friend a rare and precious commodity. Hope.

"Told you." Gil sat back down in the chair.

The glower on Isaac's face softened, not a smile, but no longer a frown. "Yeah, well, talk is cheap."

"Iz, shut up."

Isaac chuckled. It was rueful but real. He stared up at the ceiling for a bit, lost in his thoughts. His eyes got heavy and he fought the sleep. "Fuck, man," he said as the realization of his injuries really started sinking in. "This bites."

"Sucks hairy donkey balls, buddy. But this ain't nothing but a bump in the road."

"Yeah," Isaac said. Though it didn't sound like he believed the words. "Tell me you guys have a plan to catch these assholes."

Gil settled deep into the chair, putting his feet on the edge of the bed again, and filled Isaac in on what little they knew. Isaac's eyes closed, and when his breathing became slow and steady, Gil stopped mid-sentence thinking Isaac had fallen asleep.

"Don't stop," Isaac muttered. "I'm not dead yet."

"Not even funny." Gil continued, "After Finn talked to the guy you shot, this Drew Roth guy, they think there might be a way to get a guy on the inside."

Isaac's eyes opened part way, but Gil knew Isaac was glaring at him. "Tell me that you didn't volunteer."

Gil pinched the bridge of his nose, thought about lying, but didn't. "Bet your ass I did."

Isaac's gaze remained steady, but tension coiled in his body. "Don't do this for me."

"I'm not."

"*Bullshit.*"

"Fine. This one is for you. But you would do the same for me."

"Not if I just got off an eighteen-month stint undercover. Not if I'd almost lost my life." With his hand, Isaac shoved Gil's legs off the bed and said, "Look me in the eye and tell me that you're mentally where you need to be to pull this off."

"This isn't like that other op. This should be short term. A few weeks, a few months tops." It wasn't lost on Isaac that Gil hadn't given Isaac the confirmation he'd needed.

"You're going to make a mistake. You're going to get yourself killed. Then it will be me passing out the *I told you so's.*"

The doctor rounded the corner with Isaac's parents right behind. *Thank Christ.* Isaac wasn't going to talk him out of going undercover. At least now they wouldn't have to argue about it.

Gil said his goodbyes and left with a promise to be back as soon as he could.

On the way out of the hospital, he stopped by Rivera's room in ICU, but he was asleep, and there had been little change in his status. Gil paid his respects to Rivera's parents and headed out the door.

Isaac might have a point about the whole undercover gig. It wasn't like Gil was dying to go back under. But what choice did he have?

7

A sheriff's deputy came and left with Tessa's statement. She spent the next hour and a half cleaning up the wreck that used to be her house. With every shard of glass she swept up, and every piece of fluff from the couch cushion she bagged, her anger built.

This may only be a house to some, but in the time that she and Jack had moved in, she'd worked her ass off turning it into a home. She could have bought something more expensive. In the past year, Bradley had started shoving money every month into a bank account he'd set up for her under the guise of child support. But it wasn't child support.

It was manipulation.

She didn't want one penny, one dime, one nickel, from her ex. All she wanted from Bradley, was for him to leave her and Jack alone. Do kids need their father? No question. Unless that father is Bradley Martin.

Then that kid would be much better off with a dog, or a cat, or even a fucking hamster. Not a weasel of a man who used his money and his power to coerce, to frighten, to get his way.

Bradley reminded her of a toddler stuck in his terrible two's, only with more power and menace. There had been a time shortly after Bradley had disappeared that she had felt sorry for herself and her son. Until she realized they were both much better off without him.

How could she raise a good son, a moral son, when his father's moral compass couldn't find true North. Now that Bradley wanted to worm his way back into their lives, there was no telling what the future held.

As she showered for her meeting with Bradley, she steeled herself for what was to come. Nothing good. That was for sure.

Bone weary, she poured a travel cup full of coffee and headed to the quiet little Italian restaurant off the square in Murdock. The restaurant had limited seating, catering to the tourist crowd, but as far as upscale restaurants went, this was the best Murdock had.

Call her cynical, but Tessa didn't think Bradley had asked her to Mariano's to wine her, dine her, and impress her. He wanted to meet her there because it was crowded. Less of a chance for her to make a scene.

But she wasn't the same woman she'd been when he'd left years ago. She no longer cared what others thought. If he pissed her off, Bradley would know it, and so would the rest of the town.

She came through the restaurant's door five minutes early. Bradley was already there. A glass of wine in his hand, and a snake-in-the-grass smile on his face. He stood when the maître d' walked her to the table, and like the gentleman he pretended to be, he pulled out the chair for her.

The two-top table sat in a quiet corner. The dim lighting might make some people feel romantic. All it made Tessa feel was tired. At least Bradley had already ordered the wine.

"You came," he said.

"Of course, I came." She kept her voice pleasant, for now. "It was an edict, not an invitation."

"Is that attitude necessary?" He eyed her over the top of his wine glass. His voice remained deceptively calm, and his expression stayed unreadable. Typical Bradley. She hadn't known what he'd been thinking way back when, and she had no freaking clue what he thought now. Nothing she would like. The wine turned to vinegar on her tongue.

The waitress came by and offered them both a menu. Tessa waved her off, and said, "The wine is all, thank you."

"You have to eat." Bradley's concern fell short of sincere.

No, I don't. Tessa caught herself before the words jumped out. She wasn't a kid who hadn't had her nap. She settled on, "I'm not hungry."

"As you wish." Bradley gave his attention to the waitress. "I'll have the Chicken Primavera."

Tessa took a generous swallow of the wine. From experience, she knew anything Bradley had to say would be easier to digest with a little alcohol in her system. "Why am I here."

"Can't I sit down and have a nice dinner with my wife?"

"*Ex*-wife."

"About that." Bradley took her hand. She took it back. He frowned and said, "Now that we're practically in the same town, I thought..."

He flashed her that well-practiced, self-deprecating smile that she'd stupidly fallen for years ago. While Bradley had many shortcomings, low self-esteem wasn't one of them. That smile was all part of the act.

"I'm not getting back together with you." She didn't know how to say it any clearer than that.

"Don't tell me you're seeing someone." His tone was teasing, in a spill-the-beans kind of way. Like he was her best friend, her confidant, not her ex.

"That's none of your business. You gave up the right to have a say in my personal life when you walked out that door and didn't come back."

"I'm back now."

"It's too late." In case he had any doubts, she added, "It's waaay too late."

Bradley swirled the wine in his glass and took a sip. "How was your day?"

Horrendous and getting worse every second she stayed in that restaurant. "Why do you care now? You've never cared when we were married."

"Humor me."

"Just peachy." If you could call running nonstop for forty-eight hours on a couple hours of sleep, having your tire slashed, your home trashed, and oh, yeah, members of your team shot, *just peachy*, then that's what she was.

The waitress came by with some bread. Despite what Tessa had said about not being hungry, her stomach rumbled. She picked up a slice and tore it in half, dipping it into the herb spiced olive oil.

"You always were a lousy liar," Bradley said.

"Better to be a crappy liar than an accomplished one." The pettiness leaked out with her words. Bradley was an expert on pushing her buttons, and it gnawed on her to know that and to not be able to stop herself.

"I didn't come here to fight."

"Then why did you ask me here? I told you earlier I didn't have time. It's been a shit day, and all I really want to do is pick up my son and call it a night."

Bradley brushed the crumbs off his fingers and sat back. "What happened?"

Tessa polished off the rest of her wine in one giant gulp, enjoying the exasperation on Bradley's face at the way she tossed back three-hundred-dollar-a-bottle wine like it came in a box. Because she wanted to see his reaction when she answered, she met his eyes. "My house was vandalized."

He almost looked surprised. Tessa figured his honed acting skills went along with his innate ability to lie through his teeth.

"Look me in the eye and tell me you had nothing to do with it."

He feigned indignation better than surprise. "Why would you say that?"

"Because it was a chicken shit thing to do to somebody and I thought to myself, 'Tessa, who would do such a chicken shit thing?' and guess whose name popped into my head?"

"Don't be ridiculous. Things like that happen when you live on the downhill part of town. When the shit rolls through, it's going to get messy."

"Nice," Tessa said. "Funny how we never had any problems before, yet within a few months of you moving close, something like this happens. I don't believe in coincidences."

He raised in hands. "Believe what you want. I had nothing to do with it. But this incident does bring up a point I wanted to make."

This should be good. Tessa tore off another piece of bread and swirled it around in the oil.

"You need to move. I won't have my son living in that kind of neighborhood. It's not safe."

"*Our* son. That neighborhood is what I can afford."

"Why do you think I send the money if not for you to—"

The waitress delivered Bradley's dinner. He gave her one of his patented classy-guy smile, but there was a tension around his eyes that kept the smile from settling there.

"I send you that money so that *our* son doesn't have to live in squalor."

Squalor. Her bank balance may not have lots of zeros, but

they lived comfortably. Jack didn't have the newest video gaming system or a phone or a computer—he was only seven—but Jack never wanted for the things that mattered most.

"You send that money to try to control me. The way my father tried. A rotten carrot dangling in front of my nose."

"It's called child support."

"No. Money like that is borderline coercion."

"The courts might see it differently."

Tessa choked on the toasted bread. Crumbs went down her windpipe, and she coughed and sputtered. People at nearby tables turned and watched. She drank some water, but her throat still spasmed. *Courts.* Heat rose to her cheeks and sweat broke out over her hairline.

She drank more water while she gathered her composure. "The courts saw fit to give me sole custody after you'd abandoned us. They gave you visitation every other weekend, which you backed out on at the last minute on Friday."

"I want what's fair. Don't make me ask for more."

Wait. How had Bradley turned this around and made himself the victim? He was the narcissist who'd abandoned his family. *Not* her. "We've been through this already. The courts have spoken."

"Don't force my hand." He pushed his plate away, his food hardly touched.

Bring it on, came to mind, but she would be stupid to underestimate him. In the time that he'd been gone, he'd matured, and done very well financially. Like her father. Tessa would be a fool to forget the kind of power and sway money like that could wield. It wouldn't take much for him to bury her in court costs and bankrupt her.

The waitress came by. "Something wrong with the food?"

"No." Bradley stood, peeling off enough hundred-dollar bills to cover the wine and his meal. To them both, he said, "We're done here."

———

Night settled in as Tessa and Jack pulled up to Gil's cabin at the Lazy S. She reached back and tugged on Jack's foot. "Hey buddy, wake up. We're here."

Jack wiped the drool off his chin and released the catch on his booster seat. "Is this where we're sleeping?"

"Not sure which cabin yet. You can leave your backpack here until we know for sure."

They climbed out and knocked on Gil's door, but when there was no answer, they followed the sound of voices farther down the two-track road toward the older cabins. Boomer and Sidney's cabin was the hangout, where since the early years on the ranch many campfires had been lit, beers drunk, and white lies told.

The night was clear, the mass of stars almost close enough to touch. In the distance, Boomer's donkey brayed. Dink, Jenna's old cattle dog, trotted up out of the darkness, and pulled his lips back and greeted Jack with a toothy doggie smile. Jack ruffled Dink's fur and chased him down to the campfire, leaving Tessa to follow behind.

"Hey, munchkin."

"Quinny!"

Quinn got up from one of the logs surrounding the fire and met Jack with some sort of complicated handshake thingy that ended with a chest slap and a hip bump. "Sidney's got food if you're hungry."

Jack ran off because even though he'd eaten dinner not long before Tessa had picked him up, the kid always acted like he was half starved.

"Hey," Quinn said, meeting her at the end of the road. "How are you doing? Gil told me about your house."

She didn't want to talk about her house or her ex. But this was Quinn, her co-pilot, her partner, her friend. They'd already clocked a lot of hours of airtime together. They relied on each other, and like that first ever flight they'd taken together, they called each other on their bullshit, cementing their friendship.

"Been better." She shrugged. "Been worse, too. Nothing a solid eight hours of sleep won't make a little better." She pointed over her shoulder. "Did Mac say which cabin she was putting us in?"

"You don't want to hang out?"

"I want some Z's."

Over Quinn's shoulder, she watched Jack poke at the fire with a long stick, sending a cloud of burning red embers into the air. Jack giggled and poked some more.

"Jack," she called out. "Be careful."

"I've got him."

Tessa stepped around Quinn to see Gil on the edge of his folding chair, a finger stuck through Jack's belt loop in case he should stumble.

Tessa offered Quinn an apologetic smile. "We really should—"

"Aw, come on." Quinn took her hand and tugged until she was forced to take one large step and then another. "Sidney has chocolate, and marshmallows and—"

Chocolate. "Sold."

Quinn grinned. Her partner didn't always play fair. Tessa fell into step beside him and joined the group around the fire.

"You made it." Jenna was sitting on a blanket, one of the logs used for seating at her back, Dink already curled up and snoozing beside her.

Boomer sat on the adjacent log, his prosthetic off, his

crutches on the ground beside him. Tessa leaned in, and Boomer gave her a peck on the cheek. "Gil was telling us about your night."

Her mind shot to the sight of Gil beneath her, the way he'd filled her, satisfied her. Had Gil told—

She shot a glance at Gil, there was a spark in his eyes, but his face gave nothing away. "It was...quite the night."

"Sorry I missed it," Boomer said.

"I'm not." Sidney came out of her and Boomer's cabin, a tray in her hand loaded down with all the fixings for S'mores. "We've had enough excitement for one lifetime."

"You don't miss it?" Jenna asked Boomer. "The danger unfolding. The adrenaline flowing, the heart racing."

"Yeah, but—"

"I can't wait to hear this." Sidney was tiny, but mighty and gave Boomer a look that said he was a few misstated words away from sleeping in the dog house.

Quinn took the tray from her, and Boomer snaked an arm around her waist and plopped her on his lap. "Yeah, *but*, this is better."

Sidney gave him a quick smack on the lips. "Nice save."

"Can I have one, Mom?" Jack stood beside Gil, who'd speared three marshmallows on a long slender stick.

"Sure, let me—"

"We've got it." Gil stood and motioned Tessa toward his chair, "Have a seat."

Tessa loaded up her own stick with a couple of marshmallows and commandeered Gil's seat and stuck her marshmallows into the fire. Gil sat on the log beside her, Jack dangling from his arms between Gil's bent legs, his stick rotating in the fire.

If you didn't know Gil, you might think twice about approaching him. From his imposing frame, the thick beard, the black dragon tattoo curling around his forearm, he could come across as intimidating. But Jack had warmed up to him almost immediately. Maybe Jack could sense Gil's inherent goodness. The stick dipped down, and Jack's marshmallows burst into flames.

"Ho, now." Gil chuckled and grabbed for the stick, yanking it from the fire. "Blow."

Jack blew but giggled too hard to be effective. Gil helped with one big burst of air.

"Oh, man." Jack's little face scrunched up. "We ruined them."

Quinn broke a graham cracker in half and loaded one with four squares of chocolate. "Naw, those are perfect."

Gil handed Jack the stick and loaded the marshmallow onto the graham cracker and gave the S'more to Jack. "Squeeze."

Jack squeezed. The cracker broke. Jack laughed, as cracker and marshmallow and chocolaty goo oozed onto his fingers.

"Easy there, Squirt." Gil laughed and caught a corner of the treat as it dropped. He popped it into his mouth and licked the sticky mess off his thumb and forefinger.

Tessa eyed him, remembering how Gil's mouth had felt on her, how that talented tongue had left her wanting more. While her head told her that Gil was nothing more than a fling, her body protested. It wanted him in her bed, over her, under her, and in her. But undoubtedly that was the lust talking.

Gil caught her staring, and the corners of his mouth tipped up, knowing where her mind had gone. "Tessa." Gil's voice was low, intimate.

"Yeah?"

"Your marshmallow's on fire."

It took a moment for Gil's words to register, but he was already reaching over, lifting her stick from the fire. A flaming ball of melted marshmallow dropped into the blaze, the marshmallow sizzling as it hit the white-hot coals below. *Dang.*

Gil extricated himself from Jack's sticky hands, and he

reloaded her stick. He stood there by the fire, rotating her marshmallow over the heat, toasting it to a golden, gooey goodness, looking seven kinds of hot himself, in his low-slung jeans, his tight T-shirt, and his tattered ATF baseball cap turned backward on his head. If Jack weren't there, and if she wasn't exhausted, she might find a dark corner to drag him off to.

No. That wouldn't do. They'd had sex, *great* sex. While the helo sex might not have been more than scratching an itch and fulfilling one or two fantasies she'd had over the years, she'd needed that connection after the night they'd had, and to say that she didn't want more would be a lie.

But she didn't know what else she wanted from Gil. She wasn't looking for a relationship. But the idea of a fuck buddy, a booty call when the fancy struck or the stress and the adrenaline and the hormones had red-lined, somehow didn't sit right with her either.

"Here you go." Jack handed her a carefully crafted S'more that he and Gil had made.

"Thanks, babe." Melted chocolate dripped onto her fingers as she bit into the sugary treat. She fanned a hand in front of her mouth. "Hot, hot."

She swallowed, and Gil handed her his bottle of water. She took a quick sip, cooling her tongue and the roof of her mouth. As soon as Gil sat back down, Jack was climbing all over him like his own personal human jungle gym.

Jack had gone from holding his legs up and dangling from Gil's thighs to climbing up his back. Currently, he was kneeling on Gil's shoulders, his hands in Gil's for balance.

"Jack, go sit with Dink and give Mr. Gil a break."

"Ah, Mom, we're having fun, right, Mr. Gil?" Jack leaned over, balancing on his stomach on the top of Gil's head, his arms and feet straight out like Superman.

"Sure, kid."

"*Jack.*"

Gil and Superman Jack turned toward her. Gil said, "Really, we're fine."

The pure joy in Jack's smile squeezed her chest. Jack was naturally a happy kid, but even riding the horses hadn't put that kind of smile on her kid's face.

She had to tread with care.

As much as Jack needed a father figure, what he needed more was to not get hurt. She couldn't bring just anybody into their lives. She didn't want to see Jack get attached to Gil and then feel abandoned all over again when whatever this was between the two of them didn't work out.

On the other side of her, she caught snippets of conversation between Boomer, Sidney, Jenna and Quinn, something about the bust from the night before, but her focus was on her son. And Gil.

Gil trapped Jack's hands at his side and rolled him off his head and shoulders, catching Jack in his arms. Gil's cap tumbled off, and Jack scrambled to get it. Jack plopped it on his head, his eyes almost disappearing beneath the now mangled brim.

Gil held out his hand. "Let me see."

Jack handed over the hat, and Gil reshaped the brim. Then he readjusted the strap on the back and tossed it back to Jack. "Try that."

Jack turned the bill around and placed it on his head backward the way Gil had. Yeah, the kid who had to tie his shoes just the right way and wear his backpack on both shoulders and his baseball caps frontwards because that's how the pros wore them, voluntarily turned his cap the other way. Because that's how Gil wore his.

Oh man. Tessa was already in trouble.

"Looks good, Squirt."

"Can I have it? I already have an FBI, a DEA, and a sheriff's cap, but I don't have an ATF one."

"Jack, you can't ask—"

"It's okay," Gil said, "Plenty more where that came from."

"If you're sure," Tessa said.

Gil nodded. Jack's face broke into a huge smile. He stuck his fist out, Gil tapped down on the fist, then Jack tapped Gil's, then they fist bumped then brought their hands back, their fingers out, Gil and Jack both making a little explosion sound.

"All right, all right, you two," Tessa said. "Time for bed."

Jack frowned. "Awh, maaan."

Gil glanced up at her and grinned. It was salty and sexy and damn...

"Not you." She gave Gil's shoulder a gentle shove. "You, young man. Tell everyone goodnight."

Jack went around the group, giving hugs and fist bumps. Dink woke up and stretched.

"Goodnight, little man," Jenna said. Then to Tessa, she said, "I put sheets and comforters on the beds in the cabin next to Gil's. Mia Mann, my newest veteran, is supposed to be in sometime tonight—"

"We don't have to stay here, we can—"

"It's fine," Jenna said. "It'll only be a day or two. Mia can either bunk in the cabin with you or I can put her on a cot in my office in the barn."

Boomer massaged the end of his stump. "I'll have a look at your back door first thing in the morning. Shouldn't be too much of a problem to fix."

"Thanks, I appreciate it."

"I'll walk you up," Gil said.

Jack jumped up and down. "Yay. Can you give me a ride?"

Gil squatted down and reached a hand over his shoulder. "Put your foot on my thigh and climb aboard."

Before Tessa could object, Jack scaled Gil the way Kong scaled the Empire State Building, latching his hands around Gil's neck for support. Gil boosted Jack higher to keep from choking.

"Thanks," Tessa said to Gil as they made their way to the cabin. "You don't have to do that."

"I wanted to." Something in the way he said that made her think he might want more.

At her Jeep, they retrieved Jack's backpack and her overnight bag. While Jack went into the bathroom to change into his pajamas, wash his hands, and brush his teeth, Tessa turned down the bottom bunk while Gil worked on the top one for Jack.

"You never said how your visit to the hospital went."

"Rivera's not out of ICU. I spelled Isaac's parents for a bit. He woke up..." Gil went quiet, refolded the top sheet back and fluffed up an already fluffy pillow.

The muscle in his jaw clenched, and he stared straight ahead. Tessa stood and touched his arm, and he wrapped it around her. She held him tight. Gil was a big man. A powerful, stoic, man. But this was Isaac. His best friend.

"I basically had to tell him he might never walk again."

He leaned against the bedpost, settling her between his legs, linking his hands behind her back. There was nothing sexual about it. This was about comfort, about letting him know he wasn't alone. "It was..." The words came out tight, and he swallowed hard.

"Tough?"

His chuckle came out harsh as he shook his head, finally meeting her gaze. "That doesn't even begin to describe it."

"I wish I could have been there for you."

"Nothing would have made telling Isaac that kind of news any better, but thanks. I appreciate that."

She pressed a kiss to the center of his chest. He smelled of smoke and roasted marshmallows. His hands skimmed up her sides, traced the line of her shoulders, then higher, cupping her cheeks.

His eyes flicked down to her lips then back up again. "We never got a chance to talk about this morning."

She sneaked a glance over her shoulder. Jack still had the water running in the bathroom. "Now's probably not a good time. Besides, do we really need to talk about it? I mean it was sex, right? No strings. We were two people who needed to blow off a little steam."

That concerned look in his eyes hardened, and a crease formed between his thick brows. "Look, I..." His eyes went to her lips again. "Awh, fuck it," he said, his voice barely above a whisper as he ducked his head down for a kiss. His lips brushed hers then he deepened the kiss, pulling her up on her tiptoes, his tongue—

"Ew, gross." Jack scooted through the room as if he were riding a stick pony.

Tessa stepped back, though Gil seemed reluctant to let her go.

"Does this mean you're going to have a baby?"

"W-what?" Tessa sputtered.

Gil chuckled.

"Definitely not," Tessa said. "I'm done having kids."

"Billy said that when two people kiss it puts a baby in the lady's belly and—"

"That's not how it works, Squirt." Gil picked Jack up and dropped him on the top bunk.

Jack rolled over and propped himself onto his stomach. "Then how do babies get in there?"

"Ah..." Gil glanced at Tessa, stark terror on his face. Who would have thought the birds and the bees could bring this man to his knees? He nudged her with his elbow. "Don't stand there laughing. Help me out, here."

Jack's eyes got big, and his mouth dropped open. "Is Becky Blevins right? She said the dad puts his thingy—"

Red crept up Gil's neck, and he looked like he wanted to cover his ears with his hands and run from the cabin.

"Penis," Tessa said, "It's called a penis, right, Gil?" Now she was messing with the big, fearsome, federal agent for grins. She figured that old saying had merit, the bigger they are, the harder they fall.

He glanced at her with an amused what-the-fuck arch to his brows. Then to Jack, Gil said, "I think it's late and a little boy needs to go to bed."

"But—"

"Mr. Gil's right." Tessa decided a little mercy was in order. "If you're curious tomorrow, we can talk about it when I get home from work."

Jack flopped his head on his pillow. "Fiine. But I'm not a little kid anymore. I know the stork doesn't bring the babies. I'm undecided if the tooth fairy is real. I mean, how is she supposed to—"

"*Jack*." Tessa tried to keep the laugh and exasperation out of her voice. "Go to sleep."

She stepped up on the bottom bunk and gave him a kiss goodnight. "Love, you."

"Love, you too."

Gil socked him gently on the arm. "Night kiddo."

"Night."

Tessa left the bathroom light on for Jack and allowed Gil to lead her out the front door by her hand. He had a smile on his face and devilment in his eyes.

$$8$$

Tessa stopped at the edge of the cabin's porch, staring out at the quarter moon suspended amongst the stars. Gil stepped up and wrapped his arms around her waist, her back to his chest. Voices and laughter filtered up from the campfire. During his stay at the ranch, Gil had come to enjoy everyone's company, and now considered them friends, but this, right here, standing with Tessa in his arms, her kid asleep in the cabin... this was better. He wanted to pretend, if only for a moment, that they were together. That he had a family.

That maybe one day he'd have a kid of his own.

Then he remembered what she'd said in the cabin when Jack had asked her about having another baby. *I'm done having kids.* It shouldn't have mattered, but for some reason, it did.

Tessa leaned into him, resting her head against his shoulder. He linked his fingers with hers across her belly. "Did you mean what you said in there, that you're done having kids?"

"I don't know. Probably. One's about all I can handle."

"That would be a shame."

"What does that mean?" She had a this-should-be-good tone in her voice, but he could tell she was smiling when she'd said it.

He pulled her in tighter against him, loving the way she fit beneath his chin, her ass snugged against his crotch. "Jack's a terrific kid. You're a great mom. You not having another kid would be like Hank selling off his prize heifer."

"Oh, no," she laughed, turning in his arms and giving his chin a playful nibble. "You did not just compare me to cattle."

"Good breeding stock is good breeding stock."

"Yeah? Does this mean you are volunteering to stand at stud?"

She was teasing him—but for some reason, maybe because he'd wanted a family of his own or the fact that Isaac may never get to have one—the words weighed on him. He sobered and said, "Yeah. I mean, someday I'd like to have a kid of my own."

She leaned back, appraising him with an expression he couldn't read.

"Is that surprising?"

"A little."

Her words pricked, but he tried not to let it bother him. They were still getting to know each other.

"But after seeing the way you were with Jack tonight, I can see it. You'd make a good father, at least until it comes time to talk to your kids about sex."

He laughed and shook his head. "Did you seriously say penis in front of your seven-year-old? You can't go with winky, or ding-dong, or tallywacker? If it was good enough for my parents, then—"

"That's what it is, a penis. The experts say—"

"What do they know? Euphemisms for the win. I turned out okay."

"Except you can't hear the word penis without blushing."

Heat crept up his face, proving her point. Now all this talk about male body parts was starting to influence his. Shifting their positions, he straddled her leg. "Speaking of penises..."

He ducked his head and pressed a kiss along the column of her neck. She smelled of smoke with undertones of the JP-8 that fueled her helo, which somehow turned him on even more. He found the easy way she gripped the Sikorsky's cyclic between her legs sexy as hell.

He'd flown in helo's enough times before to know that she flew with a light touch and tight control. He appreciated that about her, but as much as she'd given of herself that morning, he wanted to know what she'd be like when she utterly, completely, unabashedly, surrendered.

He brushed her hair behind her shoulders, kissing his way up her neck, to the corner of her jaw. Her head thumped back against the porch column, eyes closed, lips parted. He dove in, their tongues meeting, mating.

"Mmm," he said, pulling back a fraction, "You taste like chocolate."

"Sorry."

"Don't be." He nipped at that luscious bottom lip. "The idea of you and me, a table, a bottle of chocolate syrup, and nothing else, makes me hard as fuck."

She reached down and palmed him through his jeans. He sucked in a breath, rough and raw, and eased into her touch. He rested his forehead on hers. "We should stop before this gets out of hand."

She huffed out a low laugh, but even in the dim light of the moon, he saw the smile slip from her face. She released him, and as she brushed her hand down his jaw, the corners of her mouth dipped down.

"What's wrong?" Whatever was going through her mind had nothing to do with the fact he'd shut them down for the night, he was sure of that.

She ran her hands down his chest, one hand stopping over his heart. It beat stout and hard beneath his sternum, but the way she refused to look at him, made his heart go *thump, clunk.* "Tessa, tell me."

Tessa shook her head, but said, "This is going to sound like a dick move, especially after how you were with Jack tonight... But I... I think..."

"I'm a big boy, spit it out."

Damn. She looked up at him then. Though her chin quivered, she met his gaze head-on. "I-I think it's best if you keep your distance from Jack."

There was a sharp pain in the middle of his chest, and his heart kicked in protest against his rib cage. "I get it." Though understanding why she was saying it didn't make it hurt any less.

"Nothing against you. It's that Jack is looking for a father figure to latch onto, and if things had been different, it wouldn't have been an issue because I wouldn't have introduced him to you unless I thought we were serious.

"Jack's a healthy, happy kid, but he's also smart and sensitive and intuitive, and even though his father left early in his life, I know that him not having a dad around has affected him. I don't want to see him get hurt."

Gil stepped back and scratched at his beard, trying to find the right words when all he wanted to do was protest.

"You're mad." She took his hand, though he could tell by the straightness in her spine and the jut of her jaw that she wouldn't take her words back.

"You're protecting your kid. That's job number one. The only thing I'm mad about is the situation. I'm not angry with you. You gotta do what you think's best for him."

It was getting late, Tessa's eyes drooped as she fought the fatigue. He took one step down the stairs, putting them near eye level. "For the record, if this thing between us gets serious, I'm good with that."

She leaned a shoulder against the column. "We had sex."

"We did."

"That doesn't make us..." She waggled her hand between the two of them as if at a loss for the right word. "...anything."

"Does it need a definition? A label?"

"No." The word came out a little soft and sad. "I'm not looking for anything that requires a label. I was upfront with you on that. That's why you and Jack..." She shrugged one shoulder and let the rest of the sentence drop.

"What if I want more? What if I want a label?"

"I'm not sure I have any more to give."

Tessa might have believed that with all her heart, but Gil didn't. Not for a micro-second. She may be freer with her body, but from what little he knew of her history, he understood her need to protect her heart.

"Consider me warned." He threaded his fingers through her hair and cupped the back of her head, placing a pleasing, promising kiss on her lips. "Sleep tight."

He stepped down and waited at the bottom of the stairs until she'd disappeared into the cabin. He ran his hands down his face and scratched his fingers through his beard. Right then, a drink almost sounded better than sex. Almost. But with the ranch's no alcohol policy in place because of the program, there wasn't a can of beer or a bottle of whiskey to be had. Probably for the best.

He should have gone to bed himself, but he wanted to wait and welcome the new veteran when she arrived. That, and he really, really didn't want to be alone with his thoughts. That would lead to thinking of Tessa, which would lead to him thinking of Tessa in the helo. Which would lead to one mother of a hard-on. It would be too pathetic for him to be rubbing one out in a one-room cabin in the foothills of the Rockies.

When he got back to the campfire, Boomer and Quinn were

alone, nursing a couple bottles of water. "Where did everybody go?"

Quinn hitched his thumb over his shoulder at Boomer's cabin. "The girls are inside. Something about Mac and baby showers." Quinn kinda shuddered. "We decided to leave them to it."

Gil flopped in the empty chair between the two men. The fire had died down, leaving nothing more than ghostly, glowing, logs. The fire popped and cracked, spitting sparks into the fresh night air.

"You were gone a long time." Boomer's tone was suggestive.

"I kinda tried to warn her off..." Quinn shrugged.

"You did *what*?" Gil reached into Boomer's cooler and uncapped a water for himself.

"I don't think she paid me any attention if that helps."

Boomer eased down in his chair, a lazy grin on his face. "From what Sidney said, Mac gave Tessa the 'if you hurt him' speech."

"You've got to be fucking kidding me." Gil should have been angry, but many times since he'd been at Healing Horses, he'd sat around that very campfire with Boomer, Mac, and Quinn, hashing out their pasts, trying to make some sense of the senseless and put it all in perspective.

While he hadn't suffered debilitating PTSD like many of his brothers and sisters in arms, it didn't mean he was unaffected or that he didn't have to come to terms with his own demons.

As much as he didn't want to believe it, being able to swap stories with people who had lived it and understood it, helped. Because for the first time in a long time, he didn't feel so alone. He felt like he had brothers and sisters, and people who had his back, even if sometimes they felt like that gave them the right to meddle in his personal life.

"I don't need any of you running interference for me, I'm perfectly capable of screwing up my own relationships."

"Relationship, huh?" Quinn teased.

Gil took a long drag on the water bottle, "It's not like that, it's—"

Headlights appeared along the dirt road, the "Taxi" sign lit on the roof.

"Jesus," Gil said, "You couldn't pick the poor woman up at the airport?"

"She refused." Quinn tossed a couple of small logs on the fire. "I'll go let Jenna know she's here."

Boomer collected his crutches and made his way to the road to meet the cab. Gil followed. The cabbie buzzed down his window. The latch on the back door popped, but Mia didn't climb out.

Boomer pulled out his wallet. "How much?"

Boomer paid but Mia remained inside. Boomer leaned in the driver's window and asked her, "You coming?"

One beat, then two, then the rear door was shoved open, and Mia Mann climbed out with reluctance and attitude. She stood about five- six or seven, but it was hard to tell by the way she held her shoulders, kind of curled in on herself.

She wore woodland green digital MARPAT fatigue pants with combat boots, topped off with an unzipped sweatshirt, the sleeves pushed up to her elbows over a white tank top. Metal pierced her left brow, and the tip of a tattoo snaked around the back of her neck from beneath her shirt. With her head shaved, she looked like the love child of the emo kid in high school and GI Jane. Only scarier.

Boomer introduced himself and shook her hand.

Gil did the same. The contact was brief, but her grip was firm. "Gil Brant. I'm also in the program."

"Good for you." She had one of those deep, Lauren Bacall

voices a lot of guys found sexy. Either she smoked a lot, or she wasn't used to talking much.

Boomer glanced at Gil, a this-should-be-fun tilt to his brow.

"You're here, finally." Jenna came up behind them, about to pull Mia in for a hug. Mia stiffened. Jenna settled for a handshake. "You want to come and sit by the campfire? I've got some food if you're hungry, some water maybe?"

"I just need some rack time."

"Yeah, sure." Jenna schooled her face, but in the cab's headlights, Gil caught the flicker of something on her face that made Gil wonder if, in less than a minute, Mia had made Jenna start rethinking the whole Healing Horses program. "A friend and her son will be sharing your cabin for a few nights, or I could put you on a cot in the barn office if you'd rather."

"I can deal."

"Somebody going to get that bag?" the cabbie called out.

Gil made a move toward the trunk. "I'll get it."

"No." Mia held up a staying hand. "I've got it."

After the taxi left, Jenna said, "Since it's already late, we'll start a little later in the morning. Meet us at the big house at eight for breakfast." Jenna pointed up the road toward the big house, even though what she'd said was self-explanatory.

"Terrific." Mia's inflection said it was anything but.

Boomer put his hand on Jenna's shoulder. "Come on, I'll help you finish cleaning up and put out the fire."

"I'll walk her up to the cabin," Gil said.

"I can find it." Mia had one of those looks on her face somewhere between get-the-hell-out-of-my-way and get-the-hell-out-of-my-life.

"I'm sure you can. But I'm going that way." Gil crossed his arms over his chest, refusing to give an inch. If she thought he was going to cower under her glower, if she thought anyone on the S would, she'd come to the wrong damn place.

She shouldered her duffel and started trudging up the hill toward their cabins, her hands gripping the straps. Both of her forearms sported vibrant tattoos, though the light wasn't good enough for him to see any detail.

"Nice ink," he said, trying to find some common ground. "Who did your work?"

She reached over and tugged the sleeves of her sweatshirt down but kept on walking. The two cabins came into view, and Gil pointed to the one that was hers. "You're there."

She grunted.

Prickly thing. All spines and sharp claws on every corner like a pissed off porcupine. "There's this tattoo parlor I found in Murdock, off the main drag. The guy does some sick—"

"*Dude.*" Mia stopped walking.

Gil raised his hands, he'd surrender now, but that battle wasn't over, not by a long shot.

She stared off into the distance. Gil waited her out. "Look," she said, "I'm not some kid looking to make a friend at sleepover camp. I'm here to do my time. That's all."

"It's a volunteer program. Not jail."

Her low laugh was ripe with skepticism. "I don't know your story. Maybe you want to be here. Maybe you don't. Frankly, I don't care. But I didn't have a choice. The judge said it was this plus probation or prison."

She glanced up and down the road. "Still not sure I made the right decision."

As Tessa walked into Spinks' standing-room-only temporary office, she realized she was the last person to arrive. All the ATF task force agents were there. Hugh Fisher, Joel Cook, and a couple of the other guys who had been on the ground when

Rivera and Lang had been shot. Quinn had propped himself up in one of the corners of the room. There were some other agents there that she didn't know, who she assumed had been brought in temporarily to help with the case.

At the front of the room, Spinks was speaking to Oliver Finn, the FBI agent who ran some of the local joint task force operations, as well as her cousin Massey.

Dressed in a suit, Massey looked all spit-polished, like a little boy dressed for his first communion. Massey glanced up and gave her a slight wave, his smile crooked, his crutch dangling from the cuff around his forearm. She returned the wave. He took a seat, then she caught Gil's eye.

He shifted and made a space for her at the back of the room. "Who's that?" He pointed with his coffee cup toward Massey.

"My cousin." She stole Gil's coffee out of his hand and took a fortifying sip.

When she tried to hand it back, he gestured for her to keep it. "What's he doing here? I didn't know you had family in law enforcement."

"I don't. Massey's the kind of geeky computer genius who makes high school Bill Gates look like the cool kid on the block. Not sure what he's doing here. Speaking of which, what are you doing here? I thought the shooting was under investigation."

"Spinks said I could come in for the brief so I'd be up to speed once I'm released to come back to work." Gil took a sip of the coffee and handed it back to her. "What did you think of Mia?"

"Never saw her, and her bed hadn't been slept in. I thought she'd gotten delayed or something. Everything okay?"

"She probably decided to take the room in the barn after all."

"What's she like?"

"Hot and prickly, like a rash you shouldn't scratch."

A whistle pierced the air, and all extraneous conversations ceased. "Let's get started," Spinks said. "The sooner we get finished here, the sooner we can catch the rest of these bastards. Quick update on Rivera and Lang. Rivera has been moved out of ICU, his condition is serious, but no longer critical. Lang is stable, but doctors won't know for a while if the paralysis is permanent. Agent Finn conducted the interview with Ross, the shooter we put in the hospital." Spinks made a go-ahead motion to Finn.

As usual, Finn looked like he belonged in one of those Rolex advertisements in Forbes Magazine. All clean lines, gold cuff-links and freshly shaved face. Always calm, always clinical, and always by the book.

"Ross isn't saying much. Yet. Fear of reprisal and retaliation against his family is keeping his mouth shut for now. Today, we're notifying the media that he died due to complications from his gunshot wounds. Hopefully, that will give him enough breathing room to get him talking. As soon as he's fit for travel, we'll move him to a safe house until we can make some arrests."

Finn turned his attention to the far end of the table. "Agent Cook, you have additional information on Ross?"

Unlike Finn, Cook's clothes looked slept in. He had a large coffee in front of him and a tiny bottle of Visine.

Cook flipped open a file. "Drew Sullivan Ross. White male. Age thirty-two. Sealed juvie record. Short rap sheet, a couple of misdemeanor arrests for marijuana possession, burglary, petty theft, ages eighteen to twenty-two. Then a judge gave him a choice, jail or the Army." Cook glanced around the room. "Guess which one our Ross chose."

Spinks stared down at him, his arms crossed, and his face sporting a get-on-with-it glower.

Cook shifted in his seat and turned a page. "Ross first trained as a Unit Supply Specialist, then later became a Logistics Officer.

Got busted down to private twice on accusations of sexual harassment—"

"Sounds like a real peach," Tessa muttered.

Spinks eyed her under his brow. Cook continued, "Until finally about nine months ago he was dishonorably discharged. That's pretty much all we have right now. I've got a call in to see if I can get the skinny on the discharge."

"Fisher?" Spinks turned his attention to the agent beside Cook.

"Right." Fisher wasn't quite as organized, he flipped through a couple pages of notes he'd jotted on a legal pad. His handwriting was all slashes and quick, hard lines as if he hid an anger issue under his otherwise laid-back demeanor. "Got some good prints off the box truck we impounded, but no hits off those yet. Contents—a grab bag of goodies. Machine guns, mortar rounds, Stingers, you know, everything your average backyard weapons enthusiast needs. Crate and weapon serial numbers are being traced. Some have come back as surplus slated for destruction. Of the few items we were able to trace, shipping and receiving records match."

"Inside job?" Gil asked.

Fisher glanced back at Gil. "That's the working theory. This SOB was passed around from base to base like a rotten potato that no one wanted to be caught with. Tracking down the guys he's worked with is like diving down a deep, dark rabbit hole. The guy that was killed, we don't have a positive ID. Fingerprints not in NCIC."

"The National Crime Information Center doesn't have everything," Gil said.

"We're also cross-referencing with military records and Interpol," Fisher was quick to point out.

"Stay on it," Spinks said.

Fisher nodded.

Then Spinks held out his hand toward Massey. "We have Massey Yates here on loan from CTS, one of the nation's top computer security firms helping us on tracking the money end."

Because Massey's CP affected his speech, Tessa knew he much preferred to work behind the scenes. He had one of those folded paper "football" triangles the kids in middle school used to always play with. He flipped it back and forth over his knuckles.

Massey dropped the "football" and tugged at his collar. "CTS has proprietary algorithms in beta testing that monitor cryptocurrency on the Dark Web."

One of the new agents on the other side of Gil leaned into him and said, "This is messed up. I can't even understand what he's saying."

The guy could use some lessons in how to whisper. Massey tried to ignore him, but he cut the guy a *what-the-fuck, dude?* glare. Gil shifted, and Tessa heard an *oompf* as if Gil had landed an elbow jab to the guy's solar plexus.

Under his breath, Gil said, "Shut the hell up and listen."

Spinks held up a hand to stop Massey. "There a problem back there?"

"We're good," Gil said. He turned to the agent beside him. "Right?"

The man managed a tight nod, but no words.

"Continue," Spinks told Massey.

Massey explained about how cryptocurrency was gaining popularity in the criminal world because of its inherent anonymity, and how his company, as part of a national security initiative, monitored large spikes in deposits and transfers in an attempt to track potential black-market buyers and sellers of large quantities of weapons, drugs, diamonds and other black-market sales.

When Massey paused to take a breath, Cook asked, "So in

English for those of us with an IQ a little closer to the double digits, what does this mean?"

"Saturday night, there was a transfer spike on CoinIt, an up and coming cryptocurrency. One of the accounts was accessed from a computer we tracked to the western part of the state."

"Why can't pinpoint the computer's location?" This from the guy Gil had elbowed. He still sounded winded.

Gil caught Tessa's eyes and hid his grin behind a sip of coffee.

"CoinIt is using a technology that makes tracing transfers nearly impossible. It routes through unusually high numbers of proxy servers all over the world. Then kind of like that Quick-Chat app the kids use where the picture or text disappears within seconds of it being read, the electronic trail of the CoinIt transfer disappears as well.

"If all three box trucks carried similar amounts of weapons, the amount of the CoinIt transfer, when you take in the conversion rate back to US dollars, is consistent with the sale of a weapons cache of the size involved in Saturday night's bust. We've adjusted our algorithm, but we won't know if it will be successful in tracking the transfer until another one is made."

Spinks ended the brief with a couple of housekeeping items and passed out various assignments. To Quinn and Tessa, Spinks said, "You two hold up, we have a quick recon hop for you."

As Gil was leaving, he caught her by the elbow and escorted her a little way down the hall. "I've got my hour with the shrink this afternoon. I'd really like to see you tonight." When she hesitated, he added, "After Jack goes to sleep."

He's trying. There hadn't been a clear demarcation in the boundaries Tessa had set, and he was feeling his way through it. It wasn't like she didn't want to see him at all, she just wanted to protect Jack.

Who's going to protect you when it all goes to shit?

Gil's not like that.

That's what you thought about Bradley, but he turned out to be as manipulative and duplicitous as your father.

Man, she could really pick 'em.

"I'd like that." She glanced down the hall. Almost everyone had filed out of the room, and she gave Massey a nod as he crutched his way down the hall.

Gil's gaze went to her lips, even as he took a step back. "You know where to find me."

When she walked back into Spinks' office, only Quinn remained. She took the seat across from him and waited for Spinks to glance up from his computer.

Spinks clicked through a document, and without looking up, he said, "There something you're not telling me, Sterling?"

Had he heard about her and Gil's extracurricular helo activities? Her scalp tingled and sweat started to bead along her hairline. She glanced at Quinn. He gave her an *I'm clueless* shrug. "Ehr...excuse me, sir?"

Spinks leaned back and gave her his full attention. "The break-in at your place."

"Oh, that." *Phew.* This wasn't about her and Gil. She wanted to wipe her brow but didn't want to do anything that might make her look nervous. Spinks didn't get to be a Special Agent in Charge because he was stupid and unobservant. "You've got a lot on your plate. The sheriff's department is looking into it."

"If there is something that affects members of my team, I want to know about it."

"Yes, sir."

"About that recon." With a blip of the remote, the big screen came to life behind Spinks with a satellite view that showed a few rectangular structures that could have been those mobile offices often seen at construction sites. There was also a more massive square building, a warehouse of some sort.

"What are we looking at?"

"It's a coal strip mine operation. Built by BBM, Big Blue Mining, but closed by the EPA a decade ago. Potentially a Superfund cleanup site, but it has been embroiled in lawsuits for years. The GPS from that box truck places it here."

"I can't see a mining company buying weapons," Quinn said.

"Our guess is whoever is buying and/or selling those weapons is using this place as temporary storage. It's off the beaten path. No close neighbors and the surrounding topography make it impossible to see from the road. With the remoteness of the mine, the newest online satellite photo is more than a year old. There is no telling what kind of changes they've made if any."

"Which is where we come in." Tessa smiled. Maybe they'd finally get to use their military-grade surveillance cameras that had recently been installed, thanks to money confiscated from a big bust the ATF had had the year before. Word was that the camera's resolution allowed you to count the gray hairs on a mouse's nuts from a mile up.

Not the manufacturer's exact words, but close.

It was the perfect tool to allow them to fly high yet get high-resolution photos of the site.

Spinks filled them in on distance and altitude parameters. They didn't want the helo to be easily seen or heard on the chance that people were guarding the site.

Tessa and Quinn beat it back to the hanger. After changing into their flight suits, she met Quinn at the helo. He'd already started on the external visual inspection.

She strapped into the pilot's chair and had picked up the pre-flight checklist when Quinn climbed in, wearing a stupid grin on his face.

"What?" Tessa asked.

"You're my hero."

"I'm your what?" She listened with one ear as she went down the list, flipping switches and checking gauges.

"Hero." He buckled in, but his grin never wavered.

She turned the APU generator switch to 'on,' and marked her spot on the checklist. She wasn't sure she wanted to hear this. "How so?"

"Sex in the back of a helo is on my bucket list. Looked like you've crossed it off yours already."

How could he know that? Even though it was a complete tell, she glanced behind her, trying to find something that would have given her and Gil away. But everything was as it should be. Except...Tessa pulled her shades to the end of her nose, to see the interior of the Sikorsky better.

Yeah, that was her bra hooked onto some webbing in the back.

There wasn't much point in denying it. "Where did you find it?"

"Between my seat and the door. The turquoise and lace was a surprise. I'd always pictured you as a gray sports bra kind of woman."

She didn't say anything. Quinn was going to give her a rash of shit no matter what she said. She knew that because they were a lot alike and if she'd found another woman's bra in the helo, it would be a while before he'd hear the end of it.

She continued down the list, calling out things for Quinn to check. They started the engines, cleared the tower and climbed to their cruising altitude without another word that didn't have to do with their flight, but Tessa knew Quinn well enough to know she hadn't heard the last from him about the sex.

As they rotored toward the strip mine, Quinn checked to make sure they weren't on an open channel. "Even before I got my wings, I've had helo sex fantasies. Not nearly as much room here as in my Super Stallion, and the '60 doesn't have the ramp, but it's obviously doable. No deets, but did the reality exceed the fantasy? Please, *please* say yes. Even if it isn't true."

She gave him a quick glance and said, "You want my advice?"

"Hit me with it, LT."

"We should stash a pair of knee pads back there."

9

GIL MUCKED OUT ONE OF THE LAZY S'S STALLS, ONE OF HIS LEAST favorite chores because it was quiet work. Raking manure into a wheelbarrow wasn't too miserable. It was combing through the shit in his head that Gil found extremely foul.

In the past, Gil's days at the Lazy S had gone by relatively fast, the manual labor, the horse training, the talks around the campfire, made each day physically and emotionally draining. Most nights, he was almost asleep before his head hit the pillow, but in the three nights since the gun bust, sleep had been an elusive beast.

As he'd lain awake, his mind had whirled. Isaac and his paralysis, the possibility of going undercover, Mia and whatever was eating at her, nibbled at him... And how the hell was he supposed to spend time with Tessa without getting near the kid? Impossible. Jack was like a cockle-burr, always showing up in the most unlikely places and impossible to shake.

Not a complaint. The kid was hard not to like.

Tessa was right to limit his interaction with Jack, because the truth was, if Gil got the undercover assignment, he could be gone a few weeks if they were lucky. Months, possibly. The

148

lowlifes always had their own schedule. They didn't care if there was a kid back home who might miss him.

Gil scraped out the pee spot in the middle of the stall and dumped the urine saturated shavings into the wheelbarrow. Out the backside of the barn, he heard a crash and Mia screamed.

He ran toward the sound. Right outside the rear barn doors, Mia lay sprawled out on the ground, a wheelbarrow across her legs, and manure and piss-soaked shavings burying her.

"Son of a bitch." Mia eyed him from the ground. "What are you laughing at?"

Gil didn't answer. Didn't have to. "I told you to come get me when you needed to dump the wheelbarrow."

She propped herself on her elbows. Dirt stuck to the sweat on her bald head, and the flies were already dive-bombing her. "You going to help me up?"

Gil dropped his manure fork. "*Now* you want my help." He dragged the wheelbarrow off her legs and locked wrists with her and helped her up.

"You're an asshole, you know that?"

"Yeah?" Gil retrieved his manure fork and started shoveling the mess back into the wheelbarrow. "You're no golden ray of sunshine, either."

She grunted in acknowledgment as she brushed off her shirt and jeans, but she picked up her own fork and started shoveling. When the wheelbarrow was full, Gil got a running start up the dump trailer ramp and made it over the lip without slipping and dropping the whole thing on himself the way Mia had.

"Thanks," she said.

How the hell could anyone put that much disdain behind one little word? "Hey." He grabbed her by the arm and stopped her before she could disappear back into the barn. She shook him off but gave him her begrudging attention. "Give it a chance. The program, and the process."

Mia bowed up, daggers in her eyes. Even though the sharp look was aimed at him, it was the first real sign of life he'd seen since she'd shown up. "You have no idea the quantum shit I've been through—"

"Try me," Gil dared. "We can go tit for tat, see who's had it worse. Better yet, I can go get Mac and Boomer. They'll want to play along. Is your shit any worse than having to put a bullet in the head of the man you were involved with? Or losing a limb, or dangling from the end of a noose?"

She didn't say anything when he took a breath, but her expression had shifted from mule-ish to something more receptive. "When you stack everything up, compare shit pile to shit pile, you may find that yours doesn't stink nearly as bad as you thought it did."

He leaned on the manure fork and lowered his voice. Losing his temper wouldn't solve anything. "We've all been through our own wicked version of hell. We wouldn't be at Healing Horses otherwise. So, don't kid yourself. You're not a special snowflake."

He tossed his fork in the empty wheelbarrow and pushed it back to the stalls. Mia followed, the tines of her manure fork scraping on the ground behind her. He couldn't tell if she'd crawled deeper inside herself or if she was quietly considering what he'd said. Her perpetual scowl hadn't shifted.

Hopefully, he hadn't royally fucked something up.

He wasn't an expert on any of this, but between his time in the Marines and his time with the ATF, he knew a little of what he was talking about. The peer-to-peer mentoring was a big part of Healing Horses.

He left Mia's wheelbarrow at the front of the stall across from his and went back to work.

Mia stood against the open sliding door. "It won't help." She sounded lost, vulnerable...*human.*

"Not if you don't let it."

"I've been in programs before."

"This is different." He didn't understand how or why, just that it was the truth. "Don't piss away the next ninety days. Do you know how many veterans are on Jenna's list? The number of people who *want* to be here? Yet out of all of them, she chose you."

"I'm a number in a slot."

"Not here you're not. As much as you try to hide, we see you, Mia Mann."

She blinked at him, turning a little green around the gills as if she'd eaten day old oyster that didn't agree with her. Down the aisle, the landline rang in Jenna's office.

Before Mia could respond, *if* she was thinking of responding, Jenna popped her head into the aisle and said, "Hey, Brant. Phone."

"Yeah, coming." Then to Mia, he said, "Give what I said some thought." He turned to go, then stopped. "Oh, and leave those wheelbarrows for me, okay?"

Something shifted on her face. She didn't roll her eyes, but the tension around them eased, and one corner of her lips twitched, the beginnings of a smile or a snarl. Gil couldn't be sure.

Jenna left him to his call. He picked up the cordless. The converted office had a desk angled to give Jenna a good view out the open door, and a window overlooking a foaling stall. "Brant," Gil said as he stepped to the counter along the back wall and washed his hands in the sink.

"Good news," Spinks said. "IA cleared you in the shooting, and I got your psych report. You passed."

Gil couldn't tell if Spinks was pleased or pissed. "You sound surprised."

"You're not?"

"No." He'd been *shrunk* enough to know what the psychologists wanted to hear. If psych evaluations were an arcade game, he'd have his initials at the top of the leaderboard. "That all you called to tell me?"

"No. Now that the fake news is out that Drew Ross died, he's started talking. Plus, it didn't hurt getting that deal from the prosecutor."

"What's he saying?"

"Gave up a guy by the name of Bradley Martin. New to the area, which might account for why we have this uptick in gun buys. Sounds like a big fish."

"But is he *the* big fish? Is he The Wolf?"

"That's for you to find out."

"I'm going in?" Gil waited for the tingle, the thrill that typically zipped through his body when he'd gotten calls like this before, but this time, all he felt was this weight in his belly and this sick, nagging feeling that maybe he shouldn't have pulled his resignation.

The resignation had been the right decision. He knew that for sure now. *One more time.* For Isaac.

"You're going in. First thing tomorrow. Meet me at the office at oh five hundred. I'll give you the particulars then."

"Give me the big picture."

"Finn got you in as part of a security detail. Coincidentally, Martin had two openings on his security team. Finn's informant is some kind of headhunter, like outsourcing for the criminal world. This is an upscale gig. Lose the hair and the beard and find yourself a suit."

Gil scrubbed at his beard and grimaced. He didn't like the beard as much as he hated shaving.

"We're putting you in deep. We don't know if Ross and his men were tipped off. Ross refused to say. If that's the case, it could have been from someone in the sheriff's department, or hell, even one of our own. Can't wait until we've got our own god damn building. But I'm not risking you. You make something up on your end about why you have to leave your program. Finn and I and the informant will be the only ones who know you're there."

"I'm supposed to trust my life to Finn's flunky?"

"No way around it. Finn vouches for him. If that makes you feel any better."

It didn't. Not at all.

It was Wednesday night, and Jack used a knife to scrape the excess pancake mix off the top of the measuring cup and poured it into the mixing bowl. "I wanted to eat at the big house tonight, with everyone else."

"You love pancake night." She added the milk and the egg to the flour mix and handed Jack the whisk.

"Yeah, but..."

"But what?"

Jack crushed the big lumps. "Mr. Gil said he wasn't going to the hospital tonight. I thought he might be there."

Gil. Tessa pinched the bridge of her nose, but it didn't ease the tension. Bradley's lawyer had visited her that morning, and ever since, she'd vacillated from shock and utter disbelief, to profoundly pissed, to scared shit-less, and back so many times she was one hit from being knocked off an emotional cliff.

Good thing she'd had Quinn to take up her slack today, she'd been in no condition to pilot that bird.

She couldn't lay her problems at her son's feet, but she'd be as honest with him as she could. "I've had a dreadful day, and I wanted some time alone. Me and you." She mostly made it through. Her voice only cracked at the end.

Jack stopped stirring and looked at her, and she blinked back the sting in her eyes. He went back to mixing. "You know when Billy has a bad day…"

Tessa tried to give Jack her full attention as she poured the batter into the hot pan, nodding encouragement and laughing in mostly the right spots, but she felt distracted and detached.

"Mom, *Mom*." Jack gave her shoulder a nudge. "The pancakes are smoking."

Smoke billowed up. She shoved the pan over to a cold burner and cut off the gas. "I'll get the windows, you go open the door."

Jack ran for the front door and threw it open. "Mr. Gil!"

Tessa turned. Gil stood on her threshold, his fist raised as if he were about to knock.

"Everything okay in here?" The smoke detector shrieked. Gil came in and waved a hand towel in front of the alarm and pushed the button to silence it as she finished opening the windows.

"Never better," Tessa grabbed the pan of burned pancakes and scraped them into the sink, keeping her head ducked and her back to Gil as she tried to regain her composure.

Gil must have known something was up because he muscled his way to the sink and took over scraping duty. "Go sit down and take a load off."

"I can clean up my own mess."

"I don't doubt that. Sit." Then he leaned into her and said, "When he goes to bed, I want you to tell me what's bothering you."

"It's the pancakes."

"Bullshit," he mumbled, as if aware that little ears were listening.

She relented. For now. But as much as she needed someone to talk to, she didn't want to taint the start of something new with Gil with the toxic fallout that had been her marriage to Bradley.

Instead of going to the table to sit, she boosted herself on the counter next to him. She handed him the hand towel to dry the pan with.

"Wanna have pancakes with us, Mr. Gil? We can make more batter, and we have a brand-new bottle of syrup. I can sit on the step stool since we don't have three chairs."

Gil glanced at her, then faced her son. "I'd love to, but..."

"You already ate?" Jack's shoulders sank, and he looked like he'd shrunk a couple inches.

"No, but... I uh..." Gil shot Tessa a quick, help-me-out-here look. He acted like he wanted to stay, but he'd been trying really hard to respect her wishes and stay clear of Jack.

"He has barn chores tonight," Tessa said.

"But, Mom, he has to eat. My teacher says that breakfast is the most important meal of the day, but Billy says it's dinner. I think all of them are important because if you skip them, then you're hungry. And if you don't eat and try to do chores then your stomach is grumbly-mumbly and mad, and all you can think about is food and, and, and I did my chores. I can help him with his. Mom, tell him he has to eat with us."

Gil raised a brow at her, a light in his eyes as he tried to hold back his smile. "Yeah, Mom." His voice was low, seductive. Sometimes he didn't play fair. "Tell me."

With the three of them living at the ranch, it didn't look like keeping Gil away from Jack was going to be as effortless as she'd thought it would. Besides, after her crap day, she could use a distraction. "Will you please stay for dinner?"

"Only if you let me and Jack do the work."

Tough bargain. Not. "Deal."

While Gil whipped up some more batter, Jack set another place at the table. Tessa wasn't sure what Gil had done to the recipe, but the pancakes came out extra fluffy and cooked to a perfect golden brown. By the time all the pancakes had been cooked, the burnt pancake smell had dissipated, and they closed the front door.

Jack slathered his food with butter and syrup and dug in. "Wow." Jack tucked the bite into the pouch of his cheek. "Mom, from now on Mr. Gil gets to cook all the pancakes."

Tessa laughed. "You little fink. My pancakes are—"

"Passable. That's what Billy calls the food at camp. It means it looks like food but doesn't taste too much like it."

Gil swallowed a big swig of milk, and to Tessa said, "I really gotta meet this Billy kid someday."

"You and me both."

Conversation came to a halt as the three of them stuffed themselves.

"Hey, can Billy come over and play when we're back in the house?"

"We'll see if we can get you two together." Tessa didn't want to commit to a play date at the house. While she didn't think Bradley was a danger to Jack or his friend, she wasn't convinced she'd seen the last of Bradley's minions, and she didn't want to take a chance they might show up while Jack had company.

"Speaking of the house, did Boomer say when he'll have your back door fixed?"

"A few days to a week maybe. That door was a non-standard size. The hardware store had to order one in."

"In the meantime, you two get to bunk with the abundantly cheerful Mia Mann."

Tessa took one last bite then pushed her plate away before she ate enough to max out her helo's carrying capacity. "It's okay. She mainly keeps to herself."

"When it's not a work night, can we get flashlights and follow her at night and see where she goes? I think she sleeps in a cave with the bears—"

Tessa nudged Jack with her foot under the table.

Gil pinned her with a look. "What's he talking about?"

"Oops." Jack ducked his head, forked another bite into his mouth, and wiped away the drip of syrup from his chin.

"Tessa?"

She gathered her and Gil's plates and dropped them in the sink as she tried to figure out how to answer that question without lying to Gil's face or betraying what little trust she'd built with her recalcitrant roomie.

"You can't say anything, Mom. We promised. Billy says if you break a prom—"

"Jack, if you're finished eating, I want you to go get your shower."

"Awh, Mom. I'm supposed to help Mr. Gil with the chores."

"I don't really have all that much to do, Squirt. Maybe you can help me another time."

After the day she'd had, Tessa needed a little peace and quiet. A short time to herself to figure out what the hell she was going to do with Bradley. She gave Jack a you-aren't-going-to-win-this look.

"Okay, okay." He put his plate in the sink and slunk off toward the bathroom.

Gil filled the sink with soapy water and started washing the plates. "You going to tell me what's going on with Mia?"

Jack ran back out of the bathroom, grabbed his pajamas and ran back in. The lock on the bathroom door clicked.

Gil glanced behind him as if to make sure that Jack was really gone. Tessa opened her mouth to speak, when Gil said, "Hold that thought."

He shook the bubbles from his hand and cupped her cheek, pressing a kiss to her lips. The tension in her shoulders eased, and all she wanted to do was sink into this man who somehow righted her world and calmed the chaos.

"I've wanted to do that all day." Then the softness left his eyes, and he dropped his hand. "Now, about Mia."

"It's not really my place to say anything."

Gil handed Tessa a plate to dry. "Then answer me this. Do you think her behavior is putting her at undue risk?"

"I don't know. I'm not a therapist."

"Neither am I. Do we need to talk to Jenna? What's your gut say?"

Her gut.

She almost laughed out loud. Her gut had a losing track record, and these days, she wasn't sure she could trust it. But she also didn't want to break the confidence of a woman who didn't seem to have a friend or even anyone batting on her team. "I think she's okay. She's unsettled. Angry, even, but I don't think she's a danger to herself if that's what you're asking."

Gil handed Tessa the last plate, plus the knives and forks. "If anything changes, I want you to tell Jenna."

"Okay, but I'll probably run it by you first, I—"

The furrow that appeared on Gil's brow had her swallowing the rest of her words. "What is it?"

"I came over here tonight because I've got something to tell you."

———

WHILE GIL DIDN'T HAVE ANY RANCH CHORES, HE DID HAVE SOME things he needed to take care of before he turned in for the night. Like packing and feeding Tessa the same sorry excuse he'd concocted and told Jenna, about why he had to leave on such short notice.

He left before Jack got out of the shower with the promise to go back later that night. He and Tessa needed to talk without interruption or little ears listening. If that time also involved a little kissing and heavy petting, well, selfish bastard that he was, he wouldn't say no.

The moon had risen high by the time Gil stepped back up onto Tessa's porch later that night. He rapped softly on the door, not wanting to wake Jack. The wait wasn't long before Tessa opened the door and stepped outside wearing a pair of old gray sweats tucked into her boots and a navy-blue hoodie that hid her slender curves.

But Gil didn't have to use his imagination to know what she looked like under those baggy clothes. He'd had her in his arms, had her breasts pressed against his chest, had her athletic thighs across his hips.

Damn if he didn't want her straddling him again.

The yellow glow of the porch's bug light couldn't conceal the red rimming her eyes and her splotchy complexion.

She'd been crying.

Awh, hell. Gil's heart squeezed.

He held out his arms, and she walked into them. "Hey, hey, hey."

There came the clomp of a boot on the steps behind him, and Mia said, "What's wrong with her?" She had that tone people get when they're afraid to get too close because they'll catch something.

As if having emotions were a communicable disease.

Mia shouldn't have worried. Gil figured she was immune.

Gil tucked Tessa tight against his chest, and to Mia said, "Can you give us a minute? Better yet, can you watch Jack for a bit? I think a little air would do her good."

Tessa swiped at the moisture on her cheeks and tried to take a step back. Gil loosened his grip, but he didn't let go completely.

"I can't ask her to do that," Tessa said. "We can stay on the porch."

Something shifted on Mia's face. Maybe her scowl softened, or the permanent crease between her brows eased. Hard to tell. "Go. I've got the kid."

"But this is when you..." Tessa made a vague motion with her hand that was lost on Gil, but Mia seemed to understand.

"Go," Mia repeated. "Before I change my mind."

Gil wasn't going to give Tessa a chance to argue or Mia the opportunity to change her mind. With a hand at the small of Tessa's back, he led her down the steps. Over his shoulder, he said, "Thanks, Snow." Short for snowflake.

Mia made a noise between a grunt and a snarl, but he'd used the nickname a few times since their confrontation in the barn and she hadn't decked him yet. She must not have hated it *too* much.

"Where're we going?" Tessa said as she slipped her hand into his.

"Wherever you want."

She didn't choose a location, but the moon wasn't very bright, so he led her up the dirt road toward the barn. This late at night, it should be deserted, but more than once he'd caught Sidney or Jenna up there at night over the past months. Seemed like the horses always made them feel better. Probably could do the same for Tessa.

A floodlight on the corner of the barn shined on one of the paddocks. Insects swirled and dived, like the bug version of a World War II dogfight.

He and Tessa leaned against the paddock rails and watched the horses graze, the rhythmic chomping as they munched on grass he found more soothing than those nature CDs with birds chirping or waves crashing.

Since she wasn't talking, he decided he'd start the conversation. "You going to tell me what's going on with you?"

One of the horses came over and sniffed Tessa's hand looking for treats. "It's my ex." She rubbed the soft velvet at the end of the horse's nose.

When she didn't elaborate, he took her hand and turned her to him. What had the asshole done this time? It took every last gram of control that he had, not to let the anger seep into his voice. "Tell me."

"Shit," she said as she swiped at her cheeks. "You sounding all concerned and sincere got the waterworks started again." She took a couple of deep, shaking breaths. The tears stopped, but her hand shook in his. "My ex filed for emergency custody of Jack. We're supposed to be in court on Friday."

"That's the day after tomorrow. What the fuck?" The words came out too fast for Gil to moderate his tone.

Tessa laughed. Dark. Stormy. "That's what I said."

"On what grounds? You're a terrific mother, what—"

"He said that I can't provide a safe environment for Jack. With the break in—"

"That's complete horse shit." Gil stalked away a few steps, then came back. "He's the one responsible for the break-in to begin with, right?"

"I can't prove it."

"You have a good lawyer?"

She nodded. "She says that my ex probably doesn't have a chance. I've got a good job. A support system for Jack while I work. He's well adjusted, and he does well in school."

Probably. Gil caught that one word. That one word that stuck out from all the others, that one word that made his gut clench and his fist want to find a wall...or a jaw.

"I'm scared." Her voice quivered, and she sniffed. "I'm so fucking scared. That's my kid. He's got no right. *He's* the one who left. *He's the one that didn't want any part of having a kid in the first place, and now he wants to fight me for full custody?*

"Jack barely even knows him. They've had a handful of visits since he's moved closer to us. If he cared at all about his son, he wouldn't take him away from his home, from me."

"I think it's clear your ex only cares about himself."

Tessa gripped the top rail of the paddock. The nails in the boards creaked under the strain. "He'll never change. I used to think he was focused on his career because he wanted to be the best husband, the best provider because he loved me. But I know the real him now. The only thing that man loves more than money and power is himself."

They heard hoof beats behind them, and out of the darkness, Eli, Sidney's buckskin gelding, aka the Houdini of Horses, came trotting up from the direction of Sidney's cabin. He jumped the fence as if it had been a log on the ground and joined the other horses in the paddock.

"Sidney must have gone to bed," Tessa said. "I can't believe Eli doesn't run off. I guess some men stick around after all."

"Hey, now." While she scratched the withers of the horse grazing nearest them, Gil wrapped his arms around her from behind. "We're not all assholes."

Because what he had to say next was true and because she probably needed to hear it, he added, "Any man would be lucky to have you and Jack to call his own. A man like your ex doesn't deserve a minute of your time. You are worthy. Don't ever forget that."

She leaned her head against his shoulder and looked up at him. "Someone like you?"

Yes... but no. She was worthy of so much more than him. "Don't settle. Look around. There are plenty of better men than me out there." He just hoped like hell she never found them.

She turned in his arms, and kissed her way up his neck, her

teeth scraping against his bearded jaw. Her hair was damp from her shower, and he caught a hint of helo exhaust beneath the spring-clean scent of her shampoo.

He backed her against the railing as she kissed her way to his lips. His mouth opened to hers, his tongue inviting and enticing her in. But he didn't want to take her up against the paddock.

He broke the kiss and held out his hand. "Come with me."

She placed her hand in his and followed him into the barn without a word. He snagged a couple of the quilted horse blankets from the tack room and led her up the stairs to the hayloft. They could have gone back to his cabin, but the bunk bed was hardly big enough for him, much less the two of them.

However, the real reason he didn't want to take her back to his cabin was that he was afraid if he did, she'd change her mind. He wasn't too proud of that, but that didn't stop him either.

Moonlight filtered in through the open hay lift door at the rear of the barn. Gil pulled the strings off a square bale, kicked the hay into a fluffy bed, and laid the blankets over the top.

Even though the night was chilly, between the heat that had gathered in the hayloft during the day, and the insulating powers of the hay, they were plenty warm as he stripped to his briefs and pulled her down beside him.

"As much as I'd always wanted to have sex in my helo," Tessa said as he pushed up her sweatshirt and started kissing his way up from her delicate belly button to her delectable breasts. "This is definitely more comfortable."

"Mmm." He pushed her sweatshirt higher and discovered she hadn't bothered putting on a bra. *Sweet Jesus.* He molded one with his hand, teasing the nipple to a peak with his thumb and taking it into his mouth to suck.

She arched beneath him, her hands going to his hair and

fisting there. A little sound escaped the back of her throat, driving his blood south.

After stripping her sweatshirt off, he took her hand and held it against his arousal. "This is what you do to me."

"I'm pretty sure if you had any woman's naked breasts in your face, it would have the same effect on you."

She was teasing, but for some reason, he couldn't let what she'd said go. "Probably. But you're the only woman who does that to me when she's fully dressed, when she's sitting at a table eating syrupy pancakes or stealing my coffee or straddling the stick in her cockpit."

"You have..." Her words dropped off as he skimmed his hand down her abdomen, under the waistband of her sweats, and cupped her through the cotton of her panties. They were damp. He had a feeling it wasn't because she hadn't toweled off after her shower. "Y-You've got a kink for female pilots?"

"When they're you I do."

She kicked off her boots, and he stripped the sweatpants down her long legs, taking her panties with them. He kissed his way up her calves and settled between her thighs, loving the way her hands held tight to his head, encouraging. He didn't make her wait, but he also didn't rush. He traced lazy circles around her clit with his tongue.

She bucked up against him, her legs moved over his shoulders as he licked and teased until he drew soft moans from the back of her throat. The sexy, sweet taste of her and the sounds she made, drove him to the brink. He needed to find that condom. Quick.

He pulled away.

"Don't stop." The frustration in her voice brought a smile to his face.

He nipped at her inner thigh, then laid across it as he

snagged the leg of his jeans and pulled them closer. "Patience, Sunshine."

His wallet fell out of his back pocket, and he dug around for the condom he'd stowed there. He sheathed himself and rolled on top of Tessa again. He was careful to take his weight on his arms, though unlike some of the women he'd been with, Tessa's height and athletic build made her substantial enough that he wasn't afraid he'd crush her or break her.

He slid his arms under her shoulders and cupped the back of her head, pressing open mouth kisses at the base of her neck where her pulse throbbed, fast and erratic.

Reaching down, he adjusted himself at her entrance, but as much as he wanted to plunge deep inside her, he held back, touching his forehead to hers. She pressed her pelvis against his, trying to take him in, but he pulled away.

A strangled sound escaped the back of her throat. "You want me to beg, is that it? Because you're killing me."

"I don't want you to beg, but I don't intend to rush this either."

She put her hands on his ass and drove him inside her. Warm, wet, welcoming. His brain seized, his thoughts scattered, and his heart tumbled in his chest. He found her hands and twined his fingers with hers above her head and met her slow, languorous strokes.

He stared down at her, amazed to have a woman like her in his life. She was tough, but sweet. Strong, yet yielding, and content to give but not afraid to take what she wanted.

He didn't want to leave.

As much as he wanted to take down the bastard responsible for Lang and Rivera, for the first time in his life he wanted something more than justice or vengeance. What he wanted, was Tessa.

Which meant he also wanted Jack, because they were a package deal.

But wanting something didn't mean he'd come close to getting it. His gaze locked on Tessa's face. On the curve of her lip, on the way her dark lashes fanned across her cheek, the look of unadulterated ecstasy on her face as he drove her higher and higher.

Opening her eyes, she gazed back at him.

"There you are," he said as he ducked his head for another kiss. He'd never get enough of her taste. Was it that awful that he didn't want to leave?

Her eyes cleared, then narrowed. "What's wrong?"

"Nothing. I'm making love to a beautiful woman. What could be wrong?"

The rhythm they'd been building slowed to a gentle, skin tingling stroke. "You're a terrible liar."

"I lie for a living. I'm actually pretty accomplished."

"Is it what you came over to talk to me about earlier?"

He didn't want to get into that right then, and not because they were making love, but because he didn't want to lie to her while he was. "Yes. Can we talk about this later?"

She stilled beneath him. "No."

Fuck. Gil almost laughed at his frustration. Not at stopping, but at himself, at how hard this lie was going to be to sell. He didn't want to do this, but he had to. Even though Tessa had stopped moving, she felt too good. He continued the slow, slick, slide in and then out to the sensitive tip and back again.

She didn't protest.

"It's my grandmother, she—" He started to feed her the same crap line he'd told Jenna about how his grandmother had died and how he had to go to her funeral and take care of her estate. But the lies didn't roll off his tongue the way they usually did.

Probably because Tessa mattered. He didn't know if that was good or bad. It just was.

"Oh, no." Tessa freed her hands and cupped his face. "Is she okay?"

"No."

"I'm so sor—"

He shook his head. "No. She's fine. Well, she's not fine, she died five years ago actually, but…" *Don't tell her.* Deep undercover was just that. The more people who knew, the higher the chances were that that information would get out, putting his life in danger. But this was Tessa. This was different. *She* was different.

"I told Jenna my grandmother passed away, but that's my cover story. Finn found a way to get me undercover with the organization we believe is behind the gun running. No one is supposed to know, but I didn't want to lie to you or disappear without explanation. You won't be able to reach me except through Spinks. I don't want you thinking I wanted to leave, because *that* would be a damn lie."

"Is it The Wolf?"

"Possibly. That's what I'm trying to find out."

She kissed him. Gentle and sweet. "Thanks for telling me the truth. I'll keep your secret safe."

Hugging him to her, she started to move beneath him. The pleasure, the tension, the heat building. He got to his knees, his hands on her hips as he drove into her, her breasts bouncing, her head thrashing, her eyes closed tight. Soft, little moans drifted to him, her breath hitching, matching his own.

He placed a hand on her mound, his thumb circling her nub as her breathing grew more and more labored. She stilled in his hands, her internal muscles squeezing, squeezing.

Her body shuddered. "*Fuck me.*"

He grinned down at her. "I'm doing my best, Sunshine."

The base of his spine tingled, and his balls got tight. He dropped down on all fours, pounding into her as the sweat slicked their bodies. His rhythm became frantic, erratic, then with one last thrust, he emptied himself inside her.

Holding her close, he rolled to his back, taking her with him, enjoying the aftershocks that wracked her body, tightening her internal muscles around him. He ran his hands down her sides to the curve of her ass, loving the feel of her breasts squished against his chest. "You feel so good, you know that?"

She folded her arms across his chest and laid her chin on her hands. "I could say the same about you."

He started going soft and as much as he wanted to lay there all night with their bodies joined, they couldn't. "I'd better take care of the condom before things get messy."

She grumbled her displeasure but rolled onto her side. Gil turned the other way, pulling the condom off. He held it up to the pale light. "Oh, shit."

She came up behind him and threw an arm over his shoulder. "What is it?"

"The condom broke."

He waited for her to get mad, to yell or holler or at least say something. She didn't. She draped and arm over his shoulder and pressed a kiss to the top of his spine.

He dropped the condom in the hay and kissed the palm of the hand. "Did you hear me?"

"I heard you." Her voice barely carried as she moved away from him.

She laid on her back, a knee raised, covering her face with her hands. Gil stretched out beside her, propping his weight on one elbow. The breeze through the open loft window cooled his skin and raised goosebumps on hers. Moonlight filtered in, making her skin glow.

Their breathing slowed, and he skimmed his hand over the

flat of her stomach, wondering what it would be like to feel her belly round with his child. Feel their baby kick and squirm. She covered his hand with hers and stared at the ceiling.

His place a light kiss on the ball of her shoulder. "I guess it's a little late asking you if you're on birth control."

"A little."

"I'm sorry." It wasn't his fault the condom broke, but still. "Not about making love to you, but the condom…"

"You don't have to apologize. Condoms break. We're both adults here. We knew the risks."

"I'm clean if that helps any. The hospital did a full screen a few months ago when I was shot. I haven't been with anyone since."

She rolled on her side, resting her head on her upturned hand. "Besides a screening when I enlisted, I haven't been tested. My ex was my first and the few guys I'd been with since we'd always had protected sex. I could get tested if—"

"Let's not worry about that right now, okay?" He gathered up her clothes and handed them to her.

They both dressed in silence, a pall cast over the evening. They cleaned up the hayloft as best they could, returned the horse blankets to their proper place, and walked back to their cabins, their fingers loosely locked together.

The door to Tessa's cabin opened before they made it to the porch as if Mia had been standing at the window waiting for them.

Mia stepped out, a pack strapped to her back. "Took you two long enough." She glanced from Tessa to Gil and back again. "Who died?"

"What?" Tessa said. "No one died."

"Coulda fooled me." Mia shouldered on past them and disappeared into the darkness, the slap and scrape of her footfalls fading away.

"Would it be awful having a kid with a guy like me?" He was kidding. Mostly.

"No. It's not that."

"Then what is it?"

"I'm a pilot. I make my money flying. If I'm pregnant, I'm no good to the task force if I'm grounded."

"I've got some money saved and—"

She pressed a finger to his lips, shutting him up. "I think we're getting ahead of ourselves. We don't have to solve this tonight, and with luck, there won't be anything to solve."

With luck? The words prickled though he knew she didn't mean to hurt his feelings. But this wasn't about him, he understood that.

"When I go undercover, you won't be able to contact me whenever you want. I understand that this could have a more profound impact on your life in the short term than mine. While I'm gone, I want you to know, that if you have to make any decisions, I know you will make the right one."

"This isn't up to me. I'm not the only one my decision would affect."

"I get that. But I'm leaving it up to you to make the best choice for you. Promise me you'll do that."

"You need to go undercover and do what you need to do to catch these guys. Then we can make *our* decisions together."

He wrapped her in his arms and nuzzled crook of her neck, taking in her scent. "I'll do the best I can."

10

———

The condom broke.

Tessa strode through the doors of the sheriff's office out of sorts and ten minutes late. Sleep had been elusive, and then when it came, it came crashing down on her. She'd slept through her alarm. If it hadn't been for Jack, she'd still be in bed.

The condom broke.

Those words kicked around in her head leaving her shaken and reeling as if she'd lost all rudder control and her helo—her life—was spinning out of control.

Was it her imagination, or was everyone either blatantly staring at her or trying to pretend like they weren't but failing miserably? One of the women deputies glanced away and giggled. Did Tessa have a freaking tattoo on her forehead that said *I had astonishing hay sex and I could be pregnant?*

Then Gil, the sweet, rotten bastard, had left any decisions she might have to make up to her. *Un-freaking-believable.* He probably thought he was being understanding, supportive even, but it was nothing like that because no matter what he said, her decision would affect them both for the rest of their lives

171

because she already knew that if she *had* to decide, she was having the baby.

With him or without him.

For her, there wasn't any other option. Yeah, she would be grounded. Yeah, she could lose her job, even with the discrimination protections in place, but Spinks probably had enough on her to fire her for cause already.

But, that was a decision for another day. Today she was going to fly the shit out of her helo and make it damn hard for Spinks to even think about replacing her.

Spinks was in the middle of his brief as she walked into the big conference rooms at the sheriff's office. She tried to squeeze her way to the back, as unobtrusively as possible, but in a packed room, all eyes went to her. Spinks stopped mid-sentence.

She glanced at Quinn, saw a woman on his right, in a flight suit. *What the frack?*

"*Sterling.*" Spinks' voice boomed. "In my office."

"I'm sorry I'm late, I—"

"Now."

She glanced around the room at her colleagues. No one met her eye except Quinn. He had one of those apologetic looks on his face as if he'd wanted to stop a train wreck but hadn't known how.

When she didn't turn to follow, Spinks stopped in the doorway and said, "*Lieutenant.*"

She turned on her heel. Murmurs erupted behind her. A few chuckles too. "Enough," she heard Quinn growl behind her.

Spinks took a seat behind his desk and said, "You're going to want to close the door."

She did. Spinks kicked out the seat next to him. It rolled toward her. She caught it and sat.

"What is this about, SAC?"

His eyebrows went up. "You really don't know do you?"

When she shook her head, he plopped the newspaper in front of her. The headline above the fold read: *Misappropriation of Government Property*. The sub-headline said: *Has illicit spending made the county hard up for cash?*

The reporter must have laughed his ass off after turning those headlines in.

The picture accompanying the headline was grainy, the lighting low, but not so blurry that she couldn't recognize her face in profile. As well as her bare breasts as she straddled Gil's hips in the open doorway of her helo.

"Care to explain that?"

Instead of explaining, because in her mind it was pretty damn self-explanatory, she said, "Who's seen this?" Dumb question. It was in the newspaper.

"I think maybe you should be asking, who hasn't seen it."

The words, "It's not what it looks like," tumbled from her lips even though, clearly, it was what it looked like. Had Gil seen it? If he had, he would have called her.

"Who is he?"

Spinks doesn't know.

She glanced at the photo again. Gil's head and shoulders were hidden behind the helo's fuselage. "I'd rather not say."

"It's not really up to you."

"I would want to talk to him first and—"

Spinks handed her the receiver to his landline. "Talk away."

"It's not that easy."

Spinks dropped the receiver in the cradle with a loud crack. "Do you even know his name?"

"*What?* Of course, I know his name." Who the freaking fat fuck did Spinks think she was that she'd screw some random guy on the back deck of her helo?

"Consider yourself suspended, without pay, pending further investigation, *and* until I have a name."

Tessa jumped up from her chair, it shot back and knocked against the wall. "You can't do that."

"Oh, lieutenant, I certainly can." He stood as well. "Tell me who he is. Give me a reason *not* to fire you."

Tessa shrank back. "I think I should call the union rep and retain representation."

"You know, lieutenant, that's the first *right* thing you've said all morning. Dismissed."

The first person she'd called after leaving Spinks' office was her union rep, requesting representation during the investigation. Then she had the pleasure of calling her lawyer to update her on the suspension.

The first unguarded words out of her lawyer's mouth were, "Oh, shit." Not what Tessa had wanted to hear. Not with the custody hearing less than twenty-four hours away.

Tessa pulled into the Lazy S after two hours of driving the back roads of Wyoming, getting lost, then finding her way back again. Hard to follow your phone's GPS when it seemed like the whole fracking state was one big, fat dead zone. The only thing she accomplished was emptying her gas tank. Her thoughts were scrambled, and she couldn't get ahold of Gil without possibly tipping off Spinks.

You would have thought being suspended would have made her lose her appetite, but as she headed for her cabin, she felt a full-on stress binge coming on.

Near the barn, Mia was working with Sidney, brushing out one of the horses. Mia had her arm stretched out, her body as far away from the horse as she could get and still have the brush touching. Mia might be tough, or she might be full of bluster. She definitely wasn't comfortable around horses.

Jenna was walking from the barn to the big house and flagged Tessa down. She wanted to keep driving. The last thing she wanted was company, but she also didn't want to be rude.

Especially since, because of Mac, Jenna had graciously given her and Jack a place to stay.

Tessa stopped and buzzed her window down.

"What are you doing home in the middle of the day." Then Jenna got a good look at her and said, "Is it Jack?"

"No." The word squeaked out as if her lungs had run out of air. She couldn't say any more, afraid she'd completely break down.

But Jenna didn't give her a chance to say anything else. She opened the door, and pulled the keys from the ignition. "Come with me."

Tessa stared at Jenna's proffered hand, before finally taking it and letting Jenna help her out of the Jeep. With a protective arm around her shoulder, Jenna led her up the back steps and into the kitchen.

"Sit," Jenna ordered.

Tessa pulled out one of the stools and sat at the bar that separated the kitchen from the dining area. Jenna went straight for the freezer and pulled out a half-gallon of Rocky Road ice cream. *Rocky Road.* Seemed appropriate.

Tessa sat and plopped the tub between them. They each picked up a spoon, and dug in. In silence, they whittled away at the ice cream until it was almost half gone. Tessa felt a little sick to her stomach, but that didn't really slow her down much.

Jenna dug out a chunk of marshmallow. "You wanna talk, or you wanna eat ice cream?" She dove back in for one of the walnuts and crunched it between her molars. "I'm game for either. But it might be nice to be able to explain to Angel the next time I ride him why I've suddenly gained ten pounds."

Tessa took her time answering. Nibbling at the spoonful of ice cream as she looked around the kitchen deciding what she wanted to say. If anything.

While Jenna was waiting for her to answer, she reached

across the bar and grabbed the rolled-up newspaper. She went to free it from the plastic cover, but Tessa stopped her. How had she thought she could keep this from anyone at the ranch? Even if they hadn't had a paper, the way news traveled around there, no one would be able to step a foot off the property and not hear what had happened.

Tessa pulled the paper from the sleeve and laid the front page out in front of Jenna. Tessa dug in for another spoonful of ice cream and waited for the questions to start flying.

"Oh, wow." Then Jenna looked closer at the picture. "*Oh, wow.*"

"You said that."

"That was before I could see it was you." She stabbed her spoon in for another bite. "Quinn's been begging me for helo sex. *Begging.* Is it as uncomfortable as it looks?"

Tessa laughed despite herself. As far as questions went, *that* hadn't been one she'd expected. "Not as uncomfortable as you might think. The bruises on my knees are almost healed."

Jenna bumped Tessa's shoulder with her own. "I know in a small town there is bound to be a bunch of crap coming your way, but before we get into all that can I point out the silver lining in all this?"

Tessa almost choked on a chocolate chunk. "There's a silver lining?"

"Sure." Tessa motioned with her spoon for Jenna to continue. "You have a rocking silhouette."

"Gee, thanks." Tessa ladled on the sarcasm on the way the southern boys ladle gravy on a chicken fried steak, thick and heavy.

What to say? What to say? If Tessa was going to talk, she was going to throw it all out there. It felt as dangerous as letting go of the stick and flying with no hands. "That silver lining won't be around for long. Between the ice cream and possibly another pregnancy."

"Back that train up. But hold that thought, we need to get comfortable for this." Jenna grabbed the Rocky Road, and Tessa followed her past the long dining table to the big brown leather couch in the den. The room was warm and rustic, with a deer head mounted over the big rock fireplace. It was the type of idyllic place she pictured large families gathering around at Christmas time.

Jenna let Tessa hold the tub on her lap but sat close enough to reach it. "Start from the beginning."

"Well, you already know about the helo sex." She hitched her thumb over her shoulder indicating the newspaper article. "I got into work late this morning. Spinks stopped the briefing and called me into the office. Basically, he wants to know who I was with, and he suspended me without pay pending further investigation."

"What did Gil say?"

"I never said it was Gil."

Jenna gave her a look that said *puh-lese*. "Who all knows?"

"You. Quinn... I think. He would have to be extremely slow not to have connected the dots as to who it is." Tessa went for another bite, but her stomach rolled over. She set the tub on the coffee table.

"He won't say anything. You don't have to worry about that."

"It may be a moot point. If I want to keep my job, I may have to tell the investigators, but I wanted a chance to talk to Gil first. Mine's not the only career this could affect."

"Call him. He wouldn't want you losing your job over this."

"I can't—" She was about to say she couldn't contact Gil while he was undercover, then she remembered the story he'd given Jenna about his grandmother. "He's got enough on his plate dealing with his grandmother's death. He doesn't need this too."

"He's a big boy, Tess, he can handle it. In fact, he'll probably be mad if you don't tell him right away. He'd want to know."

Tessa shrugged, and because she didn't want to get into why she couldn't call Gil, she told Jenna about the emergency custody hearing the next day.

"Damn. That sounds bad." Jenna wasn't one to blow sunshine up your ass. Tessa appreciated that.

"It's not good."

Tessa went to get up. She couldn't wallow all afternoon. She had to…she had to…crap. She had nothing she had to do. She wasn't flying anytime soon.

Jenna grabbed her arm and sat her back down. "Where do you think you're going?"

"I don't know, but—"

"You can't basically tell me you think you're pregnant and walk out of here without spilling."

Crap. How could she have forgotten about that? Tessa collapsed into the corner of the couch. It was thick and cushy. Maybe if she were lucky, it would swallow her whole. "I probably have nothing to worry about."

"Was it from that day?"

"No. Last night. The hayloft. I think we owe you for a bale of hay." Tessa scrunched up her nose. "Sorry about that."

Jenna waved her hand as if to say not to worry about it. "The hayloft is an excellent choice. Hard to find privacy around here sometimes."

"Maybe, but after the helo and the hayloft, a bed is looking mighty good."

"No protection?"

"Condom broke, and I'm not on birth control. I haven't had a reason to take them these past few years."

"If it was last night, you could see a doctor, it's not too late for to prescribe—"

"I thought about that, but the doctor couldn't see me today and tomorrow I'm in court and then it's the weekend, and then that window of opportunity is pretty much closed. But in truth, I don't think I would have taken it anyway."

"You're a pretty kick ass mom, and Gil would step up. He's that kind of guy."

"I know, but if he didn't, as hard as having another baby would be, I also know I can go it alone."

———

Spinks had assigned Gil a late model Chevy Tahoe from the motor pool that had been confiscated during a big drug bust a few months back, thanks to Finn and his task force. It smelled like Cheech had been smoking weed in there for years. Good pot from the smell of it.

Unfortunately, the air vent deodorizer couldn't touch the stench.

He pulled up to the gate of an estate nestled in the shadow of the Rockies about twenty-five minutes outside of Murdock. The hilly topography of the land made it impossible for him to see the house from the road, but early that morning, Spinks had pulled up the aerial view online.

The large house—more like a mansion—was tucked in behind the rolling hills, with a large swimming pool, and what had looked like several outbuildings that could be horse barns, or they could have been the perfect buildings to stash a bunch of weapons. But if this guy was The Wolf, Gil doubted a man as cautious as that would hide stolen military weapons on his own property.

If Finn's sources were right, this was their guy. Now all Gil had to do was find some evidence to prove that. Gil glanced at the folder beside him one last time before he pressed the button at the gate.

There was a short write up about Bradley Martin. Financier, from what the guys could dig up in the short time they'd had. What a financier was doing in the middle of Wyoming was anyone's guess, and Gil's guess was it was all a front for weapons smuggling.

Whoever answered the gate, buzzed him in. It was about a five-minute drive up to the house. The driveway ended in what he could only describe as a large cul de sac. The mansion on the left, all stone and log exterior with soaring roof lines and enough windows to need a window washer on staff. On the right, a matching six-car garage with an outside staircase to what looked like some sort of living area over the top.

Gil parked in front of the house, turned the rear-view mirror toward him one last time. Seeing the new him, the military haircut, with his face shaved clean was a sight he hadn't seen in too long. It took him back to his first day as a recruit when he was lean muscled and baby-faced. A time when he didn't know how innocent he'd been until the military turned him into a man. He tucked those thoughts away as well as his thoughts of Tessa... and the broken condom.

He ran his hand through what was left of his hair, and that did more to bring him back to reality than anything else. He took one last look and slipped into character. For the foreseeable future, he was no longer Gil Brant, but his alter ego he'd played for eighteen months, Gil Goodman, aka Moose.

The street cred he'd earned as one of El Verdugo's top men had been crucial in helping to set up this undercover operation. Luckily, those who'd known him before then were either dead or in prison for a very, very long time.

He climbed out of the SUV, retrieved his suit coat from the

back seat and shrugged it on. This wasn't a black T-shirt and black tactical pants, AR-15 strapped across your chest kind of gig, like it had been for El Verdugo. This was upscale. Business suits and shoulder holsters. Gil tugged at the collar of his white dress shirt. Damn shame.

Before he could make it to the front door, someone called out to him from the top of the stairs of the garage. Gil walked over and met the man halfway with an outstretched hand. "Gil Goodman."

"Nigel Burton, head of security."

Burton was about six foot. Broad chested. Thick arms. Had a nose that probably had been broken more than once. He had the same short hair as Gil and was wearing the black tactical pants, except he'd mixed up the look by going with a dark gray T-shirt instead of the black. Maybe Gil was overdressed after all. He could only hope.

Gil hitched a thumb over his shoulder toward the mansion. "I'm supposed to be meeting with Mr. Martin in about ten minutes. He inside?"

"He's on a conference call, fighting fires. Had some things come up. I'm supposed to get you settled and get you on the gun range. He should be done by the time we are."

"Gun range?"

"We gotta make sure you can shoot as well as you say you can. Plenty of guys say they can." Burton shrugged. "But they can't. We don't take that kind of chance when our lives and more importantly, Mr. Martin's life, could depend on it."

"You guys really see a lot of action?"

"Not usually. But Mr. Martin is a powerful man. He's made more than his fair share of enemies along the way."

"As a financier?"

Gil fell into step as Burton turned and they walked toward

the garage. "You'd be surprised. You gotta step on a lot of necks to get to the top."

Burton showed him around the top floor of the garage which amounted to a large den with a couple of extra-long, black leather couches in front of a big screen TV, a kitchen area with a table that could seat eight, a communal bathroom, and six doors that all opened onto the central area. A typical open concept space, except for the oversized gun safe tucked into one corner.

Burton unlocked the number 3 door and held it open for Gil. Burton walked in behind him. "Nothing fancy, but at least you have a full-sized bed, a bedside table, and a closet. Not huge, but it's enough. Sure as hell beats an army cot in a tent in the desert."

No joke.

"How long you been a merc?" There was no doubt in Gil's mind this guy had served. It wasn't unusual for some guys to find jobs as mercenaries, guns for hire, after getting out of the military. Guns were what they knew, and the para-military life seemed to suit them. Though most were legit.

"Since I got out. Six years. You?"

"About the same."

"You like it?"

Gil cut him a grin. "Pay's a hell of a lot better."

"No shit." Burton chuckled. "Anyway, there are a couple employment forms on the table you need to sign. W-2. Non-disclosure. That sort of thing. Then we'll hit the range. You might want to change before we head out there. You'll have a chance to shower and get cleaned up before you meet with Mr. Martin after."

"Sure." They walked out, and Gil found the paperwork and a pen and claimed one of the chairs.

"I'm going to head on out to the range." Burton pointed away from the mansion. "Follow the path and the sound of gunfire. You can't miss me."

Gil filled out the forms and changed into his tactical pants and T-shirt in record time and met Burton out on the range. There were gun ranges, and there were *gun ranges*. This wasn't a paper target at twenty yards kind of thing. They had multi-shooting stations, different distances, cover to hide behind and shoot, targets that popped out and you had to decide shoot or don't shoot. All with a high berm behind to protect against stray bullets. It was an impressive, top-notch range.

Burton ran him through various scenarios. He'd probably run seven magazines of ammo through his Glock before they moved onto the rifle range. Again, more of a tactical setup than a point and shoot. For this Burton handed over an M-4. A real one. Complete with the burst selector switch. Not one of those M-frauds sold in the civilian market.

Legally, there were few ways to get your hands on a weapon like that. *Illegally*... that was an entirely different scenario. "Haven't held one of these babies since I got out. Where did you dig this up?"

"I could tell you, but then I'd have to kill you." Burton said it with a smile. Gil figured he was most likely kidding.

"Fair enough." Gil would let that drop. He was in no hurry to arouse any suspicions.

Burton ran him through another set of close quarter drills. They ended the session by burning through a clip on full-auto, because, hell, why not?

"Damn nice range," Gil said.

"Thanks." Burton's chest puffed out a bit. "Mr. Martin gave me a budget and set me loose. A few things I might change if I had to do it over again, but overall I'm happy with it."

Gil picked up his Glock from a nearby table and replaced it

in his shoulder holster. Burton slung the M-4 across his shoulder and clapped Gil on the back.

"Did I pass?" No question in Gil's mind that he had. Besides his military training, he'd had extensive training with the ATF. Even with time off since he'd been shot, he was pleased with how sharp he'd been.

"Close enough," Burton said, but there was clear admiration in his eyes. "Let me guess. MP?"

Military police. "Good guess. What gave it away?"

"You look like a cop."

Gil scoffed. "Why would you say that?"

"A feeling." Burton slowed and eyed Gil a second. "Maybe it's the way you carry yourself."

Gil laughed him off. "I'm just walking, dude. But shit. No. Not a cop. I mean I tried. They didn't want me. Had a few issues with authority in my younger days. Besides, better pay in the private sector. No regrets."

"Word is, you were with El Verdugo for a while."

"Yeah." Gil glanced at Burton, curious as to where he was going with this. "So?"

They'd almost reached the garage. Burton stopped, his hands on his hips as if he had something to say. "Did it ever bother you? Working with... questionable employers?"

Gil played it cool. Acted like he was contemplating his answer when what he was really doing was trying to figure out if Burton was playing Gil or if maybe Burton knew something and was himself questioning his own loyalties. If so, Burton might turn out to be an ally if shit went sideways.

Gil settled on an equivocal, "I get paid to protect. That's what I do. The rest is above my pay grade."

Burton's expression shifted. Gil couldn't tell if the man was satisfied or disappointed with Gil's answer.

Burton's phone buzzed. He pulled it out of one of his thigh

pockets and read the text. "Mr. Martin will be ready for you in fifteen."

———

THE INTERIOR OF THE MANSION WAS WHAT GIL WOULD DESCRIBE as rich rustic. All wood and rock and aged leather. He and Burton walked past a two-story rock fireplace with the typical assortment of animal heads stuffed and mounted and looking rather pissed.

Down a short hallway, Burton led Gil through an open office door. Bradley Martin was hanging up the phone as they entered.

"Mr. Martin, this is Gil Goodman, the new security hire I told you about."

Martin came around the desk. Gil didn't pay much attention to men's designer business wear, but that suit had to cost more than a crate of M-4s.

The man couldn't have been more than five foot ten on a good day. Younger than Gil would have expected. Mid-thirties at most, but he had this cocky, self-assured air that chaffed at Gil before the man even said a word.

Gil stuck out his hand. "Mr. Martin."

Martin left him hanging. Gil cleared his throat and dropped his hand. He hoped like hell Martin was The Wolf. He'd have one hell of a good time taking this asshole down.

"Leave us," Martin said to Burton. To Gil, he said, "Have a seat."

As Gil sat, Martin walked back around his desk and sat. "I usually hire security based on personal recommendation only, but it seems I have an urgent need that couldn't be filled by normal means."

Gil crossed his ankle over his knee but didn't say anything. There hadn't been a question.

"You came highly recommended. Though I do have a couple questions for you."

"Yes, sir." Gil figured Martin was the kind of guy who would get his rocks off with the deferential "sir." Especially coming from a larger, stronger, man. Martin reminded him of a young prince who'd ascended the throne way too young and was enjoying the sudden power trip.

"You were one of El Verdugo's men."

"Correct."

"When his place was raided, correct?" Martin narrowed his eyes as if he could read Gil's mind. News flash. He couldn't.

"Yes, sir."

"How did you manage to not get picked up like the rest of them? You get scared? You run?" Martin poked.

Gil poked back. "You a cop?" Gil stood, planted his hands on the desk and leaned into Martin's personal space. "You got a camera? A wire? This a set up?"

"I'm not a cop." To prove the point, Martin untucked his shirt and pulled it up to the middle of his chest. "No wire. Answer the question."

Gil was slow to sit, his expression set to *better not be fucking with me*. Finally, he said, "Cops swarmed the mansion. I took two bullets trying to protect El Verdugo, but he was apprehended. In the storm and the confusion, I slipped away unnoticed."

"With two bullet wounds?" Martin sounded incredulous.

"Yes, sir." Gil wouldn't do himself any favors by elaborating. Short and direct, that was the ticket with this guy.

"The hospitals didn't report the gunshot wounds?"

"The wounds were through and through. My shoulder and abdomen. Nothing vital hit. I have an old medic buddy from my military days who patched me up." Plausible and hard to disprove.

Martin sat silent, eying him. If Martin thought he was intimidating, he hadn't looked in the mirror in a while. Gil stared back. He could play this game all damn day.

A knock came at the closed office door. It opened before Martin could say "come in."

"This better be good, Sloan." Martin stood, re-tucking his shirt.

Sloan handed Martin a newspaper. "Burton wanted you to see this."

The man didn't hang around, as if shooting the messenger could be a real issue. Martin laid the newspaper out on his desk and studied the front page. When he glanced up at Gil, red had infused his face, and a vein had popped out on his forehead.

"You ever been married? Kids?" Martin asked, the leashed rage burning him up from the inside.

"No, sir."

"Sloan," Martin called out. "*Sloan.*"

No answer. Martin raised his hands in disbelief, like *where did the man run off to?*

Martin stormed out of the office, presumably to find Sloan. Gil stood and turned the paper around. His breath caught, and his stomach dropped and twisted. On the front page of the Bison County Enquirer was a picture of Tessa riding him in the back of the helo. He wasn't proud that his dick was the first to respond to the image.

The *how*, as in *how did this get in the newspaper?* wasn't hard to answer. Gil had been right from the beginning. That hadn't been a kid who'd been at the back fence of the muni airport, but a reporter.

The question was, why did Martin care?

He heard voices approaching. He turned the paper back around and reclaimed his seat.

From down the hall, he heard Martin's raised voice. "I want you to get my lawyer on the phone. Now. I don't care if he's golfing, screwing his secretary, or arguing a case before the Supreme Court. You have him call me. Tell him it's urgent."

Martin stormed back into the room, the rage had bled out, leaving behind an excited, frenetic energy that Gil didn't quite understand.

"Everything okay?" Gil asked as Martin returned to his chair behind his desk.

Martin folded the newspaper over twice and tossed it in a trash can. "Nothing a decent lawyer can't take advantage of."

11

———

Before walking into the courtroom, Tessa and her lawyer were cautiously optimistic. Their case was being handled by a divorced judge with kids of her own. Even with Tessa's recent suspension, they could conceivably walk out with a win.

Then they walked in.

Instead of Judge Nicolls, Judge Hart was presiding. Two lawyers were at the bench, the judge's pudgy hand over the microphone as the lawyers argued their point.

Tessa's lawyer, Patricia Dunn, dropped her briefcase at her feet and sat heavily in a chair at the back of the courtroom. She leaned into Tessa. "This isn't good."

One of the things Tessa really liked about Patricia was she didn't sugar coat things and didn't hide what she thought to spare someone's feeling. Mostly that was a good thing, but Tessa's throat went dry at her comment.

"Where's Nicolls?"

"No clue." Patricia whipped out her phone and blasted off a quick text to her office, Tessa assumed. "Let's see what my assistant can find out."

Maybe a minute passed before Patricia got a return text. It felt like an hour. Patricia's frown deepened. She tossed her head toward the rear doors, and Tessa followed her out and down the hall for additional privacy.

"Turns out Judge Nicolls called in sick. Judge Hart is filling in from a nearby county."

"What's the problem with getting him?"

"Because he can be bought."

"You don't think..."

"You're the one who said Bradley had money."

"But if people know Judge Hart can be bought, how is he still on the bench?"

Patricia leaned against the white marble wall of the old courthouse. "I said he could be bought. I didn't say he was stupid."

Bradley and his lawyer walked up the stairs. Bradley's eyes raked over Tessa, a flash of an inward smile on his face, the one a snake might give the mouse right before he struck.

"*Bradley.*" Before Tessa got two steps away, Patricia caught her by the arm.

Turning her back to the two men, Patricia whispered to Tessa. "Don't say anything. Stay calm. Stay cool. We're going to fight it out in there, not out here."

They were called into the courtroom a few minutes later. Bradley's lawyer held the door open for them, "Ladies."

The condescension in his tone made Tessa bristle. Patricia grabbed her elbow and ushered her to the front of the stuffy, wood-paneled courtroom. Tessa's palms went sweaty, but her skirt was silk, and she didn't dare wipe her hands on it.

What happened next was a blur. Long and short, despite Tessa's lawyer's numerous objections, Bradley was awarded sole emergency custody of Jack. Until Tessa could find a more suitable environment to raise her son, and oh, find a solution to the no job thing. A couple of outbursts and the threat of being charged with contempt of court, may not have helped, but Tessa couldn't keep her mouth shut.

The only thing the judge had conceded was allowing Tessa to wait until Sunday evening to deliver Jack to Bradley, and that was only because she had temporary housing at the ranch.

The judge would allow the issue to be revisited in a month. *A month!*

Tessa collapsed on one of the benches outside the courtroom. Bradley walked out, shaking his lawyer's hand and clapping him on the back. Then the slick smile slid from Bradley's lips as he caught Tessa's eye. His features shifted, turning impossibly cold. Tessa was amazed at how a nice suit could camouflage the devil's own tail.

Bradley wasn't doing this to protect his son, he was doing it to punish his ex-wife.

Bradley turned and spoke in hushed tones to his lawyer. When his lawyer left, Bradley approached her. Patricia hopped to her feet, but Tessa put a staying hand on her arm.

"A word?" Bradley asked, his hand outstretched toward the end of the hall.

Patricia made a disapproving face, but Tessa excused herself and followed Bradley until they were out of earshot.

"Why are you doing this?"

Instead of answering, Bradley brushed a strand of her hair away from her face. Her shoulder flinched as she held back a full cringe. "You can come with Jack. I have plenty of room."

"Is that what this is? You want me under your thumb?"

"No, Tessa. I want you under my roof. Permanently. Think about it."

Bradley didn't give Tessa a chance to respond. He turned on his heel and disappeared down the stairs.

She didn't have to think about it. Her answer was simple. No. Way. In. Hell.

Now Tessa was on a mission. She would get her son back. She hadn't wanted to take a dime of Bradley's money, but she would spend every last red cent of it to buy her and Jack a place in a better part of town.

The job... the job could be a little bit trickier. If Tessa went to Spinks and told him Gil had been with her, it didn't guarantee she would get to keep her job. More than likely they would both get kicked loose. Was it better to keep quiet—to protect Gil— and hope her exemplary record would trump any detrimental recommendations stemming from the investigation?

Her head spun, and she saw black dots floating in her peripheral vision. The general hub-bub of the people in the hall sounded like it was coming from a hundred feet away not a few yards. She felt a hand press against her back forcing her head between her knees.

"Breathe, Tessa," Patricia said. The voice was disembodied, almost ethereal.

In and out, slow and steady. Tessa breathed until the sounds around her became clear, and her world came back into focus. But when she looked up, everything wasn't quite right either, because while objects may have come back into focus, the axis of her world had a precarious tilt.

"Better?" Tessa asked.

Tessa made a non-committal sound in the back of her throat. How could she be better? Her son had been taken away from her. Tears didn't fall. She didn't wail. That didn't happen when your emotions had been stripped from your soul leaving you numb and dumb.

She had to pick Jack up from camp. Had to tell him... oh God oh God oh God... how was she going to explain to Jack that he had to go live with his father?

Patricia caught her when she stumbled and helped her back to the bench. "Give me your phone. Let me call someone for you."

Jenna and Mac came and picked her up, and since they all agreed Tessa needed a chance to pull herself together before seeing Jack, they'd arranged for Evie to pick him up from camp and bring him to the ranch after dinner.

That evening, Tessa came out of the master bath of the big house dressed in Jenna's fluffy terrycloth robe after Jenna had poured her a hot, lavender bath. It was supposed to have been soothing, but all it had done was drain what little energy she'd had left after Bradley had ripped her life to shreds.

Tessa flopped in the corner of the couch opposite Jenna. "How much longer until Jack's here?"

Mac paced in front of the fireplace. Back and forth, back and forth like a pregnant yellow duck at the shooting gallery. Would that be Tessa in four months? Walking around with a bulge in her belly? Tessa squeezed her temples, trying to contain the questions, the thoughts, the fears, the emotions, the outrage.

Jenna glanced behind her at the clock on the wall. "Ten minutes, tops. You ready for this?"

Not even close, but when she had less than forty-eight hours to spend with her son, she didn't want to waste another millisecond. "I'll never be ready."

Hank walked in the back door and Mac went to him. He wrapped an arm around her shoulder, and his hand instinctively covered her belly for a quick touch.

"Any luck?" Mac asked him.

Hank had been talking to another local lawyer, getting a second opinion. "No. Not really. Best advice was to do what the judge suggested—move to a better location, make sure the job is secure, and hope like hell that in a month's time the judge will reverse his decision."

"Bradley doesn't want Jack. He's *never* wanted Jack." Tessa had said those same words a hundred times but couldn't help repeating herself. "I don't know what his game is, or why he wants back in our lives when he's wanted nothing to do with us for years." The backs of Tessa's eyes stung, and her voice shook with her anger and frustration and the complete unfathomability of the entire situation. If unfathomability was even a word. At this point, her brain was too scrambled to tell. If it wasn't, it should be.

They heard the crunch of gravel under tires, and Hank stepped over to the screen door and looked out. "He's here."

He held the door open. Jack came bounding in, his eyes ablaze with excitement. Evie was a few steps behind, with a red, splotchy complexion and a fake, tabloid smile.

Jack ran over and gave Tessa a hug, she held on extra tight and extra-long as if she could keep that moment frozen in time. The moment when he was still innocent. The moment when he still didn't know that he was being taken away from the only parent he'd ever known. Tessa's chest constricted, her lungs froze, and her heart tumbled beneath her feet.

Boomer and Sidney came through the back door, hand in hand. "Great news," Boomer said. "Tessa's door came in early, and we finished the install, you can move back any time you want."

"Boom," Mac said, her mouth tight, her voice a shoddy stage whisper. "Didn't you get the message?"

Sidney's smile cratered. "We'd left the phones in the truck. What message?"

Jack glanced around the room at the fake smiles and confused faces and the tears that were now streaming down Tessa's cheeks. "Why are you crying?"

———

THREE DAYS. THREE DAYS GIL HAD BEEN AT THE MARTIN ESTATE and the only thing he had to show for it was blisters on his heels from walking the perimeter of the property while on duty.

He wasn't going to get any valuable information if he couldn't get close to Martin. Sometimes the undercover game was a long one. Criminals didn't stay free long if they trusted too easily. All he could do is a good job and try to ingratiate himself to Martin as much as he could. He'd rather put his nuts in a vice and screw it down tight than suck up to Martin, but if that's what it took, then he'd ingratiate away.

Maybe tonight he'd have some luck. Martin was throwing an afternoon pool party, and Gil had been pulled in closer to the house.

From his spot at the back side of the pool, Gil had a clear line of sight through the windows at the back of the house to where Burton was working the front door, checking invitations, and for any obvious bulges that could indicate a potential weapon.

Pool parties had changed since he'd been a kid.

More people filtered through the house and into the backyard, milling around the buffet table, the line at the open bar growing longer by the second.

He recognized a member of the Wyoming House of Representatives from a news piece he'd seen on TV while he'd been laid up after being shot. There was a city councilman from a couple towns over and a local semi-celebrity who was more infamous than actually famous, who'd been drafted by the NFL a few failed years before. Gil remembered hearing some charges had been filed, intoxicated manslaughter he thought, but they'd never stuck.

Gil wracked his brain trying to figure out how these people were mixed up with The Wolf. If Martin was The Wolf. To date, he'd seen nothing that might corroborate that theory. Besides the M-4 and the security detail.

Or maybe it was all on the up and up—a businessman throwing a party and doing a little networking.

Riiight.

The front door opened again, and Gil almost stumbled off the foot-high wall at the back edge of the pool deck.

Tessa.

And Jack.

What the ever-loving hell was going on?

Gil shifted off to the side where the clump of people mingling around the bar wouldn't make him stand out. He'd cut his hair and shaved off his beard, but it wasn't like he was unrecognizable. A man his size never went unnoticed.

He watched over the heads of the small crowd. Martin was at the front door, a proprietary hand on Jack's shoulder. Burton carried in a kid-sized suitcase. Tessa bent down giving Jack a long, long hug. Then the door closed, and she was gone.

He needed to call Spinks and see if he knew what the hell was going on. Gil's initial concern after Martin had seen the newspaper, ramped up.

Tessa was involved, he just didn't know how.

Then his mind went to a dark and disturbing place, one that he had to consider no matter that he'd been balls deep inside her four days ago. No matter that she could be pregnant with his child. Was Tessa working with Martin?

Was Martin The Wolf and she the mole?

He'd told her he'd gone undercover. Did she know he was here? Did Martin know he was a plant?

The skin between his shoulder blades itched as if he could feel the target she'd slapped on his back. He eyed the other security guys, but none of them paid him any extra attention.

As the evening wore on, he kept a close eye on the kid. Not

only did he want to make sure Jack didn't spot him and inadvertently blow his cover, but Jack was a young kid by a pool. No one paid him any attention. Not Martin, not any of the guests. There weren't even any other kids for Jack to play with.

Jack filled a plate with food and carried it to the end of the low diving board perched over the deep end. Jack had on a button up western shirt, jeans, and his cowboy boots. Despite the fact the pool was heated, this wasn't the kind of pool party where people actually swam.

Jack set his plate on the end of the diving board and sat, his legs straddling either side, the tip of the board dipping toward the water. Gil wanted to call out, to tell Jack to get off the board before he fell in. You know, like any reasonable adult would. But he couldn't take that chance. Too much was riding on this assignment. Including his life.

Martin mingled with a drink in one hand, not paying Jack any attention since the kid had arrived.

There came a loud crash. A woman screamed. Gil spun toward the sound, his heart ramping up a notch as his hand went to the butt of his gun beneath his suit coat. Then the laughter came, and one of the waiters bent down and started picking up the shattered wine glasses and setting them on the serving tray.

Gil turned back around, his eyes scanning, making sure that wasn't some sort of diversion. Conversations had returned to normal levels, another song, the volume set low, played through the outdoor speakers.

When he was confident no external threat existed, he returned his attention to the pool to check on Jack.

He wasn't there.

Burton came up to Gil. "Take fifteen. This is gonna be a long night."

"Where's the kid?"

"How should I—"

Gil pushed past him before Burton could finish the sentence. He jogged over to the deep end of the black bottom pool. Jack's plate was still at the end of the board. He glanced down into the pool, but with the black bottom and the fading light reflecting off the surface, he couldn't see the bottom.

Then the automatic outside lights clicked on, then the pool lights.

There.

Jack. At the bottom of the pool.

Gil didn't hesitate. He didn't take off his shoes or take the time to toss his cell phone or his gun. He dove in, kicking hard with his legs, pulling with his arms, the weight of his wet clothes restricting his movements making it a struggle to reach Jack.

Gil felt like he was trying to free-dive the wreck of the Titanic.

The pressure built against his eardrums, the steady thrum of his heart the only sound he could hear. Jack lay at the bottom of the pool, his eyes stark, his arms paddling, his legs kicking, but he barely moved.

Jack blinked, and a rush of bubbles escaped from his mouth. Gil saw the moment water rushed into Jack's lungs, witnessed Jack's eyes go wild, his body flail, his mouth open, as if to scream.

Fuck. Fuck. Fuck.

Gil kicked harder, and fisted his hand around Jack's belt, pulled him against his chest and shoved off the bottom of the pool with all the strength he possessed.

Hang on, Jack!

Gil fought his way to the surface, not daring to think about how devastated Tessa would be if anything happened to her son. His mind couldn't go there, not without threatening to shut him down. He pushed that terrifying thought into that box in the back of his brain reserved for all the horrors and tragedies and deaths he could do nothing about.

He broke the surface, grabbing the edge of the pool. Hands reached down, hauling Jack out of his arms. There was some shouting, but Gil couldn't focus on the words. He climbed out of the pool and crawled the couple feet to where they had Jack laid out. Jack's lips were blue, and there was no rise or fall of his chest.

Gil rolled Jack to his side, the water flooding out of the boy's mouth. A quick touch of his finger to Jack's carotid artery.

A pulse.

Faint.

Gil pinched Jack's nose, tilted Jack's head back and covered the boy's mouth with his, blowing into Jack's lungs. Once, twice. Jack's chest convulsed. Jack coughed and gagged. More water came up. Gil rolled him to his side again.

"Jack," Gil patted him on the cheek. "Jack, come on, son."

Then Jack took a large heaving breath, then another and another, coughing and sputtering and crying. In the distance, Gil heard sirens. Jack's color shifted from blue to gray to pale pink as oxygen returned to his system. Jack's eyes fluttered as he started to regain consciousness. As much as Gil wanted to gather Jack up in his arms and hold on tight, as much as he wanted to tell him everything was going to be okay, he couldn't.

He couldn't risk being recognized.

This wasn't a game.

This could be life and death.

Someone must have found Martin because he showed up about the same time the paramedics arrived. Martin started giving orders, and the guests fell away.

Gil made it to one of the patio tables before his knees gave way. He collapsed into one of the chairs, his forearms on his knees, his head hanging between his shoulders, water pooling beneath him.

His chest tight, Gil's breaths came in harsh pants. It had nothing to do with his exertion and everything to do with how he couldn't get that flash, that moment out of his mind when Jack couldn't fight the overwhelming need to breathe.

The biggest mind fuck of all was that now that Jack was safe, Gil's brain kept flashing the what ifs. What if he hadn't found Jack in time. What if he had to tell Tessa her son was dead. She would crumble, she would shatter, she would never be whole again, and there wouldn't have been a damn thing he could have done to make it any better.

Ever.

A hand clapped him on the shoulder. Gil sat back and looked up. Burton stood beside him, his expression a stoic shit-that-was-close.

"You all right?" Burton quickly regained his composure. His tone came out even, one of those questions you throw out when you know everything is okay as if Gil had stubbed his toe, but the tension around Burton's eyes gave him away.

"Sure," Gil said, maintaining the ruse. After all, the kid was supposed to be nothing to him, right?

Gil peeled off his suit coat and shrugged out of his shoulder harness, chlorinated water pouring out of the leather holster.

"How do you know the kid?"

He pulled his phone out of the pocket of his pants and set it on the table beside his holstered gun, proud of himself for not letting his movements falter. "I don't."

"You called him Jack."

"Did I?" Water continued to pool at his feet, the puddle ever expanding. He tugged on the front of his sopping wet shirt, the breeze off the mountains stealing the heat from his body. He suppressed a shiver by giving what he hoped looked like a half-hearted shrug. "Must have heard someone use his name."

Burton's eyes narrowed. Gil took him for a naturally suspicious man and then throw in the fact Martin paid him to be even more so, meant that Burton didn't give up until he was satisfied. "You had to have been watching him awfully close to notice him falling in when no one else had."

Gil stood and turned it around on Burton, taking advantage of his superior size. Tough guys never admitted it intimidated them, but Gil knew that on some level it always did. "I do something wrong here? I get paid to be observant, to watch for danger, to notice inconsistencies. I was doing what Mr. Martin pays me for. My job. No more. No less. Is that a problem?"

Burton took a half-step back, unconsciously giving ground. Before he could answer, Martin walked up. "Burton, reorganize the men so Goodwin can get dried off and changed."

"Sure thing, boss." Burton stepped away, barking orders at the closest security guy.

For the first time since he'd pulled Jack out of the pool, Gil tuned back into his surroundings. The music still filtered out of the outdoor speakers, guests still milled about, though they gave the paramedics who were packing up their gear room to work. Off to one side of the pool, a few women had started to dance. Then it hit him. The party hadn't ended, it was just getting started.

"Thanks." Martin stuck out his hand, a look of chagrin on his face as if it would have been embarrassing... no embarrassing was incorrect... *inconvenient*, if things hadn't turned out the way they had.

Gil shook his boss's hand. He didn't quite know what to say. Somehow 'you're welcome' didn't quite seem appropriate. "I should get changed."

"Hold up. The kid wants to meet you. Says you're a hero."

Martin made a noise in the back of his throat as if that idea was preposterous. Not that Gil considered himself a hero. He wasn't. He'd been at the right place at the right time. That was all. "That's what happens when his mother surrounds him with law enforcement types. Makes the kid think caped crusaders are real."

One of the paramedics gave Jack a hand off the gurney. Jack's color was off, but he was steady enough on his feet. The other paramedic stacked the gear on the stretcher and started wheeling it away. Wait. They weren't taking the kid to the hospital? "Shouldn't he go to the hospital, get checked out?"

"He's fine," Martin said. "Besides, it's not your call."

Martin turned toward Jack, his arm outstretched. "Come here, son."

Son. Gil had suspected, but now Martin confirmed it. Gil didn't know what that meant for the investigation. All he knew was he was about three seconds away from having his cover blown by a seven-year-old.

———

"You weren't at dinner," Mia said with a hint of accusation.

Mia noticed? Tessa glanced up from the stall she was stripping down to the dirt. She'd needed something physical and mindless to keep her thoughts off Jack. Jenna had obliged with the back-breaking chore. Though she had blisters on her hands despite the gloves, and sweat rolling down between her breasts, her mind raced, and she had this pain in her chest where her heart used to be.

"Wasn't hungry," Tessa said.

Mia crossed her arms over her chest and leaned against the

open stall door, the laces loose on her desert colored combat boots. "I heard."

Tessa knew she was talking about Jack. Chatty Cathy, Mia was not, but there was no need for elaboration. Tessa kept on shoveling. Mia had made a statement. Tessa had nothing to add. In fact, she preferred not to talk at all. If she'd wanted company, she would have joined the others at dinner, not hidden away in the barn.

Mia sat in the doorway, wrapping her sleek, muscled arms around her legs, making Tessa wonder if Mia spent all her free time doing push-ups. "Those fuckers always win." Mia spat as if the thought had turned bitter on her tongue. "Sucks."

Intrigued, and because there were so many to choose from, Tessa asked, "Which fuckers? You have to be more specific."

One side of Mia's lip lifted, more smile than sneer. "The ones with all the power."

With a boot to one arm of the manure fork, Tessa went in for another scoop of dirty shavings. They weren't talking about Jack anymore. Tessa laughed, bitchy and bitter. "Tell me about it."

Night had fallen and with it had come the cold, but even in a T-shirt with the sleeves torn off, there were no goosebumps on Mia's arms. Tessa figured that deep-seated anger she wore like an avenger's cloak kept her plenty warm twenty-four/seven.

"What are you going to do?"

"Fight. For my job, for my kid." Tessa dumped another forkful into the wheelbarrow. The muscles in her arms burned and her back complained as if she'd been stacking bales of hay all day. "That's all I can do."

Her real estate agent had two houses lined up for her to see the next afternoon after her preliminary meeting with Internal Affairs, IA.

Tessa had enough drama in her life, but because she needed

something, anything to keep her mind off her own problems and because she had the sense that Mia wanted to share, Tessa asked, "What about you?"

Mia's two-hundred-yard stare focused back on Tessa. "What about me?"

"Are you going to fight?" Tessa held eye contact long enough to let Mia know she wasn't going to pry, but she would listen.

Mia stood and brushed the dirt off the seat of her jeans, her shoulders slumping under the weight of her own problems. "You know what they say... you can't fight Uncle Sam."

Mia turned to leave, and Tessa said, "Bullshit."

Mia turned back. "What?"

"That's bullshit. You, me, and every other woman in the military have been fighting Uncle Sam from the get-go. Clawing our way in, fighting for our right to fight for this country like the men. We fought, we *are* fighting, and we *are* winning. Whatever issue you have, you should fight, too."

"Hard to battle back when you've been dragged down a back alley and had the shit stomped out of you."

"You seem like the kind of woman who would come back up swinging, not huddle in the grime on the ground and give up."

"I didn't give up." This time Mia did smile, thin and grim. "I self-destructed. At least that's what the shrinks all said."

———

GIL SHIFTED, PUTTING MARTIN'S BODY BETWEEN HIM AND JACK, but that would be like the Hulk trying to hide behind a tree sapling. Jack started walking over, his steps slow, but steady, the towel draped around his pint-sized frame dragging along the pool deck.

Jack's eyes traveled past his father, landing on Gil.

Shit was about to get real. Gil laid a hand on the patio table near his gun, unsure if he was going to have to shoot his way out or make a run for it.

In slow motion, Gil watched the whole thing, the anticipation on Jack's face turning to recognition and then confusion. Jack's steps faltered, then Jack's grin spread on his boyish face.

In that splinter of time, when Gil was still Goodman, all sound faded, his vision narrowed, and his knees went weak. He leaned his hip against the table to steady himself. Had anyone *ever* looked at him that way before? No fear. No judgment. Just pure joy and unabashed adoration?

It wasn't deserved, but that didn't take away the power of the emotion that almost toppled a giant. Even as adrenaline seeped into his system, preparing his body for fight or flight, the backs of his eyes stung, and as much as he tried, he couldn't keep the return smile off his face.

Off to his left, someone called out for Martin. His boss stepped away as Jack took the last five or six steps at a run, his sopping wet sock feet leaving a trail behind him. Gil went to a knee and pulled Jack in for a hug. He didn't know who'd needed it more, him or Jack. The boy shook in his arms, Jack's chin quivered. Then the brave front Jack had put on had disintegrated.

"Mr. Gil," Jack choked out.

"Shhh. Shhh. Shhh." Over Jack's shoulder, Gil took a quick glance around. Martin was gone. Burton was calmly talking with one of the men, not shouting and telling his men to get Gil. There were no guns pointed at his head. In fact, no one paid them any attention.

When Jack's hitching breaths slowed, Gil held him out at arm's length. "You okay?"

Jack coughed and nodded, his hair damp and falling into his bloodshot eyes. The chlorine wafting off them both stung his eyes.

"You want to call your mom?" Gil didn't know how he was

going to manage that, but if Jack wanted to, he'd find a way to make it happen.

"My dad would be mad. He says big boys don't go crying to their moms." Jack hiccupped, and Gil cupped his cheek and brushed away the tear.

Gil didn't know what to say, but for some stupid reason, "I can talk to him," came out, as if the kid didn't already pose a serious risk to his cover.

Jack swiped his sleeve under his nose and dried his cheeks with the palms of his hands. He stood straighter and shook his head. "What are you doing here?"

The only way Gil thought he could buy the kid's silence was to tell him the truth, or at least the stripped down, G-rated, Disney version of it. "Can you keep a secret?"

Gil sat him in one of the patio chairs. He took one of the others, not caring that the cushions probably cost more than his suit. He glanced around again. Burton's eyes skimmed over him but kept going. The voices and laughter of the guests had picked up along with the alcohol consumption. Jack and the near-drowning already out of their minds.

"I can keep a secret." Jack's eyes lit, and he leaned in. "This year I found out the Easter Bunny isn't real, but I never told Mom, because Evie says Mom likes hiding the Easter eggs and I didn't want her to not hide them and be sad."

Yeah, this was not close to the same thing. "This is a different kind of secret, but just as important. I'm on a secret mission. No one can know that you know me from before today. No one can know who I really am, not even your dad." Gil added a wink. It made Jack smile.

"Like Bruce Wayne is really Batman? He fights the evil guys, but no one knows it's him."

"Yep. Only I don't have the cool suit."

"Does that make me Robin?"

Gil smiled. "Yeah, Squirt, I guess it does."

12

MONDAY MORNING, TESSA WALKED INTO THE SHERIFF'S OFFICE with a knot in her belly and determination steeling her spine. IA investigations were never pleasant. This one wouldn't be either.

She held her head high as she walked down the halls toward Spinks' office where the IA interview would take place. She got a couple of sideways glances from the deputies and one of them said something along the lines of how he'd like the chance to rev her engines, but she ignored them. Punching an LEO right before an IA interview wouldn't help her situation.

Even if it would feel good.

At Spinks' open door, she rapped on the door frame. She was a few minutes early, and the IA investigator hadn't arrived yet.

"Come in," Spinks said. "And close the door."

Tessa hesitated. The last time she'd closed the door, it hadn't gone well. She stepped inside and did what she'd been asked.

"Sit."

She sat.

Spinks closed the lid on his laptop and gave her his full attention. "Heard from Brant this morning."

Tessa's mouth went dry, her palms went sweaty, and the

room felt ten degrees too hot. What was that supposed to mean? Why was he telling her? Had Brant seen the newspaper?

Tessa blanked all expression from her face even though her jaw wanted to hit the floor and her eyes wanted to pop out. The struggle was real.

"What is your relationship with Bradley Martin?"

This time her jaw did drop. Of all the things she'd expected Spinks to say, the least of which was nothing short of a Trump-like 'you're fired!' was for him to bring up her ex.

"Complicated," was what she decided on, but when Spinks' expression went flat at her non-answer, she added, "He's my ex, sir."

Spinks scrubbed his face with his hands as if it was midnight, but it was only a little after eight in the morning.

"What is this about?"

"Massey found a money trail. We have reason to believe Bradley Martin is The Wolf." His words landed like a harpoon to the gut, yanking her insides out.

Tessa let those words sink in as she tried to catch her breath. Then she shook her head. "He's a lot of things. Brash, cutthroat, arrogant, total bastard, being the first ones that come to mind, but The Wolf? Nuh, uh."

"What do you know about his business dealings?"

"Not much. He's in some sort of finance, I think. I don't really know much. He's my ex. We aren't close, and he's been out of my life until the past few months."

"Then why is he here?"

"He wants my son and me back. He doesn't like to hear the word 'no.' Surely, Bradley isn't the only man with money to have moved to the area in the past few months."

But how many of them had business problems pop up over the weekend like Bradley had? Was the gun buy the reason he couldn't take Jack last weekend?

Could Spinks be right?

If Bradley is The Wolf, what kind of danger did that put Jack in?

More importantly, Tessa didn't know if Bradley was the type of man who would protect his son or use him as a shield.

"What do you want me to do?"

"Brant's on the inside," Spinks said. If he'd expected it to surprise her, it didn't. "He's part of Martin's new security detail, but he's the FNG." *Fucking new guy.* "He's having trouble getting close and gathering any actionable intel. You. You could get close."

Tessa laughed. "We've been separated six years. Divorced for three of them. I'm the last person Bradley would trust."

Spinks leaned forward. "This is important. Massey has picked up some chatter on the Dark Web. He has reason to believe The Wolf is building a large stash of weapons to send overseas. Somalia is heating up. With the prices the way they are, selling to Syria is also a possibility. You have M-4s going for as much as six thousand dollars each over there."

"Jesus." It didn't take a mathematician to calculate that you could make big money selling on the black market.

"Can you get inside? Can you earn his trust?"

Her and Bradley's conversation in the courthouse ran through her head.

You just want me under your thumb.

No, Tessa, I want you under my roof.

The air seemed thinner. Tessa took a couple of deep breaths. "Yes, sir. I think I can. As soon as IA is done with me, I'll see what I can do."

Spinks waved her off. "The investigation is on hold. Let me deal with the mayor and the public backlash. The Wolf takes priority." Then he pulled two cell phones out of his desk. "Encrypted phones, courtesy of Agent Finn. Slip one to Brant when you see him."

The heat rose to her face, and it wasn't from embarrassment. Anger pitched her voice into the next octave. "You sent Gil in without means of communication?"

"There was a mishap." Spinks' gaze slid from hers.

Her heart dropped in her chest, and she had that floaty, disconnected feeling she got when her helo dropped from sudden wind shear. "What kind of mishap? Is he okay?"

"*He's* fine." She didn't like the way Spinks emphasized 'he,' but by the closed look on the SAC's face, he wasn't going to elaborate. "Better to let him fill you in."

Spinks didn't look at her. Something was way off, and he wasn't going to tell her. She opened her mouth to press him, but he beat her to it. "Dismissed, lieutenant."

She pocketed the phones and hadn't even made it to the door when he added, "Lieutenant Sterling? Why didn't you tell me that it was Brant in the helo with you?"

Gil must have seen the papers. Must have told Spinks that he was the guy. Further proof of the honorable man Gil was. Tessa took a shallow breath, her lungs refusing to expand. "Would it have mattered?"

Spinks shrugged, not in an indifferent way, but in a you-should-have-trusted-me way. Then his expression softened as much as it ever did. Which meant you had to be paying close attention to notice it. "*You* should have told me, though I do respect that you didn't throw him under the bus to save their own ass."

———

It was early yet as Gil rubbed the last of the gun oil off and reassembled his Glock. The phone in the apartment only had a direct line to the house, requiring Gil to wake up early to find a phone in the main house that had an outside line to give

Spinks an update. Turned out that line had been in Martin's office.

He'd wrestled all night with his concerns over Tessa's involvement with Martin and had concluded it had less to do with Martin possibly being The Wolf and more to do with Martin being an asshole ex. He'd given Spinks the skinny on how he'd taken his phone for a swim as well as Tessa's connection to Martin. If nothing else, she might have insight or a way for him to get closer to his new boss.

Burton came through the front door of the apartment, a scowl etched so thick on his face it might never come out.

"Martin wants to see you."

Gil slid a full magazine home, racking the slide to chamber a round. He replaced his weapon in a spare shoulder holster one of the other guys had lent him until his dried out. "Anything I need to know?"

"He'll fill you in." Burton's hands were on his hips, and he stared at Gil like there was more he wanted to say.

"What?" If Burton had something to say, Gil didn't want it festering.

"You sure you've got no connection to the kid?" Burton met Gil's gaze head-on. Watching for any kind of tell that he was lying. Gil would be doing the same if the roles were reversed. Burton had good instincts, Gil had to give him that.

"None. Why?" The key to lying for a living was remembering that the less you elaborate, the less you need to keep straight.

"Kid keeps asking for you. The little shit doesn't shut up."

What else had Jack said? Had he given him away? Is that why Martin wanted to see him? Gil hid his concern behind a broad, guileless smile. "I saved the kid's life. Hero complex. That makes me better than Batman, and Optimus Prime all rolled into one."

"Opti-*what*?"

Gil clapped Burton on the shoulder as he walked by. "Man,

you gotta expand your horizons. There's more to life than targets and gunpowder."

A half-hearted 'fuck you' followed Gil out the door and into the glare of the early morning light. The sky was blue and bright. The kind of sky without a cloud and visibility that would go on for miles and miles. The kind of sky Tessa would love.

He didn't run into any of the other security guys this early in the morning. After they'd all had a late night with the party, everyone had been sent to bed leaving only two on guard for the rest of the night. One patrolling the outside and one roaming somewhere inside the house.

Martin's office door was open as it had been in the past. Gil wasn't sure if it was because he had an open-door policy for his staff or if he was paranoid and wanted to make sure he didn't miss anything significant.

Martin was on the phone but waved Gil in as Sloan brushed past Gil with a short stack of papers for his boss to sign. Martin scrawled his signature over the documents without reading them.

"I assure you," Martin said to whoever was on the other end of the line, "It doesn't matter what NASDAQ or the bond market is doing, I can get you double their return. Yeah. Yeah." Martin pointed to one of the black leather chairs in front of his desk, and Gil took a seat. "Have your secretary send the money by Wednesday at the latest. You won't be sorry."

Martin hung up, the lines around his eyes tight as if he were fighting a headache and wanted to press his fingers into his temples and massage the pain away. Gil didn't know if it was a hangover or the phone call that was making his boss's head hurt.

Martin plopped in his chair behind the desk. He was one of those obsessively neat guys that only had a keyboard, computer monitor and a couple other necessary odds and ends on his desk. On the bottom right corner sat a leather-bound journal, the attached silk ribbon marking a page a third of the way through.

Gil's fingers itched to open it. Martin didn't seem like the type of man who trusted technology with his deepest, darkest, rankest secrets. Those he would keep close at hand.

"I've been thinking." Martin leaned back and crossed his ankle over his knee in a move that appeared relaxed, but somehow wasn't. "I need another man I can trust. One who's observant. One who isn't afraid to put his life on the line."

Martin didn't seem like a man who tolerated being interrupted, so Gil didn't speak. "You saved the kid."

Finally. Some sort of verbal acknowledgment of what had happened. Not that Gil needed any validation from Martin, though it was a surprise to see that the bastard wasn't the Tin Man. Maybe he did have a heart and a soft spot for his son.

"Anyone would have done the same." Standard, no-I'm-not-a-hero response. Sounded legit.

Martin inclined his head, conceding. "That would have been a headache. One I don't need right now."

This prick was cold.

Really *fucking* cold.

How had Tessa ever fallen for him? How had an intelligent woman like her been taken in by his bullshit?

"Burton said you wanted to see me?" Gil's most delicate way of getting Martin back on point. He knew he had to get closer to his boss, it was part of his job, yet Martin had quickly reminded him how great it would feel to resign.

"Effective immediately, I'm putting you on my personal detail. Good work has its rewards."

"Thank you, sir."

Martin glanced at his watch. "I have meetings all day. Starting in fifteen minutes. Take a break. Get some coffee. Then come back here. It's going to be a long day."

Gil excused himself and made his way into the kitchen. After his late night, the early morning, and all the tossing, turning, and mind racing in between, he could certainly use another jolt of caffeine.

He stopped short at the sight of Jack sitting alone on a tall stool at the black granite kitchen island. Jack looked up from a comic book he was reading, a spoonful of milk drenched Fruit Loops in one hand.

"Whatcha reading?"

Jack shoved the spoon in his mouth and held up the cover of the comic book, smiling around the spoon in his mouth. Batman and Robin. Appropriate.

Gil glanced at the clock on the oven and went to pour his mug of coffee. "Shouldn't you be at camp already?"

Jack pulled the spoon out of his mouth and quickly chewed and swallowed. "I got to stay home today on account of I almost drownded."

Taking a fortifying sip of coffee, Gil pulled out the stool next to Jack and sat. "How are you feeling?" Then, Gil noticed Jack's bloodshot eyes. "You get any sleep?"

Jack shrugged. "I kept coughing and waking up, and then I heard a noise and got scared and went to find my dad only the hall was dark and then I didn't know where his room was. I hid in the closet." His words ran together, the emotion made Jack's chest hitch, which made him cough. He sounded like a winded seal.

Jesus Christ.

Before Gil could say anything, Jack said, "Can you keep a secret?"

"If you're going to tell me Santa Claus isn't real, I'm not going to believe you."

Jack giggled, then coughed. Gil handed him the glass of milk next to his cereal bowl. Jack took a couple gulps and said,

"Everyone knows Santa is real."

"Bet your bottom." Gil winked and leaned in. "What's the big secret?"

The smile slipped from Jack's face. "Don't tell mom, but I always wanted to live with my dad, because dads are cool and fun and play catch with you. Billy said they don't even make you eat your vegetables."

"I get it," Gil said.

"But, living with a dad isn't as fun as I thought it would be."

———

TESSA ROLLED UP TO BRADLEY'S MANSION A LITTLE BEFORE NOON after getting home from her meeting with Spinks and shoving clothes into a suitcase. Even though Bradley had said he wanted her at his house, she wasn't sure what he would do when faced with that option, so she'd decided against calling first, hoping it would be harder to tell her no to her face.

Instead of jeans and a T-shirt—that Gil and the rest of her friends were okay with—she'd thrown on a casual day dress that accentuated what curves she had. She'd even applied a little makeup. All for Bradley. All for the game she was playing.

If Spinks wanted her to get close, then she'd get close, no matter how much the idea made her skin crawl.

She knocked on the thick wooden door and was led into some sort of sitting area off the main hall while she was 'announced.' Like a peasant waiting for the king to grant her a scrap of his time.

Bradley hadn't had much money when they'd married, but somehow, the ostentatiousness of the house and the doorman/assistant guy seemed to fit what she'd expect of Bradley. He had to have a red Lamborghini stashed somewhere as well. Maybe a smoking robe and a Playboy Bunny or two for those lonely nights.

She heard footsteps coming down the hall. An older gentleman with a briefcase, and a younger, fitter, I-may-be-wearing-a-suit-but-I-can-still-kill-you kind of man trailing a few steps behind.

Then one of Bradley's men, Sloan she thought he'd said his name was, saw the men out and escorted her through the den—complete with the soaring ceilings and requisite mounted animal heads—and then down a hall on her right.

They rounded the corner of Bradley's office as her ex closed the door on a wall safe. Her eyes shot to Gil. He stood with his back to the large plate glass window.

He was all suited up and clean shaven. His eyes followed Tessa, but his expression never wavered. He swallowed hard behind his buttoned-up dress shirt and tie, but that was the only indication that he'd recognized her.

Her heart sped up, blood pooled low in her belly, and she stopped her hand before it could cover her womb where his baby might be growing. But now wasn't the time for that.

She must have made some primal sound in the back of her throat at the sight of Gil, because Bradley turned, and said, "Don't worry. He looks like a beast, but I assure you he's perfectly tame when required."

"Do you always talk about your employees like they're the gum beneath your shoe, or is he special?"

Bradly closed the gap between them, grabbing her lower jaw, his grip a hair shy of painful.

Out of the corner of her eye, she saw Gil's hands unclasp and fist at his sides. "Don't." Though her eyes never left Bradley's edgy gaze, the words were meant for Gil. He wasn't the lion on a chain Bradley thought he was. At least not where she was concerned.

Bradley released her, the smile on his face as slimy as an oil slick. "Don't forget who's in charge here."

"I didn't come here to argue."

Bradley stepped away and gestured toward the chairs in front of his desk. She took a seat as he settled against the front of his desk with his back to Gil. "Why did you come then?"

"To stay. For Jack."

He stared at her, a finger stroking his chin the same way her father had always done. Had Bradley spent so much time with her father that the gesture had rubbed off on him, like a father to a son?

Dread danced up her spine at seeing her father in her ex. She'd always known that Bradley had admired her father, envied him.

"What do you want with this game?" she demanded. "Taking Jack? I'm not a fool. We both know you don't want him. Tell me what you *do* want?"

"You. Reconciliation." His arms went wide as if encompassing the whole house. "All this could be yours. You wouldn't have to work. A full staff to do your bidding."

"I'm sure there are plenty of women who would love to spend your money and order your staff around. I'm not that woman, so why me? Because I'm the one that got away?"

Bradley shrugged one shoulder covered in beautiful Italian fabric. "All men have goals. Dreams. *Desires*. Otherwise what is the point?"

"I'm not a prize you can mount on the wall above the fireplace."

That's how you're going to get closer to your ex? By antagonizing him?

Bradley smiled. It was softer, more real than any of the others that she'd seen over the past few months. "I *have* missed you, you know."

She couldn't say the same, but in the interest of the assignment and more importantly, her son, she dropped the edge in her voice. "Maybe this will give us time to get to know each other again."

When she stood, he had a schooled look of triumph on his face she would never forget. Bradley had changed since their divorce. But not for the better.

Bradley stepped into her personal space, brushing the back of his hand along her cheek and down her jaw. Over Bradley's shoulder, Gil shifted and stretched his neck from side to side as if readying for a fight.

She took a step back before Bradley could try to kiss her and Gil went ballistic. She didn't like that she had to worry what Gil might do to Bradley if provoked, but she didn't hate it either.

It meant that he cared.

It meant that she mattered to him, the same way he mattered to her. Whatever Gil had started out being in her life, a distraction, a little sexy fun, he had quickly become much more than that.

Bradley glanced at his watch—which had probably put a Swiss watchmaker's kid through college. "Time for some lunch." He turned to Gil. "Bring the lady's luggage in and show her to the Blue room. I wasn't expecting guests. I'll have Sloan send someone in to make up the room."

Gil cleared his throat. "Yes, sir." He stepped away from the window and gestured toward the office door. "After you, Mrs. Martin."

"Sterling. It's *Miss* Sterling." Gil gave her elbow a light squeeze. Tessa cut her eyes to Bradley. "For now."

She turned in the doorway, and Gil almost bumped into her. To Bradley, she said, "I would like to be the one to pick Jack up from camp today."

"Sloan will be the one picking him up on camp days."

Bradley had settled behind his desk, his phone already in his hand. "You're no longer on the approved pick up list."

Of course, she wasn't. But before she could argue, Bradley said, "But he's not at camp today anyway."

"Why not?"

"He's sick."

"He was perfectly healthy when I dropped him off last night."

"Go get settled." Bradley looked away and started dialing, then held the receiver to his ear. "It's nothing. Really. I'll tell you all about it over lunch."

———

THE BLUE ROOM WAS... BLUE. SLATE BLUE CURTAINS, MATCHING the bedspread on the four-poster mahogany bed, and the fabric on the armless chair in the corner. Even the towels, and the dish of soap Gil saw in the attached bathroom matched.

Everything sparkled. The scent of lemon furniture polish hung in the air. Nothing out of place or askew, all of it staged like a movie set as if none of it was real.

Gil laid Tessa's suitcase on the padded bench at the foot of the bed and turned toward her. "Close the door."

Tessa took a step back, the latch clicking as she leaned against the door. In three long strides, he was in front of her, one hand braced on the door beside her head, the other caressed her cheek. He rubbed his thumb over the light bruise that had popped up on her jaw.

If this weren't an assignment, if there weren't so many lives depending on them to stop a weapons shipment, there would have been little that could have kept him from breaking Bradley over his knee like a broomstick.

"You okay?" he asked.

She nodded, tucking a finger through his belt loop and tugging him closer. He ducked his head and pressed his lips to hers. That one touch, that one taste. He knew he would never get enough of this woman. His chest felt heavy, and his heart felt light.

"*Jesus,*" he said. "You have no idea what you do to me."

He kissed her again. Instead of her usual ponytail, she had her hair down around her shoulders. He fisted the luxurious strands in his hand, as her arms went around his neck, deepening the kiss. She ground against his erection, and he had to bring his hands to her hips and stop her before he took her against the door in a house that wasn't his, during an operation they couldn't blow.

He broke the kiss and rested his forehead on hers as they caught their breath.

"I missed you," Tessa said.

He leaned away enough to see her face. She didn't look thrilled with her admission, but there was a look in her eyes that told him he was more than a fling or a mercy fuck on the back deck of a helo after an op gone wrong.

This could get very complicated.

He didn't need any more complications in his life.

But he'd be damned if he wanted to make it any simpler. "I missed you, too."

"How's Jack?"

He took her hands and led her to the bed where they could sit. How the hell do you tell the woman you love that her kid almost died?

Love?

No.

But even as he denied it, he knew it was true. The one thing being deployed and then undercover all that time had taught him, it was life was way too short. That if you found something good, something remarkable, something that stopped your heart and at the same time started it again, you held on tight and never let go.

She would want to know all of it, not want to be coddled. Gil loved that about her. She was so tenacious, so resilient, so... "First, I'm going to tell you that he's okay. All right?"

She nodded. If she was breathing, Gil couldn't tell.

He squeezed her hand and told her the truth. Detail, by brutal detail. He left nothing out. From the panic that had shot through him when he found Jack at the bottom of the pool, to the deep dive that seemed to take hours, to the terror of seeing Jack suck in the water. He told her about the faint pulse on the pool deck, the mouth to mouth, the paramedics, the oxygen, to the first smile and the moment Gil's heart started beating in his chest again.

"Oh, God." Her breath hitched, and she took in several heaving lungsful of air as the tears gathered in her eyes. His went misty, and he blinked them away.

"But he's okay? You've seen him?"

"I saw him this morning. He seemed good. Had a bit of a cough, but otherwise okay. Missing you, I think."

"I don't even know how to thank you. If... if—"

"No ifs," he said, and he certainly didn't need her thanks or gratitude. This wasn't the type of thing where the accolades made you feel any better. This was the type of thing where the positive outcome was the reward.

He kissed the moisture from her cheek. "Better get cleaned up and down to lunch before Martin sends Sloan up to find you."

She traced a finger down his beard-free face. "You look different."

"Good different or bad different?"

"Just different."

Her thoughts turned inward. She was still touching his face, but she was no longer seeing him. He knew what he'd told her was a lot to take in. He caught her hand and pressed a kiss on her palm. "What is it?"

"How do you do it?" Her eyes searched his, though he knew she wouldn't find the answers there because the hell of it was, he didn't know. "How do you pretend and lie and live this double life? How am I supposed to go down there and look at the father of my child and pretend Jack didn't almost die? How do I not take your gun and end all this with one bullet?"

"It's not easy, but we do it because we have to. Innocent lives are at stake, and as much as we'd like to, we can't take the law into our own hands. We pretend. We bury the hurt and the anger and the sometimes-overwhelming desire to pull the trigger, so we can do our jobs and do what's *right*. They're the monsters. Not us."

———

"Mom!" Jack jumped up from his seat at the long table in the dining room and ran to her, his grip around her waist fierce. He coughed, sounding like that time he'd had the croup.

She peeled him off her and felt his forehead. He wasn't hot, and he was alive, and... and... *you can do this. You. Can. Do. This.*

It took her swallowing twice before the stricture in her throat eased. "That's some cough, you got there, buddy." Taking his hand, she walked him back to the table.

"Yeah, I—"

"Come back to your seat, Jack," Bradley commanded, indicating the chair directly on Bradley's left with a half-eaten PB and J.

There was another plate on Bradley's right. With a bowl of

soup and a salad and some sort of fancy sandwich with a tooth-pick holding it together.

As Jack took his seat, Bradley stood and held out the chair for her. She sat and laid the cloth napkin on her lap. She half expected a waitress to ask for her drink order, but Bradley reached for the carafe of water on the table and filled her glass before retaking his seat.

"You were going to tell me why Jack's not at camp today."

Bradley forked some fresh spinach leaves and a grape tomato. "Like I said. It was nothing really. Jack decided to go for a swim. A little bit of water got in his lungs. Gave him a bit of a cough is all."

Jack had that look on his face he always got when he had a lot to say, and everyone was going to hear about it. He opened his mouth, but Bradley put his hand on Jack's shoulder and gave it squeeze.

"*Ouuch.*" His mouth went mulish, and he crossed his arms over his chest.

"*Bradley.*"

"Finish your lunch, son." To Tessa he said. "About time the boy learned some manners at the table. You're too soft on him. If he wants to be a man—"

"*He's seven.*"

"You can't coddle him."

"Maybe," she conceded. She wouldn't get anywhere with Bradley if she antagonized him. The sooner she got on his good side, the sooner they discovered the truth about him, the sooner she and Jack could get far, far away. "But with a cough like that, he should see a doctor."

"All taken care of." Bradley tucked the bite of sandwich into his cheek. "I had Sloan call a doctor in. He should be here by two."

"What if he needs X-rays?"

"Don't go buying trouble."

"Answer my question."

"Then we will get him X-rays. But I'm sure he's fine. The whole thing is being blown out of proportion." He turned his attention back to his son. "Finish your meal."

"I'm not hungry."

Bradley pulled Jack's chair away from the table. "Go to your room then. Your mother and I have things to discuss."

As much as Tessa wanted to protest, what she had to discuss with Bradley shouldn't be overhead by little ears.

Behind Bradley was an open door leading to the kitchen, and she caught a glimpse of Gil as he walked in and started pulling food from the fridge, but knowing Gil he was there to eavesdrop, not to make a sandwich.

Bradley contemplated her over the top of his water glass. "Despite what you might think, I really would like this to work."

"This?"

"Us."

Man, he was a piece of work. Tessa kept the anger out of her voice. It wasn't easy. "By taking my son?"

"It got your attention."

"Am I supposed to fall into your bed? Pretend like the last six years never happened?" She knew she had a role to play and sucking up to her ex was part of it, but she wouldn't be believable if she gave in from the start.

"Not yet, but eventually, yes. But first..." He leaned forward. "Who was he?"

There was no need to pretend she didn't know who 'he' was. In the kitchen, Gil stilled, a knife loaded with mayo halfway between the jar and a slice of bread.

"He was a nobody." Bradley leaned back and gave her the eye, and she added a huff and a disdainful laugh, "It was sex,

Bradley. It scratched an itch. You know? A warm body. A big cock. Nothing more."

Gil lathered the mayo on his bread and slapped it on top of his meat. He turned, his eyes boring into her as he tore a bite from his sandwich. Even though he had to know she was playing a part, what gave her words the jagged teeth, was that they had been true. At least in the beginning.

"You've always had a big mouth on you."

"You never complained about the size of my mouth before."

The double entendre wasn't lost on either man. Bradley uncrossed his legs as if his slacks were suddenly too tight. Gil stopped chewing and tossed the rest of his sandwich in the trash. Tessa almost smiled. Jealousy looked good on him.

While Bradley suffered from a rare loss of words, she asked, "What kind of business brought you to Wyoming?"

"Personal business. As in you. The rest..." With his fork, he rolled a grape tomato around on his plate and shrugged one shoulder feigning nonchalance. "Professionally, the business could be done anywhere."

"Which is?"

"Financier and expediter of humanitarian efforts."

Tessa laughed, but Bradley didn't crack a smile. "You find that funny?"

"You? A humanitarian? Yes. That's hysterical."

"Being a financier puts me in contact with people with bottomless pockets. The humanitarian side gives them a way to donate and feel good about themselves as they stuff their Swiss bank accounts."

Time to do her job and dig for a little intel. "I can't even begin to guess what and where."

"Would you believe feminine hygiene products to Syria?"

Her interest perked at the mention of Syria. She snuck a glance at the kitchen, but Gil was no longer there. It sounded like a load of bull, but Bradley wasn't lying, she would bet her wings on it. "You mean to tell me, the guy who was too embarrassed to buy me pads at the pharmacy is now supplying the third would with tampons?"

Bradley grimaced. So, not as evolved as he pretended to be. "Not everyone has access to what women here take for—"

"Yeah, yeah, cue the tears, the soulful music, and the infomercial sob story. What's next? Condoms for the Mongolian monasteries?"

Bradley chuckled, and for once the smile reached his eyes. For the briefest of moments, she saw the man she'd fallen in love with. The guy who was always up for a little clean trouble. The guy who'd put her before him, chasing dreams, not dollars.

Where had that man gone?

"I don't get to choose what goes where. I make it happen. After Syria, it's school supplies to refugees in Turkey, then water well pumps to Mozambique."

It didn't escape her that any of those places would be prime locations for illicit arms shipments as well.

"Great," she said as she plopped the last bite of her sandwich into her mouth. "How can I help?"

The disbelief on Bradley's face was genuine.

"What? You really didn't think I'd sit around here soaking up the sun by the pool and baking cookies all day?"

"I suppose not."

"Let me help." When he didn't look convinced, she added, "If I don't have a job, I'll go crazy."

"I'll see what I can do."

13

———

Wednesday morning found Gil unable to decide which circle of hell he was spiraling. Whichever circle it was, it was the one between watching your woman get hit on by her ex and the one where there wasn't anything he could do about it.

In the two days since Tessa had arrived, there had been a steady parade of luxury cars and briefcases packed with more cash than Gil had made in his lifetime.

In that same time, he'd contacted Spinks twice. Something was happening soon. Through Spinks, the word from Massey was that chatter on the Dark Web indicated an international shipment of weapons was imminent, and from the stuffed briefcases streaming through the door, Gil was convinced more and more they had the right guy.

All that security, all that firepower Burton and his men had, wasn't to protect a shipment of tampons. But he also didn't believe all these old codgers knew what their money was buying. Oh, they had to know it was illegal or skirted the line, you didn't get the kinds of returns Martin promised from investing in savings bonds.

Martin *was* a financier. A financier funding weapons. Classic buy low, sell high, use someone else's money to do it, and reap the rewards for himself and his "investors."

Gil glanced at his watch and rolled his shoulders as one more gray-haired man with a briefcase strode into the office looking frazzled and windswept.

The man tugged on the cuffs of his suit coat as Martin shook the proffered hand. "Cutting it close, Mr...?"

"Smith," the man said.

Sure, it was. And Gil was Tiny Tim.

"Frank Hanley highly recommended you," Mr. Smith said. That was the third Mr. Smith that week, but Martin gave him a unique number, and contact details like Martin's own little version of a Swiss Bank account.

Mr. Smith laid his briefcase on the desk and unlocked the clasps. "Coming up with this amount of cash on such short notice proved more problematic than I'd anticipated, but the projected returns seemed worth the headache."

"I assure you, you won't be disappointed," Martin said.

Unless the task force arrests every last swinging dick. Then the investors will be *sorely* disappointed.

With practiced ease, Martin counted the banded bundles of hundreds, recording the transaction in his leather-bound journal. Martin swept the money, and the journal into the safe, careful to close the door and spin the dial.

With the transaction finished, Sloan saw Mr. Smith out as Burton walked in. He cut a quick glance to Gil and said to Martin, "The men and I will be leaving within the hour. I want to make sure the area is secure before the shipment arrives."

"We'll take Goodman with us."

"Goodman? *Us?*"

"It's our biggest shipment to date. I have a lot riding on this. We need all the security we can bring. And yes, *us*. I'll be accompanying you."

Burton raised a brow, but Gil gave the man credit for not voicing the what-the-ever-loving-fuck-are-you-thinking expression that was carved into his face. A face that was as simple to read as a kindergarten primer. "Yes, sir, but..."

Burton glanced at Gil as if he didn't want to speak in front of him.

Gil kept his face neutral, if not a little bored, while on the inside his interest spiked and the hairs on the back of his neck prickled.

"Spit it out, Burton. We haven't got all day."

"I think Goodman should stay here. He's new, he's—"

"*I* think his reputation speaks for itself, and he proved his loyalty the other night."

"Just because—"

"Need I remind you we are a man short? If things go like they did ten days ago, we'll need a man with his skill and training."

Gil's attention meter pinged to red. That was the first time he'd heard any reference to something going wrong. Martin could be referring to anything, but Gil had a feeling it had to do with the task force's gun bust. It almost had to be.

He watched and listened. It would do him no good to argue in his favor. He didn't want to look too eager, even though this could be a big break for the case, and for the task force.

If Martin went with them, could Tessa find a way to get in the safe, get her hands-on Martin's journal, and feed that information to Spinks?

"No, sir." Burton did a decent job keeping the aggravation out of his voice. At least enough that it didn't register with Martin who was already tidying his desk. "You finished with Goodman then, sir?"

Martin glanced up from shutting down his computer. "For now."

"You're with me, Goodman," Burton said as he turned on his heel.

Gil caught up with him in the hallway. They were alone, but Gil didn't call Burton on his concerns about him. There was nothing Gil could say to ease Burton's distrust. Gil's actions would have to speak for him.

On the way back to the apartment, Gil spotted Tessa and Jack out by the barn feeding carrots to a rather rotund, black and white pony. He needed to talk to her, but he needed to shake Burton first.

At the apartment, he and Burton met with the rest of the men, changed into tactical pants, boots and T-shirts. Then they checked, and double checked their weapons, loaded up with extra magazines, their Glocks in their thigh holsters and M-4s ready to sling over their shoulders.

Burton even handed out the newest bulletproof vests. The ones Gil had only read about online. Hopefully, he wouldn't get to see for himself how much more effective they were. Then Burton pulled up an aerial view of where they were going, giving each man an assigned position. It was the mine.

Martin was The Wolf.

When the two SUVs were loaded with their gear, they had a few minutes of downtime before they had to leave. Burton had gone back up to the apartment and Gil skirted down the path to the barn.

He found Tessa on the backside of the barn, supervising Jack as he finished tacking up the pony for a ride.

"Hey," Gil said, as he came up behind her.

Her lips curved into a smile, but the worry line between her brows remained. "You shouldn't be here. If anyone sees you with me—"

"I'd tell them I was checking on Jack." He turned his attention to her son as Jack put his foot in the stirrup and swung his leg over. "How are you feeling, Squirt?"

"Terrible. I missed archery day, and Billy's mom was supposed to bring brownies."

———

Jack clucked to the pony, and the two started walking down the paddock's fence line. Gil stood close to Tessa, his black T-shirt stretched across that thick, broad chest. The intricate black dragon tattoo curled up his arms like a living, breathing creature, and disappeared beneath the short sleeve banding Gil's bicep.

That undercurrent of electricity that always pinged her nerves and made her hormones go haywire whenever he was near, triggered again. Having to pretend she didn't know him hadn't been easy, and her concern someone might catch her staring at him like a love struck sap was real.

As if her attraction to Gil wasn't enough of a worry, there was also Jack to deal with. Trying to keep her son's interaction with Gil to a minimum was like trying to pull a rare earth magnet off a solid block of charismatic steel. Jack couldn't stay away any more than she could.

Something about Gil drew her to him. Stronger than the magnetic pull Gil had on her son. Stronger even than the gentle, unrelenting, tug of the moon on the tides. Being around Gil changed her in ways she couldn't articulate but felt at her very core as if the structure of her DNA would unravel without him.

As an independent woman, it scared her shitless.

Luckily for her, Gil, and the mission, Bradley didn't know Jack's fascination with being in his father's office had nothing to do with Bradley and everything to do with Gil.

She focused on his face, on the hardscrabble of his features, the thin press of his lips. Something was going down. The spit dried in her mouth. "What's happening?"

"We're heading to the old mine. The same one the truck was tracked to. Martin's expecting a big shipment coming in by rail. Spinks' previous orders stand. We are observation and intel gathering only. The task force will move in once the merchandise is ready to ship out."

"That could be too late. What if—"

"Not our call. Spinks is a little gun shy with one suspect dead and two of his men in the hospital. He wants to make sure all the T's are crossed, the I's are dotted, and everything is authorized and signed in quadruplicate.

"I don't like it," Tessa said. "You have no backup."

"I'll be fine."

From the open doors at the back of the barn, they could see straight down the barn aisle as Burton's men gathered by the black Tahoes, all tacked up and looking like the presidential security detail.

Gil placed a hand on her elbow and guided her out of direct line of sight. Jack glanced up long enough for his eyes to light and send Gil a smile, but he was too busy guiding the pony through the series of cones they'd set up in the paddock to bother coming back over.

If this relationship crashed and burned, she didn't know who would take it harder. Her or Jack.

Gil stared down at her, his hard gaze turning to mush as he brought a hand to her face and brushed a lock of hair back from her forehead. Everywhere he looked, her eyes, her cheeks, her lips— was the gentlest of caresses that made her heart trip and her stomach falter. Ducking his head, he skimmed his lips over hers, the barest, briefest of touches—a foot skidding on the edge of an abyss—as if he were afraid that if he pressed harder, longer, he'd tumble and never hit bottom.

"I need your help."

"Anything." Deep down inside, she knew she didn't just mean the mission.

He hesitated. Could he hear her thoughts, feel her sincerity? He shook his head as if clearing his mind. "Martin's going with us. I need you to try to get in his safe and get a look at that journal. He keeps *everything* in there. If you could get photos, send them to Spinks, maybe he could have Massey run down the other end of the money trail."

"Sure." There was no hesitation even as she felt the color drain from her face. The boulder that had been sitting solidly in the pit of her stomach since Bradley had taken Jack, shifted. Bradley wasn't a man to trifle with. If she got caught—

Gil cupped her face, and she met his eyes. "No worries, yeah? Martin and the rest of the men will be gone. All you need to do is slip past Sloan, and you're in the clear. You've got this."

She wanted to curl up into him, but she stood straighter and nodded. Compared to Gil, she had the nonhazardous job. She wasn't the one who would be surrounded by a bunch of men with M-4s strapped across their chests. Men who could turn on him with one word from Burton or her ex.

He traced the pad of his thumb across her lower lip, and his eyes went hot and dark as he closed the thin gap between them. Boots scuffed in the aisle, and they jumped apart like two kids caught kissing in the corner at the Sadie Hawkins dance.

Burton came out the back, his gaze shifting from Gil to her and back again. Gil, the poster boy for calm, cool, and collected hitched his thumb over his shoulder at Jack and said, "Checking on the kid. Cough's much better. We ready to go?"

She probably looked like she'd pinched a candy bar from the gas station.

Burton didn't answer. He gave her a disapproving look and turned on his heel. Gil followed and that boulder in her stomach not only shifted, it started to roll. How long had Burton been standing there? Had he seen them together? More importantly, had he heard them?

———

GIL AND BURTON WERE IN ONE TAHOE. TWO OF THE OTHER security guys, Wu and Price, were in the another. And Martin, Carter—who was at the wheel—and Young, were in the S class Mercedes, with a trunk full of money.

Burton wasn't much of a talker when the conversation didn't center around guns and tactics and women, but the uneasy quiet that settled between them gave Gil no doubt that Burton had heard or at least seen something back at the barn.

Someone without Gil's undercover experience might be fighting the urge to stick a finger under his collar and give it a tug. But Gil wasn't the kind of guy who tugged at a tight collar, he was the type who tightened it around his opponent's neck. "If there's something you want to say, then say it."

Burton's right arm rested on the center console, his fingers inches away from the Glock in his thigh holster. Gil subtly shifted his weight to his left hip, to make his own gun more easily accessible. He wasn't expecting the inside of the Tahoe to become a shooting gallery, but Uncle Sam, the ATF, and life, had taught him to that even the best plans don't survive first contact.

"A word of advice." Burton took his eyes off the road long enough to give Gil a look. The same kind of look Gil's dad used to give him when his father knew he was probably wasting his breath. "Stay away from Martin's woman."

"I was checking on the kid."

Burton didn't have to say, "Riiight." The snort of derision said it for him.

Better to make Burton believe he had a thing for Tessa than for Burton to start suspecting the truth. "She's not Martin's woman. At least not anymore."

They were in the rear car, and Burton kept a close eye on the rear-view mirror for signs of trouble, but as they made their way through the foothills toward the mine, there was little traffic. "You think you know her?"

"Enough." Gil allowed.

"I'm trying to look out for you, buddy. Not a guy here that doesn't think about bending her over Martin's massive mahogany desk. But trust me, no piece of ass, no matter how nice, is worth getting on Martin's shit list."

Bending her over the desk. Piece of ass.

If Gil had been a younger man, with a quicker temper, he might not have been able to keep from knocking a couple of Burton's teeth in. Luckily, Gil wasn't the hothead he used to be.

"What can I say? I saved her kid. She's got some of that hero worship thing going on. You can't blame me for taking advantage of the opportunity." Gil turned to Burton and gave him one of those you-with-me-bro? smiles. "You've seen that ass, right? Totally worth it."

Burton just shook his head. "It always is... at the time."

"Got any other words of advice, *Dad*?" Gil broke the tension. "You could give me the birds and the bees speech."

Burton flicked Gil a glance and chuckled. "You're a dick, man." But there was hardness in Burton's eyes that made Gil wonder if Burton had heard more of his and Tessa's conversation than he'd let on, but before he could ask any questions, Martin's car pulled off the road at a scenic overlook.

"What the hell?" Burton pulled in behind the Mercedes and as he went to get out, said to Gil, "Get out and watch our six."

Gil got out, as well as Wu and Price who were in front of the Mercedes in their Tahoe. Burton approached the Mercedes as

Martin's blacked out window behind the driver buzzed down. From where Gil stood, he couldn't hear the conversation, but from the grip Burton had on the door frame as he leaned down, Burton wasn't happy.

After a brief conversation, Burton stepped back, the window buzzed up, and Burton waved at Wu and Price to get back in their vehicles and follow him.

Gil climbed into the Tahoe as the Mercedes drove back the way they'd come. "What's going on?"

"Martin forgot something. He's going back."

Back? Gil's chest squeezed, and his heart whooshed behind his eardrums. He glanced at his watch. They'd only been on the road ten minutes, maybe fifteen at most. Would Tessa try this soon to get in the safe, or would she wait a little longer?

"Shouldn't we be following him? That's a hell of a lot of money not to have an armed escort."

"He's more worried that we get in a defensive position before the shipment arrives. He says he won't be long. I don't like it, but he's got Carter and Young with him. Carter can out drive anyone, and Young was never one to hesitate to pull a trigger if need be."

The way Burton said it, it was like he was trying to convince himself as much as Gil.

"You didn't tell him that was a bad idea?"

"I told him, and he's paying me good money to ignore my advice."

As they sped toward the mine, Gil said, "How much further?"

"What are you? Five? You need me to stop the truck so you can take a piss?"

No. So he could pull out his encrypted phone and send a warning to Tessa. "Actually, yeah."

"You have got to be shitting me."

Gil put his hands up and did his best to look embarrassed. "Sorry, man."

"It's only like fifteen more minutes."

In fifteen minutes, Martin could be back at the house, and it could be too late. "Either you pull over, or I'm pissing in the truck. Your call."

Burton huffed out an exasperated sigh, but he pulled over. "I can't fucking believe this."

"Two seconds." Gil stepped out of the truck before it had come to a complete stop. Keeping his back to the truck, he took a piss as he fished the phone out of his pocket and fired off a quick text to Tessa, hating that he didn't have time to wait for an answer.

As soon as Gil and the rest of them had left, Tessa pulled Jack off the pony, stripped the saddle and bridle off and turned it loose into the paddock by the barn before high-tailing it back to the house.

The window of opportunity to try to get into Bradley's safe was narrow. There was no telling how long he would be gone, and more importantly, how long it would take her to get into the safe.

If she could.

In her mind, she ran through possible number combinations Bradley might use for the combination. Short of guessing or finding the numbers written down, her chances of getting in were slim, but she had to try.

Tessa plopped Jack in his room in front of his favorite cartoon channel with a bowl of dry cereal full of sugar and tiny marshmallows, feeling like the worse mom ever, but she didn't have much choice.

She reached for the bedroom door and started pulling it closed behind her.

"Mooom," Jack whined, "why can't I go with you?"

She stuck her head back in the room. *Because you can't ever not talk, and I can't take the chance that Sloan will hear us.* "It'll just be a few minutes. When I'm done, we can finish the Spiderman puzzle. Deal?"

Jack rolled his eyes and let out an exasperated sigh. "Fiiine."

"Stay here," but Jack had already turned back to the cartoons and tuned her out.

Tessa worked her way back downstairs, keeping her ears out for Sloan, but that guy was like some kind of personal assistant Ninja. You never seemed to hear him coming. One second, he was nowhere, and the next he was behind you.

She swung through the kitchen hoping to find him there to keep an eye on his whereabouts, but he wasn't anywhere around. Not wanting to waste any more time, she headed straight for Bradley's office.

Standing outside the door, she put her ear to the thick wood but heard no noise coming from the other side. The brass knob was cold to the touch as she turned it and pushed the door open.

"Can I help you?"

Tessa slapped a hand over her chest and barely managed to keep her heart behind her sternum. Her pulse beat at her temples and sweat immediately formed along her hairline. "I'm going to have to put a bell around your neck if you don't stop slinking through the halls." She cracked a smile.

Sloan didn't.

She pointed a finger inside the office. "Bradley said I could use his computer for the investor reports until he could get a chance to get me my own laptop."

"Did he now?"

"Yes," Tessa tossed in a healthy dose of irritation to match Sloan's. It wasn't difficult. "He did."

He still looked suspicious.

Tessa pulled her phone out of her pocket and held it out to Sloan. "You can call and ask. He wanted them done before he got back tonight. I don't have much time."

He eyed her phone, but she knew as well as Sloan did that Bradley wouldn't want to be interrupted with a phone call while he was in the middle of conducting important business.

"Can I get you anything? Coffee? Tea?"

"Some peace and quiet."

Closing the door, she waited on the other side for Sloan to open the door or find an excuse to come in. She waited about a minute, and when he hadn't come into the room, she hurried over to Bradley's desk and started searching through the drawers.

She must have spent five minutes checking drawers, even going as far as pulling each one out and looking underneath in case he had taped the combination to the bottom of a drawer, but no luck. Not a complete surprise. Bradley didn't strike her as the type of man who would leave something like that laying around.

That left trying to run through possible number combinations on the safe's tumbler. Bradley wouldn't use something as simple as a birthday or anniversary as the combination. He wasn't sentimental like that. But that was all she had to go with.

She had about exhausted all the possible number combinations she could think of when she heard the latch on the office door click. She turned to scramble back to the desk when a little brown head appeared around the door.

"Mom?"

Tessa pinched the bridge of her nose and called on every last rag-tag shred of her tattered patience to keep from raising her voice at Jack. "I told you to stay in your room."

"I know, but—"

She waved him in. She didn't want Sloan to see him standing in the hall. "Come in. Close the door behind you."

She turned back toward the safe. She had two more number combinations to try. If those didn't work, then they were out of luck. "What did you need, big guy?"

Jack said something, but she was too focused on the spin of the dial, trying not to overshoot the last number, that she didn't catch what he'd said. She grabbed the handle and gave it a twist, but like all the other times, it didn't turn. *Crap.*

Several beads of sweat slipped down her spine, and her heart ratcheted up a notch as she stole a glance over her shoulder to make sure the office door remained closed. She wasn't cut out for undercover work, that was for sure. Give her a helo sucking fumes in the middle of a kick-your-ass, blackout sand storm any day of the week.

She sucked in a breath and held it, then slowly let it out.

"Mom."

"Give me one more sec—"

"Your phone went off."

Her phone was in the front pocket of her jeans. She shook her right foot, but no phone rattled in her boot. She spun on her heel and snatched the encrypted phone from her son's hand. "Thanks."

She went to enter the code for the lock screen when Jack said, "Why don't you use the keypad like dad uses?"

Her fingers stilled mid dial spin, and she glanced up at her son. "What do you mean? What keypad?"

"The one for the safe."

She glanced at the office door again. "Show me."

Slipping the phone into her back pocket, she turned back to

the safe. Jack stood on his tiptoes and slid his hand between the safe and the cabinet surrounding it. There was a soft click, and a hidden drawer in the cabinet opened with a keypad attached.

She ghosted her fingers over the number pad as she glanced back at the old safe. Was this some sort of electronic upgrade? Was that even possible?

Apparently, it was.

Would she be locked out if she entered the incorrect numbers?

She glanced at her son, almost afraid to ask. "Do you know what the numbers are."

He shook his head.

She let out a long breath. Of course it wouldn't be that easy.

"Dad presses corner, corner, side, bottom, top, corner."

No way. She gasped at her son. He had the biggest, brownest, most intelligent, innocent eyes. "Show me."

He smiled and used his pointer finger to press the keys in sequence. She tried the handle. Nothing.

"Oh, wait." Jack pressed another key. "I forgot the star." Jack pressed the 'star' key, and Tessa heard a muffled click.

She placed her hand on the lever, and it turned. She smiled at Jack. "You did it."

"No," came the voice from behind them. "Now, *you've* done it."

Tessa spun around, almost knocking Jack to the ground. She latched onto his arm and kept him from falling. "B-Bradley." All the saliva evaporated from her mouth. The *what are you doing here?* stuck on her tongue.

With a hand on Jack's shoulder, she eased her son behind her. Heat burned up Bradley's neck, a deep crimson settling into his cheeks, a color she'd only seen on a lobster in a boiling pot.

Bradley strode across the room until he was mere inches from her. "Jack," he said, "Go to your room."

"M-Mom?" Jack's voice was too fragile to hide the quiver.

"Go," Tessa said, not daring to glance away from Bradley.

Jack didn't move.

"Go!" Bradley roared, his eyes never leaving hers.

She flinched. Jack ran.

Bradley placed his hand around the base of her neck and pushed her back against the cabinet and held her there. He glanced away long enough to reach his hand into the safe and pull out the journal. He slapped it against her chest, and she caught it, holding it against herself like a leather-bound shield.

"Is this why you're here, Tessa?" He actually sounded hurt.

"I'm here because you gave me no choice. Because you took my son."

"No," he said. "Why are you in my safe?"

"Money. What else."

He shook his head, then leaned in close, his mouth by her ear, his breath hot, dangerous. "You had plenty of my money but refused to spend it. Try again."

The encrypted phone in her back pocket vibrated, reverberating through the wood.

Bradley leaned back. "What was that?"

"Nothing."

It buzzed again, and Bradley reached toward Tessa's back pocket. With the thick journal in her hand, Tessa cocked her arm and swung at Bradley's head. He must have caught the movement out of the corner of his eye. He shifted, the blow glancing off the side of his head.

Instead of knocking him unconscious, it just pissed him off.

He batted the journal out of her hand and slammed her against the cabinet. Her head smacked against the dense wood. Pain radiated around her skull, and stars skipped and danced across her vision. Her knees buckled. Only his hand around her throat kept her on her feet.

He reached for the phone again, and she let him. Her only focus now was making sure she got out of that office alive. Jack was the only thing that mattered.

His safety.

His life.

She would do whatever she had to do to make that happen.

Bradley touched the home button, and the lock screen appeared. "What's the code?"

"I don't—"

"What is the code?" Bradley shouted. His face went beet red, and spittle landed on her cheeks, her lips. His grip tightened around her neck.

Sloan popped his head around the edge of the door. "Can I help you, sir?"

Tessa had never seen Bradley's eyes go that dark before, as if all reason, all humanity, had drained from them. Her pulse hammered at her temples as Bradley's grip tightened and the pressure built in her head and behind her eyes.

"Get the master key," Bradley said. "Lock the little brat in his room."

"N-No." Unable to swallow, the saliva pooled in her mouth making her cough. "This isn't about him."

She gripped Bradley's wrist with both hands, but he was too strong, and the growing lack of oxygen in her system made her too weak to really fight. Bradley glanced over his shoulder, though his grip never loosened. "Did I stutter, Sloan?"

"No, sir."

Sloan disappeared, taking Tessa's hope with her. Her lungs burned, and her legs felt as heavy as concrete blocks. "F-five," she managed, though the word was barely audible, even to herself.

Bradley released his grip, and Tessa gulped in air, her chest heaving, her body wracked with coughs. She braced her hands on her knees and pressed her butt against the cabinet to keep from falling to the ground.

"Five, what?"

She glared up at him. His color had returned to normal, and his eyes had lost most of the crazy. "Five, seven, four, four, one."

Bradley punched in the numbers.

Tessa slid to the ground and held her head in her hands. The black dots cleared, and her breathing started returning to normal, but as Bradley began thumbing through her texts to Gil as well as Spinks, a chill swept through her body, settling deep into her marrow. Her hands started to shake.

What scared her most was she had no clue what Bradley was capable of, but she was afraid she was about to find out.

As Bradley skimmed through the texts on Tessa's encrypted phone, it vibrated again. Bradley glanced down at it. "Awh, how *sweet*," he said, the sarcasm dripping from his words as artificial as saccharine and potentially as deadly. "He's worried about you."

Bradley crossed his arms over his chest. "Was it him? Was he the guy you were screwing in the helo?"

Tessa didn't answer, but then again, she didn't have to, the way the blood drained from her face said it for her.

He didn't outright call her a whore, but the disdain etched across his features said that *whore* would be putting it mildly. Never mind that it had been six years since she and Bradley had split.

Bradley read out his response as he typed. "I am safe. Don't worry about me." He glanced up, his words as flat as the luster in his eyes. "I added the kissy emoticon. Seemed appropriate considering you're fucking him."

Then he slipped the phone into the inside pocket of his suit. "I'll be keeping this for now."

She was fucked. Gil was fucked. The task force was fucked,

and she didn't know what she could do about it. But everyone's safety paled in comparison to her son's. She would do whatever she had to do to protect him.

He stepped to his desk and draped one leg over the corner, his focus on the safe as he fit all the pieces together. Tessa saw when it all clicked, that moment when his gaze refocused and landed on her with this calm detachment she hadn't expected from a man who'd had his hands around her neck mere moments before.

Her thoughts pinged in her head, different scenarios of where Bradley would go from there. None of them good. That rolling boulder in her stomach gathered speed, she felt like a bowling pin, and this gargantuan ball was spinning, rolling, and sliding in for a strike. She couldn't take the uncertainty any longer. Around the stricture in her throat, she said, "What are you going to do?"

He glanced at his watch, then stood and closed the gap between them. Tessa scrambled to her feet. She wanted to fight, wanted to run, but that was impossible without Jack.

He stepped closer, crowding her personal space.

"It's not what I'm going to do. It's what you are going to do for me."

"It's not what you think." Tessa's denial was *waaay* too late. Like closing the barn doors after the horses had run out, jumped the fences, and high tailed it toward the mountains.

"It's *exactly* what I think. You. Goodman, and that governmental alphabet soup you're working for."

She opened her mouth, but the words didn't come. There was no doubt in her mind that Bradley didn't possess an ounce of mercy or compassion or empathy. Maybe he never had. She wasn't sure how to get the upper hand, but she knew cowering before him wasn't the way.

She stood up straighter and swallowed down the thick, ropey

saliva. "You're selling military weapons slated for destruction to terrorist groups in third world countries. We can't let you do that."

"What do you care if the terrorists blow each other up? What does anyone care?"

"What about the civilians caught in the crossfire? What about the women, the children? If you supply the weapons, thousands of innocent people could die."

"It's business, Tessa. *Big* business. If they don't buy from me, make no mistake, they'll buy from someone else. I want my due, my piece of the pie."

His *due*. If she had any say in it, he would get that.

"What are you going to do? Send your son's father to prison?"

"Leave Jack out of this."

The tips of his lips curved up—a semblance of a smile—one that he'd probably practiced in front of a mirror to make it look authentic.

"I have to go. You're playing for my team now. You will do exactly what I say when I say it. That is if you ever want to see your son again."

"You don't want Jack. You never did."

"No," Bradley said, the most agreeable he'd been since he came back into her and Jack's life. "But you do."

14

GIL LAY PRONE ON THE BLACK TARRED ROOF OF ONE OF THE warehouse buildings at the abandoned mine, staring through the scope of the M-4, as he and the rest of Martin's men waited for the shipment to arrive by train. Somewhere off to his left, an industrial-sized generator supplying power to the warehouse and surrounding buildings chugged away, the thick diesel exhaust drifting by him.

Which explained why Spinks couldn't find any records from the power company going to the site.

Down below, a crane started up and inched toward the train tracks. A couple other men in forklifts drove out of the open doors of the warehouse below him. These guys had been at the facility when he and the rest of the men had arrived.

"Five minutes," came Burton's voice through Gil's earpiece.

"Roger that," Gil said into his mic.

Wu and Price checked in as well. Burton was leaning against one of the SUVs with his M-4 pointed down, but ready. Wu was laid out on top of a portable office trailer about fifty yards to Gil's right, and Price was positioned behind a rock on the rise across the tracks midway between Gil's and Wu's position, like their own little choke point.

A cool breeze blew through, and the sun would set behind the mountains soon. The sweat beading on his brow had less to do with the fact he was lying atop a black roof, in black clothes, without any cover, and more to do with the fact that Tessa hadn't texted him back yet.

By his calculation, Martin should be on his way back from the house by now. He shifted positions and pulled his phone from one of the side pockets of his pants. He typed in: *U R worrying me. Let me know u got my text.*

He set the phone down in front of him so he wouldn't miss Tessa's reply.

"One minute," Burton reported.

In the distance, Gil heard the chug of an approaching train. One of the men below worked a manual switch on the track that would divert the train off the main line and onto one where they could offload the shipment.

Still nothing from Tessa. He unlocked his phone and typed in: *??!*

Then the little moving dots showed up as Tessa started her response. The train rolled in, and Gil caught the incoming text before he placed his right eye back on the scope of the gun. *I am safe. Don't worry about me.*

Followed by what looked like a kissing emoji. Tessa wasn't the emoticon type, and it struck him as odd since she knew as well as he did that Spinks was monitoring their texts to stay in the loop. But he had more important things to worry about than the judicious use of emoticons.

The relief from receiving her response eased the tightness in his chest, and he blew out a breath. The train's engine stopped in his crosshairs, a nagging sinking feeling burned in his gut like one-hundred-and-ninety-proof moonshine. What was he missing?

"Showtime, boys," Burton said.

The air brakes hissed, the train groaned, and six armed men scrambled to the ground.

Gil scanned the train with his scope. The two men who had climbed down from the engine were at the wrong angle for him to cover, but the two from the caboose were a simple shot if need be. Into the mic, he said, "I've got the two at the rear."

Wu piped in, "I've got the two at the front."

Another man descended from the engine with only a sidearm at his hip. The two men in the middle flanked him on either side, their rifles ready, but aimed at the ground.

"I've got the three assholes in the middle." That from Price.

Burton stood and approached the man in the middle. They shook hands. Without Burton's mic button depressed, he couldn't hear what he was saying, but the man in the middle crossed his arms over his chest, not looking pleased. His two goons settled the butts of their rifles into their shoulders but didn't raise the barrel of their weapons. From their demeanor, Gil assumed Burton had told the man that the money and their boss hadn't arrived yet.

One man was in the engine, though by his clothes, he looked like a civilian. The guys at the business end of Gil's scope were dressed in fatigues, but these guys were *not* military. At least not active duty if the longer hair, scruffy faces, and disheveled clothes were anything to go by. The uniforms were likely Army surplus, like the rest of the shipment.

Tensions mounted on both sides as time ticked by, one slow second and then another as they waited on Martin, and more importantly, the money. Fifteen minutes. Twenty. Thirty. Sweat pooled at the base of his spine. The longer the train waited, the more exposed everyone was, but unloading couldn't begin until the cash arrived.

"The cocksuckers by the engine are getting antsy," Wu said. "Where the hell is Martin anyway?"

"No, shit," Price said, "I'm tired of laying out here with my dick in my hand."

"Mark this day on the calendar boys, Price got tired of masturbation," Wu shot back.

"Fuck you, Wu." Price chuckled. "Listen to me, I sound like Dr. Fucking Seuss."

Burton turned away from the three men and growled into the mic, "You girls need tampons and chocolate for this little slumber party? Or you do you think you can quit your bitching and do your jobs?"

A cloud of dust rose over the top of the scarred earth on the far side of the abandoned mining site. "Incoming," Gil said.

Burton notified the three men in front of him. The head honcho called out to the other four men, who closed in, their hands going to the grips on their guns, their fingers indexed next to the triggers.

Not long after Martin arrived, the cash was counted and exchanged, and the men on the crane and the forklifts got to work. From his vantage point, Gil was able to get photographs with his phone. The quality from that distance wasn't as good as he'd hoped, but at least with his phone working off satellites, he could send the photos in real time to Spinks instead of having to wait to upload them in secret back at Martin's.

Tensions eased as the offloading continued. The two guys Gil was covering were leaning against the caboose, their guns hanging from their neck tethers, their hands cupped to cut the breeze as they lit up a couple of cigarettes.

Nothing exciting happened. The men worked quickly, trying to finish before they lost the light. Containers were lowered, and the forklifts emptied the steel containers of unmarked, large wooden crates, and then the empty containers were reloaded onto the train's flatcars.

Then it happened. On the last container, one of the hoist straps broke, and the steel container crashed into the dirt with the groaning of metal and reverberations that shook the ground beneath him. All the men on the ground dropped to the dirt and covered their heads as if they were expecting an explosion.

None came.

The men slowly stood, brushing dust from their clothes. The sounds of nervous laughter wafted up. Someone sputtered and coughed. The container lay bent and twisted, the rear doors ajar.

Burton shouted at the men, and they worked hard to pry the steel doors open. One by one, the men entered the wrecked container and one by one they came out with a steady supply of shoulder-fired SAM's.

Surface to air missiles.

Christ. Gil shifted and swung his gun until the back of Martin's head centered in his sights. He could end this all right here. Right now. His finger ghosted over the trigger.

In his head, he could hear the report of his rifle, feel the thump of the butt against his shoulder, smell the gunpowder in his nose, see the spray of blood and brain matter as he rid the world of Bradley Fucking Martin.

If he did that, the likelihood of Gil escaping unscathed was about as slim as the chances of his big mug ever gracing the cover of *GQ*. He could take a handful of them out before the guns were turned on him. But it wasn't the thought of dying that stopped him, it was the thought of living with even more blood on his hands that did.

His time at the Lazy S had helped him see that there was a life on the other side of law enforcement waiting for him. A life with Tessa and Jack, and he was afraid to screw that up.

He'd do what he was sent in to do and get the three of them out of there as fast as he could. Then he'd give Spinks that letter of resignation and never look back.

Between Drew Ross, who Spinks had singing like an operatic canary, and all the task force's angles of investigation pointing to Martin as being The Wolf, they'd had no physical proof until now. Gil clicked away with the camera and uploaded a sample batch to Spinks with a succinct, *Merry fucking Christmas* as the subject line.

Gil smiled to himself. He could count the time he had left undercover in days, maybe even hours. They would get these bastards. They would lock them up, throw away the key and if Gil were lucky, if Gil played his cards right and the stars aligned, he'd have five minutes alone with the asshole who'd shot Isaac.

———

Tessa stared out of her second story window. The moon was high, and her spirit, her resolve, her hope, was at an all-time low. Like Jack, she'd been locked in her suite. From her vantage point on the semicircular balcony, she'd seen the men return from the mine. Even if size weren't a factor, from that distance, she could have singled Gil out from the confident, fluid way he carried himself.

A flood of emotions washed through her. Relief, shock, guilt. A part of her hadn't really believed that she would see Gil alive again, not after Bradley had found out the truth about him. About *them*.

Maybe the fact that he knew that Spinks and the rest of the task force were keeping close tabs on them had kept Bradley from doing anything too stupid. Killing an officer of the law in cold blood wasn't Bradley's style.

What about Lang and Rivera?

No. That was a bust gone bad. That wasn't the same as Bradley directly ordering someone's execution.

She clutched at the railing, wanting to call out to Gil, but she didn't dare. Without her phone, she had no way to warn him of the impending danger.

She considered sliding down the drainpipe near her balcony once it got dark, but the night patrols around the house were frequent, and she hadn't maintained the upper body strength she'd gained while in the Army. No way could she climb back up.

As much as a part of her couldn't believe Bradley would cause any physical harm to their son, she also didn't want to be caught outside her room and find out she was mistaken.

A key worked in the lock of the bedroom door, and Bradley entered, careful to lock the door behind him.

Bradley had said he wanted her, but he sure as hell didn't trust her.

Cold, spindly fingers of dread gripped her stomach and refused to let go. "How's Jack?"

"He's fine," Bradley said, more of a blow off than an actual accounting of her son's mental and physical wellbeing. Had he even checked on him?

"I swear to you, if you—"

He closed the gap between them, grabbing a fistful of hair and yanking her head back. Fire seared her scalp. "You're in no position to threaten me, wife. Do as I say, and no harm will come to the boy."

The boy. Dread's grip tightened and squeezed bile up the back of her throat. He said 'the boy' as if Jack didn't even belong to him. That he was nothing more than a pawn in the world's most deadly game of chess.

If Bradley really wanted her back, did he think this was how to do it? "I'm not your wife."

Bradley loosened his grip and brushed her hair behind her ear. A smile toyed with his mouth. "Just because a judge has signed some papers doesn't mean you aren't mine."

He leaned in, pressed a kiss at the corner of her jaw and nibbled at her ear. The muscles in her legs twitched, her body wanting her to flee but her brain making her stay. In her ear, he whispered, "To be clear, fucking another man, doesn't make you his."

He took a half-step back. "Not much longer and we'll be together, and this will all be behind us."

He had to be batshit crazy to think that she would ever willingly be with him again, but that wasn't what scared her the most. When she looked into his eyes, what frightened her the most was that he *wasn't* crazy. She didn't even think he was delusional. No, what she saw was the confidence of a man who knew what he wanted and stopped at nothing to get it.

"How much longer?"

If she could get an idea of when the shipment was going out, maybe there was some way she could get the word out to Spinks. The only outside phone line was in Bradley's office, and she didn't think she should chance going in there again, even if she had the opportunity. She and Jack would not voluntarily go anywhere with Bradley. No. Fucking. Way.

Leaning in, he pressed his lips to hers, the tip of his tongue tracing the seam of her lips. "Open for me." His hands tightened in her hair again, and pain zipped across her scalp. It wasn't a request.

She opened her mouth, and his tongue darted in, invading, taking. The urge to fight back, to kick and scream and punch and bite and scratch and claw almost overwhelmed her, but she had to keep her composure. For Jack if not for herself.

If she played the part, would he start to trust her? She kissed Bradley back, deepening the kiss and letting loose a fake little moan in the back of her throat that she almost choked on.

Bradley pulled back, leaving the taste of whiskey in her mouth. She didn't think she would ever be able to drink alcohol again. "That's my girl." He reached into the inside pocket of his suit coat and pulled out her phone and held it out to her.

She hesitated, her hand partially outstretched, and he said, "It's not going to bite."

She took it, immediately suspicious. "Why are you giving this back to me?"

"I had it cloned."

"It's encrypted."

"New phone. Old style encryption. Might as well not even have it."

The phone that had been a lifeline was now an anchor. She couldn't text Gil without Bradley knowing about it.

He went on to explain that he would be able to see every text, email, phone call, web search, as well as her GPS location. If she pressed any button on the phone, he'd know about it.

The way their phones were connected, anything she typed to Gil, Spinks would see as well. She had to find a way to get word to Gil that Bradley was on to them, but how?

"What am I supposed to do with this?"

"We're going to use it against your little friends. I'll let you know when the time comes. For now, know that I'm watching, listening. Don't screw it up. This is our chance to be happy again."

At one in the morning, Gil lay fully clothed on top of the covers on his bed. The moon shone through the open blinds. All was quiet, except for Wu's steady snore coming from the room next door.

He'd had a brief text stream with Spinks after getting back to the house, a text stream that Tessa would have seen. A text stream that she didn't comment on.

Something was off.

Since they'd been back from the mine, he hadn't been able to relax, even after going through magazine after magazine on the range behind their apartment until Burton had come around and told him to lay off.

Gil palmed his phone from his nightstand, thumbed to his last text from her and stared at the screen. Tessa's message stared back at him. *I am safe. Don't worry about me.*

Those words should have put his mind at rest, but they didn't. Where the hell was her update? Had she been able to get in the safe or not?

His thumbs hovered over the screen, debating. He wanted to say he missed her. That he wanted to see her, but Spinks would get the text notification. Not that there was anything to hide anymore as far as his and Tessa's relationship went, since he'd notified Spinks he'd been in the helo with Tessa. Though he doubted Spinks wanted to be a witness to any of it.

He also didn't want to alarm Spinks by asking if she was okay again. Spinks would want to know if there was a problem. Gil didn't *know* there was a reason for concern and trying to explain to his boss how his skin felt too small, and his gut felt like some overeager Boy Scout was using his intestines to practice for a knot tying badge, didn't sound detached and professional.

His thumbs flew over the tiny keyboard, as he got to the point. *Success?* His thumb hovered over the send button. He erased it. Typed it back in. Erased it again.

What was he missing? *I am safe. Don't worry about me.*

The text didn't sound like her. She wasn't like other women

he'd texted before. She used the shortest texts to get to the point. She would have said *safe*. Not *I'm safe* and certainly not *I am safe*. And *no worries* would have sounded more like her. Not *Don't worry*. And what was up with the apostrophe? She never used them with contractions, she'd once told him it was too much trouble to bother putting them in.

If her phone didn't automatically capitalize the first word in a sentence, it would be lower case as well. That was the type of woman she was. She didn't stand on ceremony or waste her time on things that weren't important.

One thing he knew for sure, he wasn't getting any sleep until he found out what was up.

What's up? You want her in your arms. Want to feel the warmth of her skin, hear her gentle sigh as she leans in against you before you roll her beneath—

That wasn't helping.

Gil needed to know Tessa was *safe*. He sat up and scrubbed a hand over his jaw, not used to feeling stubble instead of his beard. Since when had his old undercover persona felt more natural?

Into his phone, he typed in: *meet me at the barn*. Yeah, that wouldn't sound like a booty call to Spinks when it alerted his phone in the wee hours of the morning.

Gil erased the message and dropped the phone into the side pocket of his tactical pants. He hadn't changed since they'd returned from the mine. He needed a shower, a change of clothes.

Down boy. He laughed to himself. It didn't matter that his clothes were dirty, or that he smelled. This was *not* a booty call. He adjusted himself before reaching for the doorknob.

Gil slipped out and descended the apartment stairs and tried not to think about how long it had been since he'd kissed her. *Really* kissed her. The barn hadn't counted. Somehow that had felt more like a goodbye, even though he knew it wasn't. It was a promise of later.

He waited in the shadows until one of the guards, Price, he thought it was, turned the corner on his patrol of the grounds. As he hurried over to her balcony, he couldn't wait to touch her again, to feel her heat against him. His mind drifted to the last time they'd been together.

He'd never be able to smell hay again and not think about smooth skin, sultry sex, and sweet surrender.

Taking the drain pipe in his hands, he hauled himself hand over hand up the pipe, the brick mostly smooth, not giving him much purchase with his booted feet.

He grunted, and his breathing became more labored as his triceps, biceps, and deltoids burned. Though mostly healed, his shoulder ached where the bullet had blasted through. Reaching over, he hoisted himself over the top rail of Tessa's balcony and dropped down on the other side with little sound, absorbing the hard landing with his knees.

The balcony door stood ajar, allowing the breeze and moonlight in. Tessa's form was clearly visible, as she lay on her side, her back to him. She hadn't stirred when he'd landed on her balcony. He thought she was asleep, but as he pushed open the door, he saw her shoulders shake and the unmistakable hitch in her breath as she wept.

"Awh, baby," he crooned, his voice low, soothing.

She didn't startle—maybe she'd heard him after all—but she didn't turn to him either. Reaching up, she swiped at her cheek, curling her hand back under her chin.

The mattress dipped under his weight as he settled behind her on top of the covers. He wrapped his arm around her waist and pulled her up against him. She didn't pull away, in fact, she wormed her way back against him as if the molecule of air that separated them was too much.

Wearing nothing but her panties and a long T-shirt, her skin was cold to the touch. He rubbed his hand up and down her arm to warm her. "Why are you upset?"

She took a shuddering breath, and then another. He'd half expected the usual "nothing," or "I'm fine" or some other line women had always fed him when something was wrong and they didn't want to talk about it.

Instead, Tessa blew out a shallow breath and said, "We're fucked."

Those words should have filled him with alarm, but despite everything, her choice of words made him chuckle—though he knew there was nothing funny. Tessa Sterling wasn't like any other woman he'd ever been with, and that was one of the many things he loved about her.

He pressed a hand to her shoulder until she wiped her cheeks and turned to face him. Unshed tears glistened in her eyes, those big, brown, beautiful eyes so vulnerable, so broken.

Swallowing hard, he clamped down on the emotion that threatened to crush him. He cupped Tessa's cheeks and kissed her forehead. "Look at me," he said as he pulled back to see her better.

She did. He saw fear and hope, helplessness and determination swimming, swirling, simmering in her eyes. "I love you."

Gil rolled out his profession of love like it was no big deal. A given it seemed that her mind couldn't quite compute. "Whatever it is, we'll get through it. Together. Got me?"

She nodded, a hiccup escaping. She looked like she wanted to believe but didn't dare.

Not completely.

Sitting up, he rearranged the bed pillows behind his back and tugged her up with him. He linked their fingers and kissed the back of her hand. "Tell me everything."

THEY SAT AT THE HEAD OF HER BED, FINGERS INTERTWINED OVER his stomach as Tessa curled against him. There was so much to tell him. A part of her feared he'd break down her door and tear Bradley limb from limb.

The scariest thing?

She wanted him to.

They heard footsteps down the hall. Tessa stiffened. Gil dropped a foot to the floor, but whoever it was kept going.

Gil spoke into Tessa's ear. "The door locked?"

She huffed out a whisper-thin laugh. "Yes, it's locked. As in Bradley locked me in."

Sitting up straighter, Gil said, "What the hell does that mean?"

She distanced herself from Gil as if that would help her distance herself from the whole situation. Stupid, but that didn't change the way she felt. She settled into the middle of the bed, cross-legged and facing him. She tucked her shirt down around her. "Don't get mad."

His expression went from concern to neutral. A subtle, gentle shift. One that might come from a well-engineered, high-end luxury car. If you didn't feel it happening, you never would have known something had changed.

Despite her jumbled thoughts, the fact that he didn't make any promises, wasn't lost on her.

"Start with why Martin locked you in your room." In his voice was the detachment she expected from a true professional, but his hand fisted in his lap. If he ever got the chance to be alone in a room with Bradley, she couldn't be confident she'd recognize her ex when Gil finished with him.

She told Gil everything. About Bradley catching her in the office, about their compromised phones, about Bradley coercing her into being his mole in the task force to feed them false information, to threatening to take Jack away from her forever.

It all seemed unreal. A couple of months ago Tessa's biggest worries were making sure Jack finished his homework on time, and what she was cooking for dinner. Full stop.

Then Gil came into her life, and she'd been concerned about protecting her son from getting attached and potentially hurt. But now all that seemed insignificant compared to trying to survive the next few days.

It was a lot to take in and wrap her mind around. Gil stood and stared out the balcony door in the shadow of the curtain, his hands on his hips as he absorbed the new information.

Finally, he pushed the chair from the corner of the room and moved it next to the bed and sat, his legs spread, his forearms draped over his knees. "Our number one priority is Jack's safety. Everything else—catching Martin, stopping the arms shipment, nailing the buyers—none of that matters if Jack gets hurt."

If a part of her hadn't already been falling in love with Gil, that statement right there would have done it. Here was a man committed to her, and perhaps more importantly, to her son. Gil wouldn't get an argument from her. "Agreed."

"As much as I want to storm down Jack's door, the chances of him getting hurt in even the most well-planned rescue aren't negligent."

Aren't negligent. Understatement. Like saying Vietnam was a scuffle.

Gil continued, "Do you think Martin is capable of physically hurting Jack?"

It was a question she didn't know the answer to. A chill settled under her skin, raising goosebumps on her flesh. Tessa shifted, bringing her knees to her chest and draping the shirt over the top of them. When she didn't respond, Gil pressed. "What does your gut say?"

Her gut. Yeah, it wasn't like her gut hadn't ever led her astray. She trusted it less than mayonnaise left out in the sun at a Memorial Day picnic. Bradley wasn't a good man. He wasn't a moral man, and by most people's standards, he was a dangerous man. Men had died because of Bradley. No question. But killing his own flesh and blood?

That went beyond brutal.

Beyond depraved.

"No." She glanced up and met Gil's eyes and said it louder, as the word sunk in. "No. But kidnapping him? Squirreling him away to a dark corner of the world where I would never find him again? Yeah, I wouldn't put that past him."

"Then I think for now, as scared as he must be, he's safest in his room. Martin isn't going anywhere until this deal is done and the shipment is on its way to the buyer. The best way to keep Jack safe is to stop Martin."

"How are we going to do that when we can't coordinate our efforts with the task force? We can't even communicate with Spinks without Bradley knowing, and with Bradley reading our texts, anything Spinks relays to us could possibly put the task force in grave danger."

"I'm hoping for now our communication silence will alert them that something isn't right. I can get the word out we've been compromised, but we'll be in the dark until we can find another way to contact them. We'll have to do what we can and trust the task force to do what they do best, and that's flushing these bastards out until they're easy targets to shoot down."

There was a way to talk to Spinks without Bradley knowing? She scooted to the edge of the bed, her legs dangling over the side. A little hope crept in, making the anchor in her stomach seem lighter. "Get the word out? How?"

"Spinks and I set up a code for cases like this."

"You going to text him now?"

"I think it's best to wait until morning. We all need a good night's sleep. I don't want to send something out and be worrying all night that Martin might figure it out and take it out on you or Jack. At least I'll be in the house in the morning and be able to keep an eye on Martin in case he decides to do something stupid."

Even though Gil had a point, Tessa deflated. She wasn't cut out for the watch and wait, the lies, the constant cat and mouse, the looking over your shoulder non-stop.

"Come here." The warm compassion in his voice made her want to climb into his lap and let him wrap her in his arms, her own personal Gil cocoon to protect her from reality. That bitch.

She took his outstretched hand, and let him pull her onto his lap, as she tucked her head under his chin. Beneath the faded scent of his cologne, she smelled the tangy mix of gunpowder and dried sweat on his skin. It wasn't unpleasant. It reminded her of the kind of man he was. The kind who acted. The kind of man who did whatever it took to get a dangerous job done.

He held her tight and pressed a kiss to the top of her head, one of his thumbs tracing a lazy circle at the angle of her hip. She touched a kiss to his neck, the pulse bumping against her lips. Her tongue sneaking out, a touch, a taste.

She didn't know when the line was crossed, when the soft contented sighs turned to moans, when chaste kisses turned hot and opened mouthed, and his lightest touch morphed into a tantalizing caress.

Gil shifted, gathering her in his arms, and laid her back on the bed. He shucked his boots and knelt between her legs, taking his weight on his arms. "I should go." The kiss that followed made her back arch and her nerves short circuit.

Inside, something elemental shifted as Gil busted through the last of her defenses.

Was what they shared real? She wanted him. Not just now.

Not just for the relief, for the sex. They were good at using their bodies for pleasure, but now she wanted more from him than to scratch an itch.

This was a forever kind of feeling—breakfasts in bed on a lazy Sunday, sex in the sun, spats about who left the car on empty, Legos underfoot, apologies when you weren't at fault, a warm leg thrown over yours at in the middle of the night, loud snores...

The everyday. The mundane.

But from day one, nothing about their relationship had been ordinary, and it sure as hell hadn't been mundane. Crisis was a brittle glue that often brought people together.

It wasn't strong.

It wasn't pliable.

It couldn't be trusted.

He said he loved you.

That, for whatever reason, she trusted.

15

THE HOUSE WAS QUIET. A SMART MAN WOULD GET HIS ASS BACK TO the apartment before someone found out he wasn't in his room. But he'd be lying if he said that the element of danger, the threat of getting caught, didn't flare within him like lighter fluid on hot coals.

As much as he wanted to stay, he said, "I should go." Which was a dick move because what he really should do was get off that bed and climb down the drainpipe, and not give Tessa the option.

His heart thumped in his chest, counting out the seconds, waiting for her response.

"Stay." The surprise on Tessa's face had to match his own. "I didn't expect to say that."

"I'm glad you did. And as much as I enjoyed having sex in the back of the helo and the loft of the barn, I must admit, my knees are looking forward to making love to you in a real bed."

"The eight hundred thread count sheets are a plus."

"I may have to splurge and buy us a set when we get back." Which kind of implied they would still be together. Which he knew would kind of freak her out.

Before that slip of the tongue registered in her brain, and she could say something along the lines of 'I like you...but' he rolled onto his back, taking her with him. She came to rest in the V of his legs, his erection already strength testing the limits of his zipper.

She ground her hips against him, and he swallowed the rising groan. Reaching for the hem of her shirt, he stripped it over her head and tossed it toward the balcony. Her panties followed. His clothes landed with a soft *fruuumph* on the floor.

As they resettled on the bed, she straddled him. Gil slid his hands up her muscular thighs, skimmed them over the flat of her abdomen, and up, up to the soft curve of her breasts. In the past, he'd always preferred big breasts, but the handful Tessa had was more than enough. A cup size larger and they'd unbalance her lithe, athletic body.

Her nipples were sensitive, the slightest tug of his thumb and forefinger and she arched, digging her pelvis into his. She reached between them and in one smooth movement, sheathed him.

So tight, so right.

Their eyes locked. They didn't have a condom.

"We could stop," he offered, however insincere it may have sounded.

She shook her head.

"I could pull out."

In answer, she started moving, and his eyes wanted to roll into the back of his head. He gripped her hips and stilled her. Gritting his teeth and blowing out several harsh pants as he tried to coax his control back from the brink.

"Out of breath already, special agent?" Tessa teased as she leaned in and nipped at his bottom lip. "We haven't even gotten started."

He wanted to wrap his arms around her shoulders and hug

her against him, but she had that naughty, wicked look in her eyes and he knew if he let go of her hips, it would be all over. "Gotta give me a sec."

He swallowed hard, and those luscious lips of hers curved into a grin. "I don't have a sec. I haven't had sex in eight days."

"It had been years before that, and you survived."

"I'd forgotten how good it can be." She started moving again, breaking the hold he had on her. "Thanks to you, now I remember."

Oh, hell. Why was he fighting? If he'd worn tighty-whities, he'd wave them in surrender.

Upping the pace, her hair went flying, her breasts bouncing as he met her stroke for deep stroke. She made that little moan in the back of her throat that he already knew meant she was close.

With an arm around her waist, he reversed their positions and linked their fingers beside her head. Sweat dampened hair stuck to her forehead and he couldn't remember when he'd ever seen her look so ravishing.

He kissed her, stroking her tongue with his in a steady, sensuous rhythm. Then came that little moan again, and Gil lifted his head and smiled. Tessa giggled.

His heart stuttered for a beat. "What's funny?"

"You," she said. "You look mighty smug."

"That's because I'm about to make you come."

"Oh, ye..." By the way her voice rose, he knew it was going to come out as a question, like 'oh, yeah?' but he changed the angle and upped the pace and the word caught in her throat. She swallowed hard and arched against him. "Oh, *yeah*. Right... right... there."

He felt the tingle at the base of his balls as she locked her ankles behind his ass driving him hard and deep. Her breaths huffed in and out in short, little pants, and her internal muscles started to squeeze around him.

He covered her mouth with his and swallowed the sound of her soft cries. She was on the verge, but he couldn't hold out any longer. He was amazed he'd been able to last as long as he had. Gil reached a hand between them to grab his cock, and pull out, but Tessa locked her legs even tighter.

If he didn't pull out now—

When he reached a hand back to unlock her ankles, she said, "No, don't."

He stilled, her eyes were half-mast when their eyes locked, but even in the dim light he could tell they were clear, focused.

"Come with me." She thrust against him.

His forehead dropped to her chest. She hadn't said she loved him, but with those three little words, she might as well have. They both knew the potential consequences. Her far more than him.

For her to accept that, to accept *him*, made his throat tight and heat bloom behind his sternum.

Raising a kid alone had to be a challenge. But if she did get pregnant, she wouldn't be raising *his* kid alone, or even raising Jack alone if he had his say.

He wrapped his arms around her, their skin slick as his strokes became quick and erratic. Her muscles clamped down around him, her mouth opened to cry out as the scuffle of boots on rocks beneath the balcony drifted through the ajar balcony door.

She must have heard it too, because at the last second, her teeth latched onto his shoulder, muffling her cry, but sending him over that jagged edge. He grunted into the crook of her neck as his balls squeezed, and his cock pulsed.

She relaxed beneath him as she came back to herself and brought a hand to cover her mouth and quiet her breathing. He breathed through his nose, but the way his lungs burned and his chest bellowed, he might as well be breathing through a straw.

More rocks shifted and ground beneath someone's boots. Gil didn't dare move. The smell of cigarettes drifted up. Menthol. One of the security guys must be catching a smoke.

As Gil went soft within her, the smell of smoke dissipated and the only sounds that came from outside were the far-off yips of coyotes on the hunt.

"That was close." Gil didn't dare talk above a whisper. He pressed a kiss to her forehead and rolled onto his back. "You okay?"

She turned her head, her eyes searching his face, for what he didn't know. Her features were soft, but there was a severity in her eyes that told him the gears were already grinding in her head. "Am I okay? Are you asking about Bradley, almost getting caught in flagrante delicto, or the unprotected sex?"

How could he not love this woman? After spending all that time undercover, he found her directness refreshing. Her unflinching ability to go straight to the heart of the matter, her unwillingness to waste time and play head games was refreshing —like a sprint through the sprinklers under a scorching summer sun.

He cupped her cheek and brushed a kiss against her lips as he poured himself into that briefest of touches. This wasn't about turning her on, this was about much more than that.

They say a picture is worth a thousand words. If that was the case, if that flutter of a camera's shutter can tell a short story, then an intimate touch, no matter how brief, could speak volumes for his heart.

"What was that for?"

"To let you know I'm here. That whatever this world throws at us, I'm not going anywhere." She covered his hand with hers, her eyes drifting closed as if she were absorbing his truth. "But to answer your question, yes. I mean all three. Or more if you have them."

"I think those three are enough to deal with right now. About Bradley, I like to think that good conquers evil and that he won't win, but this isn't a Marvel movie. In real life, the bad guys get away. All. The. Time. About almost getting caught, I'm not sure I've been that scared and aroused at the same time. I don't know how I feel about that. Still processing. About the unprotected sex..."

Her gaze slipped from his and focused somewhere behind him. His chest hitched as the air backed up in his lungs. He'd forgotten to breathe. Now he was afraid to. Afraid he might find out the reason she hadn't told him she loved him was that she didn't.

"I think..." She started, then stopped, then started again. "If I made a social media post about having unprotected sex, one side would be all *#itsyourbody,* and the other side would be all *#irresponsible.* It would get ugly. Name calling would ensue, threats would be made, and I would have to shut off the comments."

"You're not the type to let your private life go streaking through social media. I want to know what *you* think?"

She locked her eyes on his. The edge, and more noteworthy, the worry, was gone. "It's... it's more what I *know*. If we made a kid, no matter what happens between us, I know he—"

"Or she."

Tessa's lips curve up. "Or she will be loved beyond measure. I know that it may not always be easy. I know that we could be judged or ridiculed or whatever people think when they are on the outside looking in. The most important thing is, I *know* I made that decision with my eyes and my heart wide open, and I know, I *know*, that you'd never let me do this alone."

Gil smiled. "You bet your ass." He didn't dare hope that she became pregnant, but on some level he still did. He brushed the hair away from her face. "As much as I hate to say this, I really *should* go."

"You've said that already." She nodded, but then said, "Stay."

He couldn't risk staying the night, they both knew it, though neither one voiced it. They got cleaned up, and dressed and ended up back on the bed, leaning against the headboard, Gil's booted feet hanging over the side, Tessa curled up against him, his arm around her waist. His eyes drifted closed, but his body was buzzing from the sex, the adrenaline, from the lazy way her hand traced the tattoo on his forearm.

"When did you get this?"

"A while ago. Soon after I got out of the Corps."

"Is it some kind of memorial?"

His usual flip response, 'I thought it was badass,' didn't make it past his lips. He didn't want to push Tessa away, he wanted to bring her closer. The only way to do that was to let her in. "You know, I was at Healing Horses for a reason, right? It helps treat—"

"I know how they help veterans. I'm not trying to pry, I—"

"I know. It's okay. The Marines. My deployments. They changed me. Not all for the worse. Not all for the better. But I'd be lying if I said I didn't need the help the program offered. This..." He wiggled is forearm indicating the tattoo, "...was my primitive way of dealing with all that. I guess deep down I'd hoped it would keep the demons at bay."

"Does it work?" If she was skeptical or thought he was a complete nutter, her tone didn't show it.

"Better than I'd thought." He blew out a breath, and a soft, rueful chuckle escaped with it. "Not as much as I'd like."

She didn't offer any empty platitudes. She was a veteran herself with shit of her own she had to deal with, Gil had no doubt. In her peaceful silence, he heard her acceptance. His past was a part of him. It always would be. He would never forget, he didn't want to, but with Healing Horses, he'd come to learn that he could live with it.

———

SLOAN SHOWED TESSA INTO BRADLEY'S OFFICE EARLY THE NEXT morning. She gripped the extra-large cup of coffee in her hand and took a fortifying sip. If she was going to have to deal with Bradley while sleep deprived, then she was going to need a mega jolt of caffeine.

Bradley leaned against the front of his desk in a pair of dark slacks and a white dress shirt. The top button was undone, with the sleeves rolled up his forearms. He hadn't even shaved that morning. Practically slovenly for him. It was the first time since he'd been back in her life that he hadn't worn a suit or been impeccably groomed.

They were alone in his office. Tessa glanced at the open door of the empty safe. When she glanced back at Bradley, he had a smile on his face, heavy on the irony, even heavier on the smug asshole.

"How's Jack?" she asked.

"I have a job for you. A way for you to start earning my trust."

Trust. Hah. Tessa wanted to throw her head back and laugh. Bradley wouldn't know trust if it came up and bit him on the balls. "Answer my question. How's Jack?" She had no leverage, but that didn't stop her. Not where her son was concerned.

"He's fine. I'm sure." *I'm sure.* As in he hasn't even seen Jack with his own eyes to be positive.

"I want to see him."

"No problem. As soon as you complete the job."

"If I refuse?"

Bradley's eyes went dark, and his grin turned ugly as he teetered on the narrow edge between practiced civility and vicious bastard. "You seem to forget who's in charge here. You finish the job like a good girl, and I'll make sure you see your son."

His words fell miles short of reassuring. Something lurked beneath his words. She didn't know if it was insincerity or deceit or plain evil that she detected, but she didn't trust one word that he said, but for now, she had to play her part in the charade. Her and Gil's only advantage, was that Bradley didn't know she'd told Gil everything.

Crossing her arms over her chest, Tessa said, "What do you want me to do?"

A knock came at the door. "Come," Bradley said.

Tessa turned as Gil came in. With her back to Bradley, she raised her brows at him, asking the un-askable question—had he been able to contact Spinks?

Gil gave her a curt nod to answer her question. "Ms. Sterling."

He came to a stop a few feet away, his stance wide, clasping a wrist in front of him. "You asked to see me, sir?"

As good as Gil looked all decked out in a suit, with his jaw smooth and his hair short, she much preferred the brawny, bearded, badass version.

"I have a last-minute investor. Someone I couldn't refuse." Bradley looked at Tessa when he said, "I need you to fly to Montana to get the money." Then he looked at Gil and said, "And I need you to ensure the money gets back to me safely."

"Montana? Are you kidding me?" The pitch of Tessa's voice jumped an octave, maybe two.

Bradley raised a brow. It was no joke.

"You got a Blackhawk stashed away up here that I don't know about?" Somehow it wouldn't surprise her if he did.

"No. A Robinson 44."

Tessa laughed and didn't bother to hide her incredulity or her frustration. "I've never flown a Robinson. All helos aren't the same. You can't just switch from one to the other. It's not like going from a monster truck to a subcompact."

"I trust you can manage."

There's that word again. "You trying to get us killed?"

Instead of answering her question he said, "You leave from Turner field at nine-thirty."

Tessa glanced at the clock on the wall. "That's less than an hour from now."

Bradley crossed his arms over his chest. He wasn't going to give an inch. Not that she'd expected him to. "I suggest you hurry, then."

At Bradley's dismissal, Gil stepped aside, his hand outstretched toward the door. "After you, ma'am."

Tessa had started to turn, when Bradley said, "One more thing, Tessa." She stopped. Then to Gil he said, "If you'll wait in the hall."

"Sir." Gil flashed her a quick look then left them alone.

Bradley crowded her personal space. "I'll be monitoring your phone's GPS. You make a detour, I'm going to know about it."

Then he leaned in, his lips near her ear. His breath was hot on her skin, and she caught a whiff of the deep undertones of his cologne which in the past she'd always described as *earthy,* but now there was a pungency that she hadn't noticed before as if the scent wasn't effective enough to cover the stench of a rotten soul. "Don't let me down. Or your son."

With only minutes to spare, Tessa finished the preflight checklist and started the engine. Gil buckled his seat belt. It was the three-point kind, like in a car. It didn't feel like enough protection. He covered his ears with a headset. He adjusted the mic boom in front of his mouth. "This thing on?"

"Roger," Tessa said from the pilot's seat to his right. Now probably wasn't the time to tell her how hot he found her single-minded focus.

He glanced over at her again, at the four, fingertip-sized bruises on the side of her neck. The room had been too dark for him to notice them last night. Cold fury spit and sparked. This he couldn't keep to himself.

Without looking over at him, Tessa said, "Did you growl?"

"Martin do that to you." It came out sounding more like an accusation than a question.

Her hand went to her neck, rubbing at the marks as if she could wipe away the fact Gil had seen them. "Really, you're going to bring that up now?"

No better time. "You're right. Forget it." But there was no way Gil could forget it. "Why didn't you tell me?"

He had to consciously dig his heel into the deck of the cockpit to keep his knee from bouncing with nervous energy. "I'm going to kill him."

Tessa flicked a couple of switches. "That's why I didn't tell you."

Gil rubbed his hands down his thighs. She was right. He couldn't remember a time when he would have gladly broken cover multiple times, endangering the success of the operation and to take matters into his own hands. All the more reason to make sure Spinks accepted his letter of resignation when this was all over.

The tarmac was wet, and water dotted the windshield from the storm that had rolled through the area not long after he'd left Tessa's room the night before. Beyond the windshield now, nothing but blue skies.

"You got those GPS coordinate handy?" Tessa asked.

Gil called the numbers out to her as she punched them into the navigation system. Burton had given them the coordinates before they'd left. Their money stop was on a path to a local airport in Montana where they'd refuel and return to Martin's.

With Martin monitoring their GPS location, they had little room to deviate from their set course.

Tessa clicked over to the external mic and got clearance from the tower. Gil kept his tongue and let Tessa do her job. After takeoff, they rose higher and higher. The skies were clear, but turbulance near the airport tossed the small helo around much more than what he was used to with the Blackhawks and Chinooks.

They hit turbulence and must have dropped fifty feet. Gil's stomach lodged in his windpipe, and he had to consciously loosen his grip on the door handle before he ripped it clean off.

When they reached their cruising altitude and settled into their two-hour flight, Tessa rolled her shoulders and resettled her grip on the stick between her legs.

"How's it feel?" Gil asked.

"Light. Maneuverable. Like I've lost a hundred pounds and went out for a jog. But I miss my bird. This thing feels as delicate as a dandelion. One massive gust and it'll disintegrate around us."

"That's reassuring."

Through the headset, Tessa's warm chuckle settled in his brain. On the one hand, it was an odd feeling as if she were in his head, but then again, she was already in his heart.

She glanced over at him. Despite what she'd said, there was a fire in her eyes. She liked the challenge—and danger—of flying a new helo.

"What did Spinks say when you contacted him?"

"Spinks couldn't say much. All the code does is tell him I'm compromised and that I'll get in touch when I can. If Burton hadn't waited at the airport for us to take off, we might have been able to use one of the phones at the security desk."

"I'm sure that's why we had the escort. You think Bradley told Burton you're ATF?"

Gil shook his head, though her focus was on the sky ahead of him and she couldn't see it. "He didn't treat me any different. No animosity. With him, what you see is what you get. I don't think he's a good enough actor to fake it."

Below them, the ground flew by, ribbons of back roads, foothills building and building higher until they crashed into the Rockies. This late in the summer, only the highest peaks had snow on them. In a field below, a herd of horses raced along the fence line.

The air smoothed out, and Gil's stomach dropped back into his abdomen. They approached a single runway airfield, and Tessa got clearance to fly through. Shortly past the airport, she said, "Ohmygod."

Instinctively, Gil gripped the door handle and glanced around them expecting to see another helo or plane headed straight for them. But there was nothing. "What? What?"

"I know how we can get in touch with Spinks."

———

As Tessa piloted the '44 through skies so clear and blue that it made a pilot never want to land, she skimmed the eastern edge of the Rockies as they flew over Yellowstone Park. She didn't know why she hadn't thought of how to contact Spinks sooner. She blamed her brain fart on trying to get the unfamiliar helo off the ground without getting them killed.

"We get a tower to patch us through to the Bison County Sheriff's Department," Tessa said. "Get them to contact Spinks.

He can direct us to a radio channel with light traffic. It will be an open frequency, anybody could overhear, but there's likely little chance Bradley is monitoring radio frequencies."

"Let's do it."

It took longer than Gil thought it would, but eventually, Spinks came over the radio and gave them a new radio frequency to switch to. They kept the conversation to the bare minimum, giving Spinks the GPS coordinates Burton had given them. Spinks was going to try to get the local sheriff's department to monitor the area, but he couldn't make any promises.

Gil told Spinks that he suspected the shipment would be moved shortly after Martin got the money from the last investor. He told him about the SAM's, and about the rest of the arsenal, all in crates newly spray painted and marked as relief supplies. He'd also told Spinks about Jack.

"Tell me you guys have a plan to move in," Gil said. "We can't take a chance these weapons get in criminal hands, over."

The radio hissed and popped and when Gil was about to ask Tessa if they'd lost contact, Spinks said, "About that..."

Fuck a duck. Gil didn't speak because he didn't want to jamb Spinks up, but he had a lot to say. Almost none of it could be reported over an open channel.

"This is out of my hands. Orders from high, high, above. At this point, we're relegated to overwatch at the mine only. The CIA's involved on the foreign end. They want to monitor the shipment. Catch the buyers on the other side. You copy?"

"I've got a bad feeling about this, over."

"Anything actionable, or just your gut?"

"My gut, at this point."

"We'll be monitoring this frequency," Spinks said. "Let us know if anything changes."

"Copy, that. Out."

Tessa switched back to their internal mic and glanced over at him. "You've got that hinky feeling too?"

"Man, it's gnawing on my gut like a goddamn starving wharf rat. I'll be damned if I know what it is, though."

They flew for several minutes with nothing but the muffled sound of the wind and rotors to keep them company. "I don't get it," Gil said, trying to work through his thought process out loud. "If Martin has already purchased all the weapons, why is he taking more money now?"

"Besides the fact that he's greedy?"

Gil huffed out a laugh. "Yeah, besides that."

"Before we left, Bradley said this was my opportunity to earn his trust. But it feels more like I'm the pesky little kid sent away to play video games so mom and dad can get some real work done."

"You think this might be Martin's way of getting us out of his hair?"

"Better than killing us." There was humor in Tessa's words, but it sounded forced.

"If the choice is a four or five-hour round-trip flight, or getting my ass shot, I'm taking the flight."

"What do you think the chances are that Bradley is taking this opportunity to get the shipment out without us underfoot?"

"Better than house odds."

After a short discussion, they hailed Spinks on the radio and filled him in on their concerns. Spinks promised to update the team they'd sent out to monitor the mine.

The next hour passed by in near silence, besides the *whomp whomp* of the rotor blades, and the whine of the engine. Gil felt like a hamster on a wheel, and even though they thought they now were on a wild goose chase, that gnawing in his gut didn't go away, in fact, the closer they got to their destination, it grew from a rat to a beaver.

"Something's still not right," Tessa said.

They were the first words she'd spoken in a long while. Gil glanced over at her, her grip on the stick so tight her knuckles blanched, which said something about the woman who usually flew controlled and loose, like the helo was a natural extension of her body.

Gil didn't disagree. Odd that she'd repeat it without a new angle on the situation. "Why do you say that?"

Instead of answering, she asked her own question. "What do you see down there?"

"Trees. Trees. More trees. Rocks. Mountains."

"Exactly."

"I'm not following."

"There's nothing out here beside mountain goats and bear shit. I don't even remember the last time I saw a paved road. The middle of nowhere is more populated than this."

"We're five miles out from the meetup, and another twenty from our fuel stop. There's no telling –"

Gil saw a bright flash, and before his brain could register a *what the fuck?*, Tessa hollered, "Hang on!"

Tessa banked the helo hard left and dove straight for the ground. Gil's body smashed against the seatbelt, a grunt escaping as the straps dug into his shoulder and across his hips. Where was that five-point harness when you needed it?

Adrenaline flooded his system demanding that he do something. *Anything.* His instinct was to grab the cyclic between his legs, but he didn't know the first thing about flying a helicopter. This wasn't his world, it was Tessa's, and as the ground rushed up, the trees and the rocks got more substantial, the last thing Tessa needed was him distracting her with questions.

Then he heard it, that all too familiar *thap, thap, thap, thap,* of bullets shredding metal.

"Motherfuckers." Tessa pulled out of the dive and zig-zagged behind a ridge. "Someone's shooting at us."

"So much for Martin not wanting us dead," Gil deadpanned.

A fireball erupted behind them, rocks exploded, and trees burst into flames, sending bits of shrapnel in all directions, raining flaming debris. The windshield cracked, and Tessa muttered another curse. She yanked the cyclic back as far as it would go, and the helo's nose pointed at the sky as they climbed higher and higher.

"Anti-tank?"

"Best guess. Been on the receiving end of one of those more than I would have liked." There was little doubt in Tessa's voice. "If it had been a guided missile, we wouldn't be here." She'd be the one to know. The helo shook and shuddered, but they cleared the blast zone. A red light on the panel blinked on, then another, as alarm bells blared.

16

Tessa didn't have to look down at the cockpit control panel to know they were screwed. Well and truly. She could smell oil burning, and from the spongy way the pedals felt, it would be a close contest between what failed next, the engine or the rudder control.

She had seconds to get their bird down before shit got real.

Tessa didn't even have time to send out a mayday. Smoke started filling the cockpit. She coughed as she shoved down on the collective and banked for a tiny scrap of bare ground among a forest of tall pines. Having not flown a Robinson before, she didn't have a good feel for her rotor clearance, but it was going to be tight, and the downdrafts on the backside of the ridge would surely be a bitch.

At least no one was shooting at them anymore.

Sweat dripped down her back and into her eyes as the Robinson bucked and yawed. When their altitude reached twenty-five feet, she lost all rudder control and started to spin, then the downdraft caught the weakened bird in its meaty grip and slammed them into the ground.

The rotors chewed through rocks and tree limbs, the

sheering of metal deafening. The right side of her head ricocheted off the door, and her world went black.

"Tessa. *Tessa.* Wake up." Gil patted her cheek, which hurt like hell, but her mouth refused to work to tell him to knock it off.

She managed a grunt, but opening her eyes seemed an impossibility. Then Gil opened one of her eyes for her, and she yanked her head away from the brightness. The motion made her head spin faster than the rotors had been. Finally, she managed to squint up at him.

It was quiet. Very, very, quiet.

The engine had stalled, and she could hear the ticking of the hot metal as it cooled, the call of a bird in a tree, the buzz of a fly near her ear.

The smell of smoke and avgas mixed as the fuel leaked from the tank or a split in a line. They had to get out of there, but her arms felt thick and too unwieldy to move.

"There you are," Gil said. "Wake up, sleepy head, we gotta get the hell outta here."

His hands roamed her body. "Where are you hurt?"

She grimaced when his hand pressed on the goose egg on the side of her head. The lower half of her right leg felt like it was on fire, but before she could get her voice, Gil's hand ran down her leg.

Pulses of pain licked up her leg, shot up her spine, and bombarded her brain. She screamed and pounded her head on the back of her seat to distract herself or knock herself out. At that point, she didn't care which.

"Whoa, whoa, whoa, hang tight," Gil said, clasping the sides of her head to keep her from moving. "We've got a situation."

The smoke got thicker and blacker, rolling out the front of the cockpit where the windshield used to be. The soot coated the back of Tessa's throat and seized her lungs. Her diaphragm spasmed and a coughing fit wracked her body. "G-get out."

"That's the plan," Gil said, his voice as thick as the smoke. "But first we gotta get your leg clear. There's a metal rod sticking through your right calf."

"Gil..." They didn't have that kind of time. The helo could explode at any second. Gil had time to get clear if he ran. Now. "*Gil...*"

"Hang on."

He stripped off his belt. Tessa grabbed the front of his shirt and gave him a shake. "Go. That's an order."

"Not a chance." His face was grim but determined.

He ran his belt below her knee and yanked it tight. Then he reached down by her leg and said, "On the count of three, ready?" Gil didn't give her the chance to nod before he started counting. "One—"

Pain soared up her leg. She'd expected him to pull the rod out on the count of two, but he didn't even give her that. She opened her mouth to scream, then the blackness blindsided her.

She woke to the sound of an explosion, and her body thrown down on a bed of rocks. Gil landed on top of her like her own personal blood and bone shield. She couldn't breathe, and it wasn't from the smoke.

She shoved at his chest. "Gil, you okay?"

He groaned and shifted, bracing his weight on his arms as he looked down at her. There was a cut over his left eye, and an abrasion scoring his left cheek. "All I can say is that, after your ex, a relationship with me looks like a no-brainer."

"You could say that again." Tessa laughed. It was either that or cry, and she didn't have time for that. Her head hurt, her ears rang, and her world got a little fuzzy again. She swiped at the moisture on her cheek.

Gil stared at her like she was something beautiful and rare, like the Hope diamond and the Star of India combined. How could he look at her like that when he'd almost died because of her? "I told you to go."

"I don't take orders from you."

Tessa scowled. "Because I'm a woman?"

"Because the last time I checked, you were on suspension, and even if you hadn't been, you're not even in my chain of command."

She reached a hand behind his neck and brought his lips to hers. "Lucky for me, then."

Gil glanced over at the burning wreckage and the black cloud blooming higher and higher as more and more trees caught fire. The summer had been exceedingly dry, the whole forest was like a box of TNT left in in the hands of a clumsy kid with a match fetish.

"We need to get downwind and find a clearing in case a search and rescue is sent in."

"What about those guys who were shooting at us?"

"It's a long hike around that ridge to the crash site. I'm hoping they're too unmotivated to come around and make sure we're dead. With a smoke plume that size, hopefully, one of the fire watch towers will see it and call it in. But first, we need to wrap that leg. We can't keep the tourniquet on for too long."

With a hand, Gil helped her sit. He stripped off his tie and dress shirt and used his pocket knife to cut it into thin strips. A bruise was blooming over his left shoulder, but otherwise, he seemed in good shape for surviving a crash. They were both damn lucky.

He bound the wound tightly, and she tried not to scream like a two-year-old who'd lost her favorite binky. She was mostly successful, but she'd be lying if she didn't say it hurt like a bitch. That adrenaline dump was no longer dulling her pain. The only thing the adrenaline was doing was making her hands shake, and her teeth rattle.

When he'd finished binding his shirt to her leg with his tie, he said, "Okay, loosen the belt. Slowly."

Her lower leg was already numb from the tourniquet. She loosened the belt a little at a time. The blood flowed in and the wound pulsed with every rapid beat of her heart. Then came the pins and needles as her nerves started regaining function.

"How's it look?" Tessa said, almost afraid to look down. It wasn't that the sight of blood bothered her, it was the thought that if they couldn't control the bleeding, they would have to reapply the tourniquet that scared her. The likelihood of a rescue anytime soon was slim, and you couldn't keep a tourniquet on too long without risking permanent damage.

A pregnancy would only keep her out of the sky for a short period of time. If she lost her right leg... she couldn't even think about that.

"Seems to be holding." They were close enough to the crash site that ash and embers rained all around them. Gil glanced up at the ridge nearby ridge. "You up for a stroll?"

She followed his gaze. The climb would be steep, and with the number of rocks and the stretch of scree field, damn slippery as well. As much as she wanted to tell him to go without her, it was too dangerous to stay. "Thought you'd never ask."

Gil stood and gave her a hand up. Gingerly, she added weight to her leg. It hurt. Damn, it hurt. Fortunately, no bones were broken. If they took it slow, she could do it.

It took them about twenty hours to make the ridge. Okay. Maybe that was an exaggeration since if she used the movement of the sun as a guide, it was probably no more than an hour. Her throat was so dry it made a clicking sound every time she swallowed, and her muscles ached like she'd gone on a twenty-klick ruck march, and she didn't even want to think about her right calf. They weren't on speaking terms anymore.

Her breathing came fast, and her heart thumped a hard,

steady rhythm in her chest. She plopped down on a rock below the top of the ridge.

"Wait here," Gil said, "I'm going to make sure no one's coming around on foot." He wasn't going to get an argument from her. "You going to be okay here?"

"As long as I don't have to move from my favorite rock, I'm good. I've gotten very attached to him."

Her forehead was grimy and sweat-stained. It didn't keep Gil from pressing a kiss there. If she'd had any doubts that his profession of love was real, she didn't anymore. "Holler if you need me. I'll check your leg when I get back."

GIL HID BEHIND A LARGE BOULDER AT THE TOP OF THE RIDGE. Down below he had a good view of the crash site and the growing fire. With the mild breeze, it wasn't spreading as fast as he'd feared it would, considering the dry conditions.

After fifteen to twenty minutes, he relaxed a fraction, having seen no movement down below from the shooters. They had to have known a fire like that would attract first responders, and they'd beat tracks back to whatever rock they'd crawled out from under.

The soreness had already started to settle into his body as he climbed down to Tessa. Every muscle ached from the impact, and his ears rang as if he'd stood next to the speakers at a heavy metal concert all night.

When he got to Tessa, she was laid out on a flat rock, her right leg propped and raised high against another rock. He jumped down beside her, landing harder than he should have, jarring his already battered body.

"How are you feeling?" he asked.

She had her arm flung over her eyes, and she didn't bother

moving it. "Like my helo crashed and someone pulled a rod out of my leg on the count of one instead of three." Her voice was thick with accusation, and a smattering of dry humor.

"I figured you knew I would pull on two, so…" He let the rest of his sentence drift off, and he shrugged, even though she couldn't see it. "Thought it might hurt less if—"

"It didn't." She dropped her arm and propped herself up on her elbows. "See anybody?"

"No activity. Also, no planes or helos or any other kind of help either. We're pretty remote. We could be here a while."

"A least we have a good fire to keep us warm."

He barked out a laugh and sat down, placing her injured leg over his lap. "You're incredible, you know that?"

Her smile fell flat before it went anywhere close to her eyes. "Not incredible enough to have figured out Bradley was trying to get rid of us permanently and not temporarily."

"Hey, hey, now." Gil made sure the bandage wasn't too tight. There was some fresh blood on the bandage, though the bleeding was well controlled. "No one saw that coming. I didn't think he would be bold enough—"

"Or dumb enough—"

"Or dumb enough," he allowed, "to try that. Martin could feel the noose tightening, he was getting desperate and—"

"What about Jack? Do you think—" Tessa's voice cracked, and Gil just shook his head because the sudden knot in his throat paralyzed his vocal cords.

Gil swallowed hard. "There's a big difference between getting us out of the way and hurting Jack. He's a kid. *Martin's* kid. No matter how indifferent he comes across, I agree with what you said, I don't think he would hurt him. This," he waved his hand in the general direction of the crash, "doesn't change that." At least he hoped like hell it didn't.

For Tessa's sake.

For his sake.

For Jack's.

Another thirty or forty minutes passed before the first spotter plane flew over the fire. Another thirty after that before the first aerial drop of fire retardant. Another hour at least before a rescue helicopter spotted Gil standing on the ridge. A basket was dropped, and they were hoisted up one at a time.

In the air, the team attended to Tessa's leg and even applied a couple of steri-strips to the cut along Gil's left eyebrow. Someone came up with an extra T-shirt and offered it to him. When they landed, one of the medics let Gil borrow his cell phone, and he called Spinks.

"You sure you're both okay?" Spinks asked after Gil had relayed the events of the crash.

"We'll live." But right then, Gil was more concerned about Jack than themselves. "Can you put some agents on the house?"

"I'll do what I can. We're stretched thin. The shipment went out by truck not train like we'd anticipated. They scattered on the roadways, we've already lost sight of two of them. Everyone is scrambling."

"You gotta get us back there. Send a plane or a helo—"

"I can't spare the manpower right now. You'll have to manage on your end."

"That's at least a six or seven-hour drive, we don't—"

"I gotta go, the head of the CIA's on the line," Spinks said. "Let me know when you get here."

Gil reared his arm back, but the medic caught his wrist before he could throw the phone. "Hey, there buddy."

Gil let the phone get stripped out of his hand. "Sorry." He was too caught up in his own problems to sound sincere. He'd lost his wallet along the way. They couldn't rent a car if they wanted to. "Any chance your crew could get us back to Murdock?"

"Murdock?" The young medic squinted as if trying to place where Murdock was.

"Wyoming," Tessa said. "Outside Alpine. It's urgent."

"I'll talk to the chief, but no promises."

———

GETTING BACK TO MURDOCK WAS SOME TWISTED TAKE ON *PLANES, Trains, and Automobiles*. In the end, it took four hours, one search and rescue helo, one single prop plane, and Boomer meeting her and Gil at the Murdock airport with a truck to get close to where they needed to be.

Boomer climbed out of the truck's cab. Followed by Hank, who was on the phone trying to placate Mac, unsuccessfully. Tessa could hear Mac cussing over the phone. From what Boomer said, Hank had practically had to tie Mac to a tree to keep her from coming along.

At the far end of the runway, one of the hanger doors opened, and a six-seater commuter plane appeared.

"We're here," Hank said into the phone. "I don't like it any more than you. If it wasn't for the kid, there's no one I'd rather have here with me." He was quiet for a minute as Mac spoke. Though Tessa couldn't make out the words, Mac must have calmed down considerably because Tessa couldn't hear her anymore. "Will do. We gotta go, Army. I'll keep you updated."

Army. Even though Mac was a Marine through and through, Sidney had once told Tessa how Hank's term of endearment had stuck. He pocketed the phone and pulled Tessa in for a quick hug and held his hand out to Gil.

"What do you need us to do." Boomer was decked out in jeans and boots, but she didn't miss the holstered Glock at his side. Hank had come similarly armed as well.

"Please tell me you've got a couple of spares." Gil pointed to the guns.

"We're going to have to make do with these for side arms," Boomer said, "Though Hank's got a .30-06, hanging in the truck."

"What's the plan?" This from Hank.

"Bradley has been keeping Jack locked in his room. With the shipment going out today, I'm hoping he left him there to keep him out of the way," Tessa said.

"Most of his men will likely be with the shipment," Gil said. "There should be minimal security at the house. But I don't want to tip our hand by driving right up. There's an old ranch road on the west side of the property. We can get within about a mile of the house and we'll have to hike in from there."

Boomer turned to Tessa. "Your leg up for that."

She appreciated that he didn't try to talk her out of going. It would be wasted breath anyway. She felt every heartbeat in her leg. Every step felt like some psycho was jabbing a stake through the muscle and enjoying every second of it. The thought of walking again made her wince with pain. "Not a problem."

"Look, if you need—" Tessa leveled a hard stare that shut Hank up.

"What I *need* is my son."

"Roger that," Boomer said.

They piled back into the truck. Gil grabbed the Remington 700 from the rifle rack above the rear seats and made sure it was loaded and a round was chambered. They peeled out of the airport and Boomer stomped on the gas as they raced toward Bradley's mansion.

"Have you called your ex?" Hank asked as they cleared the airport property.

"He thinks we're dead," Tessa said. "I think that gives us an advantage."

Boomer said, "Unless Jack's not at the house."

"According to Spinks, no one has come or gone from the house since we told him about Jack and they put a guy on surveillance."

"But how much time had elapsed since you left this morning to the time Spinks had a man on location?"

Tessa thought about it. Before she could say anything, Gil said, "Too long." His voice was grim, and Tessa's heart tumbled. There was a good chance Jack wasn't even at the house anymore.

Hank reached into his pocket and handed Tessa his phone. "Try calling him. Knowing you guys were onto him, Martin would have to be a special kind of idiot to stay at the house once the shipment has gone out."

Tessa took the phone and punched in Bradley's number. Her finger hovered over the green call button, then she pressed it. The phone picked up on the fourth ring."

"Martin." Clip and short, Bradley sounded all business. With her using Hank's phone, he wouldn't have recognized the number.

In the background, she heard Jack's voice. Tessa swallowed hard and held a hand over her sternum to keep her heart from kicking through her chest. She couldn't make out what her son was saying, but at least he didn't sound distressed. More importantly, he was alive.

"Hello?" Bradley said.

The first thing to tumble out of her mouth was, "You tried to have me killed."

There was a beat of silence on the other end. She might have heard a soft gasp, but that might have been wishful thinking on her part.

"You always were resourceful," Bradley said, "I'll give you that."

The unmistakable chug of a propeller engine spooling up came over the line. "Where are you?"

Then the engine noise got muffled, and Bradley said, "Sit down and buckle up." He wasn't talking to her.

She glanced behind them at the airport. It wasn't the closest airfield to Bradley's house, that had been the one she and Gil had flown out of, but this one wasn't that much farther.

She leaned forward and tapped Boomer's shoulder and made a turn-around motion with her index finger and pointed back at the airport.

Boomer stomped on the brakes and pulled a U-ey. The right side of her head bumped the window, and her brain sloshed around in her skull. She tried hard to ignore the wave of nausea and the stars that danced in her peripheral vision.

If Bradley wasn't at the Murdock airport, they wouldn't be too far behind schedule, but if she was right...

In her calmest, most reasonable voice she said, "Whatever you're doing you need to stop. You need to turn yourself in."

Never in her wildest dreams did she think Bradley would give up. He wasn't that kind of man. That type of man didn't become a success in his field the way Bradley had even if that field was illegal. The climb to the top must be grueling and brutal. "It's not too late to do the right thing."

Bradley laughed on the other end. It sounded genuine. "I see you've been polishing up that halo. You would have been a great asset, but your father was right to have kept you out of the family business. You don't have the heart for it."

Wait. *What?* "What are you talking about?" Her words came out so soft, she repeated herself to make sure she was heard.

"Nothing. It's time for me to go. Seeing you again was good."

No. No. No, no, no. Tessa had to keep Bradley on the line.

Boomer made a sharp left turn and somehow managed to keep all four wheels of the trucks on the ground, though the tires slid and there was probably a long skid mark on the asphalt behind them. He accelerated for one of the utility gates, a chain held the two sides together.

"Hang on." Gil braced his arms on the seat in front of him. Tessa did the same. They busted through the gate, aluminum poles and chain link went flying.

Maybe if she appealed to Bradley's practical side. "Look, I don't care what you've done, or where you go, just leave Jack. He's only going to slow you down."

Tessa's mind raced. What else could she say that would make Bradley change his mind?

"There." Hank pointed to a single prop plane that had turned and lined up on the runway.

"Is that you sweetheart?" Bradley's voice was calm. Too calm. "Valiant try, but you're too late."

Between the roar of blood behind her eardrums and the whine of the plane's engines revving up and filtering over the line, Tessa almost couldn't hear Bradley.

With Boomer already racing for the runway, Tessa pointed at the plane. All she could manage was a strangled, "It's him. Hurry."

The wheels of the plane started rolling, and Boomer gunned the gas. The truck accelerated, throwing Tessa back against the seat. They bounced in the seats as Boomer cut through the grass between runways on an intercept course with the plane. Then Boomer sped the truck ahead of the plane and slid to a stop mid-runway.

The plane was a four-seater. It didn't need that much runway. By the way the aircraft was barreling down on them, it was either going to barely clear them, or run right through them, the propellers slicing and dicing as they went.

"Bradley, Bradley, stop. This is insane, this—"

"He's slowing," Hank said.

The plane's brakes kicked in, the tires locked and skidded. The stench of smoke and burning rubber filled the air.

"He can't stop in time," Gil said.

Boomer slammed the truck into drive, but at the last second, the pilot turned. The plane bounced through the grass and came to rest parallel to the perimeter fence, the edge of its left wing brushing the chain link.

The four of them scrambled out of the truck and ran over to the plane. With Hank's phone, Tessa tried calling Spinks, but when she couldn't get through, she hung up and dialed 911.

Boomer, Hank, and Gil spread out, their guns pointed at the plane. Boomer gestured at the pilot, with a cutting motion across his throat and the pilot cut the engine. The noise died as well as the hot blast from the prop wash.

Tessa identified herself and gave her location to the 911 operator. The plane's passenger door opened. Jack stood in the entrance, Bradley hunched down behind him, one hand on Jack's shoulder the other holding a gun.

With Bradley using Jack as a shield, Hank and Boomer lowered their weapons. With the rifle, Gil shifted, for a better angle, Tessa assumed. He knelt and took careful aim at Bradley.

The thought of her son being at the other end of a rifle should have terrified her, but when the man with his finger on the trigger was Gil, all she had was faith. Pure and blind. There was nothing else.

"Hang up the phone, Tessa," Bradley said. His voice came out even as if he'd told her to change the channel on the TV, and not as if he was cornered and running out of viable options.

"Mom?" Jack's voice wavered, but she had to hand it to her kid for keeping his cool.

"Don't move, baby." Tessa raised her hands, the phone high as she used exaggerated movements to disconnect the call and lay the phone on the ground. "Every thing's going to be okay."

Injecting as much authority as she could, Tessa said, "The sheriff is on the way. Give me Jack, and you can be gone before they get here."

"You must think I'm stupid." The tension in Bradley's voice rose as sirens wailed in the distance.

Lights flashed as airport security sped around the far hanger in their utility vehicle.

Bradley raised his gun, level with Jack's chest. "You need to get them to back off. Right the fuck now."

"Hold on," Gil said to Bradley, "No need to get excited."

Hank turned to deal with security while Tessa did her best to talk some sense into her ex. Every fiber, every cell of her being wanted to scream at Jack to run.

"Tick tock, Martin," Gil said. "Give us the kid, and we'll let you go. You have our word."

How Gil sounded calm and collected, Tessa would never know. After aiming the rifle for so long, it must feel like it weighed a hundred pounds, but Gil's aim was rock solid, the end of the barrel perfectly still.

There came a ruckus behind them as airport security blew past Hank. Bradley raised the gun and put it to Jack's temple. Jack shook, Bradley's hand shook, and Tessa's knees almost gave out.

"Whoa, whoa, whoa," Gil stood, holding the rifle and his other arm to the side. "Everybody calm the fuck down."

Over his shoulder, Gil identified himself and told the airport security to back off. Gil laid the rifle on the ground and to Bradley, said, "Point that thing at me."

"Gil, no." Tessa thought she spoke out loud, but Gil didn't respond, so she wasn't sure.

"At me, Martin. At my head. Come on." Gil eased forward as he spoke. "I'm a big, fat target at this distance, you can't miss."

Tessa saw the indecision on Bradley's face.

"Do it," Gil ordered. "Do it now."

Bradley held Jack tighter against his body, but he shifted his aim from Jack's head to Gil's.

"That's it," Gil said. "I'm the one you want. I'm the one fucking this up for you. You want to take it out on somebody, you take it out on me, not the kid."

A tsunami of relief washed over Tessa at the same time guilt swamped her. Bradley adjusted his finger on the trigger, his hand shaking as no doubt the combination of stress, adrenaline, and muscle fatigue worked against him.

Tessa didn't dare move, didn't dare speak. One flinch, one false move, and Gil would be dead.

Compared to your ex, a relationship with me looks like a no-brainer.

Gil's words flashed in her head, as he took one cautious step toward the plane and then another. The truth of those words hitting her psyche hard enough to knock the breath from her lungs and all her previous reservations from her head.

This man, this big, bold, brave man was her and Jack's everything. Risking his life for her son's. He was the definition of selfless, the spitting image of integrity, the perfect picture of what a man should be.

It didn't come as a revelation that she loved him. Though she hadn't admitted it to herself, her heart, her body had known all along. It had just taken her brain some time to catch up.

The sirens were getting louder, but Bradley might still be able to get away if he hurried.

Gil eased closer and closer, his hands raised by his head, as he said, "Take me. I'm the one you want, Martin. Easy now. Easy." Though Gil's words were soothing, Tessa noticed the subtle way Gil's body tensed, reminding her of a panther about to pounce. Jack's eyes went to Gil, and in Tessa's peripheral vision, Boomer shifted.

"They're here," Hank said.

Bradley's focus shifted to the airport entrance. Sirens blared, tires squealed, and the full force of the Bison county sheriff's department bore down on them.

Bradley froze.

Gil dove.

Tessa screamed.

Bradley and Boomer fired.

———

THE SOUND OF THE SHOT DIDN'T EVEN REGISTER, AND GIL BARELY felt the bullet rip through his shoulder as he yanked Jack from the plane by the ankle, tucked him in his arms, and ducked and rolled under the plane.

They came to a stop against the fence, while the sheriff's deputies leapt from their vehicles and charged the plane. Chaos surrounded them. Shouting, yelling, sirens howling.

But in the shadow on the far side of the plane, Gil and Jack were sheltered. Gil came to rest on his back, Jack tight in his arms against his chest.

He loosened his grip and held Jack at arm's length. Gil grunted at the movement as the adrenaline started to wear off and the searing pain started taking its place. "You okay, Squirt?"

Jack nodded. Grass clippings fell out of the kid's hair, and his body shook worse than palm fronds during a Florida hurricane. But there were no tears. The kid was too much like his mother for that.

Jack scrambled off Gil and sat in the grass. "You're bleeding." There was no panic in his voice. Again, so much like his mother.

"It's not as serious as it looks." Gil should know. It was close to where the last bullet had struck him. He took in a measured breath. At least this one had only hit meat instead of lungs.

He couldn't turn his resignation papers in fast enough.

"Does it hurt? Billy's dad was shot in the leg one time while he was hunting, and he said bullets hurt like a b—"

"Watch your mouth," Gil said, though he couldn't keep the grin off his face.

"Biscuit," Jack said. "I was going to say biscuit. You thought I was going to say bitch." Jack slapped a hand over his mouth before Gil could. "Don't tell Mom I said that."

"Don't tell me you said what?"

"Mom!"

Jack jumped to his feet, and Tessa scooped him up in her arms. He wrapped his skinny legs around her waist as she held him extra, extra tight.

"Mom, I can't breathe."

Gil propped himself up against the fence and spared a glance at his shoulder. The bullet had left behind a hole and a trail of blood in the borrowed T-shirt.

Tessa sank to the ground beside him, loosening her hold on her son enough to keep him from turning blue. She ran her hands all over Jack, looking for signs of injury.

Jack giggled and squirmed. "Stop, that tickles."

"Don't move, I want to make sure you're okay."

"I'm fine. Mr. Gil's not."

Tessa shot a look at Gil. "Why didn't you say something?"

"I'm okay. Seeing the two of you together is the best medicine." Though he'd be lying if he said morphine wouldn't feel good right about then.

Tessa leaned over and pressed a kiss against his lips. "My hero," she teased, though as soon as she said it, her eyes welled, and she blinked back the tears.

Gil shifted and flashed Tessa a smile, though the painful movement made it come out more like a grimace. "Does that mean I get a reward?"

Tessa's eyes went dark and mischievous, but before she could say anything, Jack piped in. "Of course, you do. When I'm good, I get something extra special."

Gil didn't take his eyes off hers when he said, "Oh, little man, I'm counting on it."

Tessa smiled. Full of relief, gratitude, and sinful promise.

Boomer came around the nose of the plane. "Hey, little man," he said to Jack, "Is this a private party or can anyone join in?"

Gil shifted, his shoulder pounded, and he grunted against the waves of pain that radiated up and down his arm.

"Whoa," Boomer said when he got a look at his shoulder. "I think we should take this little party over to the ambulance, let the EMTs take a look at that."

"Come on, Jack," Tessa said.

Boomer reached down and locked wrists with Gil's uninjured arm and helped him up. A wave of dizziness made Gil take a stutter step to catch himself.

"You good?" Boomer asked.

Gil leaned his uninjured shoulder against the plane until the world righted itself. "Yeah, I'm good."

Twenty minutes later, Gil sat on a stretcher in the back of the ambulance, an IV in his arm and his shoulder temporarily bandaged until he could get to the hospital. His condition wasn't critical, and since he was friendly with the EMTs, he managed to talk them into letting him stay on scene until they'd gotten Martin cuffed and stuffed into the back of a cruiser and the deputies could get his statement.

It would all be in a report to Spinks later, but the sheriff's boys needed to do their jobs and truth be told, he wasn't going anywhere until Tessa had her leg evaluated.

At some point, Spinks had shown up. He must have finished

with Boomer and Hank because he headed over toward Gil, Tessa hobbling along at the SAC's side.

"Make room," Spinks said as he handed Tessa up into the ambulance.

Gil scooted over giving Tessa room to sit on the end of the stretcher. The EMT put on a fresh pair of gloves and used bandage scissors to slice the leg of her jeans to expose her wound.

"They're taking care of my leg," Tessa said to Spinks, "now tell me what's going on with the rest of the shipment."

"We believe all trucks are accounted for. They're being followed. Right now, it looks like they'll converge somewhere on the coast in the Pacific Northwest. Quincy or Everett, Washington, Massey thinks."

Tessa hissed in a breath. Her voice tentative when she said, "Quincy?"

Spinks' eyes narrowed. "Yeah, why?"

"Bradley said—" Tessa hissed again, but it had nothing to do with a revelation and everything to do with the disinfectant the EMT was applying to her calf.

"Sorry," the EMT said. "I'm almost done."

Tessa closed her eyes and breathed through her mouth a couple times, then continued. "Bradley said something about my father keeping me out of the family business."

Spinks crossed his arms over his chest. His hair was a mess, he had double bags under his eyes, and by his sour expression, he was a couple quarts low on caffeine. "What the hell does that mean?"

"My father owns a lot of businesses. A little of this. A little of that all over the world. But he specializes in logistics. That's—"

"I know what logistics is. He specializes in getting things to people who need them."

Tessa snatched her leg back from the EMT. "Okay, you're

done."

"But I—"

"No more," she said.

"I could give you something for the pain—"

"*Not now.*" Tessa pressed the heels of her hands to her temples. "Sorry, I know you're doing your job. Give us a minute, will you?"

By the strain on her face, she needed the meds as much as Gil did, but he knew she would refuse, like he had. Pain management could wait. Right now, they needed to have their minds clear. Spinks needed their help. The EMT peeled his gloves off and backed away. "I'll give you five minutes, then I'm taking both of you in. With pain meds or without."

From across the runway, Jack's laugh came fast and light as he played a game of keep away with one of Boomer's baseball hats. Jack tossed it to Hank, but Boomer roared and swept him up with one arm and dangled the kid over his shoulder. Jack kicked and screamed, his laughter sweet and high pitched.

"My father has a warehouse in Quincy. It's right on a rail line. It's his preferred port when he ships supplies because it's a smaller inland port in the middle of nowhere. It's not nearly as busy as the coastal ones."

"You really think your father's in on this?" Gil gave her shoulder a reassuring squeeze.

"I hope I'm wrong, but the more I think about it, the more I think Bradley got the idea to use an out of the way port for his illegal activity from my father's business model."

Tessa went on to supply Spinks with her father's full name, address and contact information and answered a few short questions her voice flat and hollow.

The EMT pushed in beside Spinks and said, "Times up. You can answer any more questions when they get done with you at the hospital."

17

———

Two weeks later, Gil's shoulder was well on the way to being healed. He scratched at the scruff growing on his jaw, liking what he saw in the mirror more and more each day.

And it wasn't just the hair.

It was Tessa and the kid and the man he was becoming as their lives neatly dovetailed together.

By the time Gil pulled into the parking lot of the Sheriff's Office, Spinks' car was one of the few ones there. No surprise. Gil made his way through the halls and rapped on the jamb of Spinks' open door. Spinks glanced up from his computer and silenced the CNN feed on the television behind him.

Leaning back in his chair, Spinks said, "This it then?"

Spinks had known this was coming. Gil had told him as much. "Yes, sir."

Gil laid the envelope beside the SAC's computer. Spinks sort of smiled. "You can drop the 'sir' now. It never sat well with you anyway."

There was no point in denying it. "Filed the last of my reports. You know where to find me if you have any questions."

"At Sterling's you mean?"

He wished. At least with him resigning, he and Tessa didn't have to find a way around their involvement while serving on the same task force.

"I'm at the ranch for now. Until I finish up the program and can find my own place, or..." He shrugged. Spinks was a bright enough man, he could fill in the blanks himself.

Honestly, Gil had no intention of finding his own place. He'd move in with Tessa, or they could find a place together when the time came. He was a patient man. At least now she encouraged Jack to spend time with him.

"I better get going. I'm picking up Lang and taking him to the barbecue tonight. You coming?"

Spinks shook his head. "Naw. I need to finish tying up all our loose ends. The case is being handed over to the FBI."

"Wait. That was a joint case, how the hell did the FBI run us out—"

Spinks held up his hands in surrender, his face a combination of resignation and frustration. "The Brass duked it out. Don't get me started."

So much for inter-agency cooperation.

Of all the things Gil wouldn't miss about leaving the ATF, the bureaucracy, the posturing, the fighting over cases like a pack of snarling, starving hyenas topped the long list. In the fight for recognition and promotion, sometimes the fact that they were all on the same team was lost in the minutia.

If Gil had learned nothing else in his years in the military and law enforcement, it was that there was no need for the agencies to squabble over scraps. There was enough evil in the world to go around.

They said their goodbyes and Gil hopped in his truck and headed over to Isaac's place. Gil was around the corner from his friend's house when a text came in. Pulling into Isaac's driveway, he parked and pulled out his phone.

Two words from Isaac. *Save me.*

Gil chuckled and went to type a reply. He couldn't get the text sent before the front door opened and Isaac wheeled himself out of the house and rolled down the newly finished ramp at warp speed.

Isaac didn't even wait for Gil to get out of the truck before he yanked the passenger door open. By the time Gil came around to the other side, Isaac had already hoisted himself into the truck. Gil pushed the wheelchair out of the way and helped Isaac swing his legs inside.

"What's your hurry? There's gonna be plenty of food to go around."

"I don't care about the food. Get in the truck and drive like you're the wheelman on a jewelry heist."

"*Okaaay,*" Gil said, as he folded the wheelchair and secured it in the back of the truck. His shoulder complained, but not too loudly. "You're the boss."

"Hurry." The unmitigated panic in Isaac's voice made Gil glance at his friend. You would have thought the Hounds of the Baskerville were nipping at his heels, but as Gil looked over at the house where Isaac was staring, it wasn't hellhounds that were after his friend, but Isaac's mother.

Rita hurried down the ramp, a backpack in her hand. "Izzy, you forgot your backpack. I've got water bottles in case you get—"

"Ma," Isaac tried to get a word in, but his mother talked right over him. "*Mom.*"

"...and I put extra urinary catheters in because I know how you don't like to use the collection bags when you go out and—"

"Mom. *Enough.*" The last time Gil had seen Isaac that red... scratch that, Gil had never seen Isaac that deep of a shade of crimson.

"Honey, I—"

Gil took the bag from Rita. "I'll take good care of him, Mrs. Lang. Don't you worry."

"What time will you be back?"

"Don't wait up," Isaac said. By the look on Rita's face, Isaac was wasting his breath.

She nodded, but her forehead remained creased. Gil got it. The woman had almost lost her son. Her only child. She was holding on tight, and she couldn't see how it was suffocating him.

Rita stood in the driveway and waved as Gil backed up and headed back to the Lazy S.

Isaac slumped in the seat beside him, his head back. "Sorry about that. That was TMI, I know. That bullet not only took out my legs, it obliterated my mother's verbal filter."

"Aw, c'mon. Can't be that awful."

Isaac rolled his head toward Gil. "You think I'm exaggerating? She told Pearl at the diner that I haven't gotten a boner since I got shot. Pearl shared my plight with her congregation down at the church. My dick's been added to the prayer list.

"Somehow, I would think my capacity for sexual gratification would be farther down on God's *To Do* list. Somewhere behind ending world hunger and sending the Cubs to the World Series again."

"You never know." Gil tried to keep a straight face. He really did.

"It's not funny,"

Gil chuckled. "Yeah, buddy. It kinda is."

"Screw you."

Gil took his eyes off the road and grinned at his buddy. "It's good to see you, too. You got any feeling back?"

Isaac offered a one shoulder shrug, but his expression was non-committal. "I get this tingling sensation sometimes. I don't know. The doctors won't say it's nothing, because they don't want me giving up all hope, but I can see it in their eyes, man. That look that all but says 'you're gonna have to learn to live with it.'

"What about one of those spinal specialty places back east—"

"Look, I appreciate your concern, and your help getting the ramp built at the house and all that, but can we talk about something else?"

"Sure thing."

They lapsed into a comfortable silence, the wind rushing in through the truck's open windows, the smell of fresh cut grass filling the truck as they passed a large hay field.

"You move in with Tessa and the kid yet?"

"We'll get there." Gil wasn't in the mood to discuss his relationship with Tessa. On the one hand, it wasn't where he wanted it to be, but on the other, it was much more than he'd ever imagined it would ever be.

"But things are good with you two?"

Gil drummed his thumbs on the steering wheel. "Yeah... Good. Really, really... good."

"You said that with the enthusiasm of a guy going in for a prostate exam. What gives?"

The turnoff for the ranch was coming up. Gil slowed and took the bumps and ruts with extra caution. Isaac had assured him at one time that he couldn't do any more damage to his spine than what had already been done, but Gil wasn't taking any chances.

"It's kind of personal."

"And my lack of a boner isn't?"

"I didn't ask. You volunteered."

"Doesn't matter. Spill."

They came over a rise, and the big house and the barn came into view.

"Tessa's late," Gil said, at last.

"Late for…?"

Gil gave him a pointed look, and Isaac snapped to. "Oh. *Late.* Late. As in congratulations?"

"As in, *what the fuck were we thinking.*"

"Oh." The word sat between them. Fat and pregnant.

Gil rolled on past the house and followed the dirt road back to his cabin. The two new veterans were due to arrive the next day, but he had the place to himself for one last night. He parked and killed the engine. Neither one moved to get out.

"You know, there are ways you can find out for sure if you've got something to worry about," Isaac said.

"I bought her a test two days ago."

"And?"

"She hasn't taken it."

"Why?"

He'd asked himself that about a million times over the last forty-eight hours. Tonight, after the party, he'd ask *her* that. "I don't know. I think maybe because it could change everything? Things are going great. I love her. I love her kid. All in all, the relationship is in a good place, especially for a relationship with a woman who was only looking for good time. Adding a pregnancy to the mix…"

Gil shook his head. Their decision back at Martin's to have unprotected sex weighed heavy on him. He'd only recently fully come to understand what a pregnancy would mean for Tessa. For him. Still, he didn't regret it, but often wondered if she might. "She wouldn't be able to fly, she—"

"*Or,*" Isaac raised his voice over Gil's. "Or it could make things better. Talk to her."

———

IF WIKIPEDIA HAD A PAGE ON EPIC *BONFIRES AND BARBECUES*, YOU'D find the Lazy S Ranch listed first. The buzz of voices and laughter mixed with the scent of tangy sauce, sausage, beans, and brisket.

The fire popped and cracked, sending tiny red embers into the air. There were coolers and chairs and logs to sit on. Somewhere a radio was turned to a country music station, filling the void between the chatter and chuckles.

Everyone was there. Dale, Lottie, and Pepita had returned from their trip to the UK. Dale manned the meat. Lottie stirred her world-famous beans over an open fire. Pepita had latched onto Jack, and they were off to one side, feeding treats to Sidney's beer loving horse Eli who appeared miffed to find out no one had brought any real brew to the party.

Alby and Santos settled into a good-natured argument with Hank, while Mac looked on, her hand on her ever-expanding belly and her eye on her husband. She had a white envelope in her hand, and she tapped it absently on the arm of her camp chair.

Mia was around somewhere, but Tessa didn't know where, and Massey hadn't yet arrived.

Gil had parked Isaac on one side of her and he had taken the seat on her other side. Jenna and Sidney came out of Sidney's cabin with their arms loaded with plates and cups. Boomer and Quinn right behind them with the sweet tea, napkins, and cutlery.

Tessa jumped up, her calf hardly complaining. "What can I do to help?"

Jenna set the plates down on the folding table some of the guys had dragged down from the barn. "Sit. Enjoy. We're done."

Boomer made a sharp whistle, and the conversations died. "Soups on."

A cheer went up. Gil stood, and asked Isaac, "What do you want?"

Isaac deflated. He clearly didn't want help. He glanced over at the table, and the growing buffet line, and she could see his gears whirling as he tried to figure out how he would manage his wheelchair in the dirt with a plate in his lap and a glass in his hand. Finally, he gave in and said, "A little bit of everything, I guess."

Tessa's phone rang, and she pulled it out of her chair's cup holder and must have made a face because Gil said, "Who is it?"

"It's my mother."

"You think it's happened?"

She blew out a breath and stood to take the call. "Gotta be. She never calls."

"Need me to stay?"

Needing and wanting were two different things but dealing with her mother wasn't anything he could help her with. However, knowing she wasn't in this thing alone, wasn't going through life alone, gave her strength. Before the call could go to voicemail, she accepted it and brought the phone to her ear.

He kissed her on the forehead and whispered in her other ear. "Come find me when you're done."

She nodded to Gil and said, "Hello, Mother."

"Tessa? Tessa, where are you? I can barely hear you." Was that panic in her mother's voice or was it the static?

"Hang on, let me find a quieter spot."

She put a finger in her ear to block the noise until she could walk further away. She stopped at the high spot in the road before it dipped down, and she would lose the signal.

"This better?" Tessa asked.

"They've arrested your father."

Tessa had known this was coming. Spinks had told her a judge had already issued a warrant to search her father's office and home, taking both hard copy and computer files. Between what they'd recovered, what Drew Ross had given up after being taken into custody, and now with Bradley making deals faster than a game show host to save his own skin, it had only been a matter of time.

"Tessa? Did you hear what I said?"

"Yeah, Mother. I heard you."

"I don't know what to do, I—"

She would give her mother the same advice she'd give anyone when dealing with a run in with the law. "You hire the damn good lawyer—"

"I've done that. The news... The hateful things they're saying about your father. And the reporters. They've camped outside our gates. I feel like a prisoner."

Yeah, a prisoner in a fifteen thousand square foot home on twenty acres appointed with every luxury dirty money could buy. Tessa tamped down on the guilt she felt for not feeling sorry for her parents.

They'd gambled.

They'd won.

They'd lost.

"Tell me, Mother. Tell me you knew nothing about this. That you didn't know that Dad supplied weapons to the black market. Tell me that you didn't know that that money was dirty, and that innocent women and children were dying because of his greed."

There was a long pause, and Tessa held the phone away from her ear to see if she'd lost the connection, but the call timer ticked away at the top of her screen.

Tessa pinched the bridge of her nose, but it had no impact on the pounding headache building behind her eyes. "Don't answer that. I don't want to know."

"I don't know why I called you. I should have known you, of all people, would have no sympathy."

"I'm in law enforcement, Mother. If Dad broke the law—"

"They can't have much of a case. Your father said Bradley won't talk and if their stories are straight, the law has nothing on them. I'm sure your father will make bail in no time."

If her mother only knew. Thanks to Massey and his new algorithm, they'd been able to backtrack the CoinIt data they thought had been permanently erased. Seems like that old saying was true, you can delete something, but it's never really gone.

Even on the Dark Web.

Her mother had no clue. The authorities had a case. In fact, they had a compelling case.

"Dad doesn't know what I've always known about Bradley. Bradley looks out for number one. Always. Which means he's making deals and spilling his guts."

Her mother sputtered on the other end, unable to form a coherent sentence.

"You want my advice, Mother?" Tessa didn't wait for an answer because she was going to give it whether her mother wanted to hear it or not. "I think you need to find yourself a good lawyer as well."

"*Tessa.*" Her mother scolded her like she was a little kid who'd said a cuss word.

Tessa glanced down the hill at the campfire. Dusk had settled in and shifted toward dark. Gil stood in a group with Hank, Boomer, and Isaac, with a root beer in his hand. He tossed his head back, laughing at something Isaac said.

Pepita had found a couple of riding helmets, and she and Jack were bareback on Eli, walking around with only a lead rope tied to the halter for reins. Jack laughed when Eli broke into a gentle trot around an old tree.

These people. These people were her *real* family. They'd opened their arms and accepted her in a way her parents and

Bradley never had. She'd never felt as loved and supported. They had her and Jack's back, always.

And Gil... He'd done the impossible, he'd given her back a piece of herself she hadn't even known she was missing... her heart.

"Goodbye, Mother."

Tessa hung up the phone, not waiting for a reply.

"You okay?"

At the sound of Mia's voice, Tessa spun around. "Hey. Um... yeah." But even as she said it, she shook her head no.

"Family problems?"

Tessa's laugh came quick and hollow. "How'd you guess?"

"It was either that, or guy problems, but you've got Gil, so..." Mia shrugged as if that was a complete answer.

Mia stepped closer and raised a hand. Tessa wasn't sure if Mia was going to hug her or—

Mia's hand landed on Tessa's shoulder, giving her an awkward, but sincere pat. The veteran wasn't the touchy-feely type, but she was trying. "Fuck family."

Tessa snorted. "Tell me about it."

"If you want to feel better, talk to me about mine sometime. You'll think you won the jackpot in the family lottery."

Those two sentences were probably the most Mia had said to her all at one time. It wasn't much, but slowly, it seemed like Mia was opening up.

"Are you coming down to the fire, or are you heading out." It was early even for Mia to head out into the bush for the night, but crowds weren't her thing.

Mia glanced over at everybody, a longing in her eye, instead of the usual quiet panic. It was unexpected. "I don't know. I—"

"Come on," Tessa said. No wasn't an option. Mia could leave whenever she wanted, but she was going. "One root beer, then you can go if you want."

Mia hesitated but gave Tessa one short nod. "One root beer."

At the last minute, Mia turned off and headed for the food. At least she came. Gil raised his arm and Tessa settled beneath it. To Quinn, Gil said, "Toss one of those to Tessa."

Quinn reached into a nearby cooler, twisted the top off a bottle of root beer and handed it to Tessa. She took a sip. "Thanks."

"Gil was giving us the play by play," Quinn said. By the grin on his face, you would think Quinn was talking about a sporting event and not a helo crash.

"More of a hard landing," Gil said.

Tessa pulled a face. "No. It was a crash. If you hadn't—"

Her throat tightened, and she cut herself off because she wasn't going to go *there*. Not tonight.

Quinn knew the dark corner where her mind had gone and deflected the attention when he said, "Lightweight. I'm one crash ahead of you."

Isaac stuffed a bite of brisket into his cheek and said to Quinn, "With a track record like that, the task force should give that new pilot *your* job, not hers."

"How is the new pilot?" Tessa was almost afraid to ask.

"She's good," Quinn allowed. "Not you. But yeah, she's good."

Not you, didn't mean, *not better*. She couldn't wait until she got her medical clearance and could fly again.

Mac caught Hank's attention. Hank raised a hand to her as if saying 'give me a sec,' then asked, "When do you think you'll be back in the air?"

Tessa stiffened, and the carbonation turned flat on her tongue. Gil gave her shoulder a reassuring squeeze. If she was pregnant, it could be a long time. Gil's words came back to her, the words he'd spoken the day he'd bought her the pregnancy test. *I don't understand why you won't take the test.*

It certainly would give them the answers to a lot of their questions. She wanted to take it. She did. As soon as she got it right in her mind what she wanted the outcome to be.

On the one hand, she had worked her ass off as the lead pilot for the task force. She loved her work, was proud of what she'd accomplished and didn't want to give that up. On the other hand, was Gil, and the prospect of a new baby, and all the joys and chaos that would bring into their lives.

Gil nudged her with his hip and brought her back to herself. "Hank asked you when you thought you'd be back in the air."

"IA dropped their investigation allowing Spinks to drop my suspension. The leg's healing well. If I get a clean bill of health from the flight surgeon next week, I could be back in the air shorty." Or give or take nine months. Nine months. Which would give the other pilot plenty of opportunities to win Tessa's job.

"Good for you." Isaac tipped his bottle toward her, and his smile came close to his eyes. From what Gil had told her, Isaac was struggling with his own recovery, trying to hold out hope he would make it back to the job, but his prospects didn't look promising.

But even if Isaac never regained his legs, there was plenty of good work he could do in law enforcement. It wasn't like his career was over if he didn't want it to be.

Maybe you should take your own advice. Pregnancy is temporary. It's not the end of the world, or even your career.

Just take the damn test.

Ok. Fine. She would. Tonight.

She thought making that decision would tie her stomach up in knots, but if anything, a weight lifted, and she felt hungry for the first time in days.

"I'm going to grab some food before it's all gone."

"Hurry back," Hank said as he let Mac pull him away from the group. "We've got an announcement."

———

TESSA RETURNED TO GIL WITH A FULL PLATE AND A SMILE ON HER face he hadn't seen in days.

"What's up with you?" Gil said, unable to keep the suspicion out of his voice.

"I've decided to take the test."

"Really?" Those six little words made his heart tumble, and suddenly the world sitting on his shoulders didn't feel as back-breaking. Not only had Tessa agreed to take the test, she seemed happy about the idea. What had changed in the last few minutes? The barbecue was good, but it wasn't *that* good. He grabbed her wrist and took a step toward the cabins. "Let's go."

She dug in her heels but laughed. "Later. I want to hear the announcement."

Hank and Mac stood side by side. Hank's arm around Mac's waist. Boomer climbed onto one of the logs and let out a loud whistle. "Can I get everyone's attention, Mac and Hank have something they wanna say."

Everyone quieted down. Sidney climbed onto the log next to Boomer. Pepita and Jack walked Eli to the outside of the circle of people. A van door slammed, and Massey crutched his way in from the road, stopping at the far edge.

Mac waved the white envelope. "First, we are terrified—"

"And excited," Hank cut in.

Though Mac looked more nauseated than anything. "*And* excited, to announce that we're having twins."

The crowd went nuts. Cheering and high-fives all around. Hank had a proud look on his face like he was the prize bull set out at stud.

When everyone settled down, Mac said, "I had my ultrasound. We were going to wait and be surprised on the sexes, but Hank won't believe me when I say that they're going to be boys. We decided instead of arguing, we'd find out, and he'll know once and for all that I'm right."

Hank coughed into his hand, but he clearly said, "Girl."

"That's where my money is, boss," came Alby's voice from somewhere in the crowd.

"Boy," Mac insisted.

"Lucky for me," Hank said, as he adjusted the hat on his head and widened his stance, "you're not the one who decides that. They're girls. So far I'm batting a thousand on that."

Jenna laughed. Mac rolled her eyes, and Hank reached up and tugged Mac's ponytail.

"Open it!" Isaac hollered out. There was a sparkle in his eyes that wasn't there earlier.

Gil stood behind Tessa, his chest to her back, one hand splayed across her lower abdomen. She leaned back against him and asked, "Did you spike Isaac's drink?"

Gil grinned. "That would be against ranch rules." He bobbed his chin toward Hank and Mac. "Hush up and listen."

She grumbled. Gil chuckled.

As Mac started opening the envelope, she said, "They can't be girls. I don't know what to do with one, much less two. I know nothing about Barbies, or tea parties or dresses or French braids or—" you could hear the terror rising in her voice.

Hank took Mac's hand and turned her to him. "Army, if they're anything like their Mom, they'll be knee deep in mud, as soon as they can walk. They'll be too busy riding horses and motorcycles and learning to shoot to care about the rest."

"But what if they do?"

"Then more power to them. No matter what, we've got this. I

can't think of anything more incredible than little Macs in my life."

"Glutton for punishment," Alby called out.

Hank barked out a laugh. "Damn straight." Then he turned back to Mac. "Open the envelope."

Mac ripped at the envelope and unfolded the single sheet of paper, her eyes darting across the page. She smiled, all teeth and triumph. She waved the paper in the air. "They're boys."

Cheers went up. Mac high-fived Jenna.

"Ha, I win. Told you." Gil whispered in Tessa's ear. She gave him an elbow to the gut.

"You're such a poor winner."

"Wait, that can't be right." Hank snatched the paper out of Mac's hand and held it up to the fire for more light. He reread the report, his expression shifting from disbelief to smug.

Hank's chest puffed out. He rattled it in front of Mac's face. "Read it again."

The cheers and good-natured jeers died down as Mac reread the letter. She pointed to something on the page. "Right here, says boy. Told you."

Hank pointed farther down the page. "There."

Mac huffed but did as he asked. "Baby, B, girl."

Jenna slapped a hand over her mouth to cover her laugh. Lottie swiped at her cheeks and anyone who had handed money over on their side bets, got their money back.

Gil didn't get to see Mac's reaction, because Tessa tossed her empty plate into the fire and turned in his arms, her eyes barely concealed her panic. "Maybe we should wait to take that test."

"We're not having twins, Sunshine. Hell, we don't even know if you're pregnant." He brushed the hair away from her forehead and tucked it behind her ears. She'd broken out into a sweat, that Gil was certain had nothing to do with their proximity to the fire. "We're taking the test. Tonight. Deep breath. It's going to be alright. I promise."

Tessa's eyes fell closed, and she drew in a big breath through her nose. She held it for three rapid beats of his heart before letting it out. He wrapped her in his arms and kissed the side of her head. "Let's go. We can take it right now."

Tessa took a step back. "Give me a minute. I wanna give Hank and Mac my congratulations."

"One minute," he said, only half kidding. Now that he'd gotten Tessa to agree to take the test, he didn't want to give her too much time to chicken out.

He grabbed a bottle of water and collapsed into the chair next to Isaac. "How you doing? You need anything?"

Isaac shook the ice in his red party cup. "I'm good, thanks."

Tessa returned, sitting on Gil's lap. Tessa asked Isaac a question, but he wasn't paying her any attention. Isaac pointed his cup across the fire. "Who's that?"

Across the fire, Massey and Mia had their heads angled toward each other in what looked like deep conversation. He wondered what the two were talking about. He'd never seen Mia look so animated.

"That's Mia Mann," Tessa said. "She's the—"

"Sunshine, he wasn't pointing at Mia. He was pointing at your cousin."

Tessa looked from Isaac's puppy love grin to Massey and back again. "Oh. *Oh.* That's Massey Yates."

"*Fuuuck*, he's fine." Isaac slurred his words. Maybe Gil had been a tad generous with the booze he'd snuck in for his buddy.

Gil leaned toward Isaac. "Dude—"

Dude? Really? Gil hadn't used that word since high school. "Massey's straight."

Tessa leaned in toward Isaac. "And a manwhore."

Isaac's grin got bigger. "You say that like it's a bad thing."

"Hey, I thought you liked your cousin," Gil said.

"I do. Massey's awesome." Tessa plucked at her black hair-band, still on Gil's wrist. Secretly loving that he'd refused to give it back. "But trust me, Isaac, even if he wasn't straight, you can do much better. That man wouldn't know a relationship if it bit him on the ass."

Glancing over, Isaac gave Tessa a wink. "Who said anything about a relationship?" Isaac tucked his cup between his legs and released the brakes on his wheelchair. "See you two around."

18

Tessa had to almost run to keep up with Gil as he dragged her by the hand to Mia's cabin. The barbecue would run late, and she let Sidney and Jenna and of course Gil talk her and Jack into spending the night.

Mia hadn't protested. She didn't spend her nights in the cabin anyway. While Mia would probably never admit it, Tessa had started to think the woman was developing a soft spot for Jack.

As reluctant as Tessa had been to take the test, now that she'd decided to take it, she couldn't get it over with fast enough. She hurried through the cabin door after Gil, threw her overnight bag on the lower bunk and rummaged around in it.

Where was it? She'd thrown it...

Tessa tossed her change of clothes, her nightshirt and her clean underwear on the bed, searching for the box.

"Hey," Gil said, as he picked up her nightshirt. "That's mine."

She glanced at him over her shoulder. "Not anymore."

Gil spent several nights a week at her house, but only when Jack was at a sleepover with friends or with Evie. The nights when she was alone, she liked wearing his shirt to keep him close. It was a sorry substitute for the real deal.

But something was better than nothing.

"Is that right?" There was a smug tilt to his lips and a wonderfully wicked glint in his eye.

"Don't look at me like that," she said, but it was hard to put any sizzle in her tone. "You looking at me like that is what got us in this mess to begin with."

She dug through the zippered pockets of her bag, her movements frantic.

Gil took her wrists and eased her over to him. "Slow down, Sunshine. This isn't a timed event."

She blew out a breath that fluffed her bangs. "Pepita's watching Jack and—"

"Which means Sidney's watching Jack, and Boomer and everyone else is out there. We have plenty of time."

"You're right." Her pulse thumped at her wrist beneath his loose grip.

"Did you put the test kit in your purse?"

Yes, her purse! She slumped and dropped her forehead to his chest. "I'm such an idiot."

He wrapped her in his arms until she heard the steady-eddy beat of his heart. An enduring, powerful stroke, like the *whomp* of her Blackhawks rotor, that had the power to both calm her and take her away.

"You're no such thing." He reached down and handed over her purse. She found the test and dropped her purse back on the bed. "I guess, I'll be right back."

A few minutes later, she came back out with the test, dropped it on the counter next to the sink, and threw a dish towel over the top of it. She couldn't stand the idea of standing there waiting for it to turn.

"How long does it take?"

"Three minutes."

Gil set the timer on his watch. "Now we wait."

He placed his hands on either side of her hips and boosted her onto the counter beside the refrigerator, putting them at eye level.

One of his fingers traced tiny circles on her lower back beneath her shirt. She put her hand on his jaw and squidged her fingers through his thickening beard. "I missed the beard."

He ducked his head and rubbed his scruff into the crook of her neck until she was giggling and laughing and couldn't breathe. "Stop, stop, that tickles."

"I think my beard missed you, too."

Her laughter died as she stared at the light in his eyes, the grin on his face. He was totally relaxed and at ease. Every day he brought joy to her life. He treated her like she was something precious, something to be cherished. No matter what that test showed, she wanted him to know how she felt.

Holding his face in both of her hands she pressed a tender kiss to his lips, then leaned back and said, "I love you, Gil Brant."

His smile was smug when he said, "You don't think I know that?"

She laughed. "I've never said it. I didn't want there to be any doubts. What I feel is right, is real, is everlasting."

His arms tightened around her waist as he snugged her up against him. He brought his lips down on hers, pouring himself into the kiss. The passion, the commitment, the love.

They were lost in the kiss, in the giving and the taking, when the timer on his watch went off.

Tessa stiffened.

Gil laughed. "You ready?"

Her stomach went light, and for a second, she thought she might puke.

"How are you not scared shitless?" she asked. "Or are you hiding it better?"

He took her hand and placed it over his heart, over the slow, methodical, almost lazy *tump-tump, tump-tump.* "Because I have everything I want right here. You. Jack." He glances down at the dish towel covering the test. "Maybe a baby. I don't need anything else."

When he reached for the towel, she said, "Wait. I want to ask you something, but I don't want you thinking I'm asking for the wrong reason."

"*Okaay.*" He was skeptical but smiling.

"Move in with me... and Jack." The air backed up in her lungs. The blood rushed past her ears with a deafening roar. If she took a breath she wouldn't hear his answer.

He remained silent far too long. Everything came rushing out—her breath, her thoughts, her feelings. "I love you, Gil. I don't want to find out that the test is positive and for you to think that I only want you to move in because I'm pregnant. I want you to move in because I don't want to be apart from you every night. I don't want to sneak time together. I want a family. With you. It's not something I was looking for, but I found it, and I don't want to let it go, and—"

"Do I get to say something here?"

Tessa took a couple of quick breaths and brushed her bangs out of her eyes and wiped the beads of sweat off her forehead. "Yeah. Sure. Sorry."

"Yes."

"What?"

Gil's warm, deep chuckle rumbled until she couldn't help but laugh too. "Yes, as in you'll move in?"

"Yes, as in *hell* yes. As in what are we waiting for? As in, I can have my bags packed, and we can be out the door in fifteen minutes, yes."

Tessa wrapped her arms around Gil's neck and was pulling him in for a kiss when the door burst open. Jack came running inside. Lord knew Gil loved that kid, but he had the absolute worst timing.

Ever.

Gil took a half-step back. "What's up, Squirt?"

Jack made a bee-line for the sink and started washing his hands. "We're about to cook S'mores. Pepita said I had to wash my hands first."

Jack shut off the water and yanked the hand towel off the counter. Tessa gasped. Gil grinned.

"Hey." Jack reached for the test. "What's this?"

Gil snatched it out of his hand and shoved it in his back pocket as the heat rushed up his neck. "Um... it's a lady test." If he was going to be a dad, to Jack or any other kid, he had to get better at this talking about sex thing.

"Ah," Jack said as if that answered everything. "Billy's mom took one of those tests. It made her cry."

Tessa's laugh came out strangled.

"I don't know why. I mean, if you do your homework and study, then you don't have to worry about the test. I like taking tests. I always get A's."

"It's not the kind of test you can study for," Tessa said.

"Then what kind of test is it?"

Tessa gave Gil a look that said she should have known Jack wouldn't drop the subject that easily. She opened her mouth to answer, but Mia came through the door.

"Oh, sorry." Mia reached for her backpack. The one she took out every night with her.

Tessa jumped off the counter. "It's okay. You heading out? The party not fun?"

Mia shrugged on her pack. "It didn't suck."

Which for Mia, was a resounding endorsement.

"Can I camp with her, Mom?"

Mia froze, her expression stuck between alarm and a scowl. Her eyes darting between Jack and Tessa. But there was something else there that Gil couldn't quite put his finger on. Almost as if Mia wanted to say yes but was afraid to.

Tessa started to answer, but Gil interrupted. "Sounds like a great idea, right Tessa."

Tessa gave him a look. It wasn't quite a WTF look, but it was close. "Um…"

"I've got a spare bedroll." Mia's answer came out more like a question. "That's if it's okay with you." She started backing for the door before Tessa could answer, unable to look them in the eye. "If not, no big."

Gil nudged Tessa with his elbow. She startled and said, "Um… no. I don't mind if he goes with you, as long as you two stay close."

"Yes!" Jack let out a loud whoop.

"There's a place by the hot spring," Mia said. "It's not far."

Tessa turned to Jack. "You have to promise to stay away from the water."

Jack raised his hands. "I don't wanna go anywhere near it, promise." For emphasis, he drew a cross over his heart.

Gil wasn't concerned Jack would break his promise. From what Tessa had said, since Jack's near drowning, her son stuck to showers only.

Mia went over to her trunk and pulled out the other bedroll and dropped it into Jack's hands. He ran out the door saying, "I'm gonna see if Pepita wants to come, too!"

Tessa scrunched her face up. "Sorry about that. I know that's not the quiet night you'd bargained for. I can tell him no if you want."

"I can deal," Mia said. Though her words made it sound like she was put out, Gil detected a smile underneath it all.

"Thanks, Mia," Gil said. "We owe you one."

Mia turned back at the threshold and said, "Yeah, you do."

The door closed, and Gil turned to Tessa. "If that wasn't okay, tell me, and I'll be the bad guy and tell Jack he can't go. I didn't mean to put you on the spot. I think Mia wants in. I just think she's too scared of rejection to ask for it."

"No. You're right. You've got good instincts, and while Mia has her own issues she's dealing with, underneath it all she's a good person. And besides..." Tessa reached around him and pulled the test from his rear pocket and read the results of the test.

Her expression didn't change.

His stomach did a slow roll, and his heart forgot to beat.

Then she smiled and turned the test around, and in bright pink letters, the test read *pregnant*. "You're going to have to get used to this parenting thing after all. Might as well start now."

Tessa came through her front door at five-thirty sharp. One good thing about taking the helo maintenance job Spinks had offered after they'd told him she was pregnant, was that her hours were much more predictable, and she no longer had to leave the house in the middle of the night to fly a mission.

Not that she didn't miss it.

And not that she wasn't going to get back in the air.

But for now, it could be much worse.

She shrugged her arms out of her grease-stained coveralls and tied the arms at her waist as she went straight for the sink and the industrial strength degreaser. She pumped a dollop into her hand and turned on the hot water.

The rear sliding door stood open, the air thick with the smell of lighter fluid and charcoal. Jack's voice filtered in as he talked Gil's ear off about something. She glanced out the kitchen window.

Gil removed his baseball cap, wiped his forehead with the back of his hand, the took a long swallow of his beer. Jack did the same, but soda, not beer. The ATF cap Gil had given Jack was already looking worn at the edges since Jack had barely taken it off in the two weeks since Gil had moved in.

Gil came through the back door. "You're home."

"Just." Tessa scrubbed away at the grease under her fingernails.

He came up behind her and tugged the strap of her white tank top off her shoulder. He pressed a kiss to the nape of her neck and started working his way across her shoulder.

"You may not want to do that. I'm hot and sweaty and—"

"Mmm." The sound was low and husky and did naughty things to her insides. "That's how I like my women."

"—covered in grease."

"Even better." His arms came around her waist, and he pulled her against his erection. He sniffed her hair. "Who would have thought JP-8 was an aphrodisiac?"

She gripped the edge of the sink to keep from stripping every last stitch of clothing off him and taking him in the kitchen. "You need to slow your roll before Jack gets an education that would blow his little seven-year-old mind."

Gil groaned and backed away. "I would say it would almost be worth it, but I don't think I'd be up to answering all his questions."

From the refrigerator, he removed a tray of hamburger patties and a bowl of fresh corn on the cob and set them on the counter beside her. She shut off the water and dried her hands. They were mostly clean.

"How was work? Getting back into the swing of it?" he asked.

She'd been in aircraft maintenance for a couple years before she'd qualified for pilot training. Helo maintenance was physical and taxing, but at least she felt like she could contribute. "Got a lot to study up on, but the lead mechanic is pretty cool, and loves to train people, which helps."

Something caught Gil's eye, and he reached for something on the counter behind her. "This came in the mail today."

She took the postcard from his hand. No note. No return address. It was the third one they'd received. The first two from non-extradition countries. This one was as well. Her mother had followed her advice and hired the best lawyers her father's money could buy. There was no proof the postcards were from her parents, but she knew it was. "I can't believe my father got bail."

"It was damn high. That's a lot of money he lost by skipping the country."

"Not that much when you have the kind of money my father does. It doesn't help to take their passports when he has the means to buy new identities. Sooner or later. Dad will make a mistake. They'll catch him."

She tossed the postcard back on the counter. She'd take it to Spinks in the morning, not that it would help in finding her parents. By the time the postcard had arrived, her parents would no doubt be in another country."

Jack ran through the back door and skid to a stop on the tile. "Did you do it? Did you ask her to marry you?"

"What?" Tessa glanced at Gil.

Gil wiggled his brows, his grin big behind his beard. "Surprise."

"Gil says he really loves you and me and the baby in your belly which you still haven't told me how it got there, but you should see the ring he got you it's pretty cool. Show her, Gil."

Jack made a come-on motion with his hand, and Gil reached into his back pocket and took out a velvet box. Before Gil could open it, Jack went on, "It's a black silicone band that won't show the grease, and instead of real diamonds, it has the word diamonds stenciled on it. You can wear it to work and everyone will know he belongs to you and you belong to him.

Tessa's heart beat faster than Jack was talking. Jack sucked in a big breath and grabbed the box from Gil and opened it up to show her. "I told him you'd say yes. Please say yes."

She looked at Gil. He was leaning against the counter, a hand over his mouth as he fought the grin. Her son had hijacked his proposal, but Gil looked more amused than annoyed. "Yes"

Gil stood up straight, the smile taking over his face. "Yeah?"

"Yeah."

"Yay!" Jack gave Tessa a hug around the waist and then Gil, then ran for the phone in the living room. "I'm gonna call Billy and tell him I'm gonna have a new dad."

"The ring," Gil called out to him. "I need the ring."

Jack ran back and slapped it in Gil's hand and said, "Oops," before turning and running away.

Gil plucked the silicone band from the velvet lining and took her shaky left hand in his and slipped the ring on her finger. "That wasn't how I'd planned to ask you, but—"

She shook her head as she tried to blink him back into focus as the tears started to flood in. "Best proposal ever."

"Best wingman ever. To be clear," Gil said, "I also got you a proper engagement ring, with real diamonds. It won't be ready for a few more weeks, but I decided I couldn't wait that long."

"The ring doesn't matter. Only the man behind it does."

Without taking his eyes off hers, he kissed the back of her hand. "With all that I am and all that I will ever be, I love you, Tessa Sterling.

In his eyes, she saw his truth. The soul of a good man, an

honest man. "I wasn't looking for this." She didn't care that her voice was thick. "You were supposed to be a distraction. But you got under my skin. That distraction became infatuation, that infatuation became a want. That want became a need until you filled me up and brought color to every corner of my life. To Jack's life. We are both so fortunate to have you. You are our light, Gil Brant."

Gil cleared his throat. "No, Sunshine, y'all are mine."

Then his mouth came down on hers, with heat and passion and possessiveness. He picked Tessa up and plopped her on the counter, stepping between her legs. They should stop. Jack could walk in at any minute, but Tessa locked her heels behind the most exquisite ass in Wyoming and pulled him closer.

Gil groaned, then pulled back. "Hold that thought." He threw the raw burgers and corn back in the fridge, then disappeared into the den. Jack said, "Thanks, Gil."

Jack came running back into the kitchen his eyes glowing with excitement. "This is the best day ever. I get a new dad and a new video game."

Tessa barely got to say, "That's great," before Jack disappeared again. Gil sauntered back into the kitchen, a cocky grin on his face as he scooped Tessa up in his arms. She locked her arms around his neck and her legs around his waist.

"That should buy us a good hour at least." He started walking toward their bedroom.

"Maybe two." Tessa grinned. "You seem to have a good grasp on this parenting thing already."

"What can I say, I'm a natural."

They stumbled into the bedroom. Gil locked the door and dumped her on the bed. He laid out beside her, his hand on her belly as he leaned over and said, "Hang on tight, little one, because I'm about to rock your mother's world."

A LETTER TO MY READERS

Dear Reader,

Don't worry, the chapter hasn't closed on the Lazy S Ranch, so stay tuned for more in the series.

Until then, it's time for a new adventure...

Take a step back in time, where bull riding isn't for sissies.

And neither is love.

Bull rider Silas Foss has a simple plan: Win big. Buy land. Start roughstock ranch. Before the bulls break him or bury him.

With Josephine's eye on barrel racing's top prize, she's sworn off men for the long season. Besides, she's too young to settle down.

She wants to chase cans, not kids.

With the end of the season near, her dream within her grasp, Josephine lets her guard down for a charming, persistent cowboy with his sights set on her.

When a crisis back home could force her off the circuit permanently, all she and Silas have is here and now.

Then everything that is right goes wrong.

Can Silas and Josephine come together and protect their

rodeo family? Or will distance, duty, and dreams tear them apart?

You'll want to hang onto your hat...
Luck of the Draw—is a throwback to a time you won't want to miss.
Your next adventure starts here at www.books2read.com/Luck-of-the-Draw

Also by Vicki Tharp

Lazy S Ranch Series
Cowgirl, Unexpectedly (Lazy S Ranch 1)
Must Love Horses (Lazy S Ranch 2)
Hot on the Trail (Lazy S Ranch 3)
Cowboy, Undercover (Lazy S Ranch 4)

Rockin' Rodeo Series
Luck of the Draw (Rockin' Rodeo 1)
Photo Chute (Rockin' Rodeo 2)
Reined In (Rockin' Rodeo 3)

Wright's Island Series
Don't Look Back (Wright's Island 1)
In Her Defense (Wright's Island 2)

ABOUT THE AUTHOR

Vicki Tharp makes her home on small acreage in south Texas with her husband and an embarrassing number of pets. When she isn't writing, you can usually find her on the back of her horse—avoiding anything that remotely resembles housework —smelling like fly spray and horse sweat.

Join my newsletter at: http://eepurl.com/croJgz
Join my street team and receive free Advance Reader Copies of my upcoming books at: http://eepurl.com/cWhXbD
You can find my website at: www.VickiTharp.com
I love to hear from readers. You can email me at Author@VickiTharp.com

Or you can stalk me at:

facebook.com/VickiTharpAuthor

instagram.com/author_Vicki_Tharp

bookbub.com/authors/vicki-tharp

amazon.com/author/vicki_tharp

twitter.com/vwtharp